IN SICKNESS & IN HEALTH

A PRIDE AND PREJUDICE VARIATION

FRANCES REYNOLDS

QUILLS &
QUARTOS
Publishing

Edited by Jennifer Altman and Grace Baumann

Cover by Carpe Librum Book Design

ISBN 978-1-956613-74-2 (ebook) and 978-1-956613-72-8 (paperback)

To those on the front lines of infectious disease treatment and research. Thank you.

"Well, my dear," said Mr Bennet, when Elizabeth had read the note aloud, "if your daughter should have a dangerous fit of illness—if she should die, it would be a comfort to know that it was all in pursuit of Mr Bingley, and under your orders."

"Oh! I am not afraid of her dying. People do not die of little trifling colds. She will be taken good care of. As long as she stays there, it is all very well. I would go and see her if I could have the carriage."

— PRIDE AND PREJUDICE,
CHAPTER 7

CHAPTER ONE

Elizabeth Bennet hovered anxiously in the corner of the spacious guest bedchamber at Netherfield Park as the apothecary examined her sister for the second time in as many days. She had never seen Jane in such a state before—feverish, nauseous, and complaining of the most terrible headache of her life.

Mr Jones turned Jane's face towards the window, into the sunlight streaming between the open curtains, and bade her open her mouth. He looked there with a deepening frown, then pronounced a single word which struck fear into both Bennet sisters, the sick and the well.

"Smallpox."

"No..." Elizabeth breathed.

The apothecary turned his grim look upon her. "I fear it is so. I have seen several cases at the Blake farm recently. I have required them to stay at home to reduce the spread, and Netherfield must do likewise. I shall arrange for food and medicines to be delivered here, but I must insist that no one but myself enter or leave until a full fortnight has passed without any illness."

Elizabeth's mind was racing. "The Blakes, you say? Why, Jane and I took them a basket little more than a week ago, as the children had a fever. But I am entirely well. How could she acquire it from a visit of an hour or so? And how could I not?"

Mr Jones sighed, wiping the lenses of his spectacles with a handkerchief. "Miss Elizabeth, it has long been known in my profession that the disease will generally not appear in the week after exposure, but may begin at any time in the fortnight following. Watch yourself carefully for symptoms. There will be fever, assuredly; pains in the head and troubles of the stomach, often; and within a few days, sores in the mouth and throat. This is the stage Miss Bennet is in now," he continued with a nod to the patient, upon whom he fixed his sombre gaze. "The lesions of the pox will appear very soon, Miss Bennet. You will be vastly uncomfortable, but do not rub or touch them, lest they take an infection. Take all the nourishment you can—you will need your strength."

Jane looked very frightened and seemed incapable of speech, and Elizabeth rushed to her side, taking one of Jane's hands in both of her own and saying, "Do not fret, Jane. I shall stay with you."

"No, Lizzy, you must go, before you too become ill."

"I was at the Blakes' with you, dear sister, and I have been with you in your illness for more than a day. Whether or not I also fall sick is in the hands of fate—it is far too late to avoid exposure. I shall make myself useful to you, since I feel perfectly well at present." A thought occurred to her, and she turned to the apothecary. "Jane was at Longbourn just before she fell ill—is the rest of our family in danger?"

"Everyone in the area is in danger. Smallpox spreads like scandal in a ballroom. I shall instruct your father to keep your family and servants within the estate until it passes, and we shall hope it may be confined to Netherfield and the Blake farm. I must speak with Mr Bingley immediately, for every moment increases the likelihood that someone will leave the house, perhaps bearing the disease with them. After I have done that, I shall look in upon you, Miss Bennet, and answer any other questions you or your sister may have." He bowed to them and exited the room.

Jane turned wide eyes on her sister. "Oh, Lizzy, am I going to die?"

———

Mr Jones descended the stairs and found Mr Bingley pacing the floor of the parlour as his relations and guests kept him company, looking rather bored.

"Mr Jones!" The young man rushed up to him. "How is Miss Bennet?"

"Oh, Charles, you are being ridiculous," Miss Bingley drawled from her seat. "It is naught but a trifling cold, I am sure. Shockingly inconvenient, but hardly dangerous."

Mr Jones ignored the lady. "Sir, I regret to inform you that you must place this house and all within it under quarantine. Miss Bennet has contracted smallpox."

Mrs Hurst fainted onto the shoulder of her husband, who awoke with a startled grunt. Miss Bingley leapt to her feet, shrieking like a scalded cat.

"We must leave this instant," she cried. "Bring the

carriage round! The servants may follow later with our trunks!"

"Miss Bingley, no one should enter or leave this house for at least a fortnight, longer if others fall ill," Mr Jones explained patiently, rummaging in his satchel as her brother and his friend—Mr Darcy, he recalled—fixed her with looks of censure. "If you fear exposure, I suggest you keep to your rooms." He produced a small bottle which he waved under Mrs Hurst's nose. The lady regained consciousness with a cough.

"That is an excellent idea," Mr Darcy said sharply before turning away from Miss Bingley to address Mr Jones. "Is Miss Elizabeth in danger of contracting the disease as well, given that she has been tending her sister?"

"Yes, although at present she shows no symptoms. I have asked that she inform me at the first sign of illness, and she has determined to remain with her sister and be of use as long as she may."

Mr Darcy only nodded in reply, though his expression reflected respect for Miss Elizabeth's decision.

Miss Bingley was openly appalled. "These country hoydens have brought smallpox to our house!" cried she. Taking no leave of them, she whirled and scurried from the room as though the hounds of hell were nipping at her heels. Hurst escorted his pale and trembling wife from the room in her wake.

Bingley's face was rather red when he turned back to the apothecary, but he spoke with admirable calm. "I was inoculated at university, sir—if there is any way in which I might be of assistance, I beg you will tell me."

Mr Darcy looked with raised eyebrows at his friend

and then, with a small nod, spoke. "As was I, and I would also wish to be of use."

Mr Jones looked between them and asked, "You are aware that inoculation is not infallible? There have been cases of previously inoculated persons acquiring the disease. According to the medical journals, it is rare, but not impossible."

Mr Bingley did not hesitate. "If it is to fail, let it fail in the service of my fellow man, not hiding away at Netherfield hoping to be spared."

After taking what appeared to be a moment of consideration, Mr Darcy replied cautiously, "I will place my trust in the rarity you speak of, Mr Jones."

The apothecary nodded slowly. "I had it in mind to attempt to visit every household in the area every few days, to check for new infection. If you would be willing to do this in my place, to call at houses and determine the health of everyone—family and servant—who dwells within them, I should have more time to spend with those who are ill."

Both gentlemen readily agreed with the scheme and Jones quickly sketched out several possibilities for routes. Mr Darcy and Mr Bingley decided they would go out every day, beginning early the next morning. All homes known to harbour the disease would be visited daily, and the rest twice weekly. It would make for a gruelling schedule if the infection spread, but with determination, dry weather, and good horses, it could be done. Mr Jones would make his visits to Miss Bennet in the late afternoon, that he might then receive any news they acquired in their travels.

As Jones departed after a final check on his patient, it appeared all three men felt better about the situation: two, from being of use, and one from having his burdens greatly lightened.

———

That afternoon, Darcy struggled to compose a letter to his sister which would inform her of the situation in which he found himself without causing her undue concern. This effort was hampered not only by his own jumbled thoughts, but also by Bingley's agitated pacing. Back and forth across the modest study, muttering to himself, stopping abruptly to stare out the window as though some rescue had been sighted upon the horizon, only to fling himself back into motion again so violently as to startle his friend.

With a sigh and hardly half a page written—and much of that struck through—Darcy set his pen aside. "Bingley, I doubt your landlord will be best pleased if you wear a hole in that new rug. The situation is unsettling, I grant you, but you are acting as though we are surrounded by a barbarian horde and running low on food."

"Unsettling?" Bingley cried. "It is terrifying. She is ill, Darcy! She might *die*! People do, all the time!" He canted his head back and glared at the ceiling as though he might see through the joists and plaster through sheer force of will.

Ah. This is about Miss Bennet. How like Bingley to be frantic over his latest infatuation and completely insensible to any danger to himself. For his own part, Darcy almost regretted his earlier offer of assistance. The risk was low, it was true, and would arise more from riding about the countryside as autumn became winter than from the disease itself, given his inoculated state. Yet as his sister's primary guardian and support, did he not owe it to her to keep himself as safe as possible? This was the question which had occupied him and distracted him nearly as much as his friend's perambulations. He would not go back on his word, of course, and certainly he would not leave the area, possibly carrying the infection with him, as Miss Bingley wished to do. But he wondered all the same if he had not been too hasty in agreeing to participate in the scheme.

"I cannot say that she will not die," he replied softly, and Bingley's head whipped around to regard him with wild eyes. "We must hope and pray that it will not be so, but her fate is not in our hands. Mr Jones seems more than competent and Miss Elizabeth will no doubt be diligent in her care also. Comfort yourself that she is well-attended."

"So long as Miss Elizabeth remains well."

There was a thought Darcy did not wish to confront. An image flashed through his mind: Miss Elizabeth's face, cold and pale, her sparkling eyes shut, all her joy and liveliness, her wit and laughter consigned forever to the cold ground. Bile rose in his throat, and only a lifetime of self-command and one or two deep breaths kept him from offering that fine new rug an insult far worse than Bingley's pacing.

"I will not tell you not to worry," he said at last. "I have my own fears regarding what is to come, and what *may* come. We shall, at least, have occupation and purpose through this crisis. And perhaps, if we do our work well and are fortunate, we will one day look back on all of today's fears and find they were none of them fulfilled."

In a silence and a stillness that rested unnaturally upon him, Bingley considered these words. "Yes," he answered, his usual optimism rekindling. "We will work, as will others, and all shall come right in the end. Thank you, Darcy. I was lost in my own fears, but I can always depend upon you to be rational!

"And thank you, also," Bingley continued, "for agreeing to come to the aid of this community, to which you have no tie beyond our friendship. I know you have not enjoyed my new neighbours, either, and would not have blamed you had you chosen to remain safe behind these walls until you could return to your own home. You are a good man, my friend, to give of your time and efforts, to risk your own safety, for those you do not even like."

"The risk is not so great," he demurred, abashed to be so praised for that which he had not been entirely willing to do even after committing himself. "I have faith in the inoculation, and in the abilities of Mr Jones. And I could hardly sit here and watch you ride out alone every day."

Even less safe than riding about an unfamiliar land-scape in bad weather, he reluctantly admitted to himself, would be spending the next weeks entirely confined to the same house as Elizabeth Bennet.

———

A few hours later, the two men and the Hursts waited impatiently for Miss Bingley to join them for dinner. A quarter hour after the sounding of the bell, Bingley sent a maid to find his wayward sister and instructed his butler to open the dining room.

They had progressed through the soup and into the first course before they were interrupted by the butler, with one of the house maids trailing behind. Bingley spoke rather more sharply than was his usual wont. "Mr Walsh, what is it? Is my sister unwell?"

Instead of answering, the butler directed a stern look at the girl who came forward hesitantly, wringing her hands. "Mr Bingley, sir, I tried to stop her, but she said if I told anyone I'd be turned off without a character."

Bingley set his fork down slowly. Darcy watched his friend's expression change as he apprehended that something, perhaps worse than his initial fears, had transpired. "What is it you were not to say? If you are honest with us, you shall have your character from me, should you need it."

The maid swallowed visibly. "Miss Bingley packed a valise and left with her abigail for London this morning, sir, not half an hour after the apothecary was here."

"Of all the stupid, selfish—!" Bingley threw up his hands. "That is the outside of enough—I cannot allow such intransigence." Though his words were intemperate, his expression was one of righteous anger. He looked, perhaps for the first time in his life, like a man one would not wish to cross.

Darcy, as unsurprised by Miss Bingley's selfishness as he was by her thoughtlessness, enquired as to her means of transportation. "Surely she did not take the post?"

"She and her maid took Mr Bingley's carriage, I believe, sir."

Bingley's jaw dropped. "She took *my carriage*? And my coachman, I presume?"

Mr Walsh appeared rather uncomfortable. "Yes, sir. And a groom. I have had words with the stablemaster about allowing this. He claims Miss Bingley stated that you had sanctioned her travels."

"I do not doubt it." He shook his head, then frowned

and turned to his sister. "Louisa, did you know what she planned?"

"Certainly not!" Mrs Hurst seemed somewhat offended. "I understand very well the necessity of quarantine. I would have told you immediately, had I known her intentions, and I am quite sure Caroline anticipated that. I know I tend to coddle her, Charles, but there are lives at risk, including hers."

Bingley nodded, though his expression darkened. "Certainly, her reckless behaviour must not pass without consequence, nor that of any groomsman who aided her."

"I hope you do not mean to be very harsh?" Mrs Hurst objected mildly. "She has acted wrongly, to be sure, but she is frightened, and if word of her unchaperoned trip to London gets out, she will be ruined."

Hurst patted his wife's hand. "Worry not about her reputation, my dear. We do not even know if she arrived safely." He did not seem at all troubled by the thought.

Darcy scowled, admittedly less concerned with Miss Bingley's safe journey on dry roads than he was about the condition of the horses she likely had driven at high speed.

"Louisa, I shall be harsh, for what she has done deserves no less. Permanently separating her from my household is not out of the question," Bingley replied implacably. "She has not only risked her reputation, she has possibly carried a terrible disease to Hurst's house and servants in town."

His brother frowned. "Endangering my household cannot be overlooked. I shall send an express to my housekeeper and ask after Caroline. That is all that may be done in our present situation."

CHAPTER TWO

JANE'S FEVER BROKE IN THE NIGHT, BRINGING HER immediate and welcome relief. Elizabeth stayed by her side, though her sister again urged her to leave and protect herself.

"Jane," she said reasonably, "I remind you again that I was with you in the Blake cottage and every day that passed between. Leaving now will avail me nothing, and cost me the comfort of being of use to you."

Jane had no reply to that, but continued to fret until Elizabeth reminded her that their father had lost two sisters to smallpox but never caught it himself. "Perhaps," she suggested lightly, "I am like him in that, as in so many other things."

"Oh, I do hope so. I shall never forgive myself if you fall ill from tending me."

"Enough of that, Jane. If I fall ill, it will be because we both went to deliver that basket of food. Do not you trust Mr Jones? He has said that these things keep to no certain schedule. Now," she turned the subject lightly, moving to the table where sat the few appealing volumes she had found in Netherfield's scant library, "should you like to hear Blake, Coleridge, or Wordsworth?"

The day passed quietly and more pleasantly than the two previous, for with the fever gone Jane felt quite well save for some lingering weakness and the increasing soreness of the lesions in her mouth and throat. Jane ate and drank as much as her stomach could hold, mindful of Mr Jones's exhortation on the subject, and after the apothecary's visit, during which he found nothing new to concern him, she fell into a deep sleep.

Noting the early hour, with more resolve than anticipation, Elizabeth refreshed herself, changed her dress and, having assured herself that Jane continued to rest peacefully, presented herself in the drawing room only moments before the dinner bell. Mr Bingley hurried to make her welcome and to ask after her sister, exclaiming with delight when informed that Jane was as well as could be hoped and already sleeping. Mrs Hurst added her own more sedate words of pleasure at this information, while Mr Darcy and Mr Hurst contented themselves with a brief nod of greeting and did not speak at all.

The bell then rang, and Mr Darcy offered his arm to Elizabeth, while Mr Hurst followed with his wife and Mr Bingley was forced to enter alone. Elizabeth wished she might instead take the arm of her host and wondered why Mr Darcy had not hung back and allowed matters to fall out so. He had openly declared upon their first meeting that she was not handsome enough to dance with, and following that they had hardly spoken. When they were together in company, she often found him staring darkly at her, no doubt cataloguing her many flaws of person and faults of manner. Not once had he troubled himself to attend his friend when Mr Bingley called upon her family home, Longbourn. Why he should wish to escort her into the room and, presumably, sit by her for the meal she could not fathom. Unless, she thought with an inward chuckle, he sought to examine in detail the defects he had thus far viewed at some remove.

"I was glad to hear your good report of Miss Bennet's condition, Miss Elizabeth," he said as they traversed the long dining room. "And may I applaud your courage in remaining to nurse her, now that the cause is known?"

A compliment from Mr Darcy! Only her innate civility prevented her from bursting out laughing in sheer astonishment. Instead, she allowed herself a half-smile. "As much as I am loath to disappoint you, sir, there is no courage in the case, only cold reason. I was with Jane for more than a day before we knew her illness for what it is; departing could not then protect me. Add to that the fact that I was with her when we suspect she contracted it, and you see that my continuing health is entirely in the hands of chance."

He pulled a chair out for her and saw her settled upon it, then bent to murmur for her ears alone, "You may call it reason, Miss Elizabeth, but I shall continue to think it courage." He took his seat to her left; Mr Bingley was at the foot of the table to her right, while Mrs Hurst had rejected the lonely mistress' seat at the head of the long table to place herself on her brother's other side with her husband next to her. Elizabeth absorbed this second compliment with only slightly less astonishment than the first.

As the soup was being served, Mr Bingley turned to her. "May I say, Miss Elizabeth, how delighted I am that you were able to join us this evening? I expect you may not often be able to do so, during your stay with us."

"I thank you, sir," she replied with a smile. "I fear you may be correct, though naturally I hope it is not the case." She looked about. "Does Miss Bingley not dine with us?"

An awkward silence descended upon the table. Mr Bingley cleared his throat and said briefly, "My sister has returned to London—"

Shocked, she cried, "London?"

"—against my wishes."

Conscious of having mortified her hosts, however inadvertently, Elizabeth merely nodded and lightly turned the conversation to the weather. "I hope your impression of living in Hertfordshire is not adversely affected by the chilly conditions of late, sir. Most years we are very comfortable until later in the autumn, though I recall one or two like this."

Mr Bingley laughed and said that, having grown up in York and Scarborough, he thought the present weather rather temperate for autumn, and was not at all disappointed. The difficult moment had passed, and everyone relaxed and entered into the conversation.

While the soup was removed, Mr Darcy turned to her. "Miss Elizabeth, I hope it will comfort you to know that all at Longbourn continue well."

"I am happy to hear it, but how is it that you know this, sir?" she asked in some surprise.

He gave her a small smile. "Why, the housekeeper—a Mrs Hill?—informed me when I stopped there today. Were you aware that Mr Bingley and I have undertaken to visit all the houses in the neighbourhood frequently, that Mr Jones may have early word of any new illness?"

"Indeed, I was not!" she exclaimed, looking between the two men. Mr Bingley's goodness she had not doubted, but she was quite shocked that Mr Darcy would put himself to such trouble for country folk. She looked at him more closely. "That is very good of you. And you are not concerned that you may face further exposure?"

"We were both inoculated at Cambridge. The risk is exceedingly low, and we have time and good horses."

"I think many would baulk at even the slight risk you admit," replied Elizabeth.

Mrs Hurst shuddered. "Such a dreadful disease. I had it myself, my first year at school. It was the most terrible experience of my life. I believed I would die, and though I did not, I was so very scarred." As all eyes seemed to examine her, she added quickly, "I was fortunate, for they faded to almost nothing over the next few years. Many are not so lucky."

"I remember," said Mr Bingley, with a soft smile towards his sister. "It is why I offered my services to Mr Jones. I am glad to be of help—and glad of the occupation, truth be told!"

"I wonder that the militia do not take on the task," Elizabeth commented, and it was Mr Bingley who answered her.

"I had the pleasure of speaking to Colonel Forster this afternoon," he said, "and he has decided to keep his men strictly within the camp for the nonce, until he can be assured that none of them have contracted it. He does not want it brought in if it is not already there, nor spread by his men if it is. Mr Denny, who is in town on regimental business, has been ordered to report to the regiment in Eastbourne until more is known."

"A sensible plan," Elizabeth agreed. "Please allow me to thank you both for your efforts on the neighbourhood's behalf. It is vastly reassuring to know that all my family and friends are being watched over."

The gentlemen disclaimed any merit, and the conversation turned to other topics. In the absence of the more forthright and odious Bingley sister, Elizabeth found Mrs Hurst unexpectedly pleasant. They discussed books and discovered some favourites in common, while two of the gentlemen spoke of hunting and the third, most taciturn one appeared to listen in on both conversations. She began to suspect that Mrs Hurst was the sort of woman who bent and swayed to please those nearest her, and took delight in the approbation of others. In good company, there was nothing objectionable about her, but under the influence of the Miss Bingleys of the world, she would behave as they did. It occurred to Elizabeth that she might very well be viewing the future of her own sister Kitty, who was too obliging and dependent on the approval of others for her own good.

When Mrs Hurst signalled that it was time for the ladies to depart, she and Elizabeth moved into the drawing room. Mrs Hurst rang for tea and then turned to Elizabeth. "Will you keep me company, or will you return to your sister?"

Elizabeth wavered for a moment. "I ought to look in on Jane. If she yet sleeps, I should be happy to come back."

"Of course," her hostess said immediately. "If she is awake, do tell her that we are all thinking of her and wishing her an easy recovery."

Elizabeth smiled and said she would, and made her way to Jane's room, where she found her sister sound asleep. She returned to the drawing room, and over their tea she and Mrs Hurst resumed their earlier discussion of books.

"Miss Elizabeth," Mrs Hurst said after a lively debate over the merits and shortcomings of the titular character of *Evelina*, "I believe the library here is rather sparse. I myself never travel without several novels, and for a visit of such duration I came prepared with more than a dozen. If you should like to borrow any of them, you need only ask."

It was a handsome offer, and Elizabeth felt all proper gratitude for it. "That would be a very great treat, and I am happy to accept, for Jane and I shall soon be through the few volumes I found that answer our tastes."

"I shall have some of them brought to you and your sister tomorrow."

"You are very generous!" Elizabeth replied warmly. "We shall take the greatest of care with them, I assure you. Everyone in my father's house learns early that books are precious objects."

Mrs Hurst veritably glowed from even that simple praise, and Elizabeth was reminded again of her earlier notion that she was, in essentials, very like Kitty. The sound of the gentlemen entering interrupted Elizabeth's thoughts, and she tucked them away for later perusal and set about making herself agreeable to the company.

Returning to Jane's room later, she found her sister lightly dozing. Jane awakened as Elizabeth moved across the room. "Lizzy, I am thirsty, but my throat is quite bad," she rasped.

"Wait just a moment, dearest." Elizabeth fetched the pitcher of sweet barley water which she had left on the windowsill to keep cold. She poured some of this out into a glass, and assisted Jane in drinking the cool liquid.

"That does help," Jane said quietly when she had her fill. "Did you enjoy dinner with our hosts?"

"It was pleasant," Elizabeth agreed, "and yet full of surprises." At Jane's enquiring look, she continued, "I learnt that Mr Bingley is a stronger character than I had thought, and that Mrs Hurst and Mr Darcy are kinder." She related then the events of the evening, including the mission of aid upon which Mr Bingley and Mr Darcy were to embark every morning, and Mrs Hurst's offer of novels for their entertainment.

Jane managed to speak a few words of approbation, and then Elizabeth read to her for a little time before she fell asleep once more. Too wakeful to retire, Elizabeth settled herself near the window and looked out across the park as she mused on the similarities she had noted between Mrs Hurst and Kitty and puzzled over Mr Darcy's generosity to the neighbourhood and civility to herself.

———

Elizabeth woke early in the morning, her rest disturbed more by concern for her sister than by the maid who went about raising the fire almost silently. She slipped through the connecting door into her own room to dress warmly against the chill of the morning. Returning, she reassured herself that Jane's sleep was yet deep and untroubled. In whispers, she asked the maid to have barley water and broth sent up for Miss Bennet in an hour, and moved to the window to look out upon the waking land. It was a clear morning, the grass tinged with frost, glinting with the promise of a sunny day. Elizabeth chafed to be out of doors, to breathe deep of the crisp autumnal air and move with freedom and rapidity, but she could not leave Jane for her own pleasure.

As she watched, grooms escorted two large and restless horses from the stables. *These must be Mr Bingley's and Mr Darcy's mounts*, she thought, and amused herself for a moment trying to guess which steed belonged to which gentleman. The largest was a handsome grey with fetlocks, mane, and tail the colour of clotted cream, snorting and pacing in the early light; the other was only a little smaller but broader of chest, a dappled roan who seemed to dance in place with eagerness to be off.

Her amusement faded when she recalled the purpose for which these mounts were required. She wondered again at the kindness and courage displayed by the two gentlemen, to put themselves at risk for the people of a neighbourhood only lately known to them, to whom they had merely the tenuous connexion of a leased estate.

A soft knock on the door interrupted Elizabeth's musings, and she stepped out into the corridor to find Mr Bingley, enquiring after her sister.

Her smile faded somewhat. "Her fever has not returned, which has made her more comfortable in general, but her throat has grown very painful."

A worried frown marred his handsome face. "I am sorry to hear that. If there is anything I may send for, for her comfort, I beg you will not hesitate to inform me. Mrs Dean has a fair hand with ices, if that would be suitable?"

"I should very much like to have some ices for her, if it is not too much trouble," she responded gratefully. "Cool drinks have already proved soothing. And perhaps some broth could be made up without salt? She never complains, but I can tell that the broth pains her, even when we have cooled it, though she requires its strengthening properties."

"Of course!" he replied eagerly. "I shall speak with Mrs Dean personally. I have no notion how long it takes to make such things, but you shall have them as soon as may be."

"You are very good, Mr Bingley. On behalf of my sister and myself, I thank you."

———

Bingley had just swung himself into the saddle, with apologies to Darcy for his tardiness, when they both heard the sound of galloping hooves approaching and saw, speeding down the drive on a great barrel-chested black gelding, a man in the scarlet coat of the militia.

As the soldier pulled up near them, Darcy exclaimed, "Captain Carter? This a surprise. We understood from Colonel Forster that none of your regiment were to leave the camp."

The captain doffed his shako at them and smiled. "I am glad, very glad, that I have found you before you set off. I heard of your purpose after your visit yesterday, and determined that I must be allowed to assist you. I was inoculated at Oxford, and with that protection I could not face myself in the looking glass if I only sat about the camp at such a time."

Darcy shared a look of surprise with Bingley, then turned back to their visitor. "Captain, we are both

Cambridge men, but I daresay we may be able to tolerate your company in such a cause as this," he jested.

The captain's smile turned self-conscious. "Unfortunately, my commanding officer is not convinced of the efficacy of inoculation, and so has allowed me to leave only on the grounds that I shall not return to camp until the trouble has passed." He looked at Bingley. "I fear, sir, that I must beg for a place to lay my head of an evening. A cot is all I require."

"Nonsense!" Bingley cried. "You shall be my guest, even as Darcy is."

Darcy, espying the rucksack tied behind Carter's saddle, dismounted. "Come, if there are to be three of us, we may start a little later. Bring your bag, and let us divide up our visits."

With expressions of gratitude from the soldier, all three men entered the house. The housekeeper was asked to prepare a room for the master's guest, and the captain's bag was whisked upstairs by a footman. It took them scarce a quarter hour in Bingley's study to reapportion their tasks, and at Captain Carter's suggestion they agreed to rotate these appointed rounds, for variety and in order that friends might be met with regularly.

Darcy refrained from claiming the Bennets to be his only 'friends' in the neighbourhood, for the only member of that family whose company he enjoyed was already close by, under the same roof as he. Though he must be wary of placing himself too much in her beguiling company, he could and would ensure she knew of her family's welfare every day.

CHAPTER THREE

Mrs Hurst had not forgotten her promise to the Bennet sisters, and shortly after breakfast her maid arrived at Jane's chambers bearing four novels and a short note urging the Bennet ladies to enjoy them and to have no hesitation whatsoever in requesting anything within Mrs Hurst's power as mistress of Netherfield to supply.

Elizabeth sat with her sister all day, distracting her from the mounting discomfort with conversation and readings, and busying herself with stitchery while Jane slept. She noted with resignation the early signs of the dreaded rash in the form of an increasingly red patch on her sister's forehead. By the time Mr Jones arrived in the late afternoon, he was able to feel lumps starting beneath the skin.

"Miss Bennet," he said gently, "the rash is coming on now. I wish to prepare you both for what will follow." He glanced briefly at Elizabeth, then returned his attention to his patient. "Over the next two or three days, the rash will spread; first, the face, then the upper limbs, then the trunk, and lastly the legs and extremities. It will happen very quickly, beginning with redness and followed soon by bumps beneath the skin. These will, after a few days, become cloudy and this is the most dangerous time. You will feel your worst and be at your weakest. You will be losing fluids every moment, and I cannot stress enough how important it is that you take in as much nourishing liquid as possible. You will not wish to. Your mouth and throat may still be painful, and you may feel that even swallowing is an effort beyond your capabilities. And yet you must."

He turned to Elizabeth, whose trepidation was plain. "This most trying period could last a week or more. While Miss Bennet's mouth remains painful, you may find that it is easiest for you both if you administer fluids by way of a long funnel. Ask the housekeeper if there is one here that would be suitable, and if there is not, I will bring one for you." Elizabeth nodded mutely, now even more frightened.

Mr Jones turned back to Jane. "Miss Bennet, you are young and strong, and I have every confidence in your ability to survive this. Exert yourself to take in nourishment; that is your only task for the next fortnight. In time, the lesions will dry up and scab over. I cannot say you will be comfortable, but by then your mouth and throat should be, if not healed, then greatly improved, and your health will return with rest and food. There will be scarring— there is always scarring—but it is likely to fade over time. When we have got past the worst, I will bring a salve which may help."

Elizabeth was gladdened that throughout the apothecary's lengthy explanation, his tone had been calm and kind; Jane's distress had not been made worse, even when he mentioned scarring. "Have you any questions for me, either of you?"

"Is it true that one may go blind?" Jane asked, her sore throat making her voice raspy and uneven.

"It does happen," he acknowledged. "And I cannot tell you why. I can only advise you to do everything in your power to keep the fluids from the sores out of your eyes."

Jane nodded slowly and then subsided back onto her pillows. Elizabeth rose to see Mr Jones to the door. "Thank you for your time and your information. I have nothing to ask you now, and I am sure you have others to see."

"Unfortunately, I do," he said. "I received word yesterday of three ailing servants at Haye-Park, whom I must visit today to diagnose."

Elizabeth and Jane exchanged a look of concern. Haye-Park was occupied by the Gouldings, neighbours and friends of long standing to the Bennets. The younger Mr and Mrs Goulding had three small children, and young Mrs Goulding had not many years previously been Miss Jones. "You will, I hope," said Elizabeth, "convey our best wishes to your sister, and all the family there?"

Mr Jones bowed. "I shall, I thank you." He bade them good day and left.

Elizabeth turned back to her sister. "I must insist that you do not fret over the Gouldings, at least not yet! They are not themselves ill, and could not possibly be in more capable hands."

Jane smiled slightly at her sister's teasing air and agreed that, beyond adding the Gouldings to her prayers, she would endeavour not to dwell upon melancholy possibilities.

The next morning, a soft knock again came at the door just after dawn. Jane was awake, her sleep cut short by the discomfort of the rash which was advancing rapidly over her body. Elizabeth slipped out into the passageway to find Mr Bingley, dressed for his daily excursion.

She smiled and informed him without prompting that Jane's illness was progressing as expected and that she bore it stoically. Mr Bingley replied that he was grateful for the information, and then he hesitated, seemed to consider something, and at last fixed her with a look that was equal parts determined and abashed.

"I wonder, Miss Elizabeth," he said, producing a folded sheet of paper from his pocket, "if you would be so good as to give this to Miss Bennet, if you do not think it too improper. As you see, it is not sealed, and I wish you would read it so that you may know there is nothing unseemly within."

She was surprised, indeed, as much by his boldness as by the somewhat improper suggestion. But he was their host, they resided in his home, and there was nothing of secrecy in his application. She accepted the page and opened it.

Miss Bennet,

I hope this note finds you well. Dash it, that was a silly thing to write, was it not? Rather, I hope this note finds you as well as (blot)ible in the circumstances.

I have been thinking of our last conversation, in the parlour at Haye-Park. We were speaking of travel, of the places we have been and those we should like to see, when

(blot) party broke up. I hope to continue that conversation
with you very soon. I am all anticipation to know whence
your fascination with India proceeds.
   C Bingley

She smiled and closed the note. "Very well, sir, as the
guardian of my sister's honour I shall allow this communication."

He beamed at her. "Thank you, Miss Elizabeth. I must
away on my 'rounds', as Mr Jones terms them, but the
entire household is at your disposal."

Jane received the note with trepidation and delight,
holding it unopened for several moments as Elizabeth reassured her that there can be nothing very scandalous in a
brief note from a host to an ailing guest, which has been
read by her sister beforehand. Delight won out, and she
read the short missive rapidly, then again slowly, savouring
every word which spoke to his kind heart and gentlemanly
concern. When she grew sleepy, she handed it back to
Elizabeth and asked that it be kept safe for her.

Though glad to see Jane taking so much rest, the time
dragged for Elizabeth, confined to the room with only a
few books and little opportunity for exercise save pacing. A
soft knock at the door brought a respite in the form of Mr
Darcy, come to report that he had called at Longbourn that
morning and all within had been well.

"I did my best to assuage your family's concerns for
Miss Bennet. Your father would appreciate as many letters,
notes, and witty assurances as you can manage," he added,
with what Elizabeth thought a wry smile.

"Of course he would," she replied, laughing. "And he
would direct my sister Mary to reply."

"I am happy to deliver your letters, or any messages. How is Miss Bennet today?"

She thanked him, and answered his enquiry after Jane, and was about to return to the room when Mr Darcy said, "Forgive me if I presume, Miss Elizabeth, but I think you are an active sort of person, and may find this confinement harder to bear than many ladies would?"

"I will admit that it is so," she replied. "You have read me aright. But I cannot complain, for a little dullness is nothing to what my sister suffers."

He inclined his head. "Of course, I can see you take satisfaction from being of use to her, as Bingley and I do from being of use in our way, even if we would all have chosen very different activities in happier circumstances." He bowed and wished her a good day before departing, leaving her wondering what he had meant by it all. She shrugged and slipped back into the room to watch over her sister.

When Jane awoke, Elizabeth plied her with as much cold broth and chilled barley water as she would take. She had picked up the novel to resume reading it aloud when Jane surprised her by saying, "Lizzy, I should like to respond to Mr Bingley's note."

"Jane..." She recognised the unusually determined set of her sister's jaw. "A note from a host to a guest is one thing, but a correspondence? It is not quite proper."

"Which means that it is not quite improper, either."

Elizabeth laughed. "You sound like me! Very well, I can see you are decided." She helped her sister from the bed and over to the escritoire. Jane bent over the note for a full half an hour, often pausing to consider her words before committing them to paper. When it was done, she waved it dry for a moment and then handed it to her sister.

Mr Bingley,

I thank you for your kind note of this morning. It is heartening to know that my friends, among whose number I am delighted to count you, are concerned for my welfare at this uncertain time.

I, too, look very much forward to continuing the conversation to which you referred. You mentioned having been to Italy, and I should dearly like to know more about that place and your experiences there. I will relieve your anticipation by telling you that I became interested in India through my uncle Gardiner, who conducts a great deal of business with that country. One of his associates, Mr Greene, has lived there for over thirty years, and I have since my childhood chanced to meet him several times when he visited England.

He would tell stories of the temples and the cities, of markets redolent with the scent of exotic spice, of the strange and haunting music of the natives. In my uncle's warehouse I have seen the brilliant, richly patterned fabrics in which the people garb themselves, and taken all together it inspired within me a great desire to one day experience it all for myself. It is unlikely that I shall ever have the chance to do so, but it is pleasant to dream upon, nonetheless.

I hope that you are keeping well and finding some pleasure in being master of an estate despite recent events.

Yours,

J Bennet

"Well," Elizabeth remarked, "there is nothing objectionable in the content, not that I expected any such thing from *you*. But though I trust Mr Bingley to be discreet, there is still some slight risk of damage to your reputation. Are you certain you wish that I should deliver this?"

"I am," Jane said. "Please understand, Lizzy. His friendship is precious to me in a way that I cannot describe. I know..." She paused, and hung her head. "I know it cannot now become more than that. If I survive this, I shall be scarred. One innocent exchange of notes—is that truly too much to ask?"

Elizabeth felt her eyes prickle and willed away the tears. She mustered a smile and replied, "Of course not, dearest." Placing the folded note upon the table, she helped Jane back into bed and resumed reading from the novel which they had both been enjoying earlier.

A little after the dinner hour, a knock sounded on the door. Elizabeth opened it to find Mr Darcy, who carried a slim wooden box held closed with a strap and buckle. He bowed and said, "I hope you will forgive the unexpected visit, Miss Elizabeth. I had thought that you might, perhaps, like to borrow this." He held out the box, which she accepted with an enquiring look.

He flushed slightly. "It is a small backgammon set, suitable for travel. My parents enjoyed it in the carriage, when they travelled together. On occasion I play both sides, when I am away from my home and at loose ends. It is not as entertaining as playing another, whose moves cannot be easily predicted, but it is something with which to occupy oneself when not in the mood for a book. And perhaps if Miss Bennet is feeling well enough, you might enjoy some games together." He stopped abruptly, as though embarrassed to have said so much at once, and indeed she rather thought it was the longest speech she had ever heard from him.

She smiled. "I thank you, sir. It was kind of you to think of my comfort, and I shall be delighted to take your suggestion."

He returned her smile awkwardly, as though he were not quite sure he was performing the action correctly. He bowed again, bid her a good evening, and departed. Elizabeth returned to the room, puzzling over the startling notion that perhaps Mr Darcy, with his ten thousand a year and Cambridge education, was uncomfortable in company and unsure of how to converse with young ladies.

"What is it, Lizzy?" Jane croaked from the bed. Elizabeth went to her and explained that Mr Darcy had offered the use of his backgammon set for their amusement. They then opened the box to find that it was a fine old set, with a playing surface of tooled leather, and pieces of carved and stained ivory.

"This is a handsome thing indeed!" Elizabeth exclaimed. "I am surprised he is willing to lend it to anyone, much less someone he knows so little!"

"It is very kind of him," Jane remarked. "I am not tired —shall we play?"

"Certainly," Elizabeth agreed, and they set up the board and passed one of the most pleasant hours of their stay at Netherfield with Mr Darcy's backgammon set.

CHAPTER FOUR

Waking the following morning, it was all Elizabeth could do not to recoil when she first caught sight of her sister. The bumps of the rash, which had only the previous day begun to burgeon with fluid, had swelled immensely in the night, and the face she knew almost as well as her own was now unrecognisable. Jane's hands and wrists, the only other parts of her visible above the night-gown and blankets, were at present only rather red, but she knew from Mr Jones's information that this, too, would soon change. Giving silent thanks that her sister yet slept, she took a moment to accustom herself to the radical changes in Jane's appearance, that she might disclose no sign of dismay when her sister awoke.

She was glad she had done it, for when Jane did awaken, her first words were, "Lizzy, I do not feel well at all, and I am so very thirsty."

"It is as Mr Jones predicted," Elizabeth said soothingly as she spooned broth into the sickroom funnel for Jane to swallow. "The rash is taking fluids from you. Oh, I know it is painful, dearest, but you must keep drinking." Jane nodded her acquiescence and reclined heavily, as though the mere ingestion of broth had sapped her strength. Soon she drifted off to sleep again, and Elizabeth decided to try Mr Darcy's suggestion of playing both sides of a backgammon match. In this manner she amused herself for half an hour, the dice almost silent on the soft leather, before a knock sounded on the door.

She hurried to see who it was, and upon spying Mr Bingley in the hall, she whispered, "I will be out in a moment, sir." Pocketing Jane's note, she joined him in the passage.

"How is Miss Bennet?" he asked anxiously.

Trying not to alarm him, she answered, "Her illness is progressing as Mr Jones predicted." Her delicacy had the opposite of its intended effect, as he clearly sensed she was withholding bad news and became alarmed. She hastened to reassure him, "She is more unwell today, it is true, but it is nothing we did not expect. Nothing has happened yet to indicate that she is in more than the usual danger."

This he accepted with good grace, though sensing he was not entirely reassured, Elizabeth chose to change the subject.

"Now, Mr Bingley, I must speak to you on a serious matter." He looked startled, and she continued. "My sister has replied to your note of yesterday. I will have your word as a gentleman that you will exercise the utmost discretion. My dearest Jane will be facing changes enough after this illness has passed. I am trusting you to ensure that her reputation will not be among them."

His expression was all surprise and delight. "Indeed, Miss Elizabeth, you may rest assured that I would do nothing to harm Miss Bennet in any way. You have my word as a gentleman that your sister's reputation is safe with me...*whatever the consequences*."

She inclined her head. "Very well, then." Elizabeth produced the note from her pocket and handed it to the eager gentleman. "Naturally, I have read it."

"I expected nothing else," he replied distractedly, turning the paper over and over in his hands. "If you will excuse me?" He hurried off to read his letter, leaving Elizabeth chuckling behind him.

———

Bingley came from the house that morning smiling over a piece of paper which he hastily stuffed into his pocket with an expression of consciousness. His actions instantly raised Darcy's suspicions.

"What have you got there, that makes you so cheerful?" he enquired. "I had not thought the post had come yet."

Bingley, as incapable of dissembling as he was of sustaining anger, reddened and admitted, "I sent Miss Bennet a note yesterday, expressing my wishes for her quick recovery, and she was so kind as to reply. Her hand is very elegant..." he concluded dreamily.

"Bingley," Darcy said sharply. "You cannot be exchanging notes with a young lady. Aside from being improper, it is far too intimate. You have known her but a month, and—" He steeled himself to say what must be said, unkind though it was. "It is likely she will be quite altered by her illness. You must not raise expectations you may not wish to fulfil."

His friend's amiable features took on a mulish cast. "I know that I am a shallow, trifling fellow. Or such I have been. But she..." He drew an agitated breath and seemed to grope for words. "She sees more in me. It is there in the way she looks at me, how she speaks to me. It is in every way apparent that she believes me to be a man of character and determination. She makes me wish to be that man. I *shall* be that man, even if...even if she is not there to know it. Her face, Darcy, is not what I love most about her." Having said this, he turned his attention to checking his mount's tack and saddle, his jaw clenched with strong emotion.

Darcy was taken aback to understand just how far his friend was indulging his infatuation. He must tread carefully, he apprehended, lest he drive Bingley into further rash acts from sheer rebellion.

"I do not deny your feelings," he said carefully, much as he wished to do just that. "I only ask that you consider your actions. Such a correspondence is improper—you must acknowledge that." Bingley nodded once, sharply, and Darcy continued. "What is done is done, but it cannot continue."

"I will take your advice under consideration," Bingley said, and at that moment the door to the house opened and Captain Carter emerged.

Frustrated by the untimely interruption, and very much afraid that Bingley would reject his advice forthwith, he turned to greet the soldier. As they all set off down the drive, Carter and Bingley chatted about the friends they expected to meet with that day, while Darcy stewed over the likelihood that the illicit correspondence would continue, and his friend would be further drawn in.

His own loan of the backgammon set to Miss Bennet's sister was, of course, a completely different matter. There was little of intimacy in the loan of a useful possession to an acquaintance in their time of trouble, he told himself. It was a courtesy he would be happy to offer anyone of whom he thought well; it was no different from lending a book. He had brought a number of volumes with him, knowing that Bingley's library would be inadequate at best. Should he...? No. No, absolutely not. He would not make a habit of catering to Miss Elizabeth's every imagined want.

Darcy determinedly put aside his thoughts about Elizabeth Bennet and set off on the day's rounds. His route took him through Meryton, and he frowned to see the populace going about their business as though nothing untoward were occurring. All the shops were open, customers moving from one to the next, greeting each other cheerfully and speaking of busy nothings. Witnessing two ladies embrace and kiss each other's cheeks before parting ways, he wondered darkly whether one of them might find herself feverish later in the day, having already passed the contagion on to her friend.

Was such a thing possible? He did not know; no one did. That it passed from person to person seemed undeniable, but the mechanism was a mystery, as Mr Jones had told them the other day. And was not that uncertainty cause for more caution? If there was the slightest chance that a fleeting encounter could lead to disfigurement or death, why did these people not stay at home?

He cursed himself again for never thinking to have his sister inoculated. It had been a thing he had done in university, flush with excitement over the miracles of modern science, and had promptly forgot when outside the rarefied atmosphere of Cambridge.

He had done what he could in sending an express to his housekeeper in London, ordering that at the first report of smallpox in the city only those who had survived it previously should venture from the house. He had further written to his sister and her companion, Mrs Annesley, explaining his fears that the illness would spread the short distance to town and requesting that they remain within the house and accept no callers. His particular fear was that Miss Bingley might call upon his sister, and so he had sent a third express, this one to his London butler, stating that the lady was not to be admitted.

None of this was sufficient to make a doting brother easy for his sister's safety, and he promised himself that his first act when they were reunited would be to arrange for her to be inoculated. In the midst of these thoughts, he was hailed by Sir William Lucas, who had come into Meryton with his daughters.

"Good day, Mr Darcy! What word from Netherfield?"

"Sir William, Miss Lucas, Miss Maria." He tipped his hat, as he could hardly bow from horseback. "The illness continues to spread. You would judge best to return home and remain there."

"We are just come to place a few orders to fill up our larder," the man replied cheerfully. "Your concern is most kind, but it has not reached the town. Naturally I should not bring my daughters if it had. I myself suffered through it as a child, so if it does spread to Meryton I shall have to venture forth alone, I suppose!"

"Sir, it may very well be in Meryton. Many show no symptoms for a fortnight or more after exposure, but it is not known when they begin to spread it. I must urge caution. Please, take your daughters home." Miss Lucas now wore an expression of concern, while her younger sister appeared confused.

Sir William chuckled. "Come now, sir, everyone knows that it cannot be passed by one who looks and feels well. You have been listening to young Mr Jones's strange theories, I wager. He is a good man, capital, very knowledgeable," he hastened to add. "But these young men of medicine always wish to believe they have discovered something no one else has! A worthy ambition, but one mustn't take their ideas too seriously. No, smallpox has been with us since the Flood, and all that may be known of it, is."

Miss Lucas stepped in then, curtseying to Mr Darcy. "We must be about our business—my mother expects our quick return, and we should delay *your* business no longer —but we thank you for the information, sir. If you would, please pass on my greetings and best wishes to the Miss Bennets at Netherfield." Her serious mien, more than her words, gave him to know that there was one in the Lucas home who would do what she might to limit what her father would not forbid, and he acknowledged the unspoken message with a nod.

"Certainly I shall, Miss Lucas. Good day to you all." Tipping his hat again, he rode on.

———

Darcy's final stop of the day was to the Millidges, tenants of Longbourn whose parcel bordered Netherfield's home farm. He had been here once before, and on this second visit was greeted more warmly by the lady of the house, who had been highly suspicious of the coming of a stranger the first time. She wrapped a thick woollen shawl about her ample form and pulled the door shut on the sounds of children at play as she joined him outside.

After reporting that all were healthy within, she said, "Iffen you don't mind, sir, might I ask after our Miss Bennet? She's at Netherfield with all of you, they say."

He replied that she was correct, and that Miss Bennet's illness had thus far given no cause for additional alarm.

"Ah, poor lamb. And Miss Lizzy? I expect she won't leave her sister's side. Still in health, I hope?"

"Miss Elizabeth is most devoted to Miss Bennet's care, and has thus far escaped the sickness."

"May it remain so!" the woman cried sincerely. "I remember when I first come here as a bride, ten years ago now, and Miss Bennet and Miss Lizzy come by with a basket that took both of 'em to carry, little as they were, to welcome me to Longbourn and help me start my housekeeping, they said. In all that time I've said perhaps five words to Mrs Bennet, but those two girls visit us all quite regular. Don't know as we'd care to stay here without 'em, truth be told. The master's not a bad sort, if you tell him something's broke, he'll see it fixed and all, in his own time, but he don't take an interest, nor does the lady. Every tenant on Bennet land is praying for those two as much as for their own kin."

"When next I see Miss Elizabeth, I shall tell her you were asking after her and Miss Bennet. I am sure it will comfort her to know they are not forgotten," he offered through a haze of shock. Ten years ago the two sisters would have been mere children, and yet it sounded as though they had already thoroughly taken up the neglected duties of the estate's mistress. How many girls would have had such fortitude, not to mention the wit to understand the need? His estimation of Miss Elizabeth, already high, rose further, and now he had learnt that there was more to her sister than serene good manners.

CHAPTER FIVE

A RESPONSE TO HURST'S EXPRESS HAD BEEN SLOW IN coming, but at last a message was received from Miss Bingley stating that she had indeed arrived safely in London; it closed with a remark that they were all great fools for remaining. He consigned it to the fire and over dinner informed his companions that he had heard from his sister and she was safe in town. When Darcy reminded his friend to have his horses, carriage, and driver returned to Netherfield, Bingley quickly wrote an express of his own, albeit addressing it to Hurst's butler.

"Are you writing to Caroline?"

Bingley startled, then wiped his pen and set it aside before looking up at his sister. "No, to Gregson, requesting the return of my equipage at the soonest possible moment."

Louisa's hands twisted together, and she asked, tentatively, "Would you also ask him to inform us if she falls ill? I am concerned for her. She will be all alone if she does contract the disease."

IN SICKNESS & IN HEALTH

Her face crumpled and her eyes shone with unshed tears. "She was such a bright, engaging girl. I have spent years hoping she would find that within herself again, but she has not. I begin to fear she shall not. I would gladly tend to her as Miss Elizabeth attends to Miss Bennet, but she would not do the same for me...would she?"

"I do not believe so," Bingley replied gently. "Whatever she was as a child, she is all ambition and cunning now. I do not know how or why it happened, and it is to your credit that you still hope for her amendment, but I do not think that is something either you or I have the power to affect. She ceased to heed either of us long ago."

"Do you not hope for her improvement?"

"One always hopes, Louisa. But I do not expect it, no."

She nodded slowly, her expression sad. "Perhaps it is time I moderate my expectations of her, Brother." She moved off then, to enquire after the comfort of their guests. Bingley took up his pen again and, for her sake alone, added her request to his letter.

———

Though Darcy, Bingley, and Carter were kept busy during the daylight hours, riding about the area and gathering information on the spread of the sickness, the evenings at Netherfield proved very long. A pall had settled over the house, with the knowledge of illness within and the fear of more to come. Dinners were quiet affairs, and the hours in the drawing room afterwards quieter still. Mr Hurst preferred to avoid the atmosphere by overindulging in wine over dinner and falling asleep on the sofa by the windows. Mrs Hurst would amuse herself with a novel or music.

The other gentlemen would use the time to tend to their correspondence, and then to read or converse. Carter proved to be pleasant company, willing to enter into conversation on any subject or indulge Mrs Hurst by making up a table for loo or *vingt-et-un*. Despite these mild pleasures, they often found themselves retiring early, ending the day that the next might arrive the sooner. Darcy found himself wishing that Miss Elizabeth might join them one evening; she more than deserved a respite from attending her sister and all would welcome the addition of her wit and intelligence to their conversation.

Darcy's mind was much occupied by the events of the day—the revelation of Bingley's strong feelings for and improper exchange with Miss Bennet, the obliviousness of those he had seen in Meryton, and the testimony of Mrs Millidge as to the fine characters of the eldest Bennet sisters. As they all sat in the parlour after the meal, Darcy emerged from his thoughts to hear his friend repeating his name with an edge of exasperation.

"I beg your pardon; I was not attending."

"I should say not!" Bingley exclaimed, his irritation instantly transformed to humour. "I have been trying to get your attention these two minutes at least. Your face is a picture of gloom, old friend. Pray, what troubles you?"

Darcy rubbed a hand over his mouth. "I do not know that I am troubled, precisely. I was only wondering...if it were my sister sick with the smallpox, and I had not been inoculated, would I have the courage to attend to her myself?"

Bingley's eyebrows rose. "I should be very surprised if you did not, for I have rarely seen a closer relationship between brother and sister than that between you and Miss Darcy. I imagine you would cheerfully die for her, if called upon to make such a sacrifice." He rose and moved to the decanter, pouring a small glass of brandy for each of them. Setting one before Darcy, he resumed his seat.

"You are thinking, I suppose, upon Miss Elizabeth's care of Miss Bennet. It is admirable. They are admirable ladies, both of them."

Darcy took a sip of the brandy, and then said, "Having met the rest of the family, I am forced to wonder if there was another Mrs Bennet, for I cannot conceive of either of them issuing from that woman, or being full sisters to the other three."

Bingley set his glass down and was silent for a moment. When he spoke, his voice was pitched too low to carry across the room to his sleeping brother-in-law, or to his sister and Captain Carter, engaged in a lively game of Cassino.

"Darcy, you seemed to approve the other day when I spoke my mind about my sister's disobedience, so I shall dare to be forthright again. I do not like it when you speak of our neighbours in such a fashion. Mrs Bennet may not be the most cultured lady, but she has made us very welcome here—more welcome than some of our party deserved," he added emphatically. "I have been in society long enough to see women of rank display similar manners—or worse!—and yet I do not hear you speak of them so. I beg you will do me the courtesy of disapproving of my neighbours silently. I am beneath many of them in station, if not in wealth, and when you mock their breeding, it makes me wonder what you truly think of *me*."

Darcy was shocked by this speech—shocked, and ashamed. "I do beg your pardon. I never wished to give you cause to doubt my esteem for you. I am mortified to find that I have done so. I hope that if I offend in future, you will correct me again."

Bingley eyed him speculatively, then nodded. "I thank you for that, and I do forgive you. I understand that you were raised to think meanly of anyone beneath you in consequence, and it has been the greatest compliment of my life to be counted among your friends despite it."

Darcy startled at that characterisation, but could not honestly deny it.

"I greatly admire the elder Miss Bennets," Bingley continued, "and as I said, Mrs Bennet has been very welcoming, despite first impressions."

"What do you mean by that?" Darcy asked.

"Well, after you insulted Miss Elizabeth during our first engagement with our neighbours, I would not have been surprised if Mrs Bennet had denied our entire party admittance to her home," Bingley said with a chuckle. "But aside from a little understandable coldness towards you, she has been gracious, and I am grateful for it. She is the leading lady of the neighbourhood and could have made us all very uncomfortable here, had it been her desire."

Darcy was greatly offended by the charge. "I have never insulted Miss Elizabeth!" he exclaimed, causing Mrs Hurst to look up from her cards.

"Certainly you have, Mr Darcy," she replied with a laugh. "At that little assembly we attended, you said she was not pretty enough to dance with, or something similar.

She heard you herself, and found it amusing to tell her friends what '*that conceited fellow from the north*' had to say about the beauty of the local ladies. Did you not know? It was much spoken of for a week at least."

An incredulous expression flitted across the captain's face before he could master himself, and he began to study his cards with more intensity than they warranted.

Darcy went by turns red and pale. To understand that the lady he was coming to admire so very greatly had overheard his petulant statement—forgotten by him until that very moment—and thought him a boor was mortifying in the extreme. He looked to his friend, who was gazing at him with a mixture of sympathy and amusement.

"I, too, thought you were aware that your opinion of Miss Elizabeth had been widely circulated," Bingley admitted.

"I had not the least idea." Darcy took a long sip of brandy, then declared quietly, "You are correct—it is a wonder that Mrs Bennet did not retaliate in her daughter's defence. I am amazed that Miss Elizabeth speaks to me at all."

Bingley stifled his laughter, but Mrs Hurst did not, and Darcy retreated into his thoughts and his brandy, which they kindly allowed. However, as the gentlemen ascended the stairs at the close of the evening, Carter made so bold as to recommend a maker of spectacles, Mr Pierce of Knightsbridge, to Darcy, delivering the suggestion with a slight smirk and a clap on the shoulder.

———

The next morning, Mr Bingley once again appeared at Jane's door in the early hours, and asked Elizabeth to give her sister another note. Elizabeth, brows raised, enquired, "Is this to become a regular occurrence?"

"I certainly hope so," Mr Bingley admitted with a boyish grin. "But the power rests entirely with you and Miss Bennet, and I must hope you both take pity upon me."

Elizabeth rolled her eyes a little, chuckling at his audacity. "I think, sir, you have realised that I will deny my sister nothing when she is ill, so rather say the power rests with her," she replied, slipping the note into her pocket.

Mr Bingley's grin widened for a moment, then he sobered. "I hope you know that I have no wish to burden or intrude upon either of you. If your sister, at any time, wishes that I cease to communicate in this manner, do tell me. I write as much in hope of distracting her from her troubles for a while as of coming to know her better."

Elizabeth was conscious of the risks of allowing this to continue; greater than the slight chance of discovery was the possibility that one or both of them would experience an increase in their affections, which might then be painfully ended by Jane's death or disfigurement. Yet she was conscious also of the joy her sister had received from the first communication, and she did not wish to deny Jane any opportunity for pleasure in the present circumstance.

"Well, sir," she said after a moment, "Jane was certainly delighted by your first note. If her reception should change, I will make it known to you."

Jane received this second letter with a pleasure tempered only by her illness, even rousing herself sufficiently to comment on the disgracefulness of his penmanship. "I shall not be able to reply," she remarked sadly as she handed the page back to Elizabeth to lock away inside the escritoire, for her hands were now covered in emerging blisters, and to hold a pen would surely cause pain.

"If you will take an ice, half a bowl of broth, and some barley water, dearest, I shall scribe your reply for you." Elizabeth was not above bribery to ensure her sister was fed, despite her painful throat and mouth. Jane grimaced but agreed, and it took almost two hours, with frequent and lengthy pauses, to accomplish the feat, but at the end of it, Jane had taken as much nourishment that morning as the entire day prior and Elizabeth was more than happy to pick up her pen and fulfil her part of the bargain.

———

When Darcy arrived at Longbourn that morning, he had hardly dismounted before the front door opened. Instead of Mr Hill ushering him in out of the cold, Miss Mary Bennet hurried out, fastening the clasp of a cloak with one hand while pulling the door closed with the other.

"Miss Mary." He bowed as concern overtook surprise in his mind. Usually he was admitted into the vestibule to enjoy a few minutes of warmth while speaking with Mrs Hill, who always prudently positioned herself at the far end of the small passage.

She curtseyed. "Mr Darcy. There is illness within the house. We do not yet know whether it is the smallpox, but it is best that you do not enter, sir. Please forgive my lack of hospitality, under the circumstances."

"Of course, you are correct to take precautions. What may I tell Mr Jones of the situation within?"

"My mother and my sister Lydia became feverish in the night, and not half an hour ago Mr Hill was put to bed with a fever also. Everyone else continues well." For all her cool, rational delivery, Darcy could see her hands twisting together beneath the cloak.

"I shall inform Mr Jones with all haste. You may expect him tomorrow, if not today. In the interim, he has been encouraging those in the early stages of the illness to take more nourishment than usual. If it is only a cold at Longbourn, I daresay a bit of hearty eating shall do no harm."

Miss Mary was clearly relieved to have some direction on actions to take; she thanked him warmly and urged him on his way.

————

Darcy returned to his chambers that afternoon, half frozen and vowing to spend a month complete without riding once all of this had passed. His valet met him with a serious expression. "Sir, there is A Letter."

Stevens had a way of slightly altering his inflection such that Darcy could see in his mind's eye the capitalisation of certain words. It rarely boded well, and in this case, Darcy knew instantly to what he referred. Of all the unwanted correspondence he received, only one person could send 'A Letter'. They arrived twice or thrice a year, at irregular intervals, and had done for the last several years. This one was particularly unexpected, as he had received the last only two months past. As much as he should like to ignore them, he knew he would do so at his own peril.

Darcy sighed. "I will change and warm up before I

deal with that. If you would be so good as to place it atop any others which have arrived?"

His man nodded briefly and set about divesting him of his dusty riding clothes and wrapping him in a warm robe and slippers. He settled into the chair before the fire with a pot of tea, toasting his thawing toes almost too close to the flames, while the small stack of correspondence taunted him from the little table to his right.

After only a few minutes he huffed, snatched the topmost missive, and broke the unmarked wax which sealed it shut.

> *Darcy, you smug muckworm,*
>
> *Imagine my surprise when I learnt that I had very nearly placed myself in close proximity to you. I encountered an old friend who was in town on business, and when I mentioned I had been looking to make a change, he suggested I join his regiment of militia, stationed for the winter in the town of Meryton in Hertfordshire. I do wish I could see your face as you read that.*
>
> *As fate would have it, just as we were about to depart for that place, my friend got word that there was an epidemic of smallpox in the area, and he was instead to report to a regiment at Eastbourne for the duration. My friend took the opportunity to stay a few days further, and during this time he regaled me with tales of the local society.*
>
> *You may picture my astonishment when your name and Bingley's were mentioned, and likewise my lack of same when Denny related that the whole of the neighbourhood finds you 'high and conceited', and the most disagreeable fellow they have ever had the misfortune to*

know. Only think, we might have met in the street, all unexpected, if not for the sickness. I am quite sure that in such a place, among people discerning enough to see past your wealth and family to the peevish, stiff-rumped churl you truly are, I could have made many friends.

Perhaps I shall, later in the winter. Denny said there are always landowners looking to have someone or other take a post in the militia in place of a son or nephew. I may yet oblige one of them. It sounds a fine lark—a few hours of marching and shooting, and then liberty to take oneself into the town and impress the ladies with one's scarlet coat and fine manners. But you would know nothing of impressing the ladies, would you, old monk?

Until then, I take satisfaction in knowing that you are trapped in a country house not your own, in a neighbour-hood full of those you would never deign to know, with the ever-attentive Miss Bingley and your friend's surely inadequate library to console you. You may imagine me laughing heartily, and often, as I imagine it.

G Wickham

Darcy's feelings upon reading this were more complex than was usual after one of Wickham's taunting missives. Annoyance and anger were his usual reaction, and certainly those were present, but now also horror at the thought that Wickham might have come into *this* neighbourhood and sported with the livelihoods and daughters of *these* people, whom he was coming to know and care for. Dread, too, that Wickham might yet come, filled his heart, and last but not least was shame that he had made such an impression.

———

Not long after, Darcy intercepted Mr Jones by the staircase, and grimly related the news from Longbourn.

Mr Jones assured him he would go immediately to the Bennets' home. "I thank you for the information," he said. "May I ask you to relay it to Miss Elizabeth?"

"Of course," said Darcy. "You must tend to the ill, and we shall continue as your couriers and informants." He found himself curious about this market-town apothecary, a man who appeared to be several years his junior, who spoke in educated accents and strode into the presence of disfiguring and deadly disease without flinching. But this was not the time to satiate his curiosity, so it must be swallowed, and the business of the day attended to. He bowed sharply.

Mr Jones returned the gesture. "I thank you, Mr Darcy. Without the aid of yourself and Mr Bingley and Captain Carter, my burdens would be much greater."

He watched the apothecary gather his scarf and bag before pulling up the collar of his old greatcoat, which Darcy saw had once been quite fine, against the chill November wind. The door shut behind him and Darcy turned his mind to other matters, his feet to the stairs.

CHAPTER SIX

THE SOFT KNOCK BROUGHT ELIZABETH QUICKLY TO the door of her sister's chamber. Holding a finger over her lips, Elizabeth slipped out into the hall and quietly closed the door behind her. "Jane is sleeping at last," she whispered, then regarded their visitor with some surprise. "Whatever brings you here, Mr Darcy?"

He indicated that they should move down the passage a space, and once they were farther from the chamber he spoke in low tones. "I come with news from Longbourn."

Elizabeth was not alarmed by this, for Mr Darcy was always grave, in her opinion, and she waited for him to continue with nothing more than mild interest.

"I stopped at your father's estate this morning to enquire after the household. Rather than being admitted to the house, Miss Mary came out to greet me." He paused, looked briefly disconcerted, and then fixed her with a gaze of such earnestness as to raise the alarm his solemnity had not. "I will be direct. Your sister informed me that your mother and Miss Lydia both developed a fever last night, and your servant Mr Hill began to feel unwell this morning."

Elizabeth sucked in a sharp breath, and he reached out a hand as if to steady her, but she did not waver and it dropped back to his side after hanging in the air between them for a moment. He continued, "Mr Jones has been informed, and one of us shall now call there daily as well, so you shall not lack for news. It is to be hoped that they have merely contracted an ill-timed ague."

She was silent for a long moment, her hands clenching and releasing the fabric of her skirts. "As you say, sir, we must hope for the best, and of course I have every confidence in Mr Jones. Has anyone else fallen ill with the smallpox?"

He looked briefly uncomfortable then, and nodded slowly. "Several servants at Haye-Park, where we all dined together a few nights before your sister fell ill, are now well into their illness. Mr Jones fears that everyone who was at that dinner is in some danger unless they are fortunate enough to have been inoculated or survived it previously, and he expects that we will begin to see more cases in the coming week."

Elizabeth thought back to that otherwise unremarkable dinner party, and concluded that most of the gentry in this corner of Hertfordshire had been at Mrs Goulding's table that evening. "My uncle Philips had it in childhood, and my father lost two sisters in that epidemic, but never fell ill himself. It has been many years since smallpox came to this area, and inoculation has not."

They were both silent for a moment as they contemplated the scope of the problem. If the Haye-Park servants had been contagious during that dinner, it seemed quite possible that many people were even now on the verge of succumbing.

"Have you any word of the Lucases since you saw them in Meryton?" she asked suddenly. "Charlotte—Miss Lucas—is my particular friend, and our families have been close these many years."

"When last I saw them, they were all well," he answered. "Bingley was to look in on them today, I believe. I will ask him to inform you when he returns."

"Might I—" she hesitated. "Will you allow me to belatedly accept your earlier offer to send notes to my family, and perhaps also to Miss Lucas, by way of your visits?"

"Certainly." He bowed slightly. "I, and I daresay Bingley and Carter, should be happy to oblige."

Her mind was too full to be more than faintly surprised by his easy agreement, though later she would remember it with wonder. "I thank you, sir. I will have a note for each of them ready before you depart in the morning. If you will excuse me, I should return to Jane."

He bowed again, more deeply. "Please give Miss Bennet my regards and wishes for an easy recovery," he said, and was gone.

Elizabeth took advantage of Jane's continuing rest to write a short, quick note to Charlotte and a rather lengthier one to Mary, who could be relied upon to respond more promptly than her father and more rationally than Kitty. When Jane awoke, Elizabeth fed her as much sweet orange ice as she would take, and then gently delivered the news from home. After a brief bout of quiet tears, Jane's natural optimism reasserted itself. "It may, as Mr Darcy says, merely be an ague, and the timing sheer coincidence," she remarked hopefully.

"Indeed, it may," Elizabeth agreed with more cheer than she felt. "After all, I am perfectly well, so you are obviously not very adept at spreading the smallpox." She chose not to mention the confirmation of illness at Haye-Park, where they had all dined so recently.

Jane laughed softly, then winced at the pain in her throat. Elizabeth spooned some broth into her sister's mouth, and after a moment Jane felt able to speak again. "Oh, Lizzy, I am a selfish creature, but I am so very glad you have stayed with me. I should be terribly frightened without you."

"And I should be terribly frightened to be parted from you in this, my dear Jane. Whatever is to come, we shall face it together, you and I." Her fears for their family at Longbourn, and her regret that they must all be separated at such a time, she kept firmly concealed.

———

Early the following morning, Mary Bennet, with all the strained patience she could muster, said, "I'm sorry you are bored, Lydia, but I must see to Mama as well, and you know how much she requires. Here is your novel, why do you not read a bit?"

"I cannot read, my head pains me so," Lydia whined. "And I am so hot. Open a window, Mary, do."

The middle Bennet sister closed her eyes for a moment as Lydia's request was punctuated by the sound of the bell her mother kept at her bedside. She opened her eyes and looked again at her youngest sister, who lay restlessly upon the muddled bed, squinting against the faint light of the candle on the bedside table. The fever had leached a great deal of her spirit in only a day, and she grew more tractable as it went on, leaving Mary torn between relief and concern. She marched across the hall and entered Kitty's room without even the pretence of a knock, finding her next-youngest sister awake but yet abed. Kitty looked up rather dully, and Mary's overtaxed patience turned to alarm. She approached the bed and felt Kitty's forehead.

"You are too warm," she fretted.

"I do not feel very well," Kitty admitted.

"Do you think you might be able to share with Lydia, and perhaps read to her? She is very dull but her head is too painful for reading, and it would be easier for me to care for you both if you were in the same room."

Kitty obligingly agreed to this proposition. Mary escorted her to Lydia's room, noting that she seemed a bit dizzy, and settled her into the bed next to Lydia. Only then did she answer the continuing chiming of the bell.

"Where have you been, child?" Mrs Bennet demanded querulously. "I have been ringing the bell this last hour, I am sure! And where is Hill?"

"Hill is tending to Mr Hill," Mary replied.

"Well, it is very inconvenient! I have such pains in my head and flutterings in my chest, worrying what will become of us all, with my two most beautiful daughters sure to be scarred by this terrible illness, and no one has even brought my tea this morning!"

"It is early yet, and I have been seeing to Lydia and Kitty. They also await their tea and breakfast."

"Why are you tending to Kitty? She is not ill!"

"But she is. She has got a fever in the night."

"Well, she cannot possibly be as sick as I!" Mrs Bennet declared. "Now fetch me my tea!"

Mary stood silent for a moment, fists balled up among her skirts, shaking and on the precipice of saying something for which she might never be forgiven.

And then she said it.

"Your tea can wait until I have seen to my sisters. They at least do not shout at me for taking care of them as best I can," she declared, marching up to the bedside table and snatching the little bell. "And I will be taking this!" she added with some asperity before storming out of the room, her mother's shrieks following her down the stairs.

Her fury carried her into her father's book-room, where she flung the door wide with a resounding thump. Mr Bennet startled and fumbled the book he had been reading; it fell to the floor. "Father! Kitty is ill and I cannot care for all three of them alone! You may tend to your wife or find someone who will!"

Mr Bennet sat silent, mouth agape, as his middle daughter shouted at him for the first time in her life. Mary drew a long breath before adding, more quietly but no more pleasantly, "She wants her tea." She whirled about and disappeared as suddenly as she had come.

———

Elizabeth received notes from Mary and Charlotte late that afternoon. Amazed, she looked up at Mr Darcy and smiled. "I did not expect to hear from them until tomorrow! Please do not feel you must wait on replies in the future, sir."

"I did not wait at all. I merely visited Lucas Lodge first this morning, and then again on my way back to Netherfield, and Carter did the same at Longbourn," Mr Darcy replied.

"Then I thank you both for going out of your way to collect these," she said, touched by their kindness.

"It is no trouble, and a pleasure to be of service to you and your family," he answered.

She cocked her head and looked at him curiously for a moment, then smiled and executed a curtsey. "Still, I am grateful, sir. To be separated from our family and friends at a time such as this is...difficult."

He bowed. "I will leave you to read your letters."

Returning to the room, she eagerly opened the page addressed in Mary's hand.

Dear Lizzy,

You cannot know what a comfort your note was to me. In addition to my fears for you both, which you have relieved for the moment, I have been feeling very alone in caring for the rest of our family, as Mrs Hill tends to Mr Hill and Sara will not leave her room for fear of contagion. Rest assured that Father and I continue in good health, but Kitty has now got a fever and headache.

I fear I rather anticipated your good advice to involve Father in caring for our invalids, for before your note arrived I quite lost my temper with Mother and her unreasonable demands, and then I invaded Father's book-room and shouted at him until he agreed to tend to Mother in my place. I am sure you are laughing now and saying something like 'Well done, Mary!', but I feel very bad about it. I did not show either of them the respect we are commanded to give to our parents. I will be a while reconciling the good result with my conscience, no doubt.

Though ill, Kitty is helping by reading to Lydia, whose head pains her far too much to allow her to entertain herself. This has given me time to consult with Mrs Saxby, fetch food and drink for all three of us, and reply to you. I am with them at this moment, and I will tell only you, Lizzy, that Lydia's state has begun to frighten me. She is so still that I would think her asleep if the corner of her mouth did not occasionally twitch in response to some humorous thing in the story. She hardly speaks and never opens her eyes, saying that the light of even a single candle makes her head feel as if it is splitting open. Her fever is very high, and I will ask you to send me any advice you have before I conclude this so I may prepare another cool cloth for her forehead.

You and Jane are in my prayers, as I hope we are in yours.

Mary

"Oh, Mary," Elizabeth said with a sigh, but not in the exasperated manner in which those words usually passed her lips. What she now felt towards her often overlooked sister was sympathy and no little pride. She determined that her reply must be as cheerful and helpful as possible, and set Mary's letter aside to read the other.

Eliza,

How glad I was to receive your note, and to learn that you are not ill and Jane is as well as can reasonably be hoped. Thus far we at Lucas Lodge are all very well, though we have lately been informed that we must be watchful for symptoms for a full three weeks from the date of Mrs Goulding's dinner party.

Mama asks if she ought to send a jar of marmalade for Jane (you know, of course, that she believes oranges cure all ills). She gives thanks every day that James and Nicholas are away at school and Matthew at university, and that since Papa had the disease as a child, only she and I and Maria are in any danger.

I wish more than anything that there were some manner in which I might be of assistance to you now. I shall write to you every day if the gentlemen are willing to serve as my couriers, and I will think of and pray for all your family. If there is anything else I might accomplish from here which would be of aid to you, you have only to ask.

Charlotte

Elizabeth smiled—good news at last! She checked on Jane, who slept restlessly, and sat at the desk to make her replies.

———

Darcy and Carter were engaged in a chess match in the drawing room when Bingley returned late that afternoon, in company with Mr Jones. As the two men warmed themselves by the fire, the apothecary wasted no time in relating that he had that morning confirmed the first case of smallpox within the town of Meryton itself. A son of Mr Turner's, owner of the mercantile, had shown a fever two days previous, and today presented with sores in the mouth.

"The shop cannot be closed, of course." Mr Jones sighed. "They are the only source of many necessities. I have requested that Mrs Turner, who now tends him, keep to their rooms above the shop and that any of the family who will be working below avoid the boy, but I am uneasy, and doubt they will follow my guidance so strictly as they ought."

"And moving the boy and his mother would do little good when the whole of the family has likely been exposed," added Carter.

"Precisely. I believe we may expect that this will get much worse, gentlemen," Mr Jones replied. "Particularly as a segment of the population appears determined to behave as though it cannot possibly touch them. More than one person has told me that God will protect them. At the risk of sounding blasphemous, I have yet to see any evidence of a divine hand in the workings of disease."

"It is generally said that the Lord helps those who help themselves," remarked Darcy sardonically. "And little can help a man who denies what surrounds him," he added, thinking of Sir William's happy obliviousness.

Mr Jones nodded his agreement before excusing himself to go tend to his patient.

CHAPTER SEVEN

THE EXODUS BEGAN WITHIN HOURS OF THE DIAGNOSIS of the Turner boy. Carter had seen evidence of odd, furtive activity at the great house at Stoke when he had visited late that day, and when the gentlemen next made their rounds, they found that house and several others empty. The Hunleys of Stoke had left most of their servants behind, while the Gouldings' poorest tenants, the Norrises, had apparently loaded their entire family of ten, including an aged grandmother, into their wagon and made for parts unknown. Several other families had sent their children away, and were as one defiant when confronted with the dangers of breaking the quarantine. Over the next several days, other families, other sets of children, and other individuals would quietly slip away from the area along the secluded farming tracks which wound across the landscape.

Bingley was particularly incensed at this happening. "Pure, bloody-minded selfishness, I call it!" he ranted to the other gentlemen of the household one evening over brandy. "They have been told that it is not safe, that to go about unless they have suffered it before or been inoculated may spread the sickness! Bad enough that so many were traipsing through the town as though nothing were amiss until the other day, but now they are leaving the area, and no doubt some at least will be the cause of a new outbreak in some innocent place! It is unconscionable! Something must be done!"

"I share your feelings, but nothing can be done," replied Darcy. "The magistrate declined to issue a legally binding order of quarantine when Mr Jones requested it, and now he and his family have fled. In the eyes of the law, they have done nothing amiss, though I venture to hope their Maker will judge differently."

"But why would they not listen to Mr Jones, even if the law does not compel them?" cried Bingley. "There cannot be another man in the county so knowledgeable about the disease! It is senseless to ignore the informed advice of an expert."

"Many people are senseless," Darcy answered wearily, "and will ignore sweet reason if its effect is to produce any possible inconvenience to themselves."

To this, the other gentleman had no reply.

———

Those days were difficult for the sisters at Netherfield as Jane's lesions swelled and her strength waned. The time was made drearier still by heavy clouds and howling winds which flung sleet against the windows and set them to rattling in their casements. The best part of Elizabeth's days was when Mr Darcy, cheeks reddened by the cold and looking on the whole less carefully arranged than ever she had seen him before, would hand her notes from Mary and Charlotte and ask after Jane's health and her own spirits. To see and speak with someone hale and well was a treat which she also received from Bingley's daily queries after Jane, but to acquire those precious missives elevated Mr Darcy's visits above his friend's.

She never thought to question why only he brought them, and more grateful still would she have been had she known that his route did not always bring him to Longbourn and Lucas Lodge, but he had quietly taken it upon himself to visit both at the end of every day's rounds, to collect the answers to the notes which Elizabeth faithfully sent downstairs every evening to await their morning departure.

Charlotte's second letter came with a jar of Lady Lucas's curative orange marmalade, which Elizabeth set aside for that longed-for day in which Jane might swallow without pain. The missive itself was full of just such cheerful nothings as took Elizabeth away from her own troubles for a few moments. Mary's note was brief, reporting that Kitty was unchanged and Lydia rather worse, and their mother's throat was now bad enough to largely forbid speech. Their father kept to his course and attended her.

The next day's letter from Lucas Lodge was not so light-hearted, for Maria Lucas had swooned at the dinner table and thereafter been found to suffer a high fever. Nothing was certain, for Mr Jones had not yet been by and no rash was to be seen, but as Lady Lucas was too fretful to be of use and not at her best in a sickroom under any circumstance, Charlotte was preparing herself to undertake a duty very similar to Elizabeth's and begged her old friend for any words of advice she might now offer.

Elizabeth wrote her reply as quickly as she could; there was no telling how much free time she might have between now and the morning, and she was determined that Charlotte would be answered with all possible haste.

My dear Charlotte,

I fear you will not be satisfied by this response, but the best advice I can give you is this:

Firstly, trust to Mr Jones's wise instruction and to your own good sense and tender heart. What can be done from a medical perspective, the former will guide you in; what can be done for Maria's solace and comfort, the latter will tell you.

Next, care for yourself second only to Maria. Sleep whenever you can, keep up your strength by not neglecting your meals, and when Maria sleeps, read amusing things to lighten your spirits.

Lastly, let others do those things which do not require your particular attention. This will ease your burden and allow them to feel of use to her as well.

There is so little which may be done to any effect, but that little will consume your every waking thought. There will be moments when you feel you are near to running mad from confinement, and others when you would not readily leave the room for any reason.

I shall continue to hope, until I hear otherwise from you, that Maria's illness is not Jane's, and that you and your mother continue well.

With fondest regards and best wishes for a happy resolution, I remain your friend,

Elizabeth

———

When Jane awoke the next morning, she confessed that she felt slightly better. Elizabeth was pleased to see her sister eat more than she had at a single sitting for the last several days, and yet that slight effort left her visibly exhausted. Even the revelation of another note from Mr Bingley, which had been slipped under the door while they both slept, was not enough to rouse her further than to say, "Will you read it to me, Lizzy?"

Elizabeth complied, and when it was done Jane said only, "I shall reply later. I wish to sleep now. Lizzy, go for a walk." She turned her face away from the windows and closed her eyes. Loath though she was to leave Jane for any length of time, Elizabeth recognised that she desperately needed to clear her head, and that obeying Jane's directive might very well accomplish just that.

A few minutes later, she emerged from the house with a great inhalation of cold, fresh afternoon air, to find Mr Darcy just dismounting. "Miss Elizabeth!" he said, and belatedly bowed. "Is all well?"

She curtseyed. "As well as can rationally be hoped. Jane has decreed that I shall take a walk while she rests, and I dared not disobey." Her saucy smile gave the lie to her ruse of reluctance.

"Do you go to the gardens?" At her nod, he continued hesitantly. "Might I...that is, would it be an imposition if I were to accompany you? It is pleasant to stretch one's legs after so long in the saddle, but if you wish for solitude..." he trailed off with a vague gesture.

Though she had been looking forward to a bit of time alone, his shy solicitude caused a revolution in her feelings, and she found herself glad of the promise of company which did not require her constant diligence and care. "I should be pleased to walk with you, sir. Though it is cold, the sunshine is most pleasant, is it not?"

He agreed, moving towards her and offering his arm, which she took. They set off towards the gardens, she asking after her neighbours and he replying largely in the positive. There were no new reports of illness from his visits that day, though Maria Lucas had again raised her family's concern that morning by fainting when she tried to sit up too quickly. "Oh, I have letters for you from your sister and Miss Lucas," he concluded.

"I thank you. I will remember to ask you for them when we return to the house. Do you visit the Blake family?"

"I did yesterday. All of the children are ill; the youngest lad is having a difficult time of it, but the rest go on tolerably well."

"Little Michael? I am sorry to hear it, he is a sweet boy."

"How is Miss Bennet today? I hope that her desire to sleep indicates that she is more comfortable?"

Elizabeth sighed. "Rather the opposite, I fear. Her discomfort prevents her from sleeping for more than an hour or so at a time. She sleeps when exhaustion overcomes her."

They walked on for a moment in silence, past the dried, rustling remnants of the summer's bounty. "That is unfortunate," he replied at last. "I hope this stage will pass quickly."

"Oh, so do I," she admitted, and his quiet, concerned attention induced her to admit softly, "I hardly recognise her. I look at the person dearest to me in all the world, and only her eyes are my Jane's." Her own eyes filled with tears, and overflowed. "I do not know what I would do without her, and I cannot conquer the fear that the loss of that familiar visage is an omen of a greater loss to come."

He wordlessly handed her his handkerchief, and waited until she had made use of it to say, "If she has half your strength, Miss Elizabeth, she will defeat this wretched illness easily."

She laughed shakily through her tears. "You flatter me, sir."

He looked uncomfortable, his feet shuffling aimlessly in place as his eyes darted hither and yon before at last returning to meet her gaze with an expression of remorse. "Truth is not flattery, and any compliment from me is long overdue. I learnt recently that upon our first meeting you overheard a comment I made in a moment of childish petulance. A comment which I cannot too strongly state was untrue."

Elizabeth had become rather accustomed to being surprised by Mr Darcy of late, so her wit was not now subdued by it. "'She is tolerable, but not handsome enough to tempt me'?" she queried with a lift of her eyebrows.

He winced. "Entirely false. I sought to induce Bingley to leave off pestering me to dance, but the method I chose was deplorable. Instead of telling him outright that I was in no mood to perform, I insulted a respectable *and very handsome* young lady. I am sorrier than I can say, and hope you might one day forgive me."

She tucked the soiled handkerchief into her pocket and

slipped her hand about his arm again, indicating that they should continue their walk. "I might be more inclined to forgive you if I knew why you were so very disinclined to dance that you would use such tactics to evade the young ladies of Hertfordshire," she said playfully.

He was silent for a moment. "I have never enjoyed balls, or assemblies, or indeed anything which requires many people to share a confined space," he said slowly. "But that night, I was more averse to merriment than I had been since the period after my father's death. I had just left my sister at a time at which I was particularly loath to be parted from her, to honour my promise to Bingley that I should assist him whenever he took an estate."

"Was your sister unwell?" Elizabeth asked sympathetically.

"Not in body. Only two months before I came here, I went to visit her on her seaside holiday." His jaw clenched, and she felt his arm tense beneath her hand. "There I discovered that a scoundrel—the worst sort of fortune hunter—had made my dear Georgiana's thirty thousand pounds his object. He had persuaded her to believe herself in love with him. You may imagine how I felt, and how I acted. She is but fifteen, her heart is tender and was very much hurt by this, and her confidence in her own judgment has been left in shambles." He paused, sighed, then added, "It was made all the worse by the fact that he had been known to her from the cradle. He was the son of my father's loyal steward, Mr Wickham, and a boyhood companion of mine. Wickham even attended the same schools I did, as a gift from my father, meant to secure his future in an honest manner."

Elizabeth was shocked and angered by this foul treatment of a girl so young, and likely more sheltered than her own fifteen-year-old sister. "Why, that ungrateful cad! I hope, sir, that you sent him off with a broken nose!" Her eyes flashed fire. "But your poor sister! Of course you did not wish to leave her at such a moment, and you may be assured I shall not breathe a word of this to anyone. You are entirely forgiven for your remark, Mr Darcy—though I may still tease you about it on occasion."

He smiled down at her. "Knowing that you have forgiven me, it shall be no great task to bear your teasing, Miss Elizabeth."

She laughed. "Ah, you say so now, sir!"

———

Elizabeth returned, red-cheeked and smiling, to Jane's chamber only to find her beloved sister in some distress.

"Oh, Lizzy," she said faintly. "I am glad you are back. I do not feel well at all."

Hurrying to the bed, Elizabeth found the pillow-case dampened and soiled. She helped her sister to sit up, and secured a clean pillow for her. Beneath the swellings, Jane had grown thin and pale, and even her golden hair had lost much of its lustre.

"I feel..." Jane closed her eyes for a moment, as though the effort of keeping them open was too great. "I feel as though I have got old overnight. My very bones ache."

"You need do nothing but rest and take nourishment," Elizabeth soothed her. "I shall do all else for you." Jane nodded very slightly, and fell from consciousness.

Eyes stinging with fearful tears, Elizabeth yanked sharply on the bell-pull and asked the maid to request Mrs

Hurst's attendance. A soft knock sounded only minutes later, and Mrs Hurst greeted Elizabeth with equal parts pleasure and concern when she emerged.

"Has Miss Bennet taken a turn?" she asked, seizing Elizabeth's hands.

"Her illness has reached the next stage, the one Mr Jones warned us contains the greatest danger," Elizabeth replied in a rush. "Thank you for coming so promptly—she is asleep now, but I do not know how long it shall last."

"Please tell me how I may be of assistance."

———

Within the hour, supplies of clean cloths, fresh bed linens, and two new night-rails were delivered to the room.

As Jane slept, Elizabeth recalled the letters she had received from Mr Darcy in the garden only hours earlier. Charlotte reported that Mr Jones had seen unmistakable signs of the smallpox in Maria. Mary relayed that Lydia and Mrs Bennet continued quite ill, but that Kitty's fever had broken and she was not half so exhausted as the other two patients had been at the same point in their own illness.

Elizabeth quickly replied with what hope and encouragement she could muster or feign for their sakes. The remainder of the day passed quietly, as Jane did little but sleep. Elizabeth would come to wish she had used the time likewise, for in the night she was awoken by her sister's soft weeping.

There followed the most difficult two and seventy hours of Elizabeth Bennet's life. Jane was too ill and exhausted to participate in her own care. Elizabeth pretended cheer as she turned her sister this way and that to remove and replace sheets and night-rails, sponging from her dearest Jane's limp and trembling body all the unwholesome effluvia of the disease. As her arms ached and her stomach roiled, she smiled and murmured soothing words, and in the deepest reaches of the night she pressed her forehead to the frost-laced window and silently wept.

CHAPTER EIGHT

Bingley's valet had news for him as he dressed that morning—to wit, that two of the Netherfield servants had developed a fever. He accepted this latest blow stoically, and asked his man to inform the housekeeper that he would speak with her after breaking his fast, before he left on his rounds. Pausing only to slip his daily note under Miss Bennet's door, he hastened to the breakfast room.

Darcy and Carter had preceded him there, as they always did, and Bingley informed them of the latest while he filled his plate with hot food. He sent a footman for the housekeeper the instant he was finished, and decided that a second cup of coffee would not go amiss on such a cold day.

"Ah, Mrs Tobin," he said as she entered. "I will not take much of your time. I merely wished to ask if there are servants here who have suffered the smallpox in the past?"

"Yes, sir, several," she replied.

"Excellent. Well, I mean, that is to say..." He waved off the verbal fumble with an impatient gesture. "They are in no danger now. If any of them will volunteer to tend to those who have just now fallen ill, there shall be coin in it for them, above their regular wages. Mr Jones shall also visit those who are sick, and I will pay his fees. Is there anything else that I ought to be doing?"

Mrs Tobin's smile was all gratitude. "Oh, no, sir! You are very generous! Most gentlemen would not do half so much."

"Well done, Bingley," Darcy said after the housekeeper had taken her leave. "She is correct—most gentlemen would have left the servants to sort such things out for themselves, but I am of your opinion, that their care for us earns our care for them."

Carter nodded approvingly, but Bingley shrugged off the praise. "I should think myself a poor master if I did less. Come, let us be off."

When Bingley returned in the early afternoon, chilled and hungry and bearing little in the way of good news, his sister hurried down the stairs to him.

"Oh, Charles, I am glad you are home. Gilbert is unwell, and I am frightened," she said, coming to a stop before him. He handed his greatcoat to the footman and opened his arms to Louisa, who entered his embrace gratefully.

"Mr Jones is expected soon," he told her. "I shall not allow my brother to lack for anything."

Louisa led him to the drawing room, where a fire heated the room, and a tea tray awaited them.

Bingley warmed his hands by the hearth. "Has Hurst's man had the illness? If not, I am sure Mrs Tobin could find a manservant to tend to him."

"Mulgrew did indeed survive smallpox in his youth,

but I suspect he would have remained in any case. He is very devoted. Some things my husband has said in the past led me to believe that his previous employer was both stingy and cruel," she informed him, pouring herself a cup.

Bingley nodded. "Please assure him that he need not hesitate to request anything for Hurst's comfort, or his own."

"I have already taken the liberty of doing so," Louisa admitted. "And I shall also tend to him, if only to keep him company. I feel it is my duty."

"I am certain he will like to have you there," Bingley said. "I shall visit him as well."

"I expect he would enjoy that." She sipped her tea, then changed the subject. "Has there been any further word from Caroline?"

"No. After her note that she had arrived in London safely, I did write to chastise her for her selfishness. I expect she hopes to out wait my anger." He frowned. "She will find me the more stubborn, for once."

Louisa sighed. "I wonder what will become of her, if she persists in such selfishness."

"I hardly know." He shook his head, then fixed her with an earnest look. "Sister, if ever I am so fortunate as to have children, please remind me—often!—not to be too indulgent with them. Perhaps especially the youngest."

———

As Miss Bennet's illness progressed, Darcy saw with mounting alarm that Elizabeth's pallor and the dark circles beneath her eyes did as well. One afternoon as she opened the door to accept the notes he had brought from her family, he was required to catch her by the elbow as she stumbled through the aperture.

"You are ill," he said, frowning. His eyes roved her pale features, searching for any hint of fever or the tell-tale rash.

"No, not ill, only very weary," she assured him. "Jane requires a great deal just now. It will pass."

"But will it pass before you reach the end of your strength?" Truly, she looked very ill, and he could see that she had grown thinner in only a few days.

"It must. Jane cannot be left alone, and I shall not consign her to strangers at such a time. She needs me, and I need every moment with her that I am allowed, in the event..."

She did not complete the thought, and with a small shake of her head, continued in a slightly different vein. "And yet, I do not think only of Jane. I feel as though I were being torn in two, or perhaps three. I wish to never stir from my sister's side, while I also long to be home, and to visit my friends at Lucas Lodge. I wish...I wish to take Jane home, to hear the voices of my family, to see Charlotte's smile. And I do not know how many of those things will ever be granted to me again." Tears were welling in her eyes, and she brought her hands up to her cheeks in sudden embarrassment. "Forgive me. I do not know why I just told you all of that. You cannot have wished to hear it."

"I think you very much needed to say it to someone, and your sister would hardly be the appropriate receptacle," he answered gently, his heart clenching at seeing her so fearful and unlike her cheerful self. "I have no objection to being of service in such a way."

"I thank you, sir." With what seemed a huff of impatience, she dashed the tears from her eyes. "Have you letters for me?"

"I do. From Miss Lucas and Miss Mary. I hope they contain good news," Darcy said, producing the documents. She accepted them with a tremulous smile and, having given her thanks, left him to wish once again there were more he could do.

————

Mrs Hill was put to bed with her husband after developing a sudden fever, and when the maid Sara refused again to assist with the care of the ill, Mr Bennet at last lost his patience and turned her off. The duties of Mrs Saxby, Longbourn's cook, therefore expanded to include care of both the Hills, which in turn meant that simple foods suitable for the sick were all that would be available to any in the house for the foreseeable future.

Kitty, however, continued to improve, and when Mr Jones came, he declared, to the joy of all, that her fever and sore throat had been caused by a mild infection of the sinuses rather than the smallpox. She was fit to do as she pleased, so long as she did not over-tire herself. The apothecary, having satisfied himself that Miss Lydia was no worse than she had been the day previous, went to check on Mrs Bennet, trailed by Kitty.

Mr Jones bent over Mrs Bennet, listening to her chest through a short tube of wood. He straightened with a faint frown. "Hm. The fever is reduced and the rash mild, but there may be a bit of congestion in the lungs," he said to his patient. "We will put a few more pillows behind you. Raising the head and shoulders eases the breath. And I wish that you will drink as much hot lemon-water as you can stand, Mrs Bennet. The heat will soothe the lungs and lemon is strengthening, though I understand that it will sting your throat."

"Ooh, I do not care for lemon water, Mr Jones," Mrs Bennet complained.

"You may have as much sugar or honey in it as you like, ma'am, but you must drink it." Mr Jones replied in a tone which brooked no disagreement.

"Oh, very well," his patient grumbled. "If it may be sweetened, I suppose I shall be able to bear it."

Mr Bennet resumed his place in the chair at her side. "You shall have to make the sacrifice, my dear," he said jovially, "unless you propose to leave me alone with five daughters?"

She looked at him as though he had uttered a blasphemy in the middle of Easter services. "I most certainly shall not!" she shrieked. "Bring me the wretched lemon water!"

———

When Mr Jones visited Lucas Lodge the next morning, marking the fifth day of Maria Lucas's illness, he found Miss Lucas at her wits' end with worry.

"I am glad you are come, sir," she said with uncharacteristic agitation, as she came to him in the passage outside her sister's room. "Maria's back pains her so, she cannot get rest nor comfort, though I have put her in every position we can think of."

He had come, in these last few days, to greatly admire Miss Lucas's steady good sense, in such contrast to her mother's dithering and her father's well-intentioned uselessness, that to see her so overset caused him no little alarm.

"Let me see her, then, and I shall do what I can." Inside the room, Maria lay patently exhausted, and yet in constant motion, seeking a position that would give her relief. She hardly seemed to notice his entrance, so wrapped up in her pain was she. He set his bag upon the dresser and hurried to his patient.

"Miss Maria, I must have you sit up for a moment," he said. A swift examination led him to diagnose a temporary rheumatism of the spine, likely brought on by the fever. He turned to her elder sister, who hovered by the bed. "I will leave you with some laudanum, and Miss Maria may have a few drops every four hours to ease her. A hot flannel where it pains her most may also help, and if she can tolerate willow-bark tea, I recommend it thrice daily."

Miss Lucas's relief was palpable. "I thank you, Mr Jones. Please, allow me to see you off with some hot tea," she said, as she had the last three days. Today, to his surprise as much as hers, he agreed. She escorted him down to the kitchens, where she ordered the preparation of a pot of strong tea, to be sealed in a flagon for Mr Jones to take with him. She pressed upon him a scone, and sat him at the little table in the corner, taking a place across from him as he ate and they awaited the tea.

"I hope Maria will be able to sleep now," she commented, "for I cannot but think that a lack of rest is highly undesirable in her condition."

He reached across the table to place a comforting hand upon her own, and they both startled, locked eyes for an instant, and then hastily looked away. While he saw her blush, the more worldly gentleman was no less confused.

Putting the matter aside to be thought upon later, he said, with tolerable composure, "I expect that she shall be able to get some sleep now, with the poppy's help. If she is not able to rest before my next visit, we will try something else." He peered at her over the top of his spectacles. "And you must rest as well, Miss Lucas."

"I shall try, sir. May I ask after your sister and her family?"

"Joanna and Davey have fallen ill, but their cases are quite mild thus far. Jenny is nonetheless wearing herself thin tending to them." He shook his head. "She and her husband and little Meg remain in health, for which I am thankful."

"I seem to recall that the last time I visited your shop, young Davey was proving a most able assistant," Miss Lucas said with a smile.

Mr Jones chuckled. "Indeed! Like every boy of three, he wants to know what everything is, but unlike most he is not satisfied with being told that this is medicine for nerves, and that is salve for burns, he wants to know how and why they work. If he were not to inherit Haye-Park, I would be hopeful that he might join my profession one day."

The Lucases' cook came bustling over just then, to hand him the flagon of tea, and he had no further excuse to linger. Riding away from Lucas Lodge, he allowed himself a few moments of bemusement at the potent physical attraction which had flowed between him and the eldest Lucas daughter. Soon, however, he turned his thoughts to his next stop, at Longbourn, for the question of Miss Lucas could wait, but the Bennets could not.

CHAPTER NINE

After listening to Mrs Bennet's chest for a long while, Mr Jones straightened and with a slight frown, said, "Madam, the congestion I suspected yesterday has established itself very quickly, and I do not like it."

"Nor do I," cried the lady.

"I will give instruction to your daughter—"

"Oh, what would you know, young as you are?" she replied pettishly.

He looked to the others in the room; Mr Bennet seemed amused at his wife's antics, while Miss Catherine was clearly exasperated. Neither showed the concern that was warranted in such a case. "Sir, Miss Catherine, perhaps we should discuss treatment elsewhere, and allow Mrs Bennet some peace?"

Moving to the head of the stair, Mr Jones detailed the mixture of herbs that should be boiled in a pot of water for the steam treatment, and the importance of holding a hot bladder to Mrs Bennet's chest.

"How is it that she has got two illnesses at once?" Miss

Catherine wondered. "The smallpox is not so very bad for her—certainly it is nothing to Lydia's—but this ailment of the lungs has come on very strong."

"I do not believe it is a distinct ailment," Mr Jones replied. "The smallpox takes some few people in this manner, concentrating upon the lungs instead of the skin, and behaves as a pneumonia."

Mr Bennet was quick to ask, "And is this variant of the disease more or less dangerous than the usual course?"

"I am by no means an expert," the young man hedged, "but to my knowledge the usual course of the disease is the least dangerous. Aggressive treatment of the pneumonia now, in the early stages, will give her every possible chance of survival."

"I agree," said Mr Bennet abruptly. "Kitty, go down to Mrs Saxby now and prepare the first steam treatment. We shall waste no more time."

The girl hurried to comply, and Mr Bennet waited until her footsteps could no longer be heard to turn back to the apothecary. "You have seen cases like this before, Mr Jones?"

"I have. There was an epidemic in Whitechapel during my training. I saw..." he thought for a second. "Three cases like Mrs Bennet's."

"I see," murmured Mr Bennet. "And how many of them lived?"

Mr Jones was silent for a long moment. "One."

Mr Bennet ran a hand over his mouth, and stared into nothingness for the space of a half-dozen breaths. Then he shook his head briefly, as though clearing it. "Much been gambled on poorer odds than that, so we shall hope for the best."

The following morning, Elizabeth was awake when Mr Darcy's soft knock came. As she entered the passage, his anticipatory expression quickly shifted into a concerned frown at her even more haggard appearance. "Miss Elizabeth, have you slept at all?" he blurted.

"Only a little, sir. It was not a good night," Elizabeth explained.

His anxious frown deepened. "Would that I could offer any information that might ease Miss Bennet's suffering, or your burden," he said earnestly.

"I appreciate all that you have done for us," she assured him. "We can only wait, and hope, and make dear Jane as comfortable as possible. Mr Jones remains optimistic, and so must we."

He nodded, and hesitated for a moment. "Miss Elizabeth, I attempted to speak with you yesterday afternoon, but got no answer to my knock. When I was at Longbourn yesterday, Miss Catherine informed me that Mrs Hill had the fever and your mother and youngest sister were both rather worse. Mrs Bennet had a cough and a renewal of fever, while Miss Lydia was much weakened by her illness."

Mr Darcy's gentle tone could not keep Elizabeth from a feeling of apprehension and dismay; he must have glimpsed it in her expression, for she felt his hand clasp her own. "Mr Jones has, I am sure, seen them since then, and I hope that you will have better news of your family later today, but I could not in good conscience remain silent longer."

"Of course not. I had rather have the truth, and I thank

you." Elizabeth looked down at their joined hands; much as his gesture had surprised her, it served to comfort and reassure her. "Did Kitty seem well?"

"She seemed entirely well, Miss Elizabeth," he replied with a smile, "and assured me that Miss Mary and Mr Bennet are likewise."

"That, at least, is something to be happy about. I sent my letters down last night; I assume they await you and the other gentlemen."

"If you wish to visit your family, if I could be of any assistance, when Miss Bennet is improved—"

"Darcy?"

Elizabeth stepped back into the doorway, her hand falling away from Mr Darcy's. She turned, smiling, to Mr Bingley and found him looking impatiently at his friend.

"Mr Darcy has brought news from Longbourn," she explained.

"Good news, I hope. We are in need of good news," replied Mr Bingley before he nodded at Mr Darcy. "Carter is downstairs if you wish to join him."

Elizabeth bit back a smile at the man's unsubtle attempt to rid himself of his disapproving friend. It worked, however; Mr Darcy looked at her, bowed, and disappeared around the corner of the passageway.

"Have you another note for Jane?"

"I do indeed," Mr Bingley said, and produced it.

"She has not been well enough to hear them, but every day I tell her that a new one has arrived, and I know that she takes pleasure in their mere existence, and your constancy in writing them," said Elizabeth with a look of gratitude.

He expressed his own pleasure in this knowledge, and

his eagerness for the day when Miss Bennet would once again be well enough to read them and—happy thought!—perhaps even reply. Unable to tarry longer, he bade her good day with all sincere wishes for the improved health and happiness of both sisters, and departed.

His wish was soon to be realised, for Jane grew rather better over the course of the day. She was yet very weak and ill, but was able to eat and drink more. In the evening, after sleeping deeply the whole of the afternoon, she expressed a wish to sit up and showed more alertness than she had for several days.

Mr Jones had come while Jane slept, and pronounced himself satisfied that the worst was past, and they need no longer fear for her life. Elizabeth relayed this to Jane, who remarked that while she did not remember much of the last several days, she recalled several times thinking that she must surely perish, and was rather surprised to find herself mistaken. It was all Elizabeth could do not to burst into tears at this, and she swiftly changed the subject by drawing Jane's attention to the little stack of Mr Bingley's notes which had accumulated. After being entertained with these, in which he wrote cheerfully of his trips about the neighbourhood and always closed with his hopes for her swift recovery, Jane asked if her sister might resume the novel they had been enjoying together, and so the two or three hours that Jane was able to remain awake passed very pleasantly indeed.

———

The next day, when Mr Jones called at Lucas Lodge, he returned the flagon to Miss Lucas with his thanks. After he visited Miss Maria and pronounced her no worse than was usual for this stage of the illness, he was surprised to find it handed back to him, now radiating warmth from the hot tea within, by the Lucases' manservant.

The fellow saw his look of surprise, and told him it was refilled by Miss Lucas's orders, and would be every day that he brought it with him.

He smiled to himself. "Please do thank Miss Lucas for me."

He arrived at Netherfield late that afternoon. Several possible new cases had been brought to his attention, and his continued forward motion owed more to sheer will than to real energy. Mrs Hurst hurried down the stairs to greet him.

"Mr Jones, I am glad you are here," the lady said. "My husband's fever has subsided but now a rash has appeared."

He followed her to Mr Hurst's chamber and examined with curiosity and unease the dusky, bruised patches appearing across his patient's body, following the path but lacking the form of the lesions of smallpox.

Mrs Hurst asked the apothecary if anything was amiss.

"I am uncertain," he replied thoughtfully. "The appearance of the rash is strange, and it is not developing in the usual manner. Mr Hurst, how are you feeling?"

"Feel like I've been trampled by horses. My middle pains me terribly."

"I must consult my books, and try to discover what is happening," said Mr Jones. "I hope to have an answer for you tomorrow. Until then, rest and nourishment are your only tasks, sir, and I expect you to devote yourself to both."

Mr Hurst offered a faint smile. "If I did not feel so very dreadful, that would be my idea of a perfect night."

As it would be mine, Mr Jones thought as he staggered out to his horse.

———

At Longbourn, Mary's world had rapidly narrowed to the confines of Lydia's room. The fever had gone some days previously but Lydia's energy had not returned. She drank little and ate less. Though Lydia remained enervated in body, the retreat of the fever revived her mind, and she required distraction from the pain of her sores and the sameness of her surroundings. And so, Mary Bennet read a novel for the first time in her life. She read one aloud to her sister, and then she read another. She was surprised to find that although the plots could be rather silly, and the characters morally suspect, the prose was often compelling and occasionally beautiful, and that in each exaggerated personality there was something to be seen which reminded her of real people known to her.

As the days crept by, the pox made its mark on Lydia in more obvious ways. Her poor mouth and throat were very slow to heal; she was very frightened when the rash erupted on her arms, where she could see it, and when the blisters of the pox appeared, she insisted on having a mirror. Mary brought her one, reluctantly, and Lydia viewed her blistered face in shocked silence for several minutes before handing it back to her sister without a word.

The next day, as Mary was reading, Lydia whispered

despairingly, "I am going to be very badly scarred. I am going to be ugly."

"We cannot know, until the disease has run its course. You may be lucky and have very few scars." Mary's words were not without sympathy, but neither did they offer impossible hope. "Do not worry about what may happen, for today has troubles enough. We must get you through this, and restore your health, and then we shall worry about your appearance."

Lydia smiled weakly. "I will try not to think of it, then. Thank you for telling me the truth."

"You may always rely upon me for that," Mary remarked drily, and was rewarded with a raspy giggle.

———

That evening at Netherfield was a quiet one. Mrs Hurst sat upstairs with her husband; Captain Carter was in the library writing letters to his family. Bingley took advantage of the intimate company of his friend in the drawing room by loosening his waistcoat and putting his feet on the ottoman. His loud sigh garnered Darcy's attention.

"The news is mixed from Longbourn. I hope none are suffering as Miss Bennet does."

Darcy sipped his brandy. "Did you receive further news from Miss Elizabeth in the letters I delivered?" At Bingley's demurral, he pressed further. "You sent me off because you wished to speak to her privately. Was it in regard to Miss Bennet or do you have other interests in that direction?"

Bingley shot him an uncomprehending look. "My interests are solely for the improvement of Miss Bennet's health! Until I can speak to her myself, I rely upon her sister to tell me about her progress."

"And to serve as the deliverer of notes?" Darcy's voice sharpened. "Love letters are an incautious means of concern for her welfare. I know you admire Miss Bennet, but do be careful of her reputation."

"Says the man who was holding the hand of her sister, in the corridor, in broad daylight!"

Damn, he did see, Darcy realised with chagrin. He had exerted much energy trying not to dwell on the moments he had held Miss Elizabeth's soft hand in his.

"She was upset at news about her family. I patted her hand but briefly," he lied.

"A caring but incautious gesture, it would appear."

Darcy turned away from Bingley's irritating smirk. "I believe I shall retire."

"No, please wait. I have further news," Bingley said. "Hurst's housekeeper in town has written to me about Caroline."

"Is your sister well?"

"Caroline has not fallen ill, but as she has no relation or companion in the house, she cannot go about. Mrs Burley writes to beg funds to hire a companion to serve her until we return. She does not exactly say that my sister is making the servants' lives miserable, but the implication is there."

Darcy was too well-mannered to roll his eyes. He shook his head slowly, careful to keep his expression blank. "And how shall you respond?"

"I believe I shall offer those funds instead as an incentive to remain in Hurst's service. Caroline chose to leave us and return to London when every rational impulse must suggest that she might yet fall ill. That she has not is pure chance. She has done wrong, and she ought to feel it."

Yes, she ought to feel it in full, he thought. Before expressing his agreement, Darcy enquired as to Mrs Hurst's thoughts on her sister.

"Louisa agrees. Her concerns centre on Caroline's welfare and the danger she could face alone if the smallpox spreads to town." Bingley clenched his jaw. "She chose this."

CHAPTER TEN

Early the following morning, Mr Jones arrived at Netherfield to examine Hurst. He halted Bingley from his rounds, asking him to wait just a few minutes. Understanding that such a request did not often presage good news, Darcy immediately said he would remain as well. Carter also postponed his own travels. The gentlemen enjoyed the warmth of the parlour, providing Bingley with distraction and support, until Mr Jones—accompanied by Mrs Hurst and her husband's valet—returned from visiting Hurst.

"I believe I have discovered why Mr Hurst's illness is not progressing as usual," the apothecary announced when the door closed behind them, and Mrs Hurst had taken a seat beside her brother. "It is a rare complication: in some people, very few, the disease diverts blood from its natural courses within the body and causes it to pool beneath the skin. We shall try giving him food and drink which are beneficial to the blood—beef, liver, red wine, and porter, but..."

Darcy saw Bingley gripping the arm of his chair.

Mr Jones looked at them earnestly, sorrow in his eyes. "You should prepare yourselves for the worst."

Darcy quickly glanced at Mrs Hurst; her distress was matched by that of Hurst's loyal servant, Mulgrew. Both stared at Jones in shock for several seconds, then Mrs Hurst sank slowly back against the cushions of the settee and sat quite frozen, one hand covering her mouth.

Bingley turned to the apothecary. "I cannot believe, sir, that it is as dire as all that. Or perhaps I do not wish to believe it. What are we to expect for my brother?"

Mr Jones spread his hands. "You must understand that I have never seen a case of this type before. All my information is from books, and there is little even there. All of it is grim," he said before providing them some details of the likely trauma and loss of blood in such a diagnosis.

The apothecary's horrifying disclosure was greeted with a weighty silence; Darcy feared Bingley or his sister would faint. "But some do survive?" he asked intently.

"Some few, according to the texts," he allowed. "Which is why I prescribe food and drink to strengthen and thicken the blood."

There was another silence. Then Bingley said with a decisive, even defiant, air, "Then that is what we shall do. We shall give Hurst every chance that diligent care can afford, and trust that he shall be spared."

Darcy was watching Mr Jones, and though the man smiled and nodded encouragingly, there was something in his expression that suggested his own hopes were faint. Darcy allowed a few minutes to pass, and then stood and said, "Come, Bingley, Carter, we must be about our rounds if we are to return before dark."

With a few final encouraging words for his sister, Bingley joined his friends, and they all made their way out to their horses again, as Mr Jones assured them he would now monitor Mr Hurst twice daily, and in the afternoons would also see Miss Bennet.

Darcy examined the apothecary, whose exhaustion was far too evident. "Sir, you do not look well. I hope you are not becoming ill?"

Mr Jones smiled faintly. "No, I am well in body. Yesterday I lost a patient, and I am merely tired and very sad."

"Who has died?"

"Little Michael Blake. It has been obvious for some days that his chances were not good, but one always hopes until the very last, particularly with the young."

Carter sighed heavily. "I rode to the Blakes' two days ago. I am sorry to hear of their tragic loss."

"The others in the family?" asked Darcy.

"Mr and Mrs Blake and their elder sons are recovering." Mr Jones straightened his shoulders. "Allow me, gentlemen, to thank you again for your efforts on behalf of this community. I do not know how I should have managed without such aid as you have so diligently supplied."

"Surely our daily rides, however cold, are nothing compared to your work directly with the ill," said Darcy. "It is a relief to me, and surely to everyone in the area, that you have not succumbed to the illness yourself."

Mr Jones looked faintly startled. "Oh, did I never mention that I was inoculated when I studied at St Bart's?" he asked, naming the great London hospital at which the most promising medical students received their practical training.

"No, nor did you mention your studies there," Darcy exclaimed. "So you *are* a physician?"

The apothecary's expression closed off. "I was unable to complete my studies or sit the examination for licensing by the Royal College of Physicians. I am merely an unusually well-trained apothecary."

"Whatever training you have had, I am glad of it," said Bingley with a weak show of his usual cheer, breaking the tension. "I expect you saw many cases of smallpox there, and that is what has made you so able in the present crisis."

Mr Jones inclined his head. "Yes, there was an outbreak during my training. I was fortunate to become familiar with the course of the disease and the signs of complications, at least the more common ones."

Struck by a sudden notion, Darcy wasted no time in acting upon it. "Sir, I am ashamed I have not thought of it before, but would you accept the use of my carriage and driver for your daily travels? It would allow you to conserve your energies for your patients."

Mr Jones smiled and spoke with real gratitude. "That is a very kind offer, Mr Darcy, and I am sorely tempted to accept, but I feel I must retain the freedom and speed which a horse provides. It is likely I shall need, sooner or later, the minutes which a shortcut across the fields provides."

"And your daily rounds would no doubt be quite extended in time, if not in effort, by being confined to the roads," Darcy said with a nod. "Of course. I did not think."

"You thought of my comfort and well-being, and I am grateful for it." He looked about, including them all as he continued, "Well, I must get on to Longbourn. Miss Lydia reported a pain in her eye yesterday, but I was unable to get a good look by candlelight. I mean to take advantage of this sunshine to do better."

They mounted their horses and soon parted at the gates of Netherfield. Darcy noted that Mr Jones's saddle and tack, like his greatcoat, were worn but had once been as fine as any of theirs. His horse, too, was a good mount; not spirited but strong and bred for endurance. He wondered at these disparate clues—the fine education and possessions, the overt signs of present poverty—for a moment, before he set them aside to turn to Bingley and offer his commiseration on the unfortunate diagnosis of Hurst.

"He shall be well," Bingley declared. "I refuse to believe otherwise."

"Would it not be better to prepare yourself for the worst, and rejoice at better if it comes?"

Bingley turned to him with a serious expression. "Why should I mourn my brother before he is dead? Should I not rejoice in his life every second it continues? There will be time enough for grief when there is no other option."

Darcy nodded once, slowly. "Perhaps you are correct. I will try to learn a little of your philosophy, my friend."

"You really ought to, you old curmudgeon," Bingley said lightly, and they both laughed.

———

That evening, Jane urged Elizabeth to join the others for dinner. "You have had so little society other than my own for many days, and now that I am better, I wish to see you enjoying yourself. And," she added by way of additional inducement, "it will give you an opportunity to convey my very great thanks to Mrs Hurst and the three gentlemen, who have done so much for us and our family."

Elizabeth rather reluctantly agreed; having so recently come close to losing her beloved sister she did not like to leave her at all. As the choice was between conceding and making Jane unhappy, however, she dressed for dinner and made her way down to the drawing room, where she found only Mr Darcy.

"Oh, I am sorry—I must have mistaken the time," she said.

He stood and bowed. "Not at all. Dinner was put back half an hour so that Bingley might visit with Mr Hurst. We did not think to inform you. Please, have a seat. Captain Carter is in the study finishing a letter and should be in momentarily. May I pour you a sherry?"

"I thank you, sir, that would be pleasant," she replied sincerely, treating her aching limbs to the overstuffed armchair Mr Hurst favoured above all others. It was all she could do not to sigh in relief as the softness of it embraced her.

Mr Darcy handed her the little crystal glass of amber liquid. "I believe you usually prefer orgeat. If you will be joining us more often, I shall ask Mrs Hurst to have a bottle decanted."

"Oh, please, do not create any work on my account. My preference is really quite slight." Elizabeth smiled and he bowed slightly before returning to his own seat upon the settee.

"I hope that Miss Bennet's improved health is the reason we have the pleasure of your company tonight?"

"Indeed, sir, she is much improved, and particularly desired that I enjoy some company this evening after having been so long at her side. But tell me, please, how does Mr Hurst fare?"

Mr Darcy looked briefly uncomfortable. "Not well at all, I am afraid," he answered in a low voice. "He has developed a rare complication of the disease, which does not often end happily. Mr Jones does all he can, of course, but he warned us early to be prepared for the worst."

Elizabeth's hand dropped from where it had rested briefly over her mouth. "How dreadful. We must hope that he is the exception. Is there, do you think, anything I might do for Mrs Hurst? She has been so very kind to Jane and me."

"I can think of nothing offhand, but I shall be sure to inform you if an idea presents itself." After a moment of silence, he opened his mouth, hesitated, and then spoke. "I hope you will not think me prying, but I confess that I find myself very curious about Mr Jones. He is extraordinarily capable for an apothecary. Recently he mentioned that he had studied at St Bart's but would not speak further. Given his capabilities and his education, I cannot understand why he is not a physician."

Elizabeth grimaced in sympathy. "Yes, he does not care to speak of it, as I imagine the recollection gives him a deal of pain." She glanced up at him. "I have the story from his sister, the younger Mrs Goulding." When he nodded to indicate that he understood to whom she referred, she continued.

"Their father was a successful tradesman. Of the three children, the eldest son was to inherit the business, the daughter was to marry a gentleman and so begin the process of elevating the family, and Mr Jones, the younger son, was to take up a gentlemanly profession. All was going according to plan until three years ago.

"His sister had married young Mr Goulding, and Mr Jones was in his final year of study when their father died unexpectedly. Some sort of accident on the docks, as he inspected one of his ships. The elder brother, upon attaining his inheritance, chose not to continue to pay our Mr Jones's fees. With no money of his own, he was forced to leave his studies and make a life for himself as best he could."

"Was there no provision for him in the will?" Mr Darcy asked in incredulous tones.

"It would seem that there was not. I suppose old Mr Jones expected to live long enough to see his youngest settled in his profession."

"Outrageous," the gentleman grumbled. "I should never leave any child of mine so unprotected."

"I have no doubt that the world would be a better place if everyone shared your notions on that subject," Elizabeth agreed, "but they do not, to the detriment of Mr Jones and the betterment of Meryton. It is not every small market town which can claim an apothecary who is very nearly a physician."

"I do not understand why he does not merely call himself a doctor and set up his practice. Many a man with far less education and experience has done so."

Elizabeth laughed. "You are not the first to suggest it. For your edification, I suggest you ask Mr Jones his views on the licensing of physicians. And for my own entertainment, I beg that you do so when I am present."

Mr Darcy chuckled. "Strongly in favour, is he?"

"Arrestingly so. He has not the least patience for men

such as you describe, who call themselves doctors with little more than a bag of instruments and a calling-card to support it."

"Having lost my own father to the incompetence of just such a man, I can only admire his principles."

Elizabeth, struck by his sorrowful expression, gave him a sympathetic look at this declaration, but chose not to request the details of such a personal and profound memory. "He is an excellent fellow, and I wish with all my heart that he might find a way to complete his studies and enter into that higher position to which he is so eminently suited."

Mr Darcy agreed with a solemn nod as Captain Carter entered the room. The officer expressed pleasure in Elizabeth's addition to the dinner party, enquired after Miss Bennet, and joined them in an agreeable discussion of the attributes of Netherfield which lasted until Bingley and Mrs Hurst were able to join them.

The dinner was not so pleasant as the first Elizabeth had enjoyed there, when only Jane was ill, but no one could have expected it to be so. Mrs Hurst was subdued and her brother distracted. With Mr Darcy's conversational deficiencies only increased by the strained atmosphere, it fell to Elizabeth and the captain to conduct light and congenial discourse on unobjectionable topics, to which the others might contribute or not, as they chose. The other three did attempt to join in, spurred by the obligations of civility, but only Mr Darcy was even marginally successful. Elizabeth returned to Jane's chamber soon after the gentlemen joined them in the drawing room, and her only reason to be glad that she had attended was the satisfaction of having offered some slight entertainment to those in need of distraction.

CHAPTER ELEVEN

Mr Jones,

Pardon me, sir, for intruding into what little time you now have in your own shop and home, but I must beg a favour of you. Maria's condition changed some hours after you left us this morning, and although my dear Charlotte assures us that it is nothing you had not taught her to expect, Lady Lucas has become quite frantic. If you will consent to visit us and put her mind at rest, and perhaps bring her a bottle of your marvellous nerve tonic, I will guarantee you not only your usual fee but a fine, hot meal and a glass of port as well.

Yours,

Sir William Lucas

JONES SIGHED SOFTLY AND SHRUGGED HIS COAT BACK on. Exhausted as he was, he was in no position to turn down either a fee or a good meal. So many of his present patients would not be able to pay him for months, if they paid at all, and the cost of a meal he need not take at the inn might be added to his savings. Miss Lucas had been kind enough to fill his flask and pack him a bite to eat on every visit. His professional duty compelled him to hie to Lucas Lodge, but it was the opportunity to visit with Miss Lucas that excited his anticipation.

He arrived at Lucas Lodge just as the swift-setting winter sun disappeared below the horizon, and was welcomed with much effusive thanks by the master of the house himself. When Jones had been divested of his winter garments and Sir William's gratitude had run low on words, he concluded with, "I shall stay with my wife, if you do not mind, sir. You know the way."

Jones bowed his assent and climbed the stairs to Miss Maria's chamber, where he found that she had entered the most trying stage of the illness and was quite fatigued but, her case being so mild in general, was in little if any danger.

Miss Lucas accompanied him downstairs after a brief word with her sister, entering the parlour just behind him and wincing in mortification as her mother shrilly babbled her worries at him without even giving him a chance to speak. It was some minutes before Miss Lucas and her father managed to calm Lady Lucas enough for Jones to deliver his verdict, which he did simply and promptly, adding that a quiet and restful atmosphere would aid in her recovery.

Miss Lucas had fetched a cordial glass as he spoke, and Lady Lucas hardly had time to express her thanks before he had poured a dose into it and handed it to her. She drank it down eagerly and her husband took custody of the rest of the bottle, standing and bowing to Jones.

"I thank you, sir, for attending us again. I will see Lady

Lucas settled for the night. Charlotte, please ensure he is well-fed before he leaves us."

Jones followed her into the kitchen, where she sat him at the little table they had occupied on his previous foray into the kitchens. The cook bustled over with a plate, which she set before him, removing the cover to reveal an amount of pheasant, roasted turnips, thick brown gravy, and buttered bread that he was not certain he could consume over the course of two dinners. She moved away and shortly returned with a dish of custard that she set beside his plate with a smile.

Miss Lucas took the other chair and silently enjoyed a glass of wine as he tucked into his dinner. He found that he had quite an appetite after his first taste of the finely-roasted bird seasoned with savoury herbs, so different from the tough, indifferent bits of flesh scattered stingily through the Meryton Inn's meat pies, his usual dinner. Only the presence of a lady prevented ill-mannered haste in his eating.

When at last he sat back, having devoured two-thirds of the heap of food and eying the custard speculatively, wondering if his stomach would accommodate just that bit more, Miss Lucas smiled at him. "Mrs Walsh is very good with pheasant, is she not? I shall have the rest of that wrapped up for you, if you like."

Most of what remained was turnips and bread, which was still rather better than his usual morning meal. "If it is not too much trouble, I should be grateful for it," he replied.

"Allow me to say, once again, how sorry I am that you should be called out on so slight a need." She blushed, and while he said all the expected and commonplace words to deny any particular merit on his own part, he took the opportunity to study her.

She was not pretty by any conventional standard, but her high cheekbones and the look of uncommon intelligence in her expression lent her a kind of handsomeness few would trouble themselves to recognise. A careful practitioner of the medical arts is trained to notice those things which escape the attention of the masses, and to him, Miss Lucas grew more attractive by the day.

She increased this impression when she earnestly enquired after his relations. "My sister has fallen ill, but her case, like the children's, is mild thus far," he replied. "My niece and nephew showed the first signs of the rash today, while Mr Goulding, his parents, and the baby remain unaffected."

"I should think it must be very hard, to be the only medical man in the area during such a crisis, and with your own family affected also," she said. "How do you manage to visit all the ill, every day, as you have been?"

"With a reliable horse and the invaluable help of the gentlemen of Netherfield," he replied frankly. "I should be quite overwhelmed if it were not for them. I certainly would not be able to monitor my patients so closely. I only wish I could do more for them."

He took a deep breath, thinking of the decision he had earlier made but now ready to act on it.

"One day, perhaps, we shall understand how to defeat this and all the other diseases which so readily kill us now. Some day soon, all of what has occurred these past weeks will be behind us."

When Miss Lucas nodded, he rushed ahead. "And when we reach that moment, when all of this is behind us,

I hope you will allow me to call on you. I enjoy our conversations and your company, and have come to admire you."

She blushed deeply, her mouth pulling into a pleased smile even as her habitually forthright gaze dropped to the scarred tabletop. "I would be...extremely pleased to receive you, sir," was all she said, but that was enough for him.

———

Caroline,

You will reply to this letter, or as soon as Mr Jones declares the epidemic ended, I shall order my servants to put you in the carriage whether you like it or not and bring you here so that we might assure ourselves of your well-being in person.

Charles

———

The next morning dawned clear and bright but bitterly cold. Mary watched Mr Jones shake off his chill as he entered Longbourn, where Mrs Bennet was nearly insensible with pain and fever, despite the caring efforts of Kitty and her father.

Mr Bennet stifled a yawn and looked blearily at the apothecary. "She seems to be declining, sir. What is your prognosis?"

"She is declining," Mr Jones admitted frankly, "but it is not hopeless. I have never seen a pneumonia of any kind which did not appear very dangerous at some point."

Mr Bennet nodded wearily. "Then we shall continue

to hope, and to work towards a happy resolution. Go and see my Lydia now, sir."

When Mr Jones entered Lydia's room, he asked Mary to draw the drapes before he removed the day-old covering from her sister's eye. Calling for warm water, he soaked the flannel in it and laid it again over the eye while examining her rash and listening to her lungs, which he pronounced entirely clear.

Mary watched as he again removed the flannel, gently pried open the eye, and frowned again, more deeply, at what he saw. It was Lydia who spoke first.

"It is very foggy, is that expected?"

The apothecary sighed. "I am afraid that the ulceration has spread despite my efforts. Your sight has been damaged; how far, we shall not know until it has healed. I am very sorry."

Lydia began to cry, and Mary blinked away tears before saying, "Mr Jones, how likely is it to spread to the other eye?"

"I cannot say." He shook his head as he replaced the covering on Lydia's eye. "I will return in a day or two."

"Lord, I am going to be ugly *and* blind!" Lydia wailed when the door closed.

"Only half-blind," Mary replied without thinking, and then clapped a hand to her mouth in horror. But after a moment of shocked silence, Lydia giggled.

"Yes, only half," she agreed through laughter that was borne as much from hysteria as humour. "And perhaps only half-ugly, too."

Mary sat on the bed beside Lydia and pulled her into an embrace, maintaining a patient silence as sobs and laughter alternated and her shoulder grew progressively more damp. When the storm had passed, she brushed tumbled curls off of Lydia's face as the younger girl gave a great yawn.

"Sufficient unto the day, my dear," Mary murmured. "Sleep, sister, and I shall think on how we are to get through this. Leave it all with me."

———

Having responded to Mary's frantic plea for advice on raising Lydia's spirits as best she could, Elizabeth unfolded her other letter, from Charlotte, with no notion of the astonishing news it would contain.

> *Dearest Lizzy,*
>
> *You shall never guess what has happened. Indeed, I can hardly account for it myself.*
>
> *Mr Jones has asked if he may call upon me 'when all of this is behind us', and I have consented. Oh, I wish I might have seen your face as you read that. I know I am older than he, and he is poor, but I believe I may be in a fair way to falling in love with him. I have never been romantic, you know this. I have long said that I would marry any man who asked, so long as he was respectable, but now I cannot countenance the thought of spending my life with anyone I like less than I do Mr Jones. If that is not love, then what is it? Perhaps you, my dearest friend, can tell me.*
>
> *Charlotte*

Elizabeth stared at the page for some moments. Then

she let out a peal of joyous laughter and cried, "Jane! Charlotte is in love!"

Jane raised her head from the pillow and smiled. "You cannot simply leave it at that. Come and tell me all."

"I shall do better," Elizabeth said, removing herself to her sister's side, letter in hand. "I shall read you her own words on the matter."

"Oh, how wonderful," Jane sighed, hands clasped together at her breast, once the happy recitation had concluded. "I know of none—save my dearest sister, of course—more deserving of such happiness."

"And Mr Jones is an excellent man. Though he has little enough, I am confident Charlotte would want for nothing of significance as his wife," added Elizabeth with satisfaction. "I hope very much that he will ask her!"

Jane took her sister's hand and squeezed it, beaming with joy for their friend. "And how lovely, Lizzy, that two worthy people should find each other in the midst of such sorrow and hardship."

The warmth of Jane's hand in her own recalled that of another, only days ago. The image of Mr Darcy's concerned, earnest gaze appeared in her mind's eye. *Charlotte has found a suitor among her trials, and I have found a friend among mine.* If there was an inexplicable sense of dissatisfaction lingering at the edges of that thought, she disregarded it.

As they canvassed the many ways in which they felt Charlotte and Mr Jones suited to each other, Elizabeth found her thoughts straying more and more often to the subject of Jane's heart, and Mr Bingley's. Would he—could he—maintain that inclination, so promising before her illness, now that her beauty was gone? For gone it was, at present, as much as Elizabeth ventured to hope that time would restore some of it. The scars would slowly fade from their current livid pink; if she were very fortunate, only a hint of the pitting would remain after the passage of many months. How much of Mr Bingley's affection was bound up in her appearance? And how much of Jane's heart was bound up in his affection? She fervently hoped that the answer to neither question would prove to be 'too much'.

———

My darling Georgiana,

To answer your most pressing questions, firstly, I have had no difficulty in riding about Hertfordshire. It is cold, but not icy, so have no fear for my safety. Secondly, I do not believe I shall be needed at Pemberley until the spring planting, and perhaps not even then, for a more competent steward would be difficult to find. We manage all quite well through correspondence. I shall certainly not be required to brave the winter roads to Derbyshire unless a crisis occurs.

Have you heard aught of Miss Bingley? Her own brother has no information save reports from his housekeeper that she has been going about with friends who have returned to London. She does not answer his letters, nor Mrs Hurst's.

Mrs Hurst wishes me to recommend to you a novel titled 'The Sword of Damocles', which was published in the summer, and she insists it is more refined and romantic than the title would suggest. As I have faith in her judgment in these matters, I give you leave to acquire it if you like.

I hope you will pardon such a dull letter, my dear, but I have little to relate at present that you would like to hear.

With every fond wish for your happiness and content-ment until we meet again, I remain your doting brother,

Fitzwilliam

———

Over the course of that day Mrs Bennet's breathing grew ever more laboured. She ceased to speak and hardly seemed to be conscious, even in the midst of a wracking fit of coughing. When Mr Jones came in the middle of the afternoon, blown into Longbourn on an icy wind, his grim expression as he examined Mrs Bennet faded to resignation, and both Mr Bennet and Kitty understood what was to come. When he left the room to see Lydia, the pair trailed behind him. Kitty pulled her elder sister from her post.

"Mary," Mr Bennet said, wrapping his hands around his daughter's. "I will stay with Lydia. Go with Kitty and say goodbye to your mother."

Mary's eyes widened, her questioning gaze apparently finding its answer in her father's solemn expression. Silently, Mary nodded, and allowed herself to be led into their mother's room.

When they emerged, pale with grief, a few minutes later, Mr Bennet returned to his wife's rooms, having restored his own composure and heard the apothecary's report on his youngest child. He sat by the bedside of his wife of nearly five and twenty years, and could not think of a thing to say to her.

Theirs had been a *mésalliance* borne of intemperate desires—his, for her beauty, and hers, for his station. He had known it for a mistake within months; it had taken her a little longer to understand the price of her victory. He had not been a good husband to her, he could admit that to himself, now that it was too late to remedy. He had been neither patient nor kind, when either quality in him might have blunted her anxieties and made their home and their union more pleasant for them both.

Kitty returned with their dinners, though neither of them did more than pick at the simple fare. After that, they both lapsed into silence, and later into a strange, anxious half-slumber. Kitty woke him in the early hours of the morning, whispering that her mother's breathing had changed. He bent over his wife, recognising that her breaths had become shallow and soft with long pauses betwixt exhalation and inhalation, and suddenly had the words he could not find earlier.

"Go on now, Mathilda, take your rest. I shall look after our girls. It is past time I took a turn at it, eh?"

Mrs Bennet drew a barely perceptible breath.

Kitty took her hand. "We shall hold him to that promise, Mama."

A long, rattling sigh passed through Mrs Bennet's lips, and then silence, ever lengthening.

CHAPTER TWELVE

A FEW HOURS LATER, AS THE SUN HAD JUST BEGUN TO rise, in the book-room which had been his refuge these last twenty years and more, Thomas Bennet wrote to his wife's brother in London. The black border carefully inked onto the page would give the Gardiners alarm, then grief, and the fact that Edward would not be able to see his sister buried would no doubt occasion further sorrow. He prepared another note, to go to the Philipses by way of one of the young gentlemen of Netherfield. Then, he glanced over another letter, received a fortnight before but left unanswered and largely forgotten in the upheaval of the intervening time. He picked up his pen once more.

Mr Collins,

I fear I must, at the present time, decline your generous offer to visit us at Longbourn. Smallpox has come upon the area. Two of my daughters suffer greatly as I write this, and my wife has been lost to it. You will surely understand that we cannot host you in these circumstances.

Yours,

T Bennet

These necessary tasks complete, he produced one more sheet and, after brooding over it for many silent moments, dipped his pen in the inkwell and set it to the paper.

My dear girls,

I regret to inform you that your mother died in the night. Her end was far more peaceful than the illness which caused it, and your sister Kitty and I were with her at the last. I am more sorry than I can say that I cannot go to you now and be of what comfort I might, and that you will not be here to farewell her.

Do not concern yourselves with mourning clothes; I will see to all those things with the assistance of Mary and Kitty, who have been as courageous and steady as one could wish throughout these events. Lydia continues ill but Mr Jones remains hopeful, and we here at Longbourn take heart from that.

Your father,

Thomas Bennet

Postscript: A lock of your mother's hair will be taken for each of you, and kept safe in anticipation of your return.

He folded and sealed it, and tucked all of his letters into his pocket before taking a seat in the front parlour in anticipation of the visit which he expected at any time.

Not half an hour later, a knock sounded on the front door, and Mr Darcy was visibly surprised to see the master of the house when it opened. He quickly recollected himself and bowed.

"Mr Bennet, I have brought notes from Miss Elizabeth to Miss Mary and Miss Catherine." These, he proffered, and the older man accepted them without comment. "Has there been any change in the health of your household?"

Bennet sighed. "Quite a large one, I am afraid. Mrs Bennet is dead." He produced his stack of letters and handed them to the younger man, whose face had gone white and still. "Would you be so kind, Mr Darcy, as to see these notes to their intended recipients? The ones to London and Kent need only be left at the post-counter at the inn."

"Of course, sir. Is there any other way in which I might be of assistance to you and your family?" Mr Darcy asked quietly.

"If you have time to stop at the parsonage, Mr Edwards ought to be informed. Tell him, if you would, that under present circumstances we understand the funeral rites must be simple and private."

Mr Darcy agreed to this sad errand and, having ascertained that there was nothing further to report to Mr Jones, he mounted his horse and sped away.

———

Darcy's heart was in his throat as he knocked softly on the door of Miss Bennet's room shortly after his return to Netherfield that afternoon. Miss Elizabeth smiled as she opened it, and he felt a brief, cowardly urge to fling her father's note at her and run away, that he need not witness its result. Instead, he bowed, and produced that letter and the one from Miss Lucas.

"Good day, Mr Darcy," she said, accepting the pages. "It looks frightfully cold out, I hope your rounds were not too uncomfortable?"

"Not at all."

She turned the notes over. "Why, this is not from Mary or Kitty, but my father! My sisters have not fallen ill, have they?"

"No, Miss Elizabeth. I believe they were too occupied yesterday to write to you, but as of this morning both were still in health."

Brow furrowed, she broke the seal on the perplexing note and quickly scanned the opening lines. The colour drained from her face. "No..." she breathed, and he impulsively took her arm and led her a short distance down the way to the servants' chair by the stairs.

"You are not well, Miss Elizabeth. Please sit." She hardly seemed to know he was there, but she sat down, unable to support herself and looking so miserably ill that it was impossible for Darcy to leave her, or to refrain from saying, in a tone of gentleness and commiseration, "Let me call for a maid. A glass of wine; shall I get you one? You are very ill."

"No, I thank you," she replied, endeavouring to recover herself. "There is nothing the matter with me. I am quite well; I am only distressed by this dreadful news which I have just received from Longbourn. I assume, sir, that you know of what my father has written?"

"I do," he replied solemnly. "I am very sorry for your loss."

"I thank you." Absently, she opened her father's letter again and read it through. He remained by her side, silent and patient.

"I do not know how to tell Jane," she said softly.

"There is no good way to deliver such news, but if I may be so bold as to offer advice from my own experience, dancing about the matter only makes it worse. Perhaps you might simply read her your father's words?"

"Perhaps," she agreed. "Who was it that gave you such news so poorly?"

A little surprised that she had got it right, and had not assumed it was he who had fumbled such an important communication, he replied, "My father, when my own mother died. Yours has done well to confine it to a short note, I think—the shock was not greater, and you suffered no period of mounting dread before it came."

She smiled slightly, as if in sympathy with the boy he had been. "I...I think that is it. I am shocked. I hardly know what to think, or what to do."

"You will, at the proper times, think and do everything necessary, Miss Elizabeth. For now, you need only begin to reconcile yourself to the news." He lowered himself to sit upon the floor beside her chair, an informal posture no one but Georgiana had lately seen him in, but he wished to signal that he had no intention of leaving her alone unless she particularly requested it. "Perhaps you should like to talk about her?"

"Oh, my mother..." Elizabeth trailed off, one hand fluttering vaguely as though it might complete the thought her voice had not. "She is...*was* not the easiest person, as I am sure you apprehended even during your brief acquaintance. But she was my mother, and I truly believe she did her best. That her best was as often borne of ignorance as sense was not her fault—her father had no use for daughters, and mine never exerted himself to teach or to check her."

Darcy saw tears welling in her eyes as she hesitantly went on. "She loved us, I believe, though she was not capable of understanding me and Mary particularly, and Kitty and even Jane also vexed her at times. She was diligent in teaching us the things she considered important—how to run a household, set a table, and lay a fine stitch. I spent my whole life wishing she might be different, might be more clever or understanding, but I never wished her gone. And now she is, and I shall not even be able to say goodbye." Her voice broke then and her tears spilled over, but as she buried her face in her handkerchief, Darcy patted her arm gently, ensuring she knew she was not alone in such a sad moment.

After a time, Elizabeth lifted her face, drew the sodden cloth across it, and glanced at Darcy, who still occupied the floor beside her, his long legs in their dusty boots jutting out into the passage. He looked back at her with concern, his thoughts solemn but tender.

"My apologies, sir, for subjecting you to such a spectacle," she said after drawing a deep and steadying breath. "I must look a fright."

He was silent for a moment. "Had you cared for your mother so little as to retain your appearance in the face of such news, I should have lost all respect for you."

She huffed out the seed of a laugh. "It is difficult to be honest without being insulting when answering such a statement, Mr Darcy, but you have managed it most adroitly." She turned fully towards him and smiled, her expression tinged with sadness but no less genuine for it. "I thank you sir, sincerely, for your care today. You have been a most excellent friend to me since my sister fell ill."

"It has been my great pleasure to be of service to you and your family," he answered softly.

"I wish I had done as you offered, gone to Longbourn to see my family. Even if I could not have entered the house, I could have—" she broke off, fresh tears springing from her eyes.

"Your father and sisters are there and would wish to see you," he urged her. "At your word, I will hitch a horse to the curricle."

Darcy would recall the sorrowful beauty in her expression till the end of his days. "I thank you for your kindness," she murmured.

"I am at your service."

He pressed her hand, and for a moment they sat together in silence. He heard a tremulous sigh and then she spoke in a stronger voice.

"I believe that little tempest has cleared my head, and I am ready to return to Jane, and to share this news with her if she is awake."

Darcy took that as his cue to stand, and offered his hand to assist her from her seat. She accepted it gracefully. He escorted her to the door and bade her farewell, and folded into his heart the brave smile she turned upon him before slipping through the portal and closing it between them.

Darcy stood motionless, staring at the thick oak door, his heart aching for what Miss Elizabeth faced. But he now had a problem of his own.

If she, occupied with the care of her sister and the

calamity which had befallen her family and her neighbours, had neither the time nor the energy to go falling in
love at present, *he* had no such constraints on his emotions.
Sitting beside her while she sobbed, in a position he would
have voluntarily assumed for very few people in all the
world, Darcy had allowed himself to acknowledge that his
admiration of her was not simply an appreciation of the
qualities she possessed, which it might be possible to find
in another, more highly-born lady, but was a real and
steady affection for her alone.

He turned and paced slowly towards the family wing
where his own chambers lay, his brow furrowed as he
wondered just what he was supposed to do about *that*.

———

At Longbourn, the day passed, as even the worst day will.
Mr Bennet and his daughters spoke to each other in
hushed voices, as though they might disturb she who lay
beyond hearing in the room at the end of the corridor. The
Reverend Mr Edwards—excellent man!—had sent a simple
coffin and a note proposing that the funeral take place the
morning after next. Mrs Bennet would pass the intervening time laid out within the pine box atop the dining
room table. There would be none but the residents of
Longbourn to see her so, but still, they would observe the
forms as much as they might.

Lydia, who had been the closest of them all to the
departed, occasionally fell into a quiet fit of tears, but
lacked the vitality to do more. Mary continued to devote
herself to Lydia's care, while Kitty grew more restless as
the hours passed. Mr Bennet realised, in a flash of under-

standing, that Kitty required occupation to be contented, and that the fretfulness he had disliked (and yes, mocked) in her was the fruit of idleness and lack of purpose.

"Kitty," he said, without stopping to think upon it further, "I wondered if you might assist me with a task?"

She turned to him eagerly. "Yes, Papa, what is it?"

"You girls, and your sisters at Netherfield, will require mourning clothes, and I will need armbands. I had thought Mrs Traynor would likely have all your measurements, but you would be able to give much better instructions for such things than I, if you would not mind writing to her?"

"Oh, certainly, nothing could be easier," she replied with unusual confidence. "How many ought we to get?"

He considered that for a moment. "Two for each of you now, one nicer than the other, and after you have each decided what of your wardrobe might be sacrificed to the dye bath, we may require more."

He held up a finger as a thought occurred to him, which he pondered for a few seconds. "And no bombazine. We shall all, I think, be unhappy enough without you girls chafing in that horrid stuff."

Mary insisted upon reading Kitty's instruction to the dressmaker before it was sealed, having learnt long ago not to allow anyone else the last word on her own clothing. Upon concluding her examination of the order, she handed it back and remarked that Kitty had done very well, though a plain fichu, rather than one edged in discreet beads as Kitty had requested for her, was all that was required. Kitty and her father exchanged a glance, and when her father slyly winked, Kitty had no qualms about sealing the letter without revisions.

CHAPTER THIRTEEN

Jane had taken the news as well as could be expected of someone with such a tender heart; she had wept, and fallen into an exhausted slumber with tears still wet upon her cheeks, and wept a little more when she awoke, but then exerted herself to be calm and very nearly serene for her sister's sake, as Elizabeth had done for her.

Elizabeth had slept poorly, her mind overrun with feelings of regret, sorrow, and guilt. Much as Jane had needed her at Netherfield, could she not have stolen away to visit Longbourn and offer words of hope and encouragement?

Mr Darcy had made his offer earlier and she had dismissed it, fearing not only leaving Jane, but endangering her sisters and parents. Yet Longbourn was already infected, so what had she done by staying away but refuse them her advice, her support, her love? Her mother, who had often mortified her, but always loved her, was dead. They had exchanged no letters since Elizabeth walked to Netherfield to nurse Jane; thinking on her mother's final words to her on that day elicited both a smile and a sob.

'How can you be so silly as to think of walking such a distance, in all this dirt! You will not be fit to be seen when you get there.'

Elizabeth came to a decision: she would find a way to visit her family, and soon.

Mr Darcy arrived as usual in the middle of the afternoon with letters for Elizabeth. As he handed her a letter from Mary, he kindly asked after her and Jane. When he turned to leave her to her correspondence, Elizabeth called out, "Please, sir. At your convenience, I would very much like to go to Longbourn."

He startled, but quickly nodded. "Would tomorrow suit? Bingley and I are to attend the service for your mother. We would need to take the curricle for propriety, but could follow the carriage as far as Longbourn, and you might stay with your sisters while we are at the church with your father. They will not, of course, have the usual visitors," he concluded sadly.

She supposed she had known, in the back of her mind, that there would be no visits of condolence from the ladies of the neighbourhood while the gentlemen attended the funeral, but to hear it spoken of drove a fresh spike of grief into her heart. Her mother, whatever her failings, did not deserve to have her death pass without even the observation of the most commonplace forms. The injustice of it made her catch her breath, and Mr Darcy frowned as she composed herself.

"Forgive me," she said. "I was overcome by my feelings. Yes, I believe I should like to spend that time with my younger sisters. It is not right that they should be alone at such a moment."

Darcy nodded. "I shall arrange it all."

———

Mary's letter was shorter than her usual report.

Dearest Lizzy,

By now you have learnt that our mother is gone. Sister, I wish so much that you were here. I wish that Jane was, too, but you are the resolute one and I want so much to lean upon you now. It is selfish, I know, but I so often feel too weak for these burdens.

We still fear for Lydia's survival, for she is so frail and only now entering the phase of which Mr Jones most particularly warned us, but I continue to truly fear for her spirit. She has naturally been brought low by the partial loss of her sight and the likely loss of her appearance, and Mother's death is a further blow from which I am uncertain she will recover. I do not know how to help her, though I have done my best to apply your good advice; I think my nature is more inclined to scolding than to enlivening. She has become so very dear to me, and I am now afraid that I am precisely the wrong person to tend to her. Tell me the truth, Lizzy—ought I to give her care over to Kitty?

Mary

"Oh Lizzy! Poor Mary sounds so very despondent, and I fear for Lydia, also," Jane said after reading Mary's communication at her sister's request.

"Jane, all will be well, but dearest, I must go to Longbourn. I had already intended to do so, and this makes matters even more urgent."

Jane frowned. "You do not mean to walk there, in this cold weather, do you?"

"Mr Darcy has offered to arrange it all," Elizabeth reassured her. "We will go in the curricle, so all will be proper, and we will not risk coming upon anyone who has not already been exposed to the illness. It will be cold, but much quicker than walking."

Elizabeth expected some further resistance, for Jane had never been one who bent, much less broke, rules—her correspondence with Mr Bingley the sole exception. But to her surprise, her sister only nodded and said, "Then of course you must go."

———

Charles,

I am writing to you—are you satisfied? I have been busy of late, for I was able to engage a companion and have been catching up with those of my friends who are in town. I am perfectly well, and all the better for being away from the savage society of the country and among civilised people. I attended the theatre last night with Miss Symonds and her family, and though the crowd was thin there were enough people of interest there to make an entertaining evening. Far more so than playing Cassino at Netherfield, to be certain. You really ought to join me just as soon as Hurst recovers, before the unwashed farmers of Hertfordshire bring forth another disease to assail you. Darcy must long for decent company, and Louisa would surely prefer to be here.

I have instructed the housekeeper to freshen your rooms, and anticipate seeing you all very soon. I have been invited to pass Christmas with the Symonds family, and you would be more than welcome, too, I believe. My friend asks after you often, and I know you enjoyed her company before our unfortunate relocation. Come back, Brother, and renew your acquaintance with a lady of accomplishment and fortune. There can be nothing to keep you in Hertfordshire any longer, now that Miss Bennet's pretty face is no more.

 Yours,
 Caroline

———

On the morning of Mrs Bennet's funeral, the parson's manservant arrived an hour early to assist Mr Bennet in placing the coffin in the carriage which would bear her earthly form to the church for the service. Shortly thereafter, Mr Darcy's fine coach rolled to a stop before Longbourn, and behind it, a curricle, driven by Mr Darcy and bearing also...

"Lizzy, my Lizzy!" Mr Bennet cried as the smaller vehicle came to a stop and his second daughter leapt down and ran to him. He swept her up into his embrace, both of them laughing and sobbing and gripping each other fiercely. At last she pulled back and took his face between her hands.

"Oh, Papa, how pale you are!"

"Say nothing of that!" He covered one of her hands with his own. "Are you my dear girl, or merely a bundle of twigs in her dress?"

Elizabeth laughed a little at that. "The last weeks have been difficult, but truly, I am well, and so very happy to see you. Jane sends, and I quote, every bit of her love to her dear family."

Someone cleared their throat nearby, and both of them looked up to find Mr Darcy and Mr Bingley standing by the door of the larger vehicle. The curricle and horse were being led away by Longbourn's stablemaster. "Forgive me, sir, for interrupting, but we should be getting on to the church soon," Mr Darcy said. "Will you join us in my carriage?"

Mr Bennet was suddenly conscious of the tears on his cheeks and hastily availed himself of his handkerchief. "I thank you, that will be most welcome. Let me just take Lizzy inside to her sisters."

He had not much time to indulge in watching the reunion of Kitty and Lizzy, nor was he in any frame of mind to enjoy Kitty's surprise when her elder sister appeared in the doorway at his side, but he did linger for a moment, nodding to himself as two girls who had hardly found a word to say to each other for the last several years clung to each other as sisters ought in times of trouble.

———

Elizabeth and Kitty saw their father off, bundled in his greatcoat, hat, and muffler, and then the elder turned to the younger, saying, "I should like to see Lydia, and then I must speak to Mary. Will you mind sitting with Lydia while I do?"

"Not at all. I am so glad you are here, Lizzy!" Kitty embraced her quickly, then they turned as one to ascend the stairs. The thought that the house seemed very quiet flitted through her mind, but she pushed it aside. No doubt they would speak of their mother soon, but for the moment Lydia and Mary were foremost in her mind.

Mary's eyes grew impossibly wide as she opened the door to Lydia's chamber to find Elizabeth on the other side, Kitty beaming behind her. "How...?"

"The gentlemen of Netherfield escorted me here on their way to the church. Do not worry, all was proper," Elizabeth replied with a smile.

"I had not even considered that," Mary admitted. "I was only glad you had not walked three miles in this cold." She glanced behind herself. "Lydia is stirring. She will be glad to see you, I think. Come in." She stepped aside for her sisters, and Elizabeth reached the bed just as Lydia's eyes fluttered open.

"Lizzy!" she breathed.

"Surprise!" Elizabeth smiled widely as she sat on the edge of the bed, allowing nothing of her distress to show at Lydia's shrunken form, altered visage, and clouded left eye.

"Are you home to stay?"

"No, only for a few hours. I am breaking quarantine, though I think it acceptable because I am only visiting another house where the illness dwells. Still, best say nothing to Mr Jones," she concluded with a wink, and was rewarded with a little chuckle, followed by a great yawn.

Elizabeth's concern that even that little conversation had wearied Lydia she hid as well, saying only, "Why do you not take more rest? I will visit you again before I depart."

Lydia nodded and allowed her eyes to close, and as Elizabeth stood Kitty came forward to take a place at the bedside. "Come, Mary," Elizabeth whispered, reaching out for her middle sister. "Let us speak below."

They settled into chairs by the fire in the parlour, and Elizabeth fixed her with a serious look. "Mary, I most certainly do not think you ought to give Lydia's care over to Kitty, although now...now that Mama does not need her any longer, you should certainly allow her to help."

Mary's surprise at this pronouncement appeared so great as to render her speechless, and after a moment of waiting for a response which did not come, Elizabeth continued. "You are the natural person to see our sister through this crisis of confidence. You, my dear sister, have never cared a whit for appearances. Who better to now teach Lydia to value those qualities in herself which smallpox cannot scar? And who among us has the patience to assist her in re-learning those things which will be so different now, with her sight damaged? Again, I say that it is, obviously, you."

"Do you truly believe that?" Mary asked in utter bewilderment.

"Oh, Mary." Elizabeth's head dropped, and she shook it slowly before raising it to face Mary with an expression of remorse. "I have not paid you the attention I ought to have done, as your elder. But you trusted me enough to ask me these questions, so I will request that you trust my answers. I am certain Kitty would take your place by Lydia's side if you were to ask it of her, but I do truly believe that you are best suited to seeing her through those ailments which are not of the body."

Mary looked shocked, and Elizabeth realised with no little regret that her sister had never before had anyone express confidence in her abilities. "I can hardly discount what you say, when I have specifically requested your guidance, and particularly when your wishes so neatly align with my own."

"I am proud of you, Mary," Elizabeth said emphatically. "You have performed excellently in a difficult situation, and I hope you never again doubt your own strength, for it is prodigious."

———

Mr Bennet returned in the early afternoon, weary and windblown. Kitty helped him shed his heavy coat, and Elizabeth ran down the stairs to prepare for her departure. He smiled at them tiredly. "Well, my girls, it was not the send-off your mother would have wanted, but it was better than it might have been. Mr Jones and Sir William Lucas also attended, and they and the gentlemen from Netherfield even stayed for the burial. Captain Carter has taken upon himself the greater part of their daily visits in the neighbourhood, which allowed them to attend. You must remind me, Kitty, to write a note of thanks to each of them, in a few days. Lizzy, the gentlemen from Netherfield await you. Mr Darcy is having the curricle brought round."

Elizabeth tied on her bonnet and gave her father a fond smile.

"They are a fine pair of gentlemen," he added. "It was very good of them to come, and bring you to us."

"It was, and I wish I had had more time with you today," she said sadly, after kissing him on the cheek. "But my sisters had a greater need of the little time I could be away from Jane."

"Indeed we did," said Kitty. "We have spent most of it

all together in Lydia's room, Papa, and I do believe it perked Lydia up a bit."

Not wishing to keep the gentlemen waiting, or the horses standing in the cold, Elizabeth's farewells were hurried, and sooner than any of them would have wished, she was gone.

———

Caroline,

You will no doubt notice that the hand of this message is not my own. I have imposed upon my valet to serve as secretary for me in this instance, for his hand is vastly superior to my own and I wish that there should be no opportunity for misunderstanding of those things I am about to relate.

I received on the same day your letter and another from Hurst's housekeeper informing me of the amount she will be required to disburse for the services of your companion. Let me be perfectly clear: in choosing to leave Netherfield against my wishes and all good sense, you created the need for a companion to lend you respectability, and I will not pay the price for your defiance. Her wages will come out of your funds. I have instructed my banker to release to you the quarterly interest from your dowry on or after 2 January, and if she expects her wages at the quarter-day as I suspect she does, you had best reserve it from the funds you currently have on hand. Mrs Burley has been instructed that she is not to be paid with the household. She is likely to expect a little something extra on Boxing Day as well, so I hope you have exercised prudence in your expenditures of late.

Henceforth, all bills I receive for anything of yours will be forwarded to my banker, who will pay them out of your next quarter's funds. You have eight hundred a year in your own right, Sister, and I shall no longer fund your excesses. You are now responsible for your wardrobe, fripperies, subscriptions, &c. You may remain in Hurst's townhouse for the time being, but I must caution you that he and Louisa approve of your actions no more than I do. Do not anticipate my own acquisition of a house in London, either, for I will not do so until I marry, and then will not subject any wife of mine to your selfishness and controlling ways.

It is likely that Parliament will convene in January, bringing many to the capital in advance of the Season. I advise you to use these next months well. Find yourself a husband, Caroline. Cease to wait for Darcy; he will not have you. This has been obvious to everyone for years, and only your own conceit blinds you to this reality. Find a man who enjoys London and needs your dowry, and if at all possible, try to consider the feelings and wishes of others on occasion, for this will help you secure a proposal. No man wants a wife unwilling to think of his comforts, you know.

Charles

———

Darcy was bent over the writing desk in the drawing room, too intent on his letters to greet Carter as he entered the room. Some minutes passed before he set down his pen, stretched his shoulders, and saw the man standing before the fire sipping from a glass of brandy. "Forgive me for not greeting you, Carter. I wished to set my thoughts down while they were fresh in my mind."

"Of course," the officer replied easily. "Matters of business?"

"Yes, the flour mill at Pemberley suffered a failure of the water wheel when the wheat harvest had just come in. Temporary repairs were affected, but those have now failed. I have just authorised the suspension of milling until a new wheel can be fitted. I think it will cause fewer delays than constantly stopping and starting for patch-work."

Bingley entered the room during this speech, and turned a laughing look upon his friend. "Are you boring poor Carter with estate talk?"

The officer shrugged. "Not at all. I am to have an estate one day, and so I am happy to learn how more experienced landowners deal with such problems as arise."

The other gentlemen's surprise could not be hidden. "I understood you to be a second son?" Bingley asked.

"Yes, but my uncle is a confirmed bachelor, and has long intended to leave Morton Grange to me." He bowed slightly to Darcy. "It is nothing to Pemberley, from what I have heard, but it does have a mill, and now I have learnt a little something about maintaining it."

"Well, that is fortunate," exclaimed Bingley, pouring himself a drink. "Very few second sons, I think, can look forward to being landowners themselves. Will you tell us a little of it?"

The captain moved from the fire to take a seat. "It is a tidy little estate, not far from my father's in northern

Hampshire. It is, I think, similar to Mr Bennet's in size and income, however I have a little money my mother left me, and thought to acquire more land. The farms are very productive, and though I should like to breed horses I would not wish to speculate good farmland on the venture."

Darcy found himself further impressed by the man's intelligence and common sense.

"Goodness, I feel such an idle fellow next to you!" Bingley exclaimed. "I am these three years from university and have only just acquired a lease; I have no notion yet of purchasing, much less expanding!"

"Well—that is only sensible."

Bingley chuckled. "I was entirely ready to purchase the first estate that came along! The prudence was all Darcy's!"

Darcy bowed his head in a theatrical manner. "And so it was."

They all three laughed at that, and Carter asked Bingley how he liked being master of Netherfield.

"It is a great lot of work, but I think I am beginning to catch on," he replied, with a quizzical look at Darcy.

"You are coming along very well," Darcy agreed. "The spring planting will be the first great test, but as it is some months off, you will have ample time to prepare."

"By which you mean, finish reading that great stack of books you foisted upon me!"

"For a start, yes." Darcy smirked.

"A start? Damn me, it's more than I read at Cambridge," their host objected.

Darcy turned to the other gentleman. "Do not let him

fool you, Captain. Bingley does not read for pleasure, it is true, but when he reads for information, he retains it prodigiously well. He is not half the fool he pretends to be."

Bingley only grinned and raised his glass.

CHAPTER FOURTEEN

Mr Jones was riding between Mr Johnstone's small estate and his sister's home at Haye-Park early the following afternoon, when a thunder of hoof-beats presaged Captain Carter's arrival upon Bingley's prized hunter. "You are needed at Netherfield, sir! Take Orion here, if you will, and I shall follow on yours."

"Mr Hurst?" he asked, quickly dismounting and seizing his bag.

"Yes." The officer held Orion's reins while Mr Jones mounted and tied his bag down, stepping back as the apothecary nudged the swift beast into a gallop and, bent low over its neck, disappeared round the bend.

Jones left Orion with a groom who awaited him before the house and rushed inside, waving off the footman and running directly up the stairs and into Mr Hurst's room.

"It has begun, then," he said, moving to the bed without even removing his coat or hat. He sent everyone else away and addressed the patient, who was awake if not entirely alert. "Mr Hurst, how are you feeling? Are you in any pain?"

"My belly aches like the devil," Hurst muttered, "but other than that I am only very tired. I did not know what tiredness was until today. And I may be a little faintish." He shifted uncomfortably as the apothecary palpated his stomach. "I don't expect you sent my wife and valet out to give me good news, sir. I'll take it plain and unvarnished, if you please."

"You are bleeding inside your gut," Jones answered solemnly. "I believe you have been from the beginning, but it has worsened. There is nothing that may be done, I am sorry."

"Had a feeling I wouldn't come out the other side of this," Hurst said tiredly. "How long, do you reckon?"

"Perhaps a day."

"Well then." He studied the plaster of the ceiling for a moment, as if inspiration might be found in its cracks. "Best send my wife in. Things I must tell her."

The apothecary stood and bowed, then disappeared into the sitting room, where Mrs Hurst waited alone. She looked up at him, pale and anxious, and moved past him into Hurst's room. Jones followed, hovering in the doorway, and watched as she went to her husband's bedside. He wished not to intrude, but his concern for Mrs Hurst compelled him to remain near.

"Gilbert..." she said helplessly.

"Hush, Lou. Things I need to say, but so tired." Mr Hurst closed his eyes, and for a moment Jones feared he had already gone. Then his lids lifted, slowly, and he fixed his wife with an earnest stare. "Been a good wife, Lou, want you to know that. Never told you so, but you were.

Sorry we never had children. Fine mother you'd have made."

Jones averted his gaze as Mrs Hurst began to sob.

"Stay away from that sister of yours. She makes you unhappy. Stick with Bingley, he'll see you right."

————

Elizabeth and Jane had not thought much of it when a maid had come the previous evening to inform them that there would be no formal dinner that evening, and that trays would be brought for them. It had been a frosty morning, and little warmer when Elizabeth had ventured a turn about the garden in the afternoon in one of the freshly dyed mourning gowns delivered from Longbourn. They presumed the gentlemen were fatigued from their exertions on behalf of the neighbourhood.

Mr Bingley's daily note for Jane that morning was unusually brief, and she gasped as she read it. Elizabeth regarded her with great concern; she had ceased to read them before Jane could, and for a frantic moment wondered if Mr Bingley had breached the bounds of propriety after all. Jane handed her the note, and she soon wished she had been correct.

Miss Bennet,

Please forgive me, but I am unable to write much today. Mr Hurst succumbed to his illness last night, and my sister has great need of my company.

Yours,

CB

"Poor Mr Hurst!" Elizabeth exclaimed in surprise.

"And poor Mrs Hurst," Jane added. "I do not feel I knew the gentleman beyond the barest acquaintance, but Mrs Hurst has been a real friend to us."

"Indeed she has. We must write her a note of condolence."

"Yes, and I must exert myself and respond to Mr Bingley, today of all days," Jane said.

Elizabeth eyed Jane's scabbed hands dubiously. "You will get salve all over the paper, dearest. Perhaps you had better exert yourself to dictate to me." Jane accepted the practicality of the arrangement with only a little disappointment.

> Dear Mrs Hurst,
>
> We are so terribly sorry to hear of Mr Hurst's death. The maids have mentioned more than once your devoted care of him, and we are certain that your gentle attentions and constant presence eased his final days. Jane is much better, though still abed, and if you should wish for some company that will demand little of you, please come and visit us. You know of our own recent loss. I cannot say that our spirits are cheerful, but perhaps we three may comfort each other.
>
> With all regard and sympathy,
> Jane and Elizabeth Bennet

"It is a good letter," Jane said with a sad smile. "I hope she will come to visit us. You are correct that we may comfort each other."

Elizabeth sealed the note and set it aside. Sharpening her pen with a few deft strokes of the knife, she prepared a fresh sheet of paper and said, "Now, let us delight Mr Bingley with your reply."

———

The day after her husband's death passed slowly for Louisa Hurst. She had sent her reluctant brother out upon his usual rounds with the other gentlemen, pointing out that she had letters to write, and that his dreadful penmanship would be of no help in that most urgent task, though he might, if he liked, ink the borders for her when he returned.

She wrote steadily through the morning, first to his family, who would have the grief of both his death and his burial in a place they did not know. Then she wrote to his regular correspondents, and lastly to her own friends in town and family in Scarborough. It was a task which required little thought, for once she had got through the first, most difficult letter to his parents and brother, she could write with more formality and less detail to everyone else. The last letter she wrote was to Caroline, whom they knew, from the reports of their housekeeper in London, to be enduring her isolation with little grace and a great deal of trouble to the household.

Her letter to her sister was little different to those which had gone before, save that she concluded it with a warning that their brother's temper with regard to her flight had not yet entirely abated. Reading back over it before she sealed it, she suddenly crumpled it into a ball and flung it into the fire. She sat back down and wrote a nearly identical missive, save for the warning. If Caroline was foolish enough not to anticipate Charles's continued ire, she perhaps ought to learn of her error the hard way.

Louisa and her brother sat together after he returned to Netherfield, she stitching up a set of armbands for him, and he tending to his correspondence. They said very little, until Louisa's maid left the room after informing her that the gowns she had selected had survived the dye bath and were drying. Charles then burst out, "I hope you know, Louisa, that I will take care of you!"

She looked at him in astonishment. "Of course I do, Charles. I never questioned it for a moment."

He subsided, mollified. "Oh. Well. Good. It is only that I know I have lived a scattered sort of life these last few years, and I feared you would not believe that you may depend upon me. But I am determined to settle into the respectable life of a country gentleman and devote myself to my family and estate. You will always be welcome in my homes, Louisa. More than welcome—wanted," he added firmly.

"Thank you, dear brother," she replied, blinking away tears. "I have seen you take up your responsibilities with pride these last weeks."

"Have you?" He grinned with boyish pleasure, entirely ruining the gravitas he had assumed, and she laughed for the first time in days.

———

Elizabeth and Jane were interrupted in their reading of one of Mrs Hurst's novels late that afternoon by a knock on the door. Elizabeth opened it and smiled to find Mr Darcy there, assuming he had letters for her. He gave her only one, from Charlotte, and asked if she could step out into the passage for a moment. Worried, she did so.

"Your sisters have been too much occupied with Miss Lydia to write to you," he said, "or so your father informed me. They roused him in the night and sent him for Mr Jones, for several of Miss Lydia's marks became infected and caused a fever. While he was away, it seems Miss Mary recalled something Mr Jones had said of the proper treatment in such a case, and between her and Miss Catherine, they carried it out," he related, his expression and tone full of admiration.

"Mr Jones was most impressed. He only gave them a little further advice before returning to his bed. I wish I could tell you that Miss Lydia is out of danger, but it is not yet known. The quick action of your sisters has given her the best possible chance, however—Jones said so himself, when I saw him a little while ago. I thought you would wish to know, both the good and the bad. I hope I have not erred?"

"No, you were entirely correct," she replied, torn between fear for her youngest sister and pride in the other two. "How many more complications must poor Lyddie endure?" she murmured to herself.

"Let us hope this is the last."

She turned a bleak look upon him. "I think it *must* be the last, if she is to survive. She was already so weak when I saw her." She drew in a great breath and squared her shoulders. "But I shall not give in to my fears. Lydia is too stubborn to die. I must believe that."

"If I hear anything, anything at all, you will know it at the first possible moment," Mr Darcy promised.

That evening, at loose ends and unable even to lose herself in a beloved novel, Louisa Hurst sent a maid to enquire when it might be convenient for her to visit the Bennet sisters, and received a reply that they would be delighted to receive her at any time.

She knocked upon Jane's door shortly afterwards and was admitted by Elizabeth, who greeted her warmly and expressed every proper condolence. Jane was sat up in her bed, with her hair in a plait over her shoulder and her face, now a jumble of scabs and livid pink scars, glistening faintly with Mr Jones's salve. Louisa, having not at all forgot what it was like to confront such a visage in her own mirror, greeted the elder Bennet without any sign of pity or discomfort, only taking her hand and saying how pleased she was that Miss Bennet was now out of danger. Jane thanked her, and offered her own regrets on the death of Mr Hurst.

"I cannot begin to imagine your feelings," said Jane, "but please believe that you have my deepest sympathies."

Mrs Hurst turned her face to the window for a moment, and then back to those two young ladies, with whom she had not been long acquainted, but inexplicably felt she could trust with the confusing contents of her heart.

"I could not have imagined my own feelings," she replied in a low, shaking voice. "I tried to, when I understood that he would not survive. I did not believe they would be so strong." She produced a handkerchief only to twist it in her hands. "I married to oblige my family and improve our position, and Gilbert to gain funds to preserve his family's estate from the results of some bad investments of his father's. He was not a bad man, only dull and rather selfish, like so many of his class. But he never mistreated me, and was even kind, in his way. I did not love him, but proximity in the absence of mistreatment breeds a sort of fondness..." She waved her hands vaguely, the crumpled handkerchief an inadvertent flag of surrender. "Oh, I am rambling. I hardly know what I feel, except that I miss him, and I did not expect to." She laughed without humour. "And now that I have bared my soul to you both, perhaps you had better call me Louisa."

Both of the Bennet ladies readily agreed to this, and after a moment, Elizabeth said reflectively, "I believe I understand you, Louisa. Many a woman, I think, knows that upon entering the married state she becomes, effectively, the property of her husband, to do with as he pleases with very few exceptions. Her only safeguards are his honour and his affection for her. Lacking either of those only makes her position more precarious. If, in a marriage of practicality, the husband shows his wife kindness and respect, it is natural that she should feel a gratitude that would in time become a real affection."

Jane added, "Oh, yes, Lizzy, I think you are right. Your feelings are perfectly natural, Louisa. And to so suddenly transform from wife to widow, when Mr Hurst was young and in good health only weeks ago, must be shock enough to overset anyone."

"It has been a shock," Louisa admitted. "A month ago my life was mapped out for me, and now...now I do not know what comes next."

Elizabeth moved to kneel by Louisa's chair, taking her hands in a light, comforting grip. "What comes next is a year of mourning in which you shall have very few demands on your time. Your brother will see to your welfare, you can have no doubt of that with such an excellent one as he!" She smiled. "And you will have that time to accustom yourself to these changes, and to decide what you wish to do after. You need not even consider it yet, if you do not want to. There is time to allow yourself to recover from the suddenness of it all."

"I hope," Louisa ventured, "that Charles will elect to remain here for the time being, even after we are free to travel again. I find I am more relaxed in the country, so I do not think the busyness of town would suit me as I become accustomed to widowhood. And I should not like to soon leave my new friends here," she added, shyly.

"We should certainly dislike to see you go," replied Jane warmly. "I hope we may know each other better in the coming weeks and months."

"That is my desire, as well," Louisa replied. She asked then which novels they had read lately, and they had a pleasant hour's conversation on the subject, which was a respite to them all in their mourning.

CHAPTER FIFTEEN

As had become her daily habit, Charlotte exited the house to greet Mr Jones when she saw him riding up the lane, but that morning his slumped posture and pale, shocked face told her that something was very wrong. Heedless of propriety, she rushed up to him as he dismounted, crying, "My God, what has happened?"

He seemed to struggle for words, so she took his arm and led him to the bench at the side of the house. She continued to hug his arm even after they were seated, and waited patiently for him to speak.

"My nephew, David…" he whispered at last, in tones of disbelief. "He died in the night. His case did not seem dire; I thought he would recover, but…" Tears spilled down his face.

She used her own handkerchief to dry his cheeks. "Oh, my dear, how terrible. And your poor sister…"

"What did I miss?" he wondered. "Is there something I might have done?"

"Surely there was not," she murmured, continuing her

ministrations. "You have said yourself that there is no way to be certain of the outcome until very late in the illness. Poor David had not the strength to defeat it, that is all. You are not to blame."

"This illness is so terrible for children," he said. "But when only one of the six Blake children died, I allowed myself to hope that perhaps, for some reason, it would not be so awful this time. I set aside the families I saw cut down in London, and convinced myself all of Jenny's children would be well. What if I also ignored the signs that David was failing?"

"You did not," Charlotte answered firmly. "You are the most observant person I know. Even if you wished to ignore such signs, your training and your nature would not allow it. David was a three-year-old boy with a sickness that brings down many adults. Leave off this castigation of yourself, I implore you, and instead be grateful that he died quietly, without suffering all the worst ravages of the disease beforehand."

He stared at her in open surprise for a moment before tentatively nodding. "You are correct, Miss Lucas —that is something to be thankful for." They sat in a strangely companionable silence for some moments, reflecting upon the tumult of the young day, until he turned and gathered both of her hands into his own, bestowing a kiss on the knuckles of one and then the other.

"Miss Lucas, I know I have not been calling on you for long—in truth, I cannot be said to have called upon you at all in the traditional sense—but I believe circumstances have allowed us to know each other better than months of polite conversation over tea in the parlour would. There is a question I should very much like to ask you, if you are ready to hear it."

Charlotte's heart leapt into her throat. There could be no mistaking his intent. And yet, she was too fond of him and too desirous of his affections to behave with him as she would have with another, more practical, choice. So she smiled and him and squeezed his fingers and replied, "When you have got over the shock of David's death, if you would still like to ask your question, I would very much like to hear it."

He regarded her solemnly. "I believe I know my own mind, but if you will be more certain of me at a later date, I can do nothing but respect your wishes now." He kissed her hands once more and released them. "How is Miss Maria this morning?"

"Restless."

"I dare say she is ready to leave her bed, on a limited basis. Shall we go and tell her the good news?"

——

The afternoon brought two very different notes to Elizabeth. From Charlotte came word that Maria had entirely passed through the danger, and now had only to rest and recover. From Longbourn, however, in her sister Kitty's hand, came news of a different sort.

Dearest sisters,

Forgive me if this makes little sense, for I have not slept in the last day. As I write, Father is reading to Lydia and Mary has fallen asleep next to her. We have passed a trying night, and are still in doubt of Lydia's fate. Mr

Jones remains hopeful, and so do we, but Lydia is very weak indeed. I wish you will both pray for her often.

Pardon my sloppiness, I am nodding off over the paper. I will close now.

Kitty

In their father's firm script, just below the smudged signature, was a further note.

My dear girls, how I wish you were home with us, but I take comfort every moment in knowing that you soon shall be, that Jane grows stronger daily, and in a week or two I shall look upon my beloved eldest daughters once more.

"Surely," Jane said in a shocked tone after reading it, "God would not take both our mother and Lydia away from us? I was so certain, after hearing of Mary and Kitty's swift action, that their next report would be of Lydia's recovery."

They both knew very well that smallpox could take entire families, but Elizabeth forbore from replying in such a way, instead suggesting that they obey Kitty's request and offer up prayers for their youngest sister. Jane was much relieved by the exercise, but Elizabeth could not be easy though she hid her worries behind a cheerful face.

———

For the second time in the space of a week, Darcy found himself attending the funeral of someone with whom he had not been well-acquainted. In Hurst's case, the acquaintance spanned several years, though he had known the man little better when he died than after being acquainted with him for only a month.

As the vicar read the service, Darcy glanced at his friend, whose eyes were red-rimmed. Though he knew Bingley had approved of Hurst's habits of overindulgence in food and drink no more than Darcy himself, he had recently learnt that Bingley had respected and liked the man for his rational prudence in matters financial and his kindness towards his dependents. Though even Bingley would not go so far as to call his brother 'considerate'—consideration requiring an effort, something Mr Hurst had generally disdained—he had treated and paid his servants well, and been gentle and even indulgent with his wife. Darcy and Bingley both knew many husbands who could not claim as much.

And so, he thought back with something like regret upon his shallow acquaintance with Mr Hurst. Perhaps, had he made the effort to know the man a little better, he might have learnt to esteem him before his death.

During the hymns, the voices of the few mourners echoed in the small chapel. Bingley had lamented in the carriage that Hurst's family would not be allowed to inter him with his ancestors, for fear of contagion, nor attend his funeral. Darcy shuddered to think that his own earthly form might be put to the earth anywhere but Pemberley, and hoped that Gilbert Hurst would rest in peace.

———

Kitty very nearly shoved Mary out of Lydia's room that

morning. "I shall tend to Lydia for a while. Go and have some sleep in your own bed for once."

"Oh, but..." Mary looked desperately over Kitty's shoulder towards her ill sister.

"You will be of more use to her if you are rested," Kitty replied firmly. "I shall wake you if there is a change for the worse." She stepped backwards and neatly closed the door in Mary's face, settling the question.

Knowing that she would not sleep immediately, Mary went downstairs and, donning her cloak and gloves, slipped out into the garden. The leaves crunched softly under her measured tread as she breathed deeply of the crisp air and willed her thoughts to peace. She meditated for some time on pleasant memories, attempting to settle her troubled spirits. When a man's voice addressed her from the direction of the garden gate, she turned and stared in surprise at Captain Carter, who bowed to her from beneath the archway there, framed by the bare remains of the summer's ivy.

"Pardon me, Miss Mary, I did not mean to startle you. I thought, when I saw you here, I might enquire after the household without disturbing those within."

Belatedly, Mary curtseyed, saying, "I am glad you did, Captain. We are all much as we were yesterday, but Lydia does not rest well and knocking might have disturbed her."

"I look forward to the day you tell me that Miss Lydia is on the mend," he replied. "Please do give her my regards. And the rest of your family, of course. Here are your letters from Miss Elizabeth." He handed two notes to her, one each for her and Kitty.

"I shall, I thank you. She will be pleased to know that

her friends remember her." She tucked the letters into her pocket.

He regarded her curiously. "May I ask what it is you were contemplating when I interrupted you?"

"Oh..." She blushed, looking away. "Nothing that would be of interest to a gentleman, I assure you. I was only recalling the games my sisters and I would play when we were small."

"To look back upon a happy childhood is a pleasure indeed," he replied, smiling. "One day, when we are all at leisure to enjoy a cup of tea in Longbourn's parlour, I shall trade you stories of the mischief two boys get up to for tales of that which five girls may cause."

"I-I shall look forward to it," she stammered, rather shocked that this amiable and, truth be told, handsome young man should even hint at wishing to speak with her absent the necessity of passing news in a crisis. With another bow and a jaunty wave, he was off on his rounds once again.

———

Word came to the Bennets at both Longbourn and Netherfield via the gentlemen's rounds—Mrs Long had died; Jenny Goulding would be well; two of the Simmons children were no more, but the rest would survive; Joanna Long had followed her aunt to the grave, while Joseph Turner, of whom all had despaired, had pulled through in the end. The Hills arose from their sickbeds and resumed light duties, and still, Lydia lingered in a twilight between life and death.

Jane grew stronger and began getting out of bed and

taking a turn about the room under her own power, though Elizabeth hovered nearby every moment. The itching scabs fell away, and all the tempting morsels that the kitchens of Netherfield could provide began to fill in the deep hollows of her face and collarbones.

One morning several days after the loss of Mr Hurst, Elizabeth entered Jane's room after dressing to find her sister before the mirror, regarding her scarred face with sombre intensity. She did not know what to say, so she said nothing, and some moments passed before Jane remarked, softly, "I am greatly altered, am I not?"

"The scars will fade," Elizabeth offered, "in time."

Jane took a deep breath, and let it out on a sigh, then resolutely turned her back on the glass. "It will take some getting used to, that is all," she said with forced cheerfulness. "Will you help me dress, Lizzy? I feel I have been a year in night-rails, and I would honour our mother by taking up my mourning garb."

"Of course, dearest," Elizabeth replied.

———

As Elizabeth helped Jane to dress, Mary and Kitty sat by Lydia's bedside while their father took his turn sleeping. Kitty was reading aloud from Donne and Mary was mending a torn petticoat she had found in Lydia's closet. They both paused in their activities when their sister stirred and opened her eyes, seeming confused for a moment as she looked from one to the other and back again. Then she rubbed a hand across her stomach and said in a soft voice, "Lord, how hungry I am!"

CHAPTER SIXTEEN

JANE BENNET WAS ASHAMED OF HERSELF. SHE HAD not been used to thinking of herself as vain, but having her extraordinary beauty extolled all her life must have made its mark, for despite her dearest sister's efforts in dressing her and arranging her hair, and also despite her own sense of obligation to her host and hostess, she could not bring herself to stand from the dressing table and bring her altered visage into company.

"Lizzy, I cannot," she whispered, shoulders slumping. Elizabeth quickly came around to sit beside her on the long seat and pull her into a comforting embrace. Jane hid her face against her sister's shoulder and felt very weak and stupid. She had known two days prior, when she donned a gown for the first time in weeks, that she would soon be required to behave more as a guest than an invalid, but now that the moment was upon her, she doubted that she could bear it.

"Dearest, surely you do not fear that anyone at Netherfield shall be unkind, when they have all been such great friends to us?"

"Oh, no...I do not think they would be unkind, certainly not. It is simply—" Jane gathered the courage to speak the truth. "I cannot face *him*, Lizzy, and see that he no longer admires me, when I admire him more every day. And I particularly do not want to watch as all his memories of me are replaced by...this."

"Oh, Jane..." Elizabeth murmured, her arms tightening. "I wish I knew what to say to you. I do not believe Mr Bingley would be unkind or unmannerly. And if he is worthy of you, he will not care a jot that you are a little altered by your illness."

"A little altered?" Jane's laugh had an edge of hysteria. "Lizzy, I hardly recognise myself."

"I have no such difficulty, nor shall anyone who cares for you," Elizabeth replied stoutly. "But Jane, we must go down. There can be no more excuses. Everyone knows that Mr Jones has pronounced you able to move about the house. We are expected to dinner, and Louisa has particularly asked after your favourites."

"I suppose," she replied slowly, "that I cannot in good conscience disappoint Louisa."

"Indeed you cannot. She has been very much looking forward to seeing you outside of this room."

Jane drew herself straight, took in a great and cleansing breath, and stood. "Very well, then."

They got to the doorway of the drawing room before Jane's courage failed her, and her head dropped as though the cords of her neck had been severed. Arm in arm with her sister, she felt herself led through the doorway, and heard several chairs slide backward. When Elizabeth curt-seyed, so did she, but she could not look at them, not at all.

Footsteps approached. "Miss Bennet!" Mr Bingley declared, cheerful and far too close. "How delighted we all are to see you up and about again!"

She murmured her thanks towards the tips of her shoes, and an uncomfortable silence fell.

"Miss Bennet?" Mr Bingley tried again, his tone now soft and full of concern. "Will you not look at me?"

Jane felt herself entirely paralysed save for the tears welling in her eyes. She could not do this! Her sister reclaimed her arm and wordlessly conveyed support. She flinched as a male hand reached for her scarred face, coming up under her chin to gently lift it into his view, and she squeezed her eyes shut.

"Miss Bennet...please, look at me."

She opened her eyes to find Mr Bingley's green gaze locked on hers, with no hint of pity or disgust marring his expression. Instead, he appeared...happy? Vaguely, she registered Louisa hovering at his left hand.

"Allow me to tell you, Miss Bennet, how deeply and profoundly delighted I am to see you returned to health. Although I have enjoyed our correspondence—" Louisa stifled a gasp "—to have you here to converse with is infinitely preferable. I have missed your company and conversation."

Elizabeth slipped her arm out of Jane's and moved to Louisa's side, redirecting her towards the sideboard with a request for sherry so that Jane and Mr Bingley might speak more privately. The captain and Darcy had also moved in that direction.

"You still wish to speak with me?" Jane asked, wonderingly.

"Of course I do. There is no one in the world I would rather speak with, now or at any other time. I hope to speak with you very often, and for the rest of my life," he concluded with no little daring.

Hope uncoiled within her breast, but a lifetime of being told in many ways, both subtle and overt, that her beauty was her only asset made it difficult for her to allow it free rein. "Mr Bingley, sir...I hope you know I do not consider your honour to have been engaged by the notes you so kindly sent while I was ill."

"If you will call it kindness, then call it kindness towards myself, for I could not bear to entirely lose your company even though I could not see you." He touched her hand, briefly. "As for my honour, well, we are both of us in mourning now, but when it is acceptable to do so, I truly hope to engage my honour and the rest of myself to you, Miss Bennet."

Tears pricked her eyes once more. "You do not mind that I am so terribly scarred?"

"Mind?" he replied in a tone of startlement. "I mind that you have suffered, and that you have feared the results of your suffering would alter my sentiments. But you are, and always shall be, my angel. I would never cast you aside for something so trifling as a few marks, and I beg you would not reject me because of them." His tone, his expression, everything spoke to his sincerity, and the earnest affection in his eyes could not be mistaken. "May I call upon you when we have left our deep mourning, Miss Bennet, and stand as your friend until then?"

The threatening tears fell at last, onto a face that was now smiling. "Sir, I can think of nothing I should like better."

Jane's smile, and Bingley's answering one, prompted the others to join them just in time for dinner to be announced. Mr Bingley offered his arm to Jane, Captain Carter his to Elizabeth, and Mr Darcy escorted Mrs Hurst.

———

In the drawing room after the meal, the company split into pairs. The captain drew the widow into a game of cards, Bingley and Jane continued their conversation from the dinner table, and Darcy found himself in the intoxicating position of having most of Miss Elizabeth Bennet's attention, though she did keep an eye on her sister.

"May I ask what news Miss Mary had for you today?" he enquired.

"Only good news, I am happy to say," she answered. "Lydia continues to improve, if too slowly for anyone's liking. My father is eager to have us home now that Jane is up and about again, but Mr Jones wishes that she should gain strength for a few days more before venturing out in the cold, and so we must impose upon Mr Bingley a little longer."

"I believe I speak for everyone at Netherfield when I say that you and your sister will be much missed here when you go home. You must be very happy to know that Miss Lydia is out of danger, and to see Miss Bennet so recovered," he remarked, a comment which gained him one of her radiant smiles.

"Oh, yes. And happier still to see Jane restored to the

company she prefers above all," she replied with a slight inclination of her head towards the couple by the fire, where Bingley was fussing over the position of the screen, attempting to direct even more of the warmth towards Jane.

Darcy regarded them contemplatively. "Your sister is an excellent woman. The tenants of Longbourn have been most fervent in her praise, and the esteem in which you hold her must of course influence anyone in her favour. I believe there is little doubt as to the course of her future, and I cannot imagine that they shall know anything but felicity together."

"They are well matched," she agreed. "I will admit in confidence that I was not at all sure what to expect of Mr Bingley when he saw her again. I hoped that he would act as he has, but feared he would not be able to look past the changes in her. I hope this does not offend you; I cannot claim to know him so well as you."

"When Miss Bennet first fell ill, and Bingley expressed an intention of continuing to pursue her when she recovered, I feared the same," he confessed. "But he has remained steadfast, and of everyone assembled in the room when you and she entered this evening, I believe he was the least anxious about what was imminent."

"Jane has always *deserved* a man who valued her essentials more than her appearance, but with such great beauty it always seemed unlikely that she would find one. I see you are confused. I mean that such beauty must attract those who prize beauty, and I have always wondered whether she would be able to find a man who would still value her when age and childbearing had taken their toll. Those of us who are merely tolerable," she continued with a sly grin, "have at least the advantage of knowing, should we receive an offer, that we are desired for more than our youthful bloom."

He could not be anything but amused at her jest, for her impudence robbed it of any possible sting. "I understand. For my own part, it has always seemed unlikely that I might be able to marry a woman who saw more in me than wealth and connexions, but I have dared to hope for better. Perhaps I shall be as fortunate as your sister, in time."

"I hope you shall. Just be sure, sir, that you value her as you wish to be valued," she cautioned lightly. "You cannot expect a lady to see your essential self if all you see are her appearance, dowry, and lineage."

He smiled and agreed, having no notion in that moment how often her words would repeat themselves in his mind in the coming weeks.

———

The Bennets did not stay long in the drawing room that evening, for Jane tired easily, and when they regained her chamber Elizabeth turned to her sister with a laughing gaze and declared, "Now you must tell me all, Jane! What did your Mr Bingley say to you after we all walked away? And what did you discuss so intently at table?"

"Oh, Lizzy," Jane breathed, dropping with little of her usual elegance onto the bed to beam up at the ceiling. "He still admires me. Can you believe it? He does not seem to regard the change in my appearance at all!"

Elizabeth sat down beside her sister, happy tears streaming down both their cheeks. "He is a most excellent gentleman, and deserves you if anyone could." She herself had not been at all sanguine about his reaction, and smiled at the rapidity and ease with which the question was finally settled, that had given so many previous hours of suspense and vexation.

"And what did you speak of over the meal?" she prompted, when Jane seemed likely to drift into silent contemplation before her curiosity had been satisfied.

"So many things," Jane said with satisfaction. "It was as though we had never been apart, but yet different, for we were more open with our thoughts and dreams in our correspondence than ever we had been in the drawing rooms of Meryton. We spoke as dear friends rather than as recent acquaintances."

"I can see you like him as a dear friend even more than you did as a recent acquaintance! I am happy for you, Jane."

"I am certainly the most fortunate creature that ever existed!" cried she, and for a time all the suffering and loss of the last weeks was entirely forgot.

———

Having seen Jane to bed, where her dreams would no doubt be blissful, Elizabeth found herself restless. Her thoughts turned to the previous hours, when the reunited couple had little to say to anyone else, but the remaining foursome kept up a jolly conversation amongst themselves —or rather, as jolly a conversation as might be had in a house of mourning. Mr Darcy had participated more often and more cheerfully than Elizabeth had ever known him to do, and their quiet tête-à-tête afterwards had only enhanced her opinion of him.

With sudden inspiration, she gathered up his backgammon set and returned to the drawing room in hopes that he remained. She was in luck; though Mr Bingley was not to be seen, Captain Carter and Louisa were still attempting to best each other at cards, and Mr Darcy had busied himself with a book.

She approached and held out the set when he looked up, saying, "Now that Jane is not confined to her chambers, I wished to return this to you, sir. It has afforded us both many hours of distraction in the last weeks, and I thank you for it."

"If you are not intending to return upstairs immediately, perhaps you would allow me to challenge you to a game?"

Elizabeth pretended to consider the suggestion seriously. "So long as you promise not to pout when defeated by a lady, I suppose I might."

He laughed. "Come then, Miss Elizabeth, and prove that such confidence is not unwarranted." He stood and gestured to a small table they might use.

It soon became apparent that each of them played as though the fate of the world hung upon their victory, though there was much laughter in it and nothing of meanness in the way they taunted each other over a poor roll of the dice. This fierce and rather boisterous competition soon drew the others, with Louisa cheering Elizabeth on and the captain taking Darcy's side.

In the end, Elizabeth could only shake her head at the lone piece which remained in front of her. "That, sir, was a very lucky roll!"

Mr Darcy grinned. "That it was. Well played, Miss Elizabeth."

"I thank you for the game, sir, but I ought to look in on Jane," she said, standing, which brought him to his feet as well. "I shall demand a rematch at a later date."

"I look forward to it."

CHAPTER SEVENTEEN

Dear Brother,

I hope you will forgive me for being so slow to reply that I am now two letters in your debt, though I do not think you truly expected a reply to the brief note informing me of poor Mr Hurst's death. I have of course written to Mrs Hurst. I delayed my response to you in hopes of answering a question of yours. Mrs Annesley and I have called upon Miss Bingley twice since your last reached me, and she has been away each time. I am sorry I was not able to find out more for Mr Bingley and Mrs Hurst. If I do chance to hear anything further, I shall write to you on the instant.

Please allow me to assure you that I care not how much of interest you have to relay, I always receive and read your letters with the greatest of pleasure. I apprehend that Mr Bingley has a greater need of you than I just now, but I do miss you.

I remain fondly,
Your Georgiana

———

FOR THE NEXT TWO DAYS THE ELDEST BENNETS SPENT their mornings in correspondence, their afternoons with Mrs Hurst, and their evenings in company with the gentlemen. They sent letters of condolence to the families of their acquaintance who had been bereaved, and answered similar letters condoling with them on the loss of their mother. They were pleased to find that their aunt and uncle Gardiner still intended to pass the coming holidays with them at Longbourn, but their feelings upon Mr Jones's pronouncement that they might safely return to Longbourn were somewhat mixed, for as much as they longed to return to their own home and what remained of their family, they could not rejoice in any separation from those friends with whom they had endured so many trials.

They left the next morning, conscious of how long they had imposed upon the hospitality of Netherfield, with many fond promises of calling upon Mrs Hurst. She and her brother stood without the house until the carriage was lost round the bend, and both were heard to remark in the following days how large and quiet Netherfield now seemed.

The gentlemen were to keep up their rounds for another week, out of an abundance of caution, and then Captain Carter would be readmitted to his camp, which had not after all escaped the disease. New recruits would need to be brought in to replace the men who had perished and the one who had been blinded, and the captain expected that he would find himself quite busy with their training for a time.

Jane and Elizabeth were met outside Longbourn by

their father, who gathered them into a fierce embrace and stunned them by allowing tears to fall as he clasped them to his chest. "My dear girls," he said reverently. "Home at last, and safe." Recalling himself, he hurried them inside out of the cold, only for them to be further embraced and wept over by Mary and Kitty, and it could not be said that either of the elder sisters was able to entirely restrain her tears, either.

They soon insisted on being taken to see Lydia. Just inside the doorway Jane stopped short on first seeing her robust, energetic sister reduced to a hollow-cheeked wisp of a girl. Elizabeth, having seen her in her illness, did not hesitate in flying across the room to take the youngest Bennet into her arms and exclaim her joy that Lydia had survived her final crisis. Jane soon followed, and although they did not risk tiring Lydia by remaining above ten minutes, many happy words were spoken in that time.

Elizabeth spent the afternoon in unpacking both her and Jane's things while her sister took a rest, and in sitting quietly with a book, becoming once again accustomed to the familiar walls of Longbourn. Having gone down to dinner early they were pleased to find that Mrs Hill's niece Amy had been hired on in Sara's place and now tended to Lydia while Mary enjoyed dinners with her family.

Elizabeth glanced about the table as they seated themselves, taking in her father's black jacket and cravat, the unrelieved black of her sisters' dresses and her own, and the empty chair at the head of the table from which Mrs Bennet had presided for a quarter-century. Jane's gaze had also gone to that chair, and her eyes filled with tears and spilled over. Elizabeth, apprehending the cause of her sister's distress, was soon in like state.

"Jane? Lizzy?" ventured Kitty anxiously.

Wiping impatiently at her eyes, Jane said haltingly, "I knew that she was gone, of course, but in some ways it did not seem quite real, until just this moment." Kitty put her arm around Jane, while across the table, Mary performed a like office for Elizabeth.

"It did not seem quite real that Jane had been so ill until you both returned home this morning," Mary said quietly, "but we had the joy of her return to health to smooth over the strangeness of it."

There was silence for several moments as they all availed themselves of handkerchiefs, though only Mr Bennet was at all embarrassed by the display.

"When I wake in the morning, I often feel it must have been a bad dream," said Kitty, daintily folding her sodden handkerchief, "and I find I must spend a moment in her room to shake the notion from my head."

"I think..." Jane trailed off uncertainly, then seemed to come to a decision. "I should like to visit Mama's room myself. I believe it may help me to accept what has happened. Will you come with me, Lizzy?"

"Of course I shall," she answered, and just then Hill arrived with the soup, and they all set about the business of dinner.

In the end, all four of them entered Mrs Bennet's chamber together after the meal. Mary lit the lamps, and they all stood for a moment, looking about them in silence.

Though it had been only three weeks since her death, their mother's chamber already had an unused air about it. The bottles and jars which cluttered her dressing table had been neatly arranged, the closet door was shut rather than hanging half-open, and there were no magazines or hairpins spread across the bedside table. The scent of Mrs Bennet's favourite perfume was faint now, her escritoire free of half-written letters and discarded pens. This was merely the place where she used to be.

Jane sat upon the bed, placing a hand softly upon her mother's pillow just where her head would have lain. "How strange it is, that she worried so often what would become of her when Papa died, and now she has been the first to go."

"How strange, and how sad," Elizabeth replied with a sigh. "All that worry for nothing."

"That is unfair," Mary remonstrated mildly. "She worried for us, as well, and our situation has not changed."

"Save that we shall lose months of husband-hunting in mourning her," Elizabeth joked weakly, and they all smiled a little, knowing that she surely would have fretted about that.

Kitty sat upon the bench before the dressing table and remarked, "Our situation will not be much altered immediately, but Papa and I have gone over the household accounts, and made a plan of savings. The interest on Mama's dowry will now add to the principal, and Papa has agreed to add to it all that we save by not entertaining during his year of mourning. Even afterwards, we intend that the house will be run with less extravagance. This time next year we may have as much as an extra hundred pounds each."

The other three regarded her in stunned silence. Mary, ever practical, eventually remarked, "If this were to continue for several years, and the savings from the departure of any who do marry were added to the fund, it would increase what remains for those of us who do not marry to an amount that would allow us to live together in modest comfort after Papa leaves us. A small cottage, a sensible table..."

"And thus, we have forever banished the spectre of the hedgerows," said Elizabeth briskly. Then her expression softened, and she added, "I only wish Mama could have known that we shall be well, after all."

"She must know now—that, and many things we cannot even imagine," Mary replied. "I only wish..." She dropped her eyes to her hands, clasped before her. "I wish I could ask her if she loved me, despite how disappointing I was to her."

"Of course she did!" cried Jane, appalled. "She loved us all, Mary!"

"Did she?" wondered Kitty. "You and Lydia, she certainly did. Lizzy and Mary and I, however, lived only to vex her, you will recall."

Elizabeth stood, facing her sisters. "I have been thinking on the subject myself, since her death. We shall never know how much of her fear for the future encompassed us, and how much was borne of self-interest alone. But I have come to believe, through reason rather than hope, that she did love us all. If she did not, if she cared only for herself, she would not have had all of us seeking husbands at once. If she cared only for her own situation, she would have kept the rest of us from society until Jane secured a wealthy man, and thereby Mama's future. But she wished us all settled, however she despaired of us individually, and however misguided her notions of a suitable match could be."

"Like when she pushed Mary towards the new curate when she was sixteen, though he was sixty!" Kitty interrupted with a laugh, and they all joined in. The laughter died away as the others considered Elizabeth's words and saw their mother in a new light.

"I should like to preserve the room as it is until Lydia is well enough to visit," Mary's voice respectfully broke the silence. "But then we must consider what will become of her things."

"Let us wait to sort through it all until Lydia is well enough to assist, not merely attend," Jane suggested. "For she was the closest to Mama, and her mourning shall no doubt be the greater for it."

CHAPTER EIGHTEEN

Mʀ Bɪɴɢʟᴇʏ ᴄᴀʟʟᴇᴅ ᴜᴘᴏɴ ᴛʜᴇᴍ ᴛʜᴇ ꜰᴏʟʟᴏᴡɪɴɢ ᴅᴀʏ at the close of his rounds, bearing Mrs Hurst's greetings and regards. Contrary to his habit, Mr Bennet joined them upon being informed of the presence of a guest, and, Elizabeth noted, received Bingley with real pleasure. Gratitude for the young man's care of his daughters had not been forgotten, nor for his attendance at Mrs Bennet's funeral. Mr Bingley stayed far longer than was proper, and no one minded in the least. As he was leaving, he mentioned that plans were afoot to bring visitors to Netherfield for Christmas—Mr Darcy's sister and his cousin.

"Well, Jane," said Mr Bennet with a twinkle in his eye as the door of the house closed behind their guest. "It seems that your young man's affections were not the work of shallow infatuation. I am impressed by him, and shall gladly hear him if he should one day insist upon asking to take you away."

Jane blushed, but replied with tolerable composure.

"He has said that he wishes to court me when it is proper to do so, and will be my friend until then."

"Then I shall expect him very shortly after you choose to enter half-mourning." Rising from his chair, he smiled fondly at all three of his daughters there, and retreated once more to his book room.

"Jane!" exclaimed Kitty when he had gone. "Is Mr Bingley to be our brother after all?"

"I hope it may be so," her eldest sister answered. "I shall certainly not refuse him if he asks. I had not the smallest hope that his attentions would continue when we met again," she confided, one hand unconsciously coming up to a scarred cheek. "But indeed, he was just as amiable and attentive as ever. He told me plainly that my altered appearance has no effect on him."

Kitty clasped her hands to her breast and let out a dreamy sigh. "How romantic. I should be happy to be loved half so well."

"It is best that you and I, Kitty, keep our hopes just so modest. Half the love granted to such a perfect creature as Jane is indeed a worthy goal for us mere mortals!" Elizabeth interjected, and she and her younger sister laughed while Jane blushed and protested.

Dearest Georgiana,

I am happy to relate to you that Mr Jones believes he shall be able to declare the epidemic ended within days. We are very quiet at Netherfield now, with Mrs Hurst in deepest mourning and the Bennet sisters returned to their own home.

I thank you for your efforts to contact Miss Bingley. My friend has now had word of her, for she at last answered one of his own communications. She is well.

Mr Bingley and Mrs Hurst have determined to pass the Christmas season here, and have invited us to join them. What think you, dearest? It will be a quiet celebration due to their mourning, but I daresay no quieter than our own last year, alone at Pemberley. Here, you might make friends with some of the young ladies of the area. The Bennets, I have mentioned previously; they have lost their mother to the smallpox and will also spend the season quiet and retired. I am certain you would like at least two of the five daughters of that family. But if you had rather be in town or even go to Pemberley, that is what we shall do. I shall not demand that you perform for strangers.

Please advise me of your decision by express, for time grows short to make the necessary plans in either case.

Your fond brother,

Fitzwilliam

———

Elizabeth's resolution to spend more time assisting her younger sisters when they were reunited was rather stymied by the revelations of their improvement in her absence, but it did not take long for her to determine that while their behaviour and even their understanding were greatly improved, their confidence was not. Kitty was making decisions for the household and then asking the nearest person if she had done right; she remained on the whole rather too obliging—perhaps a desirable trait in a sister, but one which would not serve her well in the greater world. In Mary's conversation it seemed that wry self-deprecation had replaced arrogant piety; she acknowledged to Elizabeth that her faith had been strengthened by her recent experiences. Elizabeth conjectured that with greater certainty came less need to speak of it, and to quote Proverbs.

Impressed by the fortitude of her younger sisters, Elizabeth wondered how, and even if, she had changed. Her own challenges seemed less than those faced by Jane and Lydia—who had fought illness—and Mary and Kitty, who had worked to nurse their sister, managed Longbourn's household, and mourned their mother in the midst of it. What had she, herself, done? She had nursed Jane, but she had been privileged to have Netherfield's servants and Mrs Hurst to assist her. That she had taken on the bulk of Jane's care was true, but she had known at every moment that she could have done less, had she wished or needed to. She had done so much partly out of a desperate desire to spend every possible moment with her dearest sister while she lived.

Could I have laboured so for anyone other than Jane or my father? Mary had certainly not enjoyed a good relationship with Lydia prior to these events, nor Kitty with her mother. *Could I have endured the illness with half of Jane's patience, had it struck me?* Even Lydia seemed to have learnt to esteem and respect her sisters, and to bear with a certain patience her present trials, which Elizabeth would not have expected of her.

Elizabeth realised she had not understood the depths of anyone around her prior to the epidemic. In this she included also Mr Darcy and Mr Bingley, whom she had perceived as little but prideful and amiable, respectively, and Mrs Hurst, of whom she had hardly thought at all. Had the best traits of those around her truly been so well-hidden, or had she been so blind?

She felt deeply thankful that she had seen these things, that she had come to know her younger sisters better and had been granted the friendship of the Netherfield party. Self-recrimination and concern over the depth and nobility of her own character remained, however, dogging her thoughts and even her dreams during those first days of her return to Longbourn, no matter how often she told herself that at least she had not thrown off all responsibility as had Miss Bingley and some of her neighbours.

Feeling that she could not answer herself, she sought the advice of one she trusted to always tell her the truth, and to either console or reprimand as the occasion demanded. She shut herself up in her chamber for two hours, and at the end of it sent four full pages of all her hopes and doubts, her questions and thoughts, to London. As she stepped away from the post-counter and turned her feet back towards Longbourn, she did so with a lighter heart. If anything in her required correction, her aunt Gardiner would show her the way.

———

Dear Brother,

I should be delighted to pass Christmas at Netherfield Park with Mr Bingley and Mrs Hurst, and to meet these ladies of whom you approve. I wish you would believe that I am very much recovered from my disappointment of a few months ago, and would dearly like to be of use to Mr Bingley and Mrs Hurst in their grief.

I hope I may be allowed to bring Mrs Annesley, for I have come to depend upon her good counsel, and she has no family to go to in any case—I should dislike to leave her alone during the festive season.

With love,

Georgiana

Postscript: Please do let me know if you should like us to retrieve anything for you by way of holiday tokens while we are yet in town.

———

Dear Georgie,

Of course Mrs Annesley must come, if that is your wish and hers. I shall write to our cousin Richard, and if he is able to get leave and has no other plans, I hope he will escort you here and join us for the holidays. If he cannot, I shall come up to town to fetch you myself.

I am very glad to hear that you are feeling more equal to being in company, dearest. I blame myself for your recent troubles, as it was I who failed to warn you of Wickham's character. In shielding you from the disappointment of learning from me that the boy I grew up with had grown into a despicable man, I opened you to the greater disappointment of learning it from him. I hope that you may forgive me; I do not know when or if I shall forgive myself.

You are kind to offer to do my shopping, and I will gratefully ask you to bring a few things with you. For Bingley, please have Harding retrieve a bottle of the

French brandy our father laid by before the war—he will know what I mean. Mrs Hurst is, as I believe you know, a great reader of novels, and as she is to be here longer than she expected I hope you may find one or two that have been published very recently, such that she will not yet have acquired them for herself. If the oranges have arrived from Pemberley before you depart, which they ought to have done, please bring three crates of them; we shall have one at Netherfield, and give one to the Bennets and the other to Mr Jones, whose excellent work I have related in previous letters.

It will be so very good to see you again, my dearest sister. I count the days,

Fitzwilliam

CHAPTER NINETEEN

Having acquired their father's permission to use the carriage, Jane and Elizabeth asked Mary and Kitty if they should like to join them in a call on Mrs Hurst. Mary preferred to stay with Lydia rather than visit a lady she hardly knew, but Kitty was delighted by the prospect of a jaunt, however sedate. So it was that three black-clad Bennets joined the similarly garbed Mrs Hurst in the bright morning parlour at Netherfield on the appointed day.

They spent a pleasant hour only rarely interrupted by thoughts of their recent losses, and in the carriage on the way home Kitty remarked to her sisters that she was sorry she had not earlier taken the trouble to know Mrs Hurst.

"That is a regret I believe we all share," remarked Elizabeth. "But we have each of us been changed by recent events, and I think it probable we would not have liked her, nor she us, half so much six weeks ago. Well, except for Jane, who likes everyone!"

When they returned home, Elizabeth was pleased to

discover the early arrival of a much-anticipated reply from her aunt.

> *My dear girl,*
>
> *Though I shall be with you in only two days, I will send this by express, for in every line of the letter I received from you today I felt your distress. We shall of course speak of this when we are together, unless you truly do not wish it, but for the nonce:*
>
> *Darling Lizzy, has it not occurred to you that you see no changes in yourself because you lived every moment they came upon you, whereas in others it is marked because you were separated while these events did their work upon them? For I assure you, the Elizabeth whose letter I have just received is not the Elizabeth who visited me in June.*
>
> *Yes, you were more fortunate in your situation while you cared for Jane than your sisters were when they cared for Lydia and your poor mother, but that was none of your doing. I am certain you would have rather been together at Longbourn than separated from all your family save Jane, and surrounded by those who, though they proved themselves good friends, were not well known to you when it all began. Had you been at Longbourn, I am certain you would have risen to that occasion as well as you rose to the one that was before you. Those weeks could have been more difficult, but I do not for a moment believe they were easy.*
>
> *Forgive me if what I relate next pains you, but you asked for my honesty and you shall have it. I saw in your words more than one instance in which you revised your opinion of someone on further acquaintance. You have*

long placed far too much reliance on first impressions, my dear, and now I think perhaps you have learnt the folly of that? You have not often made allowances for circumstances, or for the ability of others to learn and grow, or even for the simple fact that one's first meeting with another might by happenstance occur when they are not at their best, or conversely, when they are in unusually good form, which may lead them to appear better than they are.

Even from one letter, Lizzy, I do think you changed. In those lines I saw an introspection I have never known in you before, and that alone is a fine thing. We cannot grow if we do not consider ourselves, our actions, and our motivations. You have admitted you were wrong about your new friends when first you knew them, and that those you have known all your life, or theirs, were not entirely without mystery. But it is not only in acknowledging and beginning to correct your flaws that I see your alteration. Until life tests us, we cannot know our own strength. Life has tested you, my darling girl, and you have emerged victorious. You did not falter when many would have. You did not flee, or collapse in despair, though I am absolutely certain there were times when you must have wished to. I hope I should have done as well as you, in your place.

I shall see you soon, and until then I remain,
Your proud and loving aunt,
Madeline Gardiner

Two days later, as Jane, Elizabeth, Mary, and Kitty were sat in the parlour attending to their needlework while their father read aloud to them from Milton, and the maid attended Lydia upstairs, Mr Bingley, Mr Darcy, and Captain Carter were admitted.

"Mr Jones has declared the neighbourhood free of smallpox!" announced Mr Bingley, his delight so great as to make him rather loud. As the ladies quietly exclaimed amongst themselves over the news, Mr Bennet stood and bowed to his guests. "We thank you for the information, sir. Would you and your friends care to stay for a cup of tea?"

The invitation was accepted and Mr Bingley fairly flew to the seat nearest Miss Bennet, while Mr Darcy joined Elizabeth and Kitty and the captain sat by Mary. Mr Bennet was left to play the role of observant father— one he found he rather enjoyed, at least while it was yet a novel experience.

What the all-but-acknowledged couple spoke of, he did not know, for though their postures were proper their voices were pitched low for privacy, and the only certainty was that both were enjoying themselves. Nearby, Mary and Captain Carter spoke together easily, and smiled often. Mr Bennet could only suppose that the soldier's frequent stops at Longbourn on Mr Jones's behalf had been sufficient to put his most diffident daughter at ease in the man's company.

The conversation between the other three started and stopped awkwardly for some moments; Mr Darcy was uneasy in most company and Kitty was rather intimidated by the tall, taciturn gentleman, but when a chance comment revealed that she was newly awakened to the pleasures to be had in the less traditionally romantic forms of poetry, the talk became rather lively. Though Elizabeth certainly helped them along, Mr Bennet was pleased to see Kitty was as interested to hear Mr Darcy's recommendations in the genre as he was pleased to offer them. They spoke then for a while on Wordsworth, a favourite of all three, and Mr Darcy was brought to confess to having met the poet himself, briefly, one summer at the Lakes between terms at university.

Mr Bennet was somewhat surprised to see the gentleman unbend, though his opinion had been greatly improved by Mr Darcy's efforts on behalf of the neighbourhood of late. He noticed, too, that the young man seemed to look at his Lizzy more often than called for by the conversation, even as his inscrutable expression left his motivations a mystery. That gentleman would bear watching, thought Mr Bennet, if only for the stimulation to be had in unravelling an intricate character.

———

Darcy was lost in his own thoughts on the journey back to Netherfield, not that Bingley's incessant chatter on the subject of Miss Bennet's many perfections required his attention, and Carter was doing a splendid job of nodding and agreeing at all the right moments. It had been a mere five days, not even an entire week, since Miss Bennet and Miss Elizabeth had left Netherfield, but to Darcy that first sight of Miss Elizabeth had felt like being offered water after wandering the desert. If he had hoped that separation would dim his affections—and the part of him still concerned with status had hoped exactly that—it had been for naught. He had been raised to view eligible women in a certain way: through the lens of wealth and connexions. Affection was of course greatly to be desired, but was understood to rank well beneath dowry and lineage.

Such concerns seemed so trivial to him now. He had, in these last weeks, seen families torn apart by death. He had seen some of those who remained turn from each other in despair and even anger. But he had seen other families, among them the Bennets, begin to knit themselves back together through the kind of love which allows grief to unite rather than sunder.

Money and connexions were not healing these wounds. Certainly, such advantages had not prevented his own parents from becoming more silent and bitter towards each other as each successive attempt to provide the Darcy name with more descendants than himself alone ended in failure. Darcy had long wondered if a desire to be free of the oppressive atmosphere of Pemberley had been as much a factor in his mother's death as Georgiana's difficult birth. His father, he suspected, had given his wife scarcely a thought after consigning her body to the ground. Though both had been good, upstanding people in many ways, they had been personally incompatible, and slow to forgive any injury from the other, real or imagined.

That was not the life, or the marriage, he wished for himself. He had not known precisely what he did wish, only that he wanted to be contented at the very least, and that it would be very difficult to achieve such a state if there were little amity in his most intimate relationship. This, he considered, must be why he had always felt a visceral revulsion for the vapid heiresses and grasping social climbers from among whom he was expected to make his choice.

Such tepid images of mere complacence had been his vision of the future only weeks ago, until a bright and witty girl from a family of no consequence and his own wayward heart had conspired to make him long for more. He now knew that he wished for more than mere contentment—he wanted to love his wife, and to build with her a family that would come together in the face of even the worst troubles. He wanted his children to grow in a home filled with laughter and kindness, not with the silence of two ill-suited people and their cold, resentful civility. He wanted his sister to have a taste of such a home before she left him to form her own.

Would it all be easier if he could find the promise of that life in a woman of high standing and large dowry? Of course it would. But he might have found it instead in Elizabeth Bennet, a woman as full of spirit and laughter as she was bereft of status. He was not yet ready to declare his heart lost, though he could not deny that she compelled his notice as no other ever had. If he should come to believe that he did love her, however, he now felt that he could cheerfully bear the disadvantages of her situation.

CHAPTER TWENTY

Richard,

Georgiana and I have elected to pass the holiday with my friend Bingley and his sister Mrs Hurst, here in Hertfordshire. We, and they, hope you will join us, and Bingley will add a note to the bottom of this by way of an official invitation. It will be a quiet season, as Bingley and his sister are mourning Hurst, but not without its pleasures. Mrs Hurst sets a fine table, the sport in the area is excellent, and there are several in residence hereabouts I think you will enjoy knowing. In particular I think of Captain Carter, who I have mentioned before. The colonel of the regiment is a gentlemanly fellow also, though his taste in wives is rather suspect. Please do let me know if you wish to, and are able to, attend. If so, I shall commit Georgiana to your care for the journey.

Fitzwilliam

Colonel,

Do come. The cook here is excellent and I have a burgundy set aside for Christmas dinner that will delight you.

C Bingley

————

Fitz,

My general has been good enough to grant me leave through Twelfth Night, though it will not commence until the twenty-fourth. Georgie and I have agreed to depart for Netherfield early in the morning, putting us, with good roads, at Netherfield well before dark. Tell Bingley I will bring some cigars from the West Indies for us to enjoy after Christmas dinner. Do not ask how I came by them, for you would not like the answer.

Richard

————

THE FOLLOWING DAY BROUGHT ANOTHER VISITOR TO Longbourn—Charlotte Lucas, red-cheeked from walking a mile in the bitter wind, but willing to wait no longer to see her friends. If Jane's appearance caused her to catch her breath, her better feelings won out instantly, and she embraced the eldest Bennet, saying, "Oh, Jane, how glad I am that you have recovered!"

Jane smiled and said, "Thank you. We were delighted to hear of Maria's return to health, as well."

Charlotte then turned to Elizabeth and hugged her

fiercely. "It is good to see you again, my friend. How often I wished for you during our troubles!"

"I would have done almost anything to see you, also," Elizabeth agreed happily. "But here we are, and many would say we have been fortunate." They clustered together on the long sofa.

"It is true that between our two families, we have only lost Mrs Bennet, but I cannot think you feel it very fortunate."

"No, but we came very close to losing Lydia, too, and Jane had no easy time of it," Elizabeth replied. "It could have been much worse, and we are grateful that our family is not more diminished. That none of the rest of us fell ill seems almost miraculous, to own the truth."

"Mr Jones says that it is a capricious illness, at times striking those who have hardly been in its presence while bypassing others who are heavily exposed to it," Charlotte remarked, shaking her head. "You know that I was spared despite caring for Maria. It cannot be explained, so I suppose we must content ourselves with gratitude. Is Lydia much recovered?"

Jane and Elizabeth looked at each other with faint grimaces. "She is recovering, but very slowly," said Elizabeth. "There was, it seems, a time when your Mr Jones advised Papa, Mary, and Kitty to prepare themselves for the worst. She wasted away quite terribly—Mary could pick her up and put her in the chair when the bed linens needed changing."

"My word," murmured Charlotte, having last seen the youngest Bennet at the peak of robust good health.

"But Mary is quite determined to plump her up," said Jane fondly. "You would be surprised by our Mary. She has gained much in sense and spirit through these trials. And Lydia will not oppose her in anything, so we are assured that she will in time be well again."

"That is the best possible news," Charlotte replied. "I have come with news also, though you may already know much of it."

———

Elizabeth listened grimly as Charlotte related to them what she knew of the effects of the sickness in their area; with Mr Jones as her source, her information was excellent. The four and twenty gentle families in the neighbourhood had lost near thirty members, and many more had been ill. Among the tradespeople, labourers, and tenants, numbers had been similar in proportion, though many of the children of poorer families had perished. Three of the shops on Meryton's high street would never re-open, their proprietors dead. Their parish of above four hundred souls was reduced by sixty-eight, and Mr Edwards was on the point of asking the local gentry to purchase a plot of land into which the cemetery might be expanded.

Those who had left were returned to their homes, save several who had succumbed to the illness elsewhere. Some who had left and not fallen ill returned smug in the perceived rightness of their decision, Charlotte told them with disapproval writ clear upon her features.

Jane squeezed Elizabeth's hand as the sisters absorbed this news solemnly. They had known some of it—even in crisis, information will find its way around a village—but Elizabeth had not grasped the full scope of what had occurred while she was consumed by the illness within her own family. To Jane, it must be even more shocking.

"One must wonder if Meryton shall ever recover from such a blow," Elizabeth said in tones of consternation.

"I believe it will," said Charlotte. "Father says the epidemic in his youth was just as terrible, though the neighbourhood was smaller then. It recovered, and even grew, in the time since."

"It must have been dreadful for Mr Jones," said Jane. "So many patients, so much loss! Is he well?"

Charlotte nodded slowly. "He is. It is of course a troubling thing, an experience one would never wish to have. But his training and his own steady nature have seen him through the worst, and now that he has time to reflect, I believe he will be able to put it behind him, likely faster than the rest of us. Although he does suffer greatly from the loss of his nephew."

"Poor little Davey Goulding," Jane murmured.

"There will be special prayers for the dead at services until Twelfth Night, beginning this Sunday," Charlotte informed them. "Will your family attend?"

"Papa and Kitty and I shall, I expect," said Elizabeth. "Mary may prefer to remain with Lydia, and Jane will have to decide what her strength allows."

"I am well enough to sit in church, Lizzy, though I would rather Papa called for the carriage. Walking in the cold would be fatiguing," Jane answered mildly.

Mr Bennet did call for the carriage on Sunday, and Mary was persuaded to leave Lydia with Mrs Hill and join them. The gentry at the front of the church resembled nothing so much as a flock of crows, so many were garbed in black, she thought, desperate for some bit of levity in a place of such bereaved sadness. When Mr Edwards solemnly read the names of the departed, a task which took several minutes, the only sound other than his voice was the muffled weeping scattered through the pews.

———

Mary sought out her sisters to ask for their advice. "Lydia is insistent on being given a mirror. Certainly she has the right to understand the changes which have occurred, but her spirits are much depressed, and I fear that she might be brought lower by such an exercise."

"Let me go to her."

They all looked at Jane with some surprise, for she preferred to avoid disputes rather than inject herself into them.

"I have been through this myself," she explained calmly. "I will go to Lydia, and tell her what it was like for me, to view for the first time what had become of my appearance. If, after that, she still wishes to see herself, we should allow it."

There was little anyone could say to that; Jane was the only one among them who truly understood what Lydia would confront in the glass.

Jane entered Lydia's room and found her reading but glad to put the book aside in favour of discourse with Jane. "Did Mary need a rest?"

"No, I asked her to stay downstairs while I spoke with you," she replied, taking a seat on the edge of the bed. "I am told that you wish for a looking glass."

"I must see myself at some time!" Lydia retorted with no little frustration.

"Indeed, you must," Jane replied easily, to the surprise of her sister. "It need not be today, but it need not be later, either. I only wished to tell you of my own experience, that you might be better able to decide if you are ready. And if you are ready today, I will bring you the glass myself."

Lydia soberly agreed, and Jane proceeded to open her heart to her sister in a manner she had not done even with Elizabeth, who would have been all sympathy but could never truly understand. She described the shock and horror she felt upon first encountering her scarred face and hands, in particular, for all else might be hidden by clothing. She told of the fears that plagued her, for her future and the reactions of others; her certainty that she could not now marry and that many of her friends would be lost to her, for who would wish to look upon such a visage? And then she revealed how the bulk of those fears had thus far proved largely unfounded, for Mr Bingley still loved her, and many had greeted her at church the day prior with smiles and pleasure in her recovery. She admitted, too, that many of those smiles had been tinged with pity, and that some looked upon her with revulsion, or not at all.

"What I wish you to know, dear Lydia," she concluded, "is that while you will have cause to mourn your loss of beauty, you need not mourn your dreams. Your family and any friends worth the name will stand with you, and one day I am sure that you will meet a man worthy of you, who will care more for your heart than for your face. I do not say life will be as easy as it was before, but all of the things that truly matter are still possible."

Lydia considered all that Jane had said with a seriousness she had rarely mustered. At last, she said, "I thank you, Jane. I was not, upon reflection, ready to see myself but I believe I am now, thanks to you."

Jane held the mirror out, wordlessly, and Lydia took it after a deep breath and a moment to gather her courage. Jane watched as her sister beheld her hollowed-out cheeks dotted with livid pink, pitted scars. Lydia's left eye was clouded with the mark of the disease's incursion there, and her chestnut curls hung limp and dry in further testament to weeks of near-starvation. Gasping, she let the glass fall to the counterpane, dropped her head into her hands, and wept. Jane crawled onto the bed to pull her into a fierce embrace.

In time, Lydia calmed. She remained safe in Jane's embrace for some minutes, then sat up and retrieved the glass, taking another look.

"It is not so shocking after the first time is got over, I suppose," she commented.

"No, it is not," Jane agreed. "And you will begin to look better soon. Already I notice my scars are not so red, and I have regained much of the weight I lost. This is the worst it shall be, I promise."

"Thank you, Jane. I do feel better now, and I am not sorry I looked. Avoiding it would not have changed anything, would it?"

"Indeed not," Jane said. "I have lately learnt that I often prefer to avoid that which I cannot change, but I do not believe it has served me well. It has certainly not served my sisters well."

"If you, the most perfect of my sisters, can think herself flawed and yet still remain the ideal to all of us, then I might not be hopeless, even with these horrible scars."

Jane smiled kindly but her reply was cut short when Lydia yawned hugely and said that she would like to rest.

———

As the Gardiners were expected for Christmas the following day, the Bennet girls all assembled in their mother's room for the task of sorting through her possessions, with the intention of freeing the spacious chamber for their relations' use. Lydia was sat on the bed, in deference to the fatigue which continued to limit her activities, and commanded a view of everything in the room.

They began with the closet and wardrobe, bringing out her gowns one by one and sharing memories of times she had worn them, provoking both laughter and tears, before relegating them to one of three piles—to be donated to the poor, to be sold, and to be given to Hill for her own use or profit. Her bonnets, shoes, gloves, shawls, pelisses, and cloaks were likewise sorted, though a few of these were kept by her daughters.

While Grandmother Bennet's pearls would now be Jane's, the hair combs and pins and brooches were quickly distributed among them. Finally, all of the handkerchiefs she had stitched herself were parcelled out to her children, Elizabeth reserving the plainest of these for their father and uncle. The silver set of hairbrush, comb, and mirror would be sold, and her perfumes given to Aunt Philips, who had a similar taste in scents and would also receive Mrs Bennet's matron's caps.

"That is everything, I believe," said Elizabeth, looking about. "Once it has all been carried away, and the connecting door locked, this will be Longbourn's finest guest chamber."

CHAPTER TWENTY-ONE

THE GARDINERS AND THEIR CHILDREN ARRIVED AS planned in the afternoon. There was a bit of awkwardness just after they disembarked, when three-year-old Samuel became frightened by Jane and Lydia, despite having been told many times that his cousins had been ill and no longer looked quite the same. Elizabeth saw the sympathy in her aunt and uncle's eyes when they gazed at their nieces; the Gardiners' presence here, and the distraction of the children, would be a balm for all the Bennets.

With Samuel soon settled into the nursery with his brother and sisters, the Gardiners were able to turn their attentions to their nieces and brother. Dinner was a subdued affair, for the travellers were weary and the absence of Mrs Bennet was felt anew by all present. Mr Gardiner was a genteel and intelligent man; Elizabeth was certain he had often despaired of his loud and silly sisters, but she knew he loved them deeply nonetheless. Her uncle's grief was sincere, and it was apparent that surrounding himself with her daughters was the greatest of comforts.

That evening, Mrs Gardiner knocked at the door of the room Jane and Elizabeth shared, and was admitted gladly.

"Girls, I must confess that your uncle and I are both stunned by the changes in your younger sisters. We had, of course, expected them to be brought rather low by your mother's death, and I had Elizabeth's testimony of their alteration in a letter, but still we are amazed at the revolution in their sense and manners."

The sisters shared a look, and Elizabeth turned to their aunt. "It is no easy thing, to care for someone suffering from that disease," she said, with all the weight of certain knowledge. "Naturally, one would prefer it to being the patient, but I feel that I put aside the last of my girlhood during those weeks, and Mary and Kitty also were forced to mature very rapidly, to think and behave with sense and without giving in to their emotions, because lives truly were at stake. It is to their very great credit that they have stayed the course now that the crisis is past."

Mrs Gardiner stood and went to her nieces, kissing each upon the cheek. "May I just say, girls, how proud I am of you—of all five of you!—for not allowing such a terrible experience to defeat you, but instead choosing to be made better by your trials? Many have not half the fortitude you have all shown." With Elizabeth, she shared a long, serious look, which Elizabeth understood to indicate that her aunt wished a private conversation on this subject, and the other related issues she had shared in her letter. She gave a small nod, and her aunt appeared satisfied.

———

Darcy was conflicted and unhappy, and unfortunately for Bingley, it was making him snappish. He still had come to no decision as to what was best done about his unexpected and persistent longing for Miss Elizabeth Bennet, though he could not seem to keep himself from joining Bingley on his twice-weekly calls to Longbourn…until today.

"I know you are eager to meet these London relations, but I have some reservations," he said to Bingley. *Mrs Bennet was not well-mannered and had the advantage of many years as the wife of a gentleman. Her tradesman brother and his wife are likely to be more akin to the uncouth, grasping Mrs Philips*, he thought.

"I understand your doubts," said Bingley, "but surely you must know that simply being in trade does not make one vulgar or venal. Miss Bennet is very fond of the Gardiners—more so than of the Philipses, I gather."

"Miss Bennet is fond of everyone." Darcy sighed. "This tradesman will see an advantage in an acquaintance with us, you know. I expect we shall be asked to invest in his business, whatever it is, within the fortnight."

"You will have to meet them at some time or another, you know, if only after church. But if you wish to delay the evil day, by all means, stay here. I am calling at Longbourn." With that, Bingley turned and left the room, displeasure clear in the set of his shoulders.

Darcy felt equal displeasure in himself. If he wished to have the company and conversation of Miss Elizabeth that he had enjoyed at Netherfield, furtive and difficult though their conversations often were, he must accept that Longbourn—and the extended Bennet family—was her world.

His own sphere had difficult, unlikeable relations—in that, he and Miss Elizabeth were equals.

Bingley had donned his greatcoat and was winding a muffler about his neck when Darcy found him in the hall and called for his own winter wear.

"You are right," he said with a shrug. "The acquaintance cannot be avoided, and I do enjoy the conversations we have at Longbourn."

The gentlemen were shown into the parlour, which now contained a couple unknown to them. They were fashionably and tastefully garbed, and their reaction to making the acquaintance of Mr Darcy of Pemberley was restrained and courteous. He detected some slight curiosity from Mrs Gardiner, while Mr Gardiner seemed most interested in Mr Bingley, sparing Darcy hardly a glance after the introduction.

Though he sat with Miss Elizabeth and her younger sisters, the cosy confines of Longbourn's parlour allowed him to occasionally and discreetly eavesdrop on his friend's conversation with Mr Gardiner. Surprised by the ease of their initial introduction though he had been, he only felt the first stirrings of doubt when he realised that Mr Gardiner was not even approaching the topic of business with Bingley, but rather was skilfully drawing the younger man out and sketching his character most thoroughly. At last he seemed satisfied and released Bingley to take his place by Miss Bennet, while he joined his brother-in-law. Though their succeeding conversation was pitched low, Darcy thought he heard the words 'may even deserve our Jane' issue from the tradesman's mouth. Had that delicate inquisition been for the purpose of determining Bingley's suitability as a nephew, rather than an investor?

He had not been attending constantly to his own group, and so was startled when Mrs Gardiner addressed him directly. "Mr Darcy, are you acquainted with Mr Cole, the rector at Lambton in Derbyshire?"

His shoulders stiffened. He had taken note of the hints of the north in her accent, and now she had landed upon a mutual acquaintance. "I am. How is it that you know him?" He vaguely registered that Miss Elizabeth was giving him an odd look, but he was not at leisure to consider it—he must ward off the encroachment which was no doubt coming.

She smiled warmly. "Why, he is my father! I hope you will be pleased to know that in the letter I received from him only last week, he reported that all was well within the village."

Darcy did know Mr Cole, and thought him a fine and worthy man of the cloth. His daughter was Miss Elizabeth's aunt? "I...I am indeed pleased to hear it," he replied awkwardly, and with another smile she turned back to her nieces, apparently having said all she wished to.

She and her nieces were discussing a trip that the Gardiners had tentatively planned for the coming summer, 'if your uncle's business allows'. Mr Gardiner wished to venture to the Lake District and try his hand at the fishing to be found there, while his wife was more interested in the landscapes to be viewed.

Darcy's attention flitted between Mr Gardiner, engaged in a discussion of the war in France with Mr Bennet, and Mrs Gardiner, whose cheerful elegance of manner reminded him very strongly of Miss Elizabeth, though with some of Miss Bennet's reserve. They were intelligent, interesting, genteel people. He felt ashamed of himself for having presumed the worst about them, and annoyed that he had been open about those assumptions; he would have to admit to Bingley he was wrong.

His acknowledgment came sooner than he'd have liked, and he was required to admit his mistake shortly after he and Bingley left Longbourn. They were hardly out of sight of the house before Bingley turned to him, eyebrows raised, and said, "Well, I dare say the Gardiners were more of a surprise to you than to me."

Darcy sighed. "Yes, Bingley, you were correct. But in my defence, it was not unnatural to expect the brother to resemble the sisters."

"I should think that having known me and Caroline for all these years would have cured you of that notion," Bingley said pointedly.

"That is unfair," he huffed. "You and your sister, though very different in personality, are both educated people able to move in elevated society."

"Is it not obvious that Mr Gardiner is also an educated man, while his sisters were not given that opportunity? A situation, I might add, quite common in the previous generation, even among your class but particularly in mine. My sisters were the first women of our family to receive a formal education, you know."

"No," Darcy said quietly. "I was not aware. I know little of the merchant class."

"I am far from the only son of trade breaking into society. Wealthy merchants are on the rise, my friend, and we infiltrate your ranks because we are well-mannered and adaptable enough to fit in. Some, it is true, are crass and grasping, but I will remind you of your own comments on the Earl and Countess of Sefton and say no more."

Darcy grimaced at that reminder of the loutish earl and his shrieking harpy of a wife. They were worse by far than anyone he had met in Meryton, Mrs Philips included, yet they were accepted everywhere by virtue of their bloodlines. And then, if he were being honest about the manners of the *ton*, he would have to admit that his own aunt, Lady Catherine de Bourgh, was by no means to be preferred over Mrs Gardiner.

———

That evening after dinner, Elizabeth was drawn away by her aunt for a private conversation. Shutting themselves in the room she shared with Jane, Mrs Gardiner took her hand and said, "Now that I have met your new friends, much of what you related in your letter is clearer to me. Mr Bingley is so very amiable and Mr Darcy so solemn, that it would indeed be easy to conclude there was little else to them. Had I not your account of their behaviour during the crisis, I might have made a few ill-informed judgments of my own," she said with a smile.

"But you would not have clung to them, as I am inclined to do," Elizabeth replied wryly.

"Now that you are aware of that inclination and its pitfalls, you will not be so firm in your initial evaluation of new acquaintances in future, will you?"

"I believe I shall not. But Aunt, I still feel as though everyone about me has grown so much, and I only a little."

"Oh, Lizzy. You have grown, believe me. I see it in you as I do in your sisters. But for all your stubborn reliance on first impressions, you have always been the one in your family most willing to look reality in the eye. Your father hid among his books, your mother in her nerves. Jane wished to pretend that everything was better than it was, and Mary that all could be solved with the perfect extract from scripture or Fordyce. Kitty and Lydia preferred not to think at all. They have recently been forced to do what you long have: recognise the truth of what is passing, and act upon it where they could.

"You feel that you have not changed, when the truth is that you have changed in different ways than they. Your family required lessons in resolve and firmness of purpose. You, by contrast, needed to learn pliancy and moderation, and I think you have."

Elizabeth laid her head against her aunt's shoulder and breathed in her familiar perfume of apricot and clover. Mrs Gardiner maintained a patient silence as Elizabeth turned these thoughts over in her mind, and eventually concluded that the uncertainty she had been feeling was largely a product of having developed, all unaware, a more nuanced view of the world.

"I think I liked it better when I was certain of everything," she admitted at last. "So much seems ambiguous and indefinite to me now."

Mrs Gardiner stroked her hair and said, "I am afraid that, my dear, is maturity in a nutshell."

———

Having met the Gardiners and found them mannerly, Mr Darcy was in a very different frame of mind the following day, when Miss Bennet, Miss Elizabeth, Miss Catherine, and Mrs Gardiner were announced. Darcy elected to sit near Mrs Gardiner and, when the flow of conversation allowed, made an effort to engage with her. His first impression of her gentility and intelligence was not at all damaged by this exercise, and for part of the morning they spoke of Lambton and the surrounding area. She mentioned that Lady Anne Darcy had at times worked with her parents in service of the parish poor, and he wondered whether his sister would enjoy hearing Mrs Gardiner's memories of their mother, who had died when Georgiana was only two years old.

As the visitors were preparing to leave, Darcy quietly reminded Miss Elizabeth, "We are expecting additions to our party shortly—my sister and her companion, and my cousin, Colonel Fitzwilliam. My sister is most eager to become acquainted with...your family."

"I do recall." Miss Elizabeth smiled broadly. "I very much look forward to making Miss Darcy's acquaintance, and your cousin's, too."

"Georgiana has few friends near her own age. I believe your company, and that of your sisters, will delight her, though it may not be apparent to a new acquaintance. Like me, she is quite reticent."

"Oh, well, then I shall just have to tease her a little. It always seems to work on you," she replied lightly.

He felt he must be grinning like a fool, but made no effort to restrain himself. Before he could reply, her countenance took a more serious turn, and she added, "It is very good of you and your relations to decline all the gaieties of the season which must be available to you in London or Derbyshire, to spend this time with Mrs Hurst and Mr Bingley. I am sure it will brighten this difficult time for them, as the presence of the Gardiners has done for us."

"Oh, well, as to that..." He shrugged, feeling both

humbled and gratified. "I will not speak for my cousin, but my sister and I both prefer a quiet Christmas, though we do wish to comfort our friends, also."

She smiled at him again, pulling on her gloves. "Declaim any merit as you please, but I will continue to think well of you for it." She glanced over her shoulder; her aunt was approaching. "I will bid you farewell, sir, and wish you a merry Christmas."

"A Merry Christmas to you also, Miss Elizabeth," he murmured in return, bowing.

———

The travellers blew in from London on a wind that spat tiny shards of ice upon them as they disembarked before Netherfield. The footmen hurried them inside, where their hosts and Darcy waited with hot tea and warm smiles.

Georgiana curtseyed to Mr Bingley and Mrs Hurst, before clasping hands with the latter. "I am so very sorry for your loss, Mrs Hurst. How are you?"

Mrs Hurst smiled. "I am tolerably well, Miss Darcy, and all the better for having you here." Mr Bingley also expressed his delight at her presence and, having done her duty by her hosts, Miss Darcy presented Mrs Annesley to their acquaintance and was at last able to reunite with her beloved brother.

Colonel Fitzwilliam bowed to Mr Bingley and Mrs Hurst, to whom he was known, and they spoke for some minutes after the requisite pleasantries had been canvassed, allowing the Darcys some little privacy.

"Georgie, you do look well," Darcy said when his sister

came to him, her companion remaining a discreet distance behind.

"As do you, Brother. We have brought with us everything you requested," she informed him with a smile, "and I am glad we left town so early this morning, for our cousin says it is going to snow, and you know that he is rarely wrong on the subject!"

CHAPTER TWENTY-TWO

CHARLOTTE AND ELIZABETH GREETED EACH OTHER IN the churchyard after services on Christmas Day, and spoke quietly of the small events in their lives in the past week until Elizabeth chuckled and bent her head towards her friend's, murmuring, "I believe your young man is desiring my absence."

Charlotte cast a glance over her shoulder and smiled at Mr Jones, who waited patiently nearby. "He is to escort me home."

"As he has after every service for the past month," Elizabeth replied teasingly. "Do not keep him waiting on my account, but do call on us this week if the weather allows."

"Thank you, Lizzy. Merry Christmas."

"A very merry Christmas to you, Charlotte." They clasped hands warmly for a moment and separated, Elizabeth to join her family party, and Charlotte to approach Mr Jones, who offered his arm along with his greetings and best wishes for the holiday.

They turned their steps towards Lucas Lodge, feet

crunching through the scatter of frozen leaves alongside the road, propriety maintained by the constant stream of carriages, wagons, and walkers moving away from the church.

"Miss Lucas," he said, after they had spent some moments in quiet enjoyment of each other's company, "I have been wondering if you are yet ready to hear my question."

Happiness roared through her like fire; he still wished to ask! It had not been only the desperation of grief! She required a few seconds to master herself before she could answer, "I believe I am, sir."

He positively beamed at her, such an expression of delight as she had never expected to have directed at her alone. "There is something I wish to tell you first." He looked at her earnestly. "I have not much now, but I do not intend to be a village apothecary forever. My aspirations have only been delayed—I save very constantly, though not much, and one day I shall complete my training and become a physician of the Royal College. If you decide that you will have me, I have every hope that in five years or so I may begin to offer you a better life."

Charlotte considered this for a moment, and found that she did not really care whether he ever became more than an apothecary, except that failure would be a great disappointment to *him*. She looked him directly in the eyes, just as modest maidens are urged never to do, and said, "Ask your question."

He stopped and stood before her, gathering her hands into his. "Miss Lucas, will you do me the very great honour of granting me your hand in marriage?"

"Thank you, Mr Jones, I will," she answered, her

sedate tone belied by her broad smile and the moisture welling in her eyes.

He stared at her in wonder for a moment, rendered briefly immobile by the pleasant shock of having got all he wanted so easily.

They turned again towards her parents' home, walking more slowly and closer together.

Charlotte, incapable of being impractical for long, ventured, "I am to have five hundred pounds upon my marriage. Will that assist you in realising your ambition sooner?"

"Dear Charlotte, we shall manage. I have some hope that your father will be able to advise me on the running of my shop, and help me to earn a little more from it. He is reputed to have been a canny businessman, in his time."

"He was, and he knew how to please his customers," she agreed. "And of course, when we are married, you will not be required to close when you are called away to a patient."

"What do you mean?"

She smiled. "Only that I am not too proud to stand behind the counter and assist your customers while you are away. Indeed, I may be a help to you in other ways. I know my way around a stillroom, and if you would teach me to make some of the simpler remedies, you may devote your time to other things. I can keep accounts as well as any tradesman's daughter, too. You may find I make you more money than I cost."

"You would do all this?" He gazed upon her as though she were some strange and magical creature come to grant him his deepest wishes. "When shall we marry?"

"As soon as possible, please!" she answered eagerly,

and blushed crimson. He laughed, tucked her arm into his own, and pulled her towards the Lodge at a great clip.

"Let us waste no time making our announcement, then!"

———

Christmas passed quietly at Netherfield, as is proper in a house of mourning. The same could be said of Longbourn, though that house enjoyed two things which eased the natural sorrow of their first Christmas without Mrs Bennet —firstly, the presence of the Gardiner children, who were the main source of the adults' lightened hearts, dear and lively as they were; secondly, the delivery of an entire crate of ripe oranges, compliments of Mr Darcy. Mr Bennet's dilatory habits could not endure in the face of such a treat at such a time, and he insisted that the Netherfield servant who performed the delivery wait, with a cup of hot ale to warm him, while he wrote a note of thanks to the gentleman.

Boxing Day passed more quietly still, as the servants enjoyed their liberty and both households made do with bread, cheese, cold meats, and the leftovers of their Christmas feasts. The day following brought early visitors to Longbourn, in the form of Charlotte Lucas and her sister Maria.

The younger Lucas instantly ran to Kitty and Lydia, and for a moment the parlour was filled with the happy babble of three young friends separated for many weeks. Elizabeth waited to join in conversation with Charlotte and Jane, wishing to ensure Lydia's confidence in company.

"My goodness, Maria, you have been fortunate," Lydia remarked artlessly. "You have only a few scars on your face. In a year or two they may not be noticeable at all."

Maria took no offence, Elizabeth was happy to see; the girl's sense of her own good fortune likely had been brought to her forcefully by seeing others who had recovered, including Jane, at church the last several weeks. "I am sorry it went so hard for you, Lydia," she replied. "I heard you nearly died!"

Lydia looked away and nodded. "It is true." She took a deep breath and raised her face to her friend again. "But I am getting better. I hope to begin going about occasionally in the next week or two."

Heartened by Lydia's response, Elizabeth turned back to Charlotte and Jane, who were discussing their holiday celebrations. Suddenly Charlotte broke into a broad smile and communicated that she and Mr Jones were now engaged. Her friends were, of course, very happy for her and offered every genuine felicitation.

"Papa was a little reluctant to give his blessing," she confided, "but when we told him our plans, that I should help in the shop when Mr Jones is with patients, and that we wished his advice on making it more profitable, he warmed to the notion. And when Mr Jones told him that he is saving to finish his training, all objections were entirely forgot. He is positively dancing with anticipation of the day he may speak of his son-in-law, the physician."

Elizabeth could not but join Charlotte and Jane in laughing at this accurate portrait of Sir William, who liked nothing better than to speak of the good fortune he had known in his life.

Over breakfast, Bingley asked if any of them should like to join him in his call upon his particular friends, the Bennets of Longbourn, later. The colonel rapidly agreed, for he understood from conversation in the drawing room the night before that the house contained several amiable and lovely ladies. Darcy was amenable to the visit if his sister would also come, but Georgiana felt that it would be rude to abandon her hostess on her first morning in the house. Mrs Hurst, however, had at last been convinced that in the country a widow might call upon particular friends after the first several weeks of her mourning had passed, and announced that she would be joining in the call. Reassured, Georgiana agreed to the scheme, and at Bingley's insistence they departed as early as proper.

As the carriage bore them towards Longbourn, Darcy reminded his cousin and sister that Mrs Bennet had been lost to the recent epidemic, and that Miss Bennet and Miss Lydia had been ill but survived, information he had previously conveyed in his letters. This served also to inform Mrs Annesley, his sister's companion.

Arriving not long after the Lucas sisters departed, they entered the parlour at Longbourn to find the entire family assembled there, Mr Bennet reading to his daughters as they attended to their handiwork. Bingley made the introductions, and though Colonel Fitzwilliam was at ease in any company (and particularly that of amiable ladies), Georgiana was quite overcome by shyness. Nonetheless, she was soon eagerly participating in a conversation upon the subject of music with Miss Elizabeth and Miss Mary. Darcy, who had been watching his sister with some concern, knowing her diffident nature, saw that it had all been Miss Elizabeth's doing—she had taken Georgiana's measure in a moment and set about making her comfortable.

Once Georgiana had been sufficiently plied with tea and talk of her favourite subject, Miss Elizabeth began drawing others into their circle and allowing the conversation to range more widely. In time, the talk naturally turned to Mrs Gardiner's former residence not five miles from Pemberley, and Darcy's sister eagerly soaked up stories of her mother's charitable work with the Reverend Mr Cole and his family.

Mrs Hurst, for her part, seemed pleased to make the acquaintance of Mr Gardiner, and upon discovering that his business included the importation of drinking chocolate, engaged him in a rather intense conversation on the qualities of different varieties.

The upcoming wedding of Miss Lucas to Mr Jones formed a large part of the general conversation, as such an event will in a small neighbourhood. The engagement was news to Darcy, and apparently to Bingley also.

"Mr Jones and Miss Lucas?" his friend exclaimed. "My word! But now that I consider for a moment, they are remarkably well-matched, are they not? Well, I do wish them joy, and shall be sure to tell them so."

Miss Elizabeth turned to Darcy. "You seem a little disconcerted, sir. Is aught amiss?"

"No...no. I am not disconcerted, only surprised, as Bingley was. Were they much acquainted before the epidemic?"

"I do not believe so. Certainly they knew each other, but I do not think they had had much opportunity to converse before they were required to meet daily at Maria's bedside. It seems that was enough for each to recognise the other's excellent qualities. I know that Maria was still confined to her bed when he first asked Charlotte if he might call." She shrugged, smiling. "A sickroom is not, perhaps, the most romantic place to come to know the companion of your future life, but they are both so dear that one can only be delighted they found each other, however oddly it came about." She turned her attention then to something Miss Catherine was saying, and Darcy allowed the animated chatter to wash over him as he contemplated what he had just heard.

He knew quite well that Mr Jones had been run ragged during the sickness, yet somehow in the midst of it all he had, apparently, recognised a lady both well-suited and attractive to him and set about pursuing her. And now, less than a fortnight after the epidemic had been declared ended, he was engaged to her. How could he be so certain of his course, having come to know Miss Lucas so recently? It was likely that he had known her better by reputation than by experience, living in such a small community; thus, he would have had few concerns about her character, but it still seemed to Darcy to be almost heedless to decide and arrange the entire course of one's future with such speed.

While his rational mind fixed upon the dangers, he could not help but feel a certain admiration for Mr Jones's decisive action. In the midst of tragedy, and despite poverty, he had seen a chance at happiness and seized it with both hands. It spoke of a certain courage, and a definitive understanding of his own desires—something Darcy wished he could claim for himself.

When opportunity presented itself, he discreetly asked Miss Elizabeth, "How will they get on? Mr Jones does not seem to have much income."

"Oh, they will be rather poor at first, I expect," answered she, "but Mr Jones is saving to complete his training, and Charlotte intends to help him in the shop, so they have every expectation that their situation will improve in a few years."

"That is well, I suppose, though one wishes the period of poverty were not necessary. He deserves better than his current situation, as does your friend."

Elizabeth gave him a warm look that made him feel the intimacy of their conversation. "I can only agree, but they are very much in love and surely that will ease their burdens until their fortunes rise. She is as determined as he, in her way, and no doubt their friends will help them along with frequent invitations to dinner."

Darcy nodded, but before he could think of a response, he saw that Georgiana was quite caught by the romance of it all—a young couple, desperately in love but short on funds, resolved to work together to better themselves—and spent the rest of the visit gleaning every detail she could about Miss Lucas and Mr Jones.

Later that evening, Darcy would recall Miss Elizabeth's words, 'their friends will help them along', and begin to consider a plan which might be most easily solidified in town.

———

"How amazing that I should meet someone who knew my mother in a county I have never before visited!" Georgiana exclaimed during the ride back to Netherfield. "I liked all of them very much, Brother, but Miss Elizabeth and Mrs Gardiner particularly. Though I hope to know Miss Lydia better, as we are of an age, but she did not seem much inclined to engage with me today. Is she shy?"

Darcy and Bingley exchanged a look at that question, having known Miss Lydia to be entirely the opposite in their early acquaintance. It was Mrs Annesley who replied gently, "I suspect, Miss Darcy, that having been so recently ill and wearing the marks of that illness now, she may be reluctant to make new acquaintances for fear of being rejected for her appearance."

Georgiana looked horrified at the very thought. "Oh, poor Miss Lydia! I confess that had not occurred to me, but now that I think upon it, she and Miss Bennet must have been as pretty as their sisters until very recently, and might feel it keenly."

"Most young ladies would, even if they had no pretty sisters to be compared to," Mrs Annesley remarked. "I know you do not like to put yourself forward, but if you wish to know Miss Lydia better you may be required to do so." As Georgiana replied that she would try, Darcy thought with satisfaction that they had indeed, if rather late, found an ideal companion for his sister, a woman of both education and kindness, capable of revealing the realities of life in such a way to inform the tender-hearted girl without damaging her spirit.

———

"So," commented Colonel Fitzwilliam as he and Darcy pulled up in a frosted field after a hard early-morning ride from Netherfield, "you spent an uncommon amount of time with Miss Elizabeth when we visited Longbourn. Is there something you wish to tell me?"

Darcy shifted uncomfortably in his saddle. "No, there is nothing."

"Come now, I have never known you to pay so much attention to a lady, much less an available one!" Fitzwilliam replied with a look of curiosity. "She is a pretty thing, and witty. Uncommonly intelligent, unless I miss my guess. Just the sort of lady who would attract you, in fact. You cannot say you are unaffected; I know you too well."

Although a little shocked that his feelings were so apparent, Darcy nodded. "She is all of those things, and you did not know her before the death of her mother and the illness of her sisters," he replied wistfully. "She brought light and laughter into every room, and no doubt shall again when her grief has passed."

"Pity her family is not suitable, though," his cousin commented. "You really ought to cease indulging yourself in the pleasure of her company, before you raise expectations you cannot fulfil."

Darcy was rather taken aback. "Cannot? I have made no declaration, but if I wish to raise her expectations, and to meet them, I am entirely at liberty to do so. The Bennets are not of the *ton*, but Mr Bennet is a gentleman. Do you truly think I require more wealth and connexions?"

"You may not need them, but it is expected that you shall get them nonetheless," came the impatient reply. "And though the father is a gentleman—just barely—the uncles are not. Are you seriously contemplating affixing the Darcy name to the stench of trade?"

Darcy huffed. "Viscount Burnley just married a trades-man's daughter; am I, a mere gentleman, to baulk at a tradesman's niece, the daughter of a gentleman?"

"Burnley needed her dowry—you have no such excuse. Think of Georgiana's prospects."

"Georgiana has wealth and connexions aplenty. I cannot see how a lively, witty, and gracious sister would harm her prospects."

"Miss Elizabeth Bennet may be all of those things, but she is not of our circles. Her acceptance would not come easily, if at all. You would be mocked for losing your head over a pretty chit of no consequence, and she would be roundly derided as a fortune hunter." Fitzwilliam shook his head as if incredulous at Darcy's naivete. "Then there's the matter of making up for Georgiana's dowry when the time comes—best think on how you'll manage that without anything from your wife. And what would you get in return for all these difficulties? A handsome armful and the care of the rest of the sisters when the father's gone."

"I would have a marriage of affection," Darcy replied frostily. "I have seen enough purely practical matches to know that I would be miserable in such a union."

Fitzwilliam's eyebrows reached for his hairline. "And just what makes you think she holds you in equal, or even comparable, affection? I have seen nothing of it. She does not seem to have any expectations of you, nor do her rela-tions." He rubbed his jaw. "It is a bit odd, now I think on it. There is usually speculation when a man of wealth pays more attention to one young lady than another, even if it truly is mere friendship on both sides, yet none of the Miss Bennets seem to consider you anything but an adjunct to Bingley, or your attentions to Miss Elizabeth more than a way of passing the time. The fact that they treat you no differently than they do anyone else must at least acquit them of fortune hunting. I will give them that."

Darcy could not disguise the disappointment he felt on hearing his worldly and perceptive cousin lay bare Elizabeth's lack of romantic inclination towards him. They had shared moments of real feeling, of her grief and his own concerns, and while he could barely acknowledge he was in love, he had thought her own amity for him was obvious. And yet the picture Fitzwilliam had just presented was not inaccurate, and he must conclude that he had most likely mistaken friendliness for a more fervent attachment. Darcy looked away, mortified and now suspecting that the friendship he had built with Elizabeth and his own role during the area's smallpox epidemic had not entirely overcome the poor first impression he had made.

He turned his horse back towards Netherfield, giving himself a moment to recover his composure, though his cousin soon pulled up alongside.

"I am sorry for your present unhappiness, Darcy, but consider: Is it not better this way? You have done nothing irretrievable. Come back to London with me after the holiday, and start looking for a lady who does not merely like you. Elizabeth Bennet will soon be forgot."

Darcy narrowed his eyes at his cousin, experiencing a sudden aversion for the company of one he had favoured since they were boys together. He knew that when he had come to Hertfordshire, he had held many of the same views Fitzwilliam now voiced. But he had since seen much that was good in this neighbourhood he had earlier disdained, and likewise in a certain lady with whom he had not then wished to dance. In truth, it was not only his view of the local society which had altered; he felt himself to be a rather different man than he had been only weeks ago.

She may merely like me now, he thought, *but that does not mean all hope is lost. Love can grow, and what better soil than friendship?*

He would not say as much to his cousin, however, so he merely sighed and muttered, "I need a gallop," before springing his horse.

CHAPTER TWENTY-THREE

THE GARDINERS DEPARTED MERE DAYS AFTER Christmas, and a great deal of liveliness and distraction left with them. The depths of winter can be trying to the spirits in the best of times, and even regular visits between Longbourn and Netherfield and the occasional calls by other friends could not do a great deal to dispel the melancholy which settled over Longbourn. Whilst Mr Bingley continued to pay attentions to Jane, Elizabeth found her happiness for her sister tempered by some confusion over the friendship she had established with Mr Darcy. She had seen his warmth and kindness, but with his gregarious cousin and eager sister in company, he now appeared content to sit quietly and almost apart during their visits.

He would watch with a little smile playing about the corners of his mouth as Miss Darcy spoke with the ladies of Longbourn, or with a faintly furrowed brow as Colonel Fitzwilliam made himself agreeable to them. He rarely spoke unless directly addressed, with Elizabeth herself the most likely to do so. She began to wonder if this reunion with his relations had made him wish to be among his own circle once more, and away from Hertfordshire.

But though his early silence had returned, his early hauteur had not. His reticence now carried an air of contemplation rather than arrogance, though upon what subject he felt the need to ponder for so many days together she could not imagine. It was worrisome, and vexing.

At the close of the first week of January, the inhabitants of Netherfield called to bid the Bennets farewell. Mr Bingley and Mrs Hurst hoped to return within a fortnight, although much of that would depend upon Miss Bingley, who had resumed her earlier practise of failing to answer their letters. Mr Darcy would re-join them at Netherfield also, though his business might take longer than Bingley's. His cousin was to return to duty, and his sister to her studies, and there was no expectation on either side of a swift reunion in those quarters.

Miss Darcy asked the Miss Bennets if she might write to them, and was delighted by the positive response. Mrs Hurst, likewise, promised to write from London, though she smilingly cautioned that she could not have very much of interest to relate. "For packing up the things I left in town will be very dull even to me," she concluded with a wry little smile. The townhouse was part of the estate, and the new heir, Hurst's younger brother, wished to take up residence in the spring.

If asked, Elizabeth would deny that Mr Darcy's farewell affected her more than the others'. She had begun to doubt he would come back with his friends, suspecting his seeming withdrawal to be in preparation for a more permanent separation. Yet when the moment came, he had bowed over her hand, giving her a searching look as he said, "I am sorry to go, and shall be happy to return. I hope very much our business will be completed quickly."

She had murmured some words of agreement; she hardly knew what. Whatever had been weighing on his mind these last days, it seemed it had nothing to do with any dissatisfaction with the company in Hertfordshire. He could be so frightfully inscrutable at times; would she ever understand him?

And why did it seem so very important that she should?

———

With their friends and relations gone, and with Charlotte Lucas naturally caught up in the details of her approaching wedding, the middle part of January passed quietly and slowly for Elizabeth and her sisters. The brightest spot in their lives was the continuing recovery of Lydia, who slowly filled out and increased in energy as the days crept by. However, as her strength grew, so did her frustration with the alteration to her vision. Nothing looked as it should any longer; one eye was as acute as ever, but the vision in the other so blurred as to only distinguish light, shadow, and motion. Her stitchery, which had been her one great accomplishment, was now as a child's, and when she used the stairs she was required to cling very tightly to the banister to avoid taking a tumble.

"Ugh!" she cried, flinging her work to the floor of the parlour and startling all her family, one afternoon in early January. "I cannot do it!"

Mary stood, picked up the discarded fabric, and put

the work into Lydia's basket. She rummaged through her own, pulling out a shirt with a great rent in the sleeve. Seating herself beside Lydia, she gave her the shirt and explained, "This is from the collection for the poor. Whoever receives this shirt will not notice that your stitches are imperfect, but instead that he or his wife or mother has been spared the labour of fixing it. I know it is not interesting work, but it will give you the practise you need to accustom yourself to stitching again. And, of course, you will be doing a service for our community."

"Will you thread the needle for me, Mary? I find it very hard."

Elizabeth watched as Mary acquiesced, and Lydia began placing a line of simple stitches through the edges of the tear. When it was finished, she accounted herself rather pleased with it. When she asked for another piece of mending, Elizabeth was only too happy to find something from the collection for the poor. The change in her sisters, the growth in maturity and patience and kindness for one another was truly the best outcome—the only good result—of what they had suffered. She glanced at Jane, as dear and kind-hearted as ever, and brave as well; her beauty remained, it was not perfect, but it was beauty nonetheless.

Her happiness with Mr Bingley was a wonderful result, as was Charlotte's with Mr Jones. Her own friendship with Mr Darcy was another unexpected and pleasing consequence of recent events. It was probable, she supposed, that once Louisa and Mr Bingley had less need of Mr Darcy and he was drawn back to his faraway estate, she might meet with him only rarely, especially once he had a family of his own to keep him even more firmly fixed in the north. Ignoring the pangs such a notion created, Elizabeth turned back to her work.

"Oh, bother." Lydia sighed. "I have dropt my thimble and do not see it."

"I will look for it," said Kitty cheerfully, setting her work aside and standing up. "It must have rolled under something, if it is not in the chair with you," she said, peering underneath the tea-cart and Lydia's chair. "I think I—oh."

Kitty reached underneath and handed Lydia her thimble without a word, then stretched her arm beneath the chair again, bringing forth an object they all recognised.

"Mama's sewing box," Mary breathed as it emerged into the light of day.

Kitty got her handkerchief out and began wiping the dust off the painted wood as her family gathered around. "Your mother always preferred using a handkerchief to stitching one," their father joked weakly, his tone more nostalgic than jocular.

"It must have been under there for many months; I do not recall when last I saw it," Elizabeth remarked, aiding Kitty in her efforts. Soon the box, a sturdy yet pretty thing, its top painted with cabbage roses and its handles wound with faded green silk, looked as it had when last they viewed it.

Kitty reverently raised the lid. The tray which covered the large compartment was filled with a jumble of needles, thimbles, buttons, and twists and tangles of thread which ought to have, but had never, been put on the snowflake-shaped mother of pearl thread winders.

"Look, there are five thimbles," Elizabeth said with a smile. "Let us each keep one."

With none of the bickering that would once have characterised such an effort, Mrs Bennet's thimbles were divided amongst her daughters. The gold one went to Jane, and the silver to Elizabeth while the three porcelain ones found homes with the younger girls.

They picked through the bundle of half-finished and hardly-started handkerchiefs, purses, and reticules. In the bottom of the compartment was a small wooden box fastened with a little brass latch. Inside lay half a dozen carefully folded pieces of plain brown paper which, when opened, each revealed a pressed primrose, browned and fragile with age. Only when they were all revealed and spread out upon the floor did the girls look up to see that tears were streaming down their father's cheeks. Concerned, Elizabeth stood and went to place her arm around him.

"Papa?"

"It was spring when I began to court her," he said, as much to himself as to his daughters. "I saw her outside the church one Sunday, just after I returned to Longbourn with my education and a brief tour to my credit. She was wearing a yellow gown and a straw bonnet with white flowers on it. She was so very beautiful, and she was laughing. I was smitten in an instant. Like the brash young fellow I was, I cast about for some means of securing her notice, and found a bunch of primroses growing in the hedgerow. So I plucked them and offered them to her with some nonsense about how *those* wild Hertfordshire roses paled in comparison to the one before me."

"And she kept them all these years," said Kitty wistfully.

Jane carefully wrapped them all up again and returned them to their box, extending it to their father. "I believe this should be yours, Papa."

He took the box gingerly, as though afraid he might shatter it, or it might shatter him. Slowly, he rose and without a word disappeared into his book-room, not to return for several hours.

————

Only a day later, Mr Bennet's dry wit seemed returned to him.

"Well, girls," he said to his family, as they were at breakfast, "I hope you will not mind an addition to our family party."

"Who do you mean?" asked Elizabeth.

"The person I refer to is a gentleman, and a stranger." He looked at them all expectantly. "It is my cousin, Mr Collins, who, when I am dead, may turn you all out of this house as soon as he pleases."

Elizabeth quirked an eyebrow at him, Kitty looked rather alarmed, and Lydia turned to Jane and said, "May I come live with you and Mr Bingley?" which made her eldest sister blush to the roots of her hair, and the others laugh.

"Yes, well, let us hope that day is far in the future, and that you will all be well settled afore it comes," Mr Bennet said drily.

"Why is he coming, Papa? I did not think you had ever met," Mary enquired.

"Ah! I will allow him to answer your question, through his letters. He wrote to me in October, but that was not a suitable time to accept his visit, so I put him off. But he has written again recently, and I can see no way to deny him this time. Let me read you his first." He pulled two letters from his pocket and opened one to read aloud.

Mr Collins's letter went on in an overblown and wordy way for two full pages, much of it congratulating himself on his own happy situation as parson to a great lady and inviting himself to attend his relations at Longbourn before concluding with flowery good wishes. "What do you think of that, eh, girls?" Mr Bennet asked as he folded up the letter. "He seems to be a most conscientious and polite young man, upon my word, and I doubt not will prove a valuable acquaintance, especially if Lady Catherine should be so indulgent as to let him come to us again."

Elizabeth, struck by his extraordinary deference for Lady Catherine and obsequious turns of phrase, watched as her amused father unfolded the second, thankfully briefer missive.

Dear Sir,

It having been two months since the lamentable loss of Mrs Bennet, and I as a clergyman neither requiring nor expecting much in the way of entertainment, such activities being largely forbidden to you at present, I hope that there can be no objection to receiving me for that visit which has so long been anticipated, I flatter myself to think, on both sides. That I may now condole with you and your amiable daughters upon your loss is, I think a great benefit which I am privileged to add to this reunification of our family. My patroness, the Right Honourable

Lady Catherine de Bourgh, has graciously condescended to allow me a fortnight complete for my travels, and thus I propose to wait upon you Monday, 27th January, and remain for twelve days in total.

With prayers for the lessening of your grief and the increase of your future felicity, I remain, dear sir,

your friend and cousin,

William Collins

"And so, you see," Mr Bennet concluded with some satisfaction, "we are to have a guest in less than a fortnight."

'*The increase of your future felicity?*' Elizabeth looked around the room at her sisters, like her, clad in their mourning blacks. How well this Mr Collins could condole with them was doubtful, but he might indeed provide them some entertainment—welcome or not.

Before their cousin was due, however, was the wedding of Charlotte Lucas to Mr Jones. The day before the event, Jane received a letter from Louisa Hurst which ended all hope that the Netherfield party would return in time to attend. Miss Bingley had been invited to live indefinitely with her friend Miss Symonds, which would save her the cost of her companion. Mr Bingley was in the process of securing to his sister the income from her dowry, that he might have less cause to interact with her in future, but the solicitors were very busy and the business proceeded slowly. He was also sorting out a number of bills she had run up in his name, and putting in place safeguards against a repeat of this spending.

Though Mrs Hurst related these events in a rational, even dry, manner, her frustration was not entirely hidden from the recipient, or Elizabeth, with whom Jane shared the missive. The young widow admitted that she resented Caroline for prolonging their stay in town, which Louisa was finding entirely too loud and busy in her present state of mind, and concluded by relating that her brother had particularly asked to be remembered to Miss Bennet.

As Jane penned a sympathetic reply, Elizabeth could only marvel at Miss Bingley's attitude. Elizabeth was quite sure she could run a comfortable household for herself and a companion with the interest from twenty thousand pounds, and wondered at the sense of entitlement which led to spending much more than that on one's wardrobe and entertainments alone. Shaking off such musings, she cheered herself with the thought that her dear Jane should not find herself sharing a home with such a sister.

When she dared to speak that notion to Jane, she did not receive the reproof she expected. Rather, Jane looked thoughtful for a moment and replied that while she felt sorry for Miss Bingley, so unhappy despite such resources, she had rather not be in the position of living with anyone who had demonstrated such selfishness.

"That is the most unforgiving speech," said Elizabeth, amazed, "that I ever heard you utter. Good girl! It would vex me indeed to see you continue to think well of her after what she has done—she might have started an epidemic in London, had she contracted smallpox here and not been forced to remain strictly at home, lest her situation—living alone without a better companion than the housekeeper—become known."

Jane visibly shuddered at the notion of a smallpox epidemic tearing through the teeming streets of London, and all because one desperate woman absconded to avoid the illness. "Well, I hope they may settle her business soon, and return to Netherfield. Perhaps it is not right to think in such a way while we mourn our dear mama, but I do miss their society."

Although Elizabeth smiled, she forbore from teasing Jane over the question of precisely whose society she missed, and instead replied, "As do I. Though your Mr Bingley is a friend to all, I have come to like Mrs Hurst and Mr Darcy very well, also. It is a pity that Miss Darcy and Colonel Fitzwilliam cannot be expected to return."

"I think there may be many opportunities to meet with Miss Darcy again in future," Jane offered with a small, private smile. "She is often with her brother, who is often with Mr Bingley."

"And you will be always with Mr Bingley, if there is any justice in the world," Elizabeth teased, and laughed at her sister's blush.

CHAPTER TWENTY-FOUR

THOUGH HE HAD BUSINESS OF HIS OWN IN LONDON, Darcy discovered that being away from Hertfordshire also allowed him the time and distance he required to think on his attraction to Miss Elizabeth Bennet with greater clarity. His cousin's words he could not discount; Fitzwilliam had been entirely correct in saying that Elizabeth had no expectations, and likely no hopes, of him. Attempting to prove to himself that his feelings were reciprocated, he had compared her behaviour towards him to her behaviour towards his cousin and had found very little difference, save that Fitzwilliam made her laugh more often.

But what of our private conversations, the consolation I offered her, and the commiseration and confidences we exchanged? Has she forgotten those moments when we appeared to be connected by shared feeling, or did they mean less to her than to me?

Unlike Jane Bennet, who could hardly be drawn from a conversation with Bingley to engage with the others present, Elizabeth was often the one to draw others into the rare private exchanges he managed to have with her. While he had sat in the parlour at Longbourn feeling as though his every yearning was writ upon his forehead, she and all her family had remained cheerfully oblivious. She was certainly not waiting in expectation of his addresses!

He felt more certain with every passing hour that he had fallen deeply and irrevocably in love with her. The difference in their stations he was now able to view with complete indifference; her lack of connexions was certainly not the great evil for which he had initially seen it. On the subject of her younger sisters, however, he could not yet be easy. If they were to revert to their old ways, he would be caught between protecting his own sister and his wife's natural desire to associate with her own.

And there you go again, old man, assuming that you could make her love you enough that it would be worth asking, he thought wryly.

On one point there was no question at all—his own love, and his increasingly passionate dreams of her notwithstanding, he would not marry Elizabeth Bennet if she did not love him. Some inequality in their affections he believed he could bear, especially at first, for surely the intimacies of married life would work upon a heart as warm as hers, and strengthen any love she already felt. But if she could not love him, that would be the end of it.

Fitzwilliam Darcy was not a man who embraced the vagaries of life. He preferred that his plans, once made, proceed without issue to their conclusions. This much he recognised about himself. It was not until he had been in London a fortnight, missing her more with every breath he took, that he knew he must attempt to turn her heart towards him, however difficult the endeavour proved to be, or how much his relations might disapprove should he succeed. Despite the disparities between their families, she was—in person and abilities—everything he wanted and needed, lacking nothing of real importance, only money and status. He might be the grandson of an earl, but in manners and consideration for others she was vastly his superior. What a mistress of Pemberley those qualities would make her! What a sister to Georgiana!

What a wife. If only he could win her.

There was the crux of the problem. The younger sisters had been affected greatly by their trials in the epidemic; a new maturity had settled on them. Still, they would perhaps remain an issue, albeit one that a loving couple could come to a loving resolution upon. But how did an unsociable, taciturn man, ill-qualified to recommend himself to a lively and gregarious lady, go about securing her affections? Certainly he could not do so by continuing to play the role of a friend. He would have to risk rejection and humiliation by being more open about his admiration, with no certainty of success. He would have to humble himself.

———

Mr Collins was punctual to his time, and was received with great politeness by the whole family. His air was grave and stately, and his manners very formal, though they failed him when he was introduced to Jane and Lydia; he visibly recoiled, and thus earned in an instant the enmity of the other three sisters.

Mr Bennet and his daughters said but little, for Mr Collins seemed neither in need of encouragement, nor inclined to be silent. Elizabeth wondered when the man would offer his condolences on Mrs Bennet's death, but soon realised he was not a man capable of understanding he was trespassing on a house of grief.

Elizabeth noticed quickly that, as his ridiculous letters promised, Mr Collins was not a sensible man, and the deficiency of nature had been but little assisted by education or society. He was singular in all he did and said, and every moment she was in his presence, Elizabeth was reminded of the heroic gentlemen who had helped during their troubles. Mr Jones, Captain Carter, Mr Bingley. And Mr Darcy.

The introduction of another name returned her attention abruptly to Mr Collins's praises of his patroness. "...as sister to the earl of Matlock, there are few who can boast of higher standing..."

Except, of course, for every noble in the kingdom whose title is not merely a courtesy, she thought with amusement. But then her mind seized upon the name 'Matlock', and she recalled that this was the earldom of Colonel Fitzwilliam's father, which would mean that Lady Catherine de Bourgh was aunt to the colonel...and to Mr Darcy!

Hastily, she bent her head over her stitchery, so as not to display the shock this revelation engendered. Having had the acquaintance of the lady's parson for mere hours, she had already deduced that the mistress of the vaunted Rosings Park was an officious, meddlesome tyrant with too much conceit and too little sense. To think such a person could be so closely related to Mr Darcy and his amiable cousin—it was scarcely to be credited. But perhaps the lady was not so bad; it was possible, even probable, that Mr

Collins's bumbling desire to present her as the most wise and splendid being upon whom the sun had ever shone was instead doing the lady a disservice.

Although granting the living serving her estate to Mr Collins does not speak well to her good sense... She drew this line of thought up short. If she were to break herself of the habit of relying upon first impressions, she told herself sternly, she certainly must not be so silly as to form one at such a distance! Either the lady was better than Mr Collins made her seem, or else Mr Darcy would avoid her company. Of that much, she could be certain. Perhaps he would be willing to satisfy her curiosity when he returned. She smiled to herself. Return he would; she had no further reservations on that score. Mr Darcy had supplied such reassurances himself, and she could not doubt him. There would be a little more time, at least, to know him better before Pemberley called him away.

For the present, Elizabeth had to consider the presence of another, far less welcome man. Having now a good house and a very sufficient income, Mr Collins intended to marry, and in seeking a reconciliation with the Longbourn family, she understood he meant to choose one of the daughters. Even more disheartening to Elizabeth, from the first evening, it was clear to all that she was his settled choice. His manner of wooing was both blatant and foolish, for he followed her about everywhere except the bed-chambers, spouting wordy compliments which he believed to be both subtle and charming.

Elizabeth, for her part, never allowed herself to be much separated from her sisters, and if a gap arose into which Mr Collins might fit, she sped to the side of her nearest sister and clung there like a limpet. To Mary and

Kitty, he was cordial, even avuncular; to Jane and Lydia, he rarely spoke and hardly looked. Mr Bennet was of no assistance; Elizabeth knew that he was enjoying his ridiculous cousin far too much to consider his daughters' opposing points of view. For her part, Elizabeth was pleased to see her father's grief eased by the ridiculousness of his cousin. In such a manner the first week of Mr Collins's visit passed, broken only by the occasional calls of their neighbours.

———

Charlotte managed to spirit Elizabeth away for half an hour on the eighth day—Elizabeth laughingly assured Charlotte that she was keeping count—by declaring that she had private matters to discuss with her dearest friend. To attain real privacy, they were forced to walk in the garden though the day was blustery and chill, but by walking briskly and clinging to each other's arms, they managed well enough.

"Well, Eliza, Mr Collins has taken quite a liking to you, and seems to have no notion that you are not pleased by it!" said Charlotte, when they were well clear of the house.

Elizabeth rolled her eyes in an unladylike manner. "Four more days, my dear Charlotte, only four more, and then he will be back in Kent and I shall not be sorry! He is not the first silly man who has attempted to win my good opinion, but he is surely the most persistent!"

"What will you do if he makes you an offer?"

"After knowing me for only a week, and while I am in mourning? Surely even he cannot be so silly and improper. I must simply hope to attract a gentleman I can admire in return, before his next visit," Elizabeth disclaimed with a laugh. "Enough about my woeful prospects, *Mrs Jones*! How are you finding married life?"

Charlotte blushed and smiled and declared with real cheer, "Why, I find I can honestly recommend the state to every young lady who can find herself a good man. It is above all things to be desired."

"I am happy for you. If your husband should happen to have any sensible, unattached friends to visit, do send them my way."

Charlotte promised most solemnly to do so, though her eyes shone with suppressed laughter. Did her friend truly not see that at least one sensible gentleman—wealthy, handsome, and earnest—had been visiting Longbourn with some frequency? *Oh Lizzy,* she laughed to herself.

Later that evening, relating her impressions of the ridiculous parson to her husband, she was struck with an uncomfortable thought. Seeing that something disturbed her, Mr Jones naturally enquired as to the subject of her unquiet musings.

"Oh, it is only that I had the sudden notion that, had I not come to know you and fallen so unexpectedly in love, I might have tried to secure Mr Collins myself, once Elizabeth had discarded him, simply to have a home and the hope of children. Dreadful thought!"

Her husband of a fortnight slid closer to her on the settee, eyes darkening in a manner she was coming to know very well. "But instead, all has fallen out as it should—you have a home here with me, and I am more than willing to continue trying to fulfil your *other* wish at any time convenient."

Charlotte found that very moment convenient indeed,

and all thoughts of what might have been were quickly banished.

———

Elizabeth's worries, slight as they were, about her father's expectations regarding her cousin's suit were to be relieved at dinner that evening, though not in a manner she would have chosen.

During the fish course, Mr Collins turned to her and asked, "Miss Bennet, I have been wondering if you are much involved with charity among the tenants of Longbourn? For charity is the most becoming accomplishment a young lady may possess, and to condescend to assist those of lower station—as Lady Catherine de Bourgh so often does!—is the mark of a true Christian."

Elizabeth said nothing, only took another bite of cod.

"Miss Bennet?" he said, somewhat impatiently.

She turned to him with a look of mock-surprise. "Were you addressing me, sir? But I am not Miss Bennet, that title belongs to Jane." She gestured towards her eldest sister, and watched the silly man blanch. "I am Miss Elizabeth."

Mr Collins smiled, a greasy, ingratiating stretching of the lips. "But you are the eldest marriageable sister, so I thought to honour you with the title you deserve."

Silence fell thick and heavy across the dining table. Kitty openly gaped; Mary gazed upon him as though he were a slug encountered on the garden path. Jane and Lydia looked wounded. Their father's expression was stern.

"You dare insult my sister, sir?" Elizabeth hissed, provoked beyond civility. "The kindest, sweetest lady who ever lived? Believe me when I say that I wish for no such honours!"

Mr Collins chuckled nervously, rubbing his hands together. "It is pleasing that you are so devoted to your sisters, yes...very becoming. But your manner of addressing me is not acceptable. When we are married, I will demand your respect in all things."

"I beg your pardon," Elizabeth exclaimed. "I have received no proposals from you, and I most certainly have not accepted. You presume too much!"

"But my attentions have been most marked, surely you have not failed to understand," he replied. "Naturally a formal proposal will be made. You are too sensible to refuse an honourable offer which will secure your future, and that of your sisters."

"Mr Collins," said Mr Bennet severely. "Let me be rightly understood. Jane is my eldest daughter, and shall be addressed as such. Any further failures of courtesy in this matter I shall consider a personal insult. And while it is admirable that you wish to offer my daughters a home after I am dead, I will not force any of them into a marriage which they find distasteful. To marry a daughter of mine, you must first gain her consent."

"Of course, of course," Mr Collins replied, entirely unperturbed, as if it did not occur to him that his proposals might be in any way objectionable. "In my desire to please Miss Elizabeth, I failed to consider Miss Bennet's feelings. I will not err so again, sir, now that I know your view of the matter."

Mr Bennet gazed at his cousin through narrowed eyes but said nothing further. The timely arrival of the roasted chicken gave them all an excuse to turn the subject.

CHAPTER TWENTY-FIVE

THE NEXT DAY OPENED A NEW SCENE AT LONGBOURN as Mr Collins made his declaration in form. His words conveyed more syllables than sense, more stupidity than sentiment. Elizabeth held back laughter as she listened. After a few long minutes of pontification, however, the man's very decency was called into question.

"...the fact is that being, as I am, to inherit this estate after the death of your honoured father—who, however, may live many years longer, though it is generally believed that widowers do not linger long in this realm, for the bachelor life is unnatural and unwelcome to any gentleman who has known the care and support of a helpmeet—I could not satisfy myself without choosing a wife from among his daughters, that the loss to them be as little as possible when the melancholy event takes place—"

It was absolutely necessary to interrupt him now. "My father, sir, is but five and forty and I expect he shall be with us another twenty years at least," she answered coldly. "For if he has not a wife to tend him, he has five daughters who will not allow him to decline, if he were disposed to do so."

He smiled condescendingly upon her and hardly paused to draw breath before continuing his conceited and insulting speech. On and on he droned; Elizabeth ignored him as best she could until she heard yet another insult. "...though there is, I think, reason to believe that your mother's funds would be most sensibly distributed between yourself, Miss Mary, and Miss Catherine, for it is impossible that the other two shall ever require a dowry, and I shall bring it up with your father when we are making the settlement. On the subject of fortune—"

Offended almost beyond words for Jane and Lydia, Elizabeth shot to her feet. "You are too hasty, sir! You forget that I have made you no answer. Let me do so this instant. I am sensible of the honour of your proposals—" *No honour at all, that is*, she thought, "—but it is impossible for me to do otherwise than decline them."

Elizabeth immediately and in silence withdrew from the dining room to find her father waiting outside the door. His obvious amusement did not improve her mood. She followed him back into the dining room, where Mr Collins sat with a satisfied smile. On the appearance of his quarry's father, his smile only widened, and he opened his mouth to speak.

Mr Bennet preceded him. "I understand, sir, that you have made an offer of marriage to my daughter Elizabeth, and she has refused you?"

Mr Collins nodded and began a lengthy peroration on the error of such a reply. It was the man's insistence that Elizabeth would provide him the 'right answer when next I raise the question' that saw anger overtake her father's amusement. Mr Collins was slow to notice that the gentleman he addressed bore a face like thunder, and his posture was neither agreeable nor obliging.

"I beg you will recall, sir, my statement of last evening, when I declared that I would not force any of my daughters into marriage. She has given you her answer, and you will not ask her again!"

"But...my position...the entail..." the clergyman sputtered.

"These have evidently not been enough to win my daughter's hand," Mr Bennet declared dismissively. "I am sorry for your disappointment—as is Elizabeth, I am sure—but the matter is settled."

Elizabeth and her father left Mr Collins to brood alone. Shortly after, into this uncomfortable atmosphere came Mr Bingley, Mrs Hurst, Mr Darcy and, in a welcome surprise, Miss Darcy, delivering themselves rather than a note to announce their return to Netherfield.

Elizabeth's pleasure in their unexpected arrival was nearly as great as Jane's, but it was their cousin who most openly exhibited his own joy. Mr Collins, upon hearing the name 'Darcy', scrambled to present himself, without introduction, to the gentleman and his sister, describing in the full flow of his wit and verbosity his connexion to their honoured, gracious, and condescending aunt. Mr Darcy eyed him with unrestrained wonder, and when at last Mr Collins allowed him time to speak, he replied with an air of distant civility.

"You must excuse us, sir—we have not yet greeted Mr Bennet or his daughters." He moved quickly past the clergyman, who was bowing repeatedly in a grovelling manner, Miss Darcy clinging to her brother's arm and equally eager to escape.

Mr Bingley and Mrs Hurst had made use of the spectacle to slip along the edges of the room, and were happily engaged in conversation with the ladies of the house. The Darcys fetched up before Mr Bennet, who regarded them with equal parts sympathy and amusement, and kept the civilities to a minimum that they, too, might join his daughters. He then did them all a great favour, by distracting his cousin for some minutes.

The five Bennet sisters and their four guests thereby received a full half an hour to speak amongst themselves. After the state of the roads had been canvassed, and Miss Bingley enquired after— "We are very disappointed with her. She believes she was correct to flee the area and will hear no other opinion," Bingley reported—Lydia then turned to Mrs Hurst and Miss Darcy and confided, "Lord, but we are glad you have come! Mr Collins has been with us for more than a week, and today he has been worse than usual, for he is angry that Lizzy refused him."

"Lydia!" hissed Elizabeth, Jane, and Mary in concert. Mary continued by saying, more gently, "That is Elizabeth's private business, Sister. If she wanted our friends to know it, it was for her to tell them."

Lydia had the grace to look rather abashed. "I am sorry, Lizzy, I spoke without thinking. But surely such good friends can be trusted to say nothing of this to anyone?"

Their guests were looking in wonder between the pompous clergyman and Elizabeth, obviously astounded that the odd fellow would think to win her with an acquaintance of only a few days, and in the midst of her mourning, no less.

The silence lengthened, the only sound in the room now the excited chatter of Mr Collins, and Elizabeth eventually dropped her hands from her burning face and nerved herself to look at her friends. "It is true. He made me an offer this morning, and I have refused it. It seems that his patroness, your aunt," she added with a nod to the Darcys, "has informed him that it is time he married. Knowing he had five female cousins who would depend upon his goodwill in the event of our father's demise, he concluded that the most expedient method of obeying would be to select one of us."

"And he chose...you?" Mrs Hurst asked, wide-eyed with incipient hilarity.

"Good God!" Mr Darcy exclaimed, though he kept his voice low. "If he meant to please my aunt, he has gone about it entirely wrong. Lady Catherine would not have taken to you at all, Miss Elizabeth. She greatly dislikes it when other ladies have opinions." He smiled at her, and Miss Darcy could not restrain a giggle at this assessment. Elizabeth thought, not for the first time, how very well a smile became him. He was always handsome, even at his most solemn, but when he genuinely smiled, she could hardly tear her gaze away.

Elizabeth was recovered enough to see the humour in this description of his aunt. "I am certainly well-supplied with opinions," she agreed with a laugh.

Miss Darcy leant forward confidingly. "I find Lady Catherine utterly terrifying. She is a very...*forceful* lady."

"My cousin seems to think the moon rises only to cast

its light upon her noble features," Elizabeth replied drily, and the group dissolved into laughter.

———

Mr Collins chose that moment to join them, exclaiming his pleasure that the esteemed Mr and Miss Darcy were so well-entertained in his cousin's humble abode.

Darcy, whose eagerness to see Elizabeth had been dampened by the presence of another caller, remained appalled by the man's presumption towards her. "Do you call Longbourn humble, sir?" he said in disapproving tones. "I should never term it so; it is a gentleman's residence and the heart of an estate, not a cottage."

"Oh, I meant no disrespect, sir, none at all!" the obsequious little man hastened to explain. "It is as fine a house as could be wished for a small estate, very fine indeed. No, I only meant humble by reference to your own home, Pemberley, which your gracious aunt has described to me, and to Rosings, which you shall soon call your own as well. Two such large and elegant houses! I only thought Longbourn must seem humble to you, but you are too gracious and egalitarian to take such a view, I now see."

Darcy stared at him in some confusion as he picked through that tangle of flattery and effrontery to glean his meaning in referring to Rosings. "Mr Collins," he intoned sharply. "You speak of matters you do not understand. Rosings is not to be mine. I will thank you to cease speculating upon the matter."

The clergyman's eyes widened in surprise and delight. "You mean to settle Rosings on your bride? How generous!

How remarkable! Lady Catherine will be extremely pleased to know it! I must write to her at once."

"You must write to no one!" Darcy said, his voice as thunderous as his expression.

Mr Collins shrank back in confusion. Darcy felt the shocked gaze of everyone in the parlour. He flushed but quickly gathered himself and continued, in more sedate tones, "Very well, it seems *my* private business is also to be canvassed before all today. Mr Collins, I presume you refer to my aunt's oft-spoken wish for a marriage between her daughter and myself. What you do not know is that neither my cousin Anne nor I wish for it, and so it shall not happen. My aunt can only desire it; she has no power to ensure its completion."

"But surely," the clergyman cried, "Lady Catherine's wishes, when combined with the approval of your own excellent uncle, the earl, must move you—"

"Enough!" said Darcy in exasperation. He glared at the silly fellow. "Now, let us move on to a different topic. You have mortified me quite enough, sir, by insisting upon this one."

Mr Collins sputtered inarticulately, seemingly torn between the desire to defend his patroness' wishes and horror that he had angered her nephew. Darcy risked a quick glance at Elizabeth; she was looking at him with sympathy, not the disapproval of his display of temper that he had feared to see.

"La, Mr Darcy!" exclaimed Lydia, drawing all eyes. "*I* would not marry anyone I did not like, not for Buckingham Palace itself! But since we have heard *all* about Rosings from our cousin—I daresay I could navigate the place blindfolded!—would you tell us a little of your Pemberley? Is it very like?"

He was pleased to see Elizabeth's relieved nod of encouragement. Darcy smiled, his posture visibly relaxing. "I believe my sister could describe it better than I, for as you know, Miss Lydia, I am a man of few words."

He was rewarded with laughter from all before he continued. "No, Pemberley is not like Rosings at all, except perhaps in size..."

CHAPTER TWENTY-SIX

Darcy had hoped to confer privately with Mr Bennet during that first visit after their return, but the intrusive presence of Mr Collins prevented it. He was only able to surreptitiously request a meeting as they said their farewells, to which the master of Longbourn agreed with raised eyebrows and a speculative expression. When he and Bingley called the following afternoon, Mr Bennet invited Darcy to join him in his study. The lack of interest the second-eldest Bennet daughter took in the summons reminded him yet again of how far he had to go to win her.

Though Mr Darcy had requested the meeting, Mr Bennet spoke first. "I had a letter from my brother Gardiner recently, in which he mentioned that you called upon him at his offices while you were in town. I recall him extending the invitation while they were here for Christmas, but I am pleasantly surprised that you took him up on it, sir. I do not imagine you find yourself often in Cheapside." He fixed the younger man with an enquiring gaze.

Darcy shifted uncomfortably, reminded of the conceit

he had only recently vowed to correct, and which he had so openly displayed prior to the epidemic. "I came to like and respect Mr Gardiner during our brief acquaintance here, and when my business allowed, I was happy to take him up on his offer to sample some new varieties of coffee which he hopes to introduce to the London market, and of course to continue the acquaintance. It was also an opportunity to speak with him about the matter I wished to canvass with you today."

Mr Bennet grinned. "And on that less than subtle hint, I shall do as expected and ask: What is it that you wished to discuss with me, sir?"

A bit disconcerted by the gentleman's sportive manner, it took Darcy a moment to gather his thoughts. "I should open by saying that I have discussed this with Bingley as well, but no one else hereabouts. I feel you are best positioned to advise me on how to accomplish this without unnecessary fuss." At his host's look of interest, he continued, briefly describing his plan and the steps he had taken to discover whether it would be possible and how it might best be done.

Darcy produced a paper from his coat, setting it before Mr Bennet. "And here I have a list of what is required."

———

Mr Bennet read over the information and asked several questions before agreeing to lend his assistance. Tucking the page into his drawer, he sat back and smiled. "Now that we have dispensed with your business, tell me, what are your intentions towards my Lizzy?"

He laughed as the young man spluttered. "Come now,

I see how often, and *how*, you look at her. If it is merely admiration of a pretty woman, I will not castigate you, but if you have hopes of my daughter I should like to know."

Mr Darcy looked at him gravely. "Just yesterday, your daughter refused one eligible man's offer. And now you ask me if I wish to put forward similar hopes?"

"I do not think you or Lizzy would compare you to Mr Collins," he replied with open amusement.

"If she should, I would hope to be judged favourably against such a man," Mr Darcy replied with a grimace. He looked thoughtful for a moment before saying quietly, "I...I do have hopes. Honourable hopes. But I do not believe she has the same hopes of me."

"No," Mr Bennet agreed. "I fancy she does not. You mis-stepped rather badly with her upon your first meeting, but after all you and the other men have done for us and all the families of the neighbourhood, I have no doubt she considers you a friend now. Still, my Lizzy is a sensible girl, and we all know that men of your sphere rarely look to ladies of ours for any noble purpose."

Mr Darcy's face reddened. "I have recently come to understand that my behaviour in the early weeks of my stay in Hertfordshire was not well-mannered." He stood and began to pace. "Since that time, I have learnt she cares nothing at all for my wealth and connexions, and have improved in my manners. Your daughter granted me her friendship only after I proved myself to be of good charac-ter. I can only hope to improve further, until I am worthy of her heart, as well."

To say that Mr Bennet was shocked by this speech would dreadfully understate the case. He had suspected a preference for his dear Lizzy on this young man's part, and had entertained himself with the notion that he might, perhaps, even propose, without ever supposing it to be at all likely. But to hear this outpouring of self-castigation, to witness the evidence of changes wrought so unconsciously by his own darling daughter upon this great man, why, it was entirely extraordinary.

In the end, he stood and offered the younger man his hand. "There is no man in the world truly worthy of my Lizzy, sir, but if you are able to win her, I expect I might enjoy calling you 'son'."

Mr Darcy accepted the offered hand and replied, "Thank you, sir. I would be honoured to be addressed so."

"Well, well," said Mr Bennet, somewhat abashed. "Go on now and join my Lizzy in the parlour. I shall be along presently." With a bow, the young gentleman exited, and Bennet was left to contemplate the possibility of his dear girl removing to Derbyshire.

———

Upon entering the parlour, Darcy was immediately accosted by Mr Collins, who in the intervening days had concocted several new but no more rational reasons why Lady Catherine should be allowed to determine Darcy's marital fate. He bore it with all the patience he could muster, for he did not wish to reinforce early opinions on the subject of his manners by being overtly rude to any member of Elizabeth's family, though the ridiculous parson was making it very difficult indeed. He was the recipient of a great many sympathetic glances from the others in the company, but none felt themselves equal to rescuing him until his sister stood, with a resolute expression, and crossed the room to take her place at his side.

In hopes of an ally, Mr Collins immediately turned to her and exclaimed, "Miss Darcy! I cannot imagine that you would be in disagreement with your most estimable and perspicacious aunt on the desirability of a union between Pemberley and Rosings."

Darcy glared at the man and then looked at his sister worriedly as surprise, combined with her natural diffidence, seemed to render her incapable of speech. Then she rallied, and taking a deep breath replied, "I am of the opinion, sir, that it is better to unite people than houses. I would wish above all things for my brother to be happy in marriage, and neither Cousin Anne nor Rosings would make him so."

"Oh, bravo, Miss Darcy!" Bingley cried as the parson sputtered. "You have said it perfectly—'better to unite people than houses'! I shall have to remember that."

As the Bennet ladies murmured their agreement, Mr Collins regained his breath and again addressed Georgiana. "But Miss Darcy, surely—"

"Enough," Darcy interjected firmly. "I have allowed you to importune me on this distasteful subject, but I will not permit you to subject my sister to a similar inquisition. Console my aunt as best you can, Mr Collins, but I will not be moved, nor will I further discuss the matter with anyone so wholly unrelated to me."

He took his sister's arm and led her back to her friends, seating himself next to her and leaving the clergyman standing stupidly near the door.

"How much longer does he stay?" he whispered to the Bennet ladies, sending Lydia into a fit of giggles and causing the others and his sister to hide their smiles behind their hands.

"Two days," Elizabeth whispered back. "Two excruciating days. We shall not blame you if you do not call again until he is gone."

Darcy shook his head. "I think I might find within myself the fortitude to bear his company for so short a time, under such an inducement as the other company to be found here."

"I do not suppose you could lend some of that fortitude to me?" Elizabeth replied, her expression droll.

"Cousin Elizabeth," Mr Collins said sternly, approaching the group, "whispering is not genteel."

"Neither is badgering a guest about a personal matter which affects you not at all," Elizabeth replied tartly. When her youngest sisters could not restrain their laughter, Darcy saw Mr Collins grow red with affront.

"I begin to feel that I have had a fortunate escape in your irrational refusal of my most eligible offers," he declared in a tone of great offence.

"Lizzy felt she had a fortunate escape the moment she said 'no'," Miss Lydia commented.

Mr Collins turned positively purple. He leant over the back of the settee, forcing Miss Bennet and Bingley to press themselves against the arms to avoid contact, and shook his finger in Miss Lydia's face. "Listen here, you little monstrosity—"

"Mr Collins!" roared Mr Bennet from the doorway. Every head whipped around to face him. He stepped into the room.

"I have warned you before about showing my daughters the proper respect. You are no longer welcome in my home. Pack your things, and I shall have you conveyed to the post station. Our association is at an end."

Mr Collins looked about the room, and all of its occupants looked back in undisguised disgust. He ostentatiously straightened his jacket and looked down his nose at the daughters of the house. "When I inherit Longbourn, you may expect from me no more civility and consideration than you have displayed today."

Bingley jumped to his feet and proclaimed, "They will not require it! It would be my honour to care for all the family when Mr Bennet dies—may he live to be a hundred!"

Darcy silently rose and stood by his friend. Faced with the wrath of two healthy young gentlemen, all Mr Collins could do was sniff disdainfully and make as dignified an exit as his odd, scuttling gait allowed.

Mr Hill was dispatched to ensure that Mr Collins packed speedily and took nothing from the house. The others settled back into their seats only to find Miss Lydia weeping silently in Mary's embrace.

The gentlemen, though sympathetic, were uncomfortable with such a display of emotion, and almost unconsciously gathered at the far end of the room to speak among themselves while the ladies worked to soothe her. Bingley offered the use of his carriage to transport Mr Collins to the post station, that Mr Bennet need not order his own, and was accepted. Minutes later, Mr Hill came down the stairs laden with Mr Collins's trunk, that gentleman following behind with a face like curdled milk. He glared into the parlour as he passed, muttering under his breath, and was gone.

The loan of Bingley's carriage necessitated that the

visitors remain at Longbourn well past the time when they ought properly to have left, and Darcy hoped to make good use of the additional time by flattering Elizabeth as a suitor ought.

He was rather stymied by the conventions of mourning; Elizabeth's black dresses and simple hairstyles did not lessen her beauty but offered little fodder for compliments. A discussion of the American protests against the naval blockade of France, however, offered him several chances to praise her knowledge and insight, and he left Longbourn with the satisfaction that she had seemed quite pleased by his efforts.

———

"Do you suppose, Lizzy," Jane wondered as she brushed her hair out that night, "that Mr Collins's interest in you spurred Mr Darcy to make his own more plain?"

Elizabeth stared at her sister, hands frozen halfway through plaiting her own unruly locks. "Mr Darcy is not courting me, Jane," she replied after a moment, continuing her work.

"Is he not? I am not so certain as you seem to be."

"We are friends. Very good friends, I dare say. But he is the grandson of an earl, and I am no one at all. Nothing more than friendship is possible."

"I do not see why not. Does he not have enough status, enough income, of his own? What would he do with more of either? But he is a very clever man, and since he obviously does not object to conversing and even debating with a woman, I think it likely he would wish for a clever wife.

Not to mention that you are now the beauty of Longbourn."

"Oh, no, that is Kitty," Elizabeth murmured, wondering how her sister could speak so easily of the loss of her appearance so soon.

"Elizabeth Joan Bennet," Jane said sternly. "Not all beauty is blonde. Our father is very handsome, and you are his image cast in a feminine mould. Sir William Lucas himself has proclaimed you one of the jewels of the county, and as you know, he has been to the Court of St James's," she added teasingly.

Elizabeth chuckled. "I suppose I must concede that I possess some modest attractions, in that case. But I do not believe that Mr Darcy has any intentions towards me beyond friendship."

Jane eyed her speculatively. "I suppose time will tell which of us is correct."

Elizabeth lay wakeful for a time after they blew out the candle, turning the conversation over in her head. Could he admire her in that way? Mr Darcy was a handsome man, a worldly man; he was a man of great wealth and high station, used to the best of everything. Surely he would expect more than a quick wit and pert opinions in the companion of his future life, even if he were willing to overlook matters of fortune? Had Jane truly seen something she herself had missed?

She knew she was not *entirely* without attractions; she had received enough unprompted attention from gentlemen since her entrance into local society to be certain of that, at least. And yet, she had never considered herself much out of the common way, having been told all her life that three of her four sisters were her superiors in beauty. Had her mother been wrong? Elizabeth had always assumed Mrs Bennet knew whereof she spoke on that account, at least—she had been, and remained until her death, the most beautiful lady of her generation in the area.

No, it was much more likely that Jane, flush with the romance of her own situation, was projecting her hopes for Elizabeth's future onto the nearest available gentleman. That she should think Elizabeth worthy of such a man's admiration was flattering, to be sure. To imagine being held in such regard by a man she knew to be among the best of his sex was alluring, but it would be foolish to assume it was so just because she and Jane both would like it to be.

Although...he had been closeted with her father for some time that afternoon. As soon as the thought came, she shook her head and silently laughed at herself. It could have had nothing to do with her! Even if Jane were correct, as unlikely as that seemed, nothing had passed between them that would require such a conference. More likely he had, while in town, chanced upon some piece of news or opportunity for investment he thought would be of interest to Mr Bennet. Satisfied with the logic of her own conclusions, she finally found her rest.

———

The Miss Bennets visited Netherfield two days later, and then a succession of rain kept the parties separate for almost a week. Darcy prowled Netherfield like a caged lion throughout, and Bingley was hardly more sanguine, though he at least had the freedom to complain openly of being separated from *his* Miss Bennet. Mrs Hurst clearly found them both amusing. At last, they woke to a dry morning, but the roads were in dreadful condition. The following day the sun came out, and by the late afternoon Darcy judged that a trip to Longbourn would be possible on the morrow. They had only just assembled in the drawing room before dinner when the butler entered.

"An express has arrived for Mr Darcy. The rider will await a reply."

Darcy felt Georgiana look at him in concern, which shifted to real worry when they glimpsed the handwriting on the letter. "I fear Mr Collins has been in our aunt's ear, Brother," she said.

"I have no doubt of it," he replied.

"Have dinner held another quarter hour," Bingley addressed the butler. "It may perhaps be longer, if Darcy must reply immediately."

Darcy nodded his thanks to his friend and broke the seal. What he read therein exposed even greater foolishness than he had expected, and he felt his eyebrows climbing higher with each line. From the corner of his eye, he saw his sister's hands begin to twist about each other in anxiety. As he reached the closing words, he shook his head and sighed, crossing the room to close the door. Everyone within knew of his aunt's wishes, but he did not care to voice her absurdity for the servants' ears.

"My aunt, it seems, hearing from Mr Collins that I denied any engagement to my cousin Anne, set off into the present inclement weather to confront me on the matter. Having been trapped at an inn not worthy of her custom for several days, she has now settled for writing to me to make her opinion known, and will visit her brother instead. I expect, though she does not say it, that she will regale my uncle with her complaints."

It was clear that Bingley and his sister felt a natural relief at not having been required to accommodate such a querulous uninvited guest, and that Georgiana was happy her most difficult relation's plans had been thwarted. He smiled wryly at them and said, "Dinner need not be held back further. It will not take me long to reply."

He moved to the escritoire and dashed off a few brief lines to the effect that no, Mr Collins had not been mistaken in what he reported. He had never intended to marry Anne and thought he had been quite clear on that point when he had visited in the spring. If his aunt had chosen not to hear *then* and was thereby inconvenienced *now*, he did not hold himself at all to blame for it. He was pressing his seal into the wax when the butler was admitted to enquire whether the party were ready to dine.

CHAPTER TWENTY-SEVEN

THE FOLLOWING DAY, HAVING DEALT WITH SEVERAL urgent letters of business which had been delayed by the storm, Darcy turned his horse towards Longbourn. There he found all five Miss Bennets about to set out to Meryton, ostensibly to purchase tea but in truth to enjoy the relatively fine weather and celebrate Miss Lydia's return to sufficient health for such an excursion. He was promptly invited to join them and accepted with alacrity. The smile Elizabeth gave him as she took his offered arm made his heart stutter. He had not always read her aright, but she was happy to see him today—of this, he was ecstatically certain!

As her other sisters hovered over Miss Lydia, she leant in and murmured, "You do not look as though you have had a good morning. When Mr Bingley called earlier, he mentioned that you had received an urgent letter from your aunt. He was too polite to say anything further, but I had the impression that rather than bearing some terrible news, it was merely an unpleasant communication."

He smiled ruefully. "It was not pleasant. She heard from Mr Collins that I do not wish to marry my cousin and, affecting great surprise, launched herself into the recent inclement weather to confront me. Being trapped at a substandard inn for several days en route did not sweeten her temper, and her heightened anger was clear in every word of her missive. I should feel fortunate that but for the muddy roads, she would have enacted a most mortifying scene at Netherfield."

When an expression of horror and sympathy crossed Elizabeth's countenance, Darcy was quick to say, "I do not understand her. I almost feel it is a kind of madness which possesses her when she is opposed."

"It has been my observation that very selfish people are truly unable to recognise that others may have wishes and opinions which differ from their own. Forgive me for alluding to your aunt in such terms, but I can think of no other explanation for such behaviour as you describe."

"It may very well be so. It is certainly preferable to think of her as selfish than as mad," he added wryly. "Though no explanation makes her a whit easier to manage."

She laughed lightly. "Do not be downcast, sir. We all have relations for whom we must blush. There is no family which may account itself perfect, much as we might wish it to be otherwise."

He was struck by the recollection that he had once scorned her for her silly relations, without recognising that his spiteful, interfering aunt was worse. "You are correct, Miss Elizabeth. I have been used to excuse her for things I would not tolerate in others, simply because she is my relation, without extending that forbearance outside my family circle. I think I must learn to be more tolerant of folly, at least where intentions are good."

"It is infinitely more pleasant to be amused by such things," she agreed. "There is enough in this world truly worthy of vexation and censure, that to laugh at what is merely silly is wise."

"My temper, I believe, is too little yielding. I do not forget the follies and vices of others as soon as I ought. It is a fault I have only just begun to correct."

She smiled up at him, making his breath catch. "We cannot correct our faults until we recognise them, so you have made a beginning. When I encounter something which angers me, I ask myself—is there anything in this I may take amusement from? If there is not, then it is truly worth my anger. And if there is, I soon laugh myself into a better mood."

He took a chance and attempted to tease her. "I shall try your technique, and see if it works for me. Have you any faults about which I might advise you in return?"

She laughed. "I have faults enough! In fact, it was you who, in a roundabout way, brought one to my attention only recently."

"Indeed!" he said in tones of surprise. "I cannot imagine what that might be."

"It is simply this—I have placed far too much weight on first impressions. My first impression of you was, as you know, rather bad, and because of it I was quite determined to dislike you forever, until you went about being so very gentlemanly and kind that I could not!" She laughed again. "You, who have so many dependent upon your welfare, largesse, and good opinion—your sister, all those who work at Pemberley or live on the estate as tenants—sacrificed your time and energy to tend to us and our neighbours in our time of greatest need. How could I dislike you? How could I not respect you?"

Darcy breathed in sharply, shocked and gladdened by the emotion in her words. As if she realised she had said too much, Elizabeth shook her head quickly and continued in a milder tone.

"Understanding how wrong I had been about your character led me to remember other, smaller instances in which my first impressions had been in error but I resisted changing my opinions—out of sheer obstinacy, I suppose."

"You were not entirely wrong about me, Miss Elizabeth. My behaviour was very bad; I can hardly think of it without abhorrence. It is, I think, natural to believe that behaviour always reflects character, for very often it does. My actions, when first we met, displayed my faults more than my virtues, and I do not blame you for thinking badly of me. I am only glad that you no longer find me quite so disagreeable," he concluded with one of his rare smiles.

"I can say with perfect honesty that I now find you entirely agreeable," she replied cheerfully, and with that he was vastly contented.

———

Elizabeth now found that her curiosity about her cousin's patroness was entirely satisfied. Her second-hand impression of the lady, drawn from Mr Collins's voluminous monologues on her every word and deed, had not been inaccurate, though it had been incomplete. The lady she had imagined was too dignified to launch herself into a storm for the purpose of enforcing her own will upon a man not easily swayed. Grand she might be, but in refinement Lady Catherine de Bourgh appeared to be greatly lacking. And deficient in sense as well, she mused. How could the lady believe that simply insisting upon her own way—and refusing to see what she did not like—would persuade a man such as Mr Darcy to oblige her?

As for her own behaviour towards the gentleman that day, she felt a little embarrassed. She had confided too much, she felt, though he had kindly repaid confession for confession. At least he did not seem to think less of her for the faults she had admitted, and she certainly could not think poorly of him for his.

An unyielding temper, he had said. Yes, she could see that in him. It was, she supposed, a rather natural outgrowth of having the prosperity and happiness of so many necessarily attached to his actions and decisions. He could not afford to be too conciliatory in his business, or too forgiving of any who abused his trust. But such firmness could easily be carried too far in cases of less moment, such as the acquisition and evaluation of new acquaintances. She was glad he understood this, and felt this self-knowledge would serve him well in the future.

They had both, she considered, improved in both civility and wisdom since their first meeting. It had been necessary for them to do so, to be such amiable confederates now. To change oneself was a painful thing, but she was finding the results most pleasing, and thought he would likely agree.

Recalling Jane's suspicion that he felt deeply for her and might be prepared to act upon it, Elizabeth found herself wishing, rather wistfully, that it could be so. Having got past their early difficulties, they now seemed to quite effortlessly bring out the best in each other. Were the gulf in their stations not quite so great, she felt she might be in some danger of joining her sister in imagining too much in their friendship.

———

Captain Carter became a regular caller at Longbourn when the new recruits were trained up a bit, appearing as much as twice a week, as his duties allowed. Lydia was very shy with him at first, for she had often flirted with him before her illness and dreaded to see any hint of disgust from one with whom she had once so blithely flirted, though with hindsight she understood that he had never encouraged her as some of his compatriots had done.

He persisted in greeting her as an old friend, and treating her likewise, and it was not very long before she was comfortable in his presence once again. His easy manners and sensible conversation made him a great favourite of the entire family, and often he would escort the ladies on a walk if the weather was fine, allowing Mr Bennet some time alone with his beloved books.

One sunny day as February drew to a close, while they ambled along the lane at a pace calculated to preserve Lydia's strength, he asked how her stitchery was coming along.

"It goes very much better if I close my bad eye, though I am sure I appear very silly," Lydia replied with a laugh. "But I am learning not to care how I look, just as I am learning how to stitch again. I am improved enough to get some enjoyment from it once more, and Mary always reminds me that is the most important thing. That, and *character*," she drawled with a look at her sister that bespoke some private joke.

Mary laughed. "Lydia likes to tease me for so often reminding her that youth and beauty are ephemeral, but a good character cannot be stolen by time or illness."

"She does this, of course," added Lydia frankly, "because my beauty was lost rather sooner than expected, and she wishes that I love myself for those qualities I yet possess."

"I hope you have taken her advice to heart, Miss Lydia," said he. "As well as your good character, your cheerful temper will always recommend you to those with the wit to see your value."

Mary cast him a grateful look, to which he responded with a smile that made her blush. For her own part, the youngest Bennet smiled and agreed, "I *do* have a cheerful temper, do I not?"

———

A few days later, it became acceptable for the Bennet girls to put off their blacks and don the lighter colours of half-mourning. There had been some discussion among them about it, for none of them wished to be disrespectful to the memory of their mother by being too eager, but neither were any of them were very fond of wearing black all day, every day. In the end they agreed they should wear their blacks to church on Sundays for a few weeks longer, that solemn day being most suited to the additional remembrance.

One sunny morning, therefore, Mr Bennet was greeted by the sight of his daughters trooping down the stairs in some of the lavender and grey dresses, trimmed heavily in black, upon which they had so diligently stitched for much of the last month. He would wear his own blacks for a six-month complete, and an armband until a year had passed.

To be so garbed cheered them, and the bright yellow daffodils which Kitty had stitched onto the length of wide lavender ribbon that now cinched the waist of Lydia's grey dress were much admired by everyone in the family.

That afternoon, true to Mr Bennet's early prediction, Mr Bingley—who, he could only presume, had received some prior intelligence of his daughter's plans—arrived alone at Longbourn and requested the honour of a private audience with Jane. With bright eyes and muffled giggles, the other sisters hurried from the parlour, and Mr Bennet paused only to wordlessly shake the young man's hand before retreating to his study to await his own interview.

———

Hardly had the book-room door closed behind him before Elizabeth, Kitty, Mary, and Lydia regained the parlour. Jane could have no reserves from her dear sisters, instantly embracing them all as best she could. Their congratulations were given with a sincerity, a warmth, a delight, which words could but poorly express, and Jane acknowledged with the liveliest emotion that she was the happiest creature in the world.

"'Tis too much!" she added, "by far too much. I do not deserve it. Oh! Why is not everybody as happy?"

"No one else deserves it as you do," cried Elizabeth, relishing the joy and laughter filling Longbourn.

Jane would not be allowed to stay only with her sisters,

for Mr Bingley's interview with Mr Bennet was short and to the purpose, and the younger gentleman had not been teased *very* much by the elder, so they soon joined the ladies.

Mr Bingley was invited to stay for dinner, and after sending a note to Netherfield considered himself quite fixed at Longbourn for the rest of the day. If Elizabeth wished Mr Darcy might join them, she did not express it aloud, for it was an occasion of no common delight to them all. Jane's happiness gratified all who loved her, while Mr Bingley's addition to the family could not fail to please. Still, the company of his friend—*her friend*—in smiles and laughter would have been a more than welcome sight.

Mr Bingley remained with them until the moon was high in the sky, taking his leave with regret and every promise of calling again on the morrow. As they entered the room they had shared from childhood, Jane turned to her and said, "Oh, Lizzy, if only Mama could have been here. How happy she would have been! Is it wrong to be so happy myself, so soon after her death?"

"If it were, surely society would decree that you might not receive a proposal in half-mourning, either. There is no cause for guilt. This is exactly what Mama wanted! You must know that if she could speak with you now, she would tell you that on no account should you let anything interfere with Mr Bingley's felicity!" She paused. "And your own, of course."

Jane laughed. "You are right. I do believe that is exactly how she would advise me."

———

Immediately upon his return to Netherfield, Bingley conveyed the news of his success to his sister and Darcy, who greeted it with pleasure but little surprise. Both listened indulgently as he extolled the virtues of his betrothed and delight in both her and the relations he stood to gain by their union.

When Mrs Hurst retired and they were left to themselves, Darcy turned to his old friend and said, "Bingley, I most sincerely congratulate you. I have no doubt that you and Miss Bennet shall be very happy together."

"Would that I could see you so happy! If we could but find such a lady for you!" Bingley exclaimed, clearly having lost not one whit of excitement in the many hours following his proposal.

Darcy smiled slightly. "I have not entirely lost hope that I may find similar happiness."

"My younger sister, I am sure, remains ready to save you from a life of loneliness," Bingley replied with a smirk.

"Forgive me, my friend, but I would rather remain a bachelor."

Bingley chuckled. "I would have been concerned had you made any other reply. Your forbearance with her for my sake all these years has not gone unnoticed, or unappreciated." He sipped again at his brandy, his expression becoming reflective. "As disappointed as I am with Caroline, I must say that I cannot repine that my bride will not be required to endure her. I think she would not have easily ceded her place as mistress of my home."

"Miss Bennet's obliging nature might have made it difficult for her to establish herself, if there were such conflict," Darcy answered carefully, not wishing to openly deprecate Miss Bingley again so soon after his impolitic jest, though he could not disagree with his friend's conjecture.

"True," said Bingley, then shook his head slightly and grinned. "But why am I allowing thoughts of what might have been to intrude upon this happy day? I shall not! Allow me, if you will, old friend, to relate to you an idea I have had for our wedding trip."

At Darcy's encouraging nod, Bingley launched into an excited narrative full of exclamations and broad gestures. The discussion of this plan and the attendant practicalities occupied them both late into the night, providing Darcy with a welcome distraction from the increasingly urgent need to secure another Bennet sister for himself.

CHAPTER TWENTY-EIGHT

"MY DEAR CAROLINE, WHATEVER IS THE MATTER?"

Caroline Bingley slowly folded the letter and raised her gaze to her friend's, uncomfortably aware that the news she would soon relay would be a disappointment. Miss Symonds—Josephine—was more plain than pretty and her dowry was a modest three thousand pounds, but her father was a baronet and she was distantly connected to the Earl of Moyne. She was also rather enamoured of Charles Bingley, which had given Caroline every hope of securing a match in that quarter when the Darcys had slipped from her grasp. She reminded herself that she surely would have lost Mr Darcy had she caught the smallpox, too, and thanks to her quick action in avoiding that fate she would still be able to secure someone worthy.

"Oh, Josie, it is the worst possible news," she lamented. "My brother has inexplicably offered for Miss Bennet!"

The young lady gasped. "The one who brought smallpox into your brother's home?"

"The very same. I was certain he was safe from her, for

she is surely quite scarred now. I could hardly bear to look upon my own sister for a year or more after her illness! I can only presume she convinced him that he had engaged his honour with her before she fell ill. Oh, my dear friend, whatever shall I do? Bad enough to see my brother joined to a woman without fortune or connexions, but she is disfigured as well! We shall be the laughingstocks of London!"

"Do you suppose that Miss Eliza of whom you have spoken played a part in this, to bring her family closer to Mr Darcy?"

"I am quite sure of it," Caroline declared. "And I shall be very sorry for him and all his family if she captures him."

Josie sipped her tea. "It is too bad that he is so attached to the countryside. If only he were a little fonder of town, you would have been the perfect wife for him."

This was the excuse Caroline had given for dropping her ambitions in his direction. She claimed that having seen him at her brother's leased estate, she had realised that he was not merely greatly attached to Pemberley, but to country life in general, and they could not be compatible. In truth, she knew that her flight from Netherfield had lowered her irretrievably in his opinion, but every time she beheld her own smooth, unblemished skin, she knew the sacrifice had been worth it.

"It is true. However, I am determined to marry a man who wishes to attend the full Season every year, and the little Season more often than not, and so Mr Darcy is not for me," she replied with seeming unconcern. "But how I am to find such a man with my brother so poorly married, I know not!"

"He is not married yet," her friend murmured. "And having been gulled into offering for such a creature, he is likely searching for a way out of this obligation. We might help him along."

Caroline's full attention was now focused upon her friend. "How might we do that?"

"Why, nothing could be easier, dear Caroline. We need only tell my mother about these Bennets, what they have done to your poor brother, and are attempting to do to Mr Darcy."

Lady Symonds was a gossip of the first order, and her husband, Sir Everard Symonds, was hardly better. Caroline's smile grew so wide it almost hurt. "And then when he is free, we shall act quickly to see him safely into a good marriage with a good woman, and I know just who will suit him," she said significantly.

Josephine's smile matched her own, and they bent their heads together to determine exactly what should be said to Lady Symonds.

———

One bright morning, Mary had just stepped out of the parsonage, trying to find a comfortable way to carry the large basket of mending the vicar's wife had given her, when she was surprised to find a soldier bowing to her. He straightened, and she smiled, trying to ignore the fluttering in her breast when he did likewise.

"Captain Carter, how do you do?"

"Quite well, Miss Mary, and yourself?"

"I find the sunshine has put me in a most excellent

mood. Is the advent of spring not lovely?" she answered shyly.

"It is indeed. One cannot help but be in good spirits on so fine a day." He gestured to her basket. "May I assist you with that?"

"I am going back to Longbourn, but I thank you."

"I am quite at liberty, and always happy to call at Longbourn. Please allow me to carry it for you," he countered with a smile.

She blushed and handed the basket to him, and he offered his other arm to her. "I am sure my sisters will be glad to see you again," she said as they turned their steps towards the lane to Longbourn. "Are you still very busy with the new recruits?"

"I am, but my Colonel is pleased enough with their progress to give me a day of liberty. I was just strolling the high street looking for a friend when you appeared."

Disappointment lanced through her, but she said what she knew she ought. "Who were you looking for, sir? I should not wish to keep you from your appointment."

He laughed. "I was not looking for a particular friend, but any friend at all, and you are the one I found. Now, may I know what is in this rather enormous basket, or is it a great secret?"

"Oh!" She blushed anew at his teasing. "It is no secret at all, but a great lot of clothing that has been donated for the poor and is in need of mending before it may be handed out. Mrs Edwards has many demands on her time, and we—I include her husband in this—expect that the next few months will go very hard for some in the area. Many have been lost, and much work went undone. This is something I can do at home and still be of use."

"I think there are very few young ladies who would willingly take on so much," he commented, hefting the basket, "for those less fortunate, even when confined by mourning. I applaud you."

"It is nothing," she demurred, and he changed the subject.

"I have heard that Mr Bingley is to be your brother."

She smiled broadly. "It is true. He and Jane are very happy, and they are so well-suited I cannot imagine that will ever change."

They spoke for a few moments about the engagement, before moving on to other topics. When they entered Longbourn the captain was greeted warmly by all the family gathered there. He spent some time in conversation with Mr Bennet, who could fairly be said to relish any opportunity for masculine companionship, and then spent a pleasant while with the ladies. He took his leave with every promise of returning when his duties allowed.

———

As March advanced, the fields and hedgerows came alive with blooms. Elizabeth returned from her morning ramble one fine, sunny day and over breakfast addressed all of her sisters. "If you will dress for a walk, Mary and I are going to take us all somewhere." Neither Elizabeth nor Mary would say any more, so they all donned their walking shoes and gamely followed along as Elizabeth led them down one of her favourite paths.

They passed the boundaries of Longbourn and ventured into the woods, and thence into a meadow festooned with all the flowers of the early spring. Mary said to Lydia, "When you were ill, you said you wanted to come picking flowers in the spring with all your sisters. Lizzy knew where they grew first and best, and agreed to tell me when it would be worth the trip."

Tears of happiness running down her cheeks, Lydia dashed off into the meadow like a little girl, seeking the prettiest blooms, and her sisters came laughing behind her. They returned to Longbourn windblown and smiling, clutching great posies with which they festooned the parlour. They all wore crowns of bluebell and cowslip, and did not remove them even when the Netherfield party called.

Elizabeth playfully set her own crown of flowers upon Miss Darcy's head, and the young lady hardly knew whether to laugh or blush. She soon decided on the former, as all her friends were similarly topped.

"What do you think, sir, will Miss Darcy set a new fashion in town?" she asked her friend's brother.

"Hm?" He startled, having lapsed into thoughts of his own. "Oh, certainly."

Elizabeth's eyebrows rose, and she was fairly sure he had no notion of what he had just agreed with. She turned back to Miss Darcy, ready to make sport of the gentleman for a little while before relieving his confusion, only to find that his sister was giving him a fretful look, and he had already ceased to pay any attention to either of them. She soon had the young lady in gales of laughter, suggesting places where she might wear her flowers: Bond Street, St. James's Court, perhaps Almack's?

Soon Kitty had engaged Miss Darcy to tell her of the delights of town, and Elizabeth was able to attract Mr Darcy's attention simply by sitting silently next to him and looking at him expectantly until he took notice. This he did, stammering an apology for failing to attend, which she dismissed with a smile. Pitching her voice low and soft, she said, "Sir, something is troubling you. Will you not tell me what it is?"

He smiled slightly. "I thought I had concealed my worries."

"You have not fooled me, nor your sister. She has been casting concerned looks at you since you arrived."

He looked startled. "The last thing I wished was to worry Georgiana." He paused. "Will you come walking with me? I will tell you, but I cannot risk it being overheard."

"Of course," she replied easily, and announced to the room that she was in need of another turn in the fresh air. Darcy volunteered to escort her, and as no one else wished to walk again so soon, it was all arranged quite easily. Mere minutes found them strolling arm-in-arm about the garden, where only a handful of daffodils and the early leaves and shoots provided any colour to break the monotony of browns and greys.

———

He watched Elizabeth turn her face to the sun and smile. She was always beautiful to him, but never more so than when surrounded by nature, even that of a denuded garden. She had taken his breath away when he had entered the parlour earlier, with her flushed cheeks and flowers in her hair. And then she had put those flowers on his sister and induced Georgiana to laugh. If only he were not so very worried; he regretted that he had not been able to better enjoy the visit.

"I believe you recall that little more than a fortnight ago I received a letter from my aunt, Lady Catherine de Bourgh, in which she berated me for refusing to follow her plans to marry me to my cousin, her daughter."

"I do," Elizabeth answered. "Has she written again?"

"No, the letter I received last night was from my uncle, with whom she stayed for some days before returning to Kent. It seems a maid in his house overheard her speaking to my cousin Anne, and word eventually reached the butler, who informed my uncle. If the girl is to be believed, my aunt was considering sending an announcement of the engagement, which has never been formed outside of her own mind, to the papers."

Elizabeth gasped.

He slanted a grim look her way. "You are too clever to miss the implications. If she succeeds, if even one paper were to print it, she could use it as evidence in a breach of promise suit. She would not succeed; even if she were to have marriage articles forged, I am confident I could prove them false, but the mere existence of such a suit could damage my reputation, and the Darcy name, for years."

"And she thinks to use your care for your name to force your compliance," Elizabeth said.

"Just so."

"And what have you done to counter her? I do not think you would be here now if you had not already acted."

This raised a faint smile in him. "Indeed, I sent an express to my man of business in London first thing, instructing him to contact every paper in town, Kent, and Derbyshire with instructions that printing any announcement involving me, which does not come directly from him or myself, would be a potentially costly mistake. He will also monitor the papers and if her announcement is printed, immediately issue a denial. I only hope we are not too late, or that she has since decided against this course. But I wonder if I should go to town, in case the worst occurs."

"Do you trust your man to carry out your wishes fully and well?"

He was silent for a moment. "I do. Mr Coulter was my father's man for some years, and I have never had reason to question his competence or his loyalty. Yet I believe my aunt would be most likely to strike through the London papers, and would it not be better if I were on hand in that event?"

"You are but half a day's travel away, and it is far from certain that your presence will be required at all. Why sit alone in your house in town, fretting over a circumstance which may never occur, when you can remain with your friends and still arrive there quickly if need be? I do not see how, if she should succeed in having an announcement printed, a delay of a day would make any difference."

He nodded, sighing. "You are correct. I feel a great need to take action, but there is little I may now do, save wait."

"And gentlemen, unlike ladies, are not used to waiting about for the actions and decisions of others to determine their own course," she said with a little smile. "You are concerned about how this will affect Miss Darcy's prospects, I imagine."

"And my own," he said. "If she were to bring such a suit, it might drag on for many months, and while it continued, she would have reason to officially object to my marriage to another, and thereby prevent it."

She looked at him curiously. "I did not know you were contemplating entering the married state at any time soon."

"I have only recently begun to." Quickly, acting instinctively if not a little impulsively, he added, "Miss Elizabeth, I have been attempting these last weeks to display my deep admiration and regard for you, though I think I have not quite succeeded." He lifted her hand from his arm and raised it, feeling Elizabeth's quiet intake of breath as his lips brushed her knuckles, soft as a spring breeze. "I will not speak further at this moment, for I can see that I have surprised you. I will only ask that you consider whether or not you could ever view me as more than a friend."

She was quiet for a moment—nearly long enough to worry him—but then, blushing deeply, she said softly, "I will certainly think upon what you have just said. And you —will you go to town, or stay?"

"Oh, I will most certainly stay. No business there could possibly be more important than the task before me." He smiled widely to see her intense blush deepen further.

CHAPTER TWENTY-NINE

Elizabeth certainly did think about what Mr Darcy had said to her at their last meeting. Indeed, she found she could concentrate upon little else! Jane, it seemed, had discerned what she had not. That Mr Darcy spoke of admiration and hinted at a desire for a courtship had astonished her. It was true that he had called her 'very handsome' during his apology for his remarks at their first encounter, but few ladies have the heart to believe themselves really handsome in a gentleman's view after hearing themselves so roundly derided, apology or no. That his second description of her was more sincere than she had believed seemed likely *now*, but his first offence, though truly forgiven, must certainly have formed the greater part of her failure to acknowledge an attraction to a handsome, intelligent, single gentleman who, in hindsight, had been paying her a deal of attention.

Another part, of course, was that the Mr Darcys of the world did not pursue the Miss Bennets—not for any honourable reason, at least. Never could she imagine him having some illicit purpose. He was too upright and honest for any such scheme, and the sort of man who would pursue a dishonourable arrangement would have taken great care to conceal his interest from her family. He certainly would not have come calling so openly.

He had urged her to consider whether she could view him as more than a friend, and this she did most seriously. He was her friend, and a dear one. *He is the best of men. How many others of his station, with his responsibilities, would do as he had done in Meryton? Few, if any*, she believed.

The revelations about his aunt's scheming, combined with her recollection of Miss Darcy's narrow escape from a fortune hunter only months ago, made her heart ache; he was beset on all sides by those who saw only his holdings, and not the admirable man he was. As a brother, he was excellent; she had not only dear Georgiana's testimony to this, but her own observation. He would not, she thought, be any less careful of a wife. The mere thought that *she* could be that wife was enough to make her knees tremble. And yet she was not concerned that he would be too cautious with her sensibilities, for he had proved again and again that he respected her mind and her desire to know the truth of things.

She began in the following days to acknowledge to herself that he was exactly the man who, in disposition and talents, would most suit her. His understanding and temper, though unlike her own, would answer all her wishes. By her ease and liveliness, his mind might be softened, his manners improved, and from his judgment, information, and knowledge of the world she must receive benefits of equal importance. His very great handsomeness did not at all harm his cause, either, truth be told. That, she had noticed from the beginning of their acquaintance, although she had kept hidden any admiration of his countenance. It was not long before she honestly felt that she could love him, if he truly wished it.

He continued to visit often, but never by word or deed pressed her for a decision, or even a hint. She rather thought that this must take some effort for a man who was surely accustomed to receiving whatever he might want, almost immediately upon conceiving the desire. His restraint and consideration were further marks in his favour.

Unbeknownst to her, Elizabeth's distraction was noticed, and after a whispered conference among her sisters it was of course Jane who came to speak with her. She invited herself along on Elizabeth's walk one morning; when they were not far from the house, she said, "Lizzy, we have all have been worried about you. You have been very quiet and serious this last week. Will you not tell me what troubles you?"

"Oh," she replied with a little laugh, "I am sorry. I have had something on my mind, but it is nothing bad. In fact, I think it might be very good." She related then the substance of Mr Darcy's admission of his feelings, and her own thoughts on the matter. Jane did not seem at all surprised, and went so far as to lift her eyebrows at Elizabeth in a very significant manner, but she was kind enough to remain silent about her earlier suspicions.

"It sounds as though you are seriously considering him, Lizzy. We all know him to be a most excellent gentleman, though I confess I had always pictured you with someone of a more gregarious nature. But that is nothing, if you really like him...if you really believe you could love him."

"I should think, my dear Jane, that it would be difficult not to love such a man, if he condescended to love me. Already he is a dear friend, his further affection an honour I had not dared hope for, and a lady could do much worse than to look at him across the breakfast table for fifty years," she added saucily, making her sister laugh. "And, of course, his sister is everything sweet and amiable, and not the least of the inducements in his favour."

"She would be a pleasant addition to the family," Jane agreed.

After a moment's thought, Elizabeth continued on a more serious note. "In practical terms, he is well able to support a wife, and any of her sisters who require a home in later years. He is too kind-hearted to ever mistreat his wife or his children, and indeed I would imagine him as a most indulgent husband and father."

"It rather sounds, Lizzy, as if you have talked yourself into falling in love with him already," Jane said lightly.

"I very nearly have, I think!" Elizabeth admitted. "I hold myself in check for two reasons—one, that he has not explicitly stated his wishes, and two, that I am not certain I could enter his sphere and fail to embarrass him. We are but country gentry—we have not had the upbringing or the education of those in his class."

Jane was quiet, and Elizabeth saw she was considering her words carefully. "I think you must discuss it with him. We may speculate all we like on what society would think of you, but he is in a position to know—it is, as you say, his sphere. And surely a man of his careful nature would consider such questions for his own part, as well."

"I can hardly imagine broaching such a subject with a gentleman to whom I am not engaged, and yet such a conversation would help me to decide, if he did propose! How would one even open it? 'Sir, you have made me no offers, but if we were to marry, I fear my country ways might mortify you in town.'" She huffed with frustration.

"Well, perhaps not quite like that," said Jane. "You are clever with words, Lizzy, and he is not disposed to be critical of you. I am sure you may find a way of delicately entering into the subject if only you were to consider it in less agitated spirits. Although I must say, if you will get so worked up about nothing more than a possible conversation with him, you may be more in love than you believe."

Elizabeth felt the heat in her cheeks. It was true she had fumbled for a reply to Mr Darcy; the sensation of his lips on her hand had taken her thoughts—and her breath—away.

Jane squeezed her hand. "Is it—forgive me, Lizzy, if I speak out of turn—but is it possible that you have been attached to him, and only your belief in his indifference kept you from acknowledging it?"

Elizabeth stopped as though she had run into a wall. The events of the last weeks flashed through her mind—the quiet of the house; the anticipation of calls to and from Netherfield, restrained in frequency as they must be; the wide-ranging conversations in which she and Mr Darcy had engaged; the fact that he always seemed to sit next to her, and the fact that she always selected a seat by an available one. In retrospect, though they had not been so oblivious to the rest of the company as Jane and her Mr Bingley, they had been drawn towards each other like magnets.

"Perhaps..." she answered slowly. "I cannot be certain.

I do feel some disbelief...it has been such a strange and difficult time. I had not at all considered him a possible suitor until he hinted at it, that is true, but he has become quite dear to me. Yet, as for my heart, I hardly know it."

"I trust that it will soon become clear to you, now that he has taken the first step. He visits almost every day—tell him your concerns, and allow him to reassure you, as I am certain he will wish to do."

Elizabeth took her sister's arm and leaned into her fondly. "When did you become so wise, Jane?"

"I make no claims to wisdom, merely to slightly more experience of being in love," she answered with a smile.

———

"So! Jane, Mr Bingley, have you given any thought to when you shall marry?" Mr Bennet asked some days after the engagement had been made, a teasing smile on his face. "I had thought perhaps you might alight upon the first week of June."

Mr Bingley did not look at all averse to that suggestion, but Jane dropped her eyes and said, "I should not wish to disrespect my mother by marrying the very moment my mourning is done." Her betrothed strove manfully to conceal his disappointment. She looked at him with a little smile and said, "But I believe mid-June might suit."

"Mama's roses will be blooming by then!" Kitty exclaimed. "You might have some in your bouquet, or your hair."

Jane looked at Bingley with a questioning expression. He smiled and shrugged. "Name the day, my love. I care only that we will be married."

"Well, then," Mr Bennet said. "We shall consult with Mr Edwards as soon as may be."

"I must return to town to alter my will and have the settlements drawn up," Mr Bingley said. Seeing Jane's downcast expression, he added, "But not for a week or two. I am enjoying being an engaged man far too much to part from you so soon!"

CHAPTER THIRTY

HARDLY HAD THE FRONT DOOR CLOSED FROM Bingley's return before he told Darcy of the date chosen for his wedding. "We are agreed that we shall be the happiest couple in England!" he added jovially, and proceeded to once again enumerate all of Miss Bennet's fine qualities. As this allowed Darcy to sit back, nod occasionally, and contemplate Elizabeth, he had no objection to hearing his friend's effusions.

The next day was sunny and warm, and as the inhabitants of Netherfield entertained Captain Carter's visit, all the Bennet ladies arrived in their father's carriage. "It is such a splendid day, Mr Bingley," said Miss Lydia eagerly, "that we hoped you might allow us to walk *your* garden for a change of scenery."

"I can think of nothing more delightful!" cried he, and within minutes they had chosen their walking partners and scattered throughout Netherfield's vast formal garden. Miss Mary blushingly accepted the captain's arm, and Miss Lydia walked with Georgiana, while Miss Catherine eagerly attached herself to Mrs Hurst, who she rather seemed to idolise. The engaged couple naturally grasped the opportunity of private conversation, leaving Darcy and Elizabeth to form the final pair, which suited them both.

"We were sorry not to see you yesterday," Elizabeth began. "Mr Bingley said you had urgent business...I hope nothing has gone wrong?"

"I received expresses within the same hour from my man of business and Lady Catherine. I felt it best to answer them both with like speed. Mr Coulter wished me to know that he had word from the *Times* and the morning post that engagement announcements naming me were received from the mother of the 'bride'," he replied, his offence and anger clear. "The editors of both contacted him for confirmation and were told the announcements were false. My aunt wrote to inform me that I could not evade the engagement now, for it would be published in today's papers. I took great pleasure in writing to one in praise of a job well done, and to the other to inform her of the failure of her plans."

Elizabeth frowned. "I can hardly believe she dared follow through with such a scheme. Had she no concern about marrying her daughter to a man who did not wish it? I should think that, if nothing else, would have stayed her hand."

His lips compressed into a thin line. "Lady Catherine is not awash in maternal sentiment. In truth, I do not know if she is capable of caring for anyone save herself." He shook his head and sighed. "I fear there will now be a permanent breach between us, which I cannot like despite her actions. She is my aunt, the sister of my mother. I did not wish for matters to come to such an end, but what could I do that would not offend her? Nothing but marry my cousin, which I would not."

"If the right thing to do were always the easy thing to do, it would be a very different world," Elizabeth mused, hugging his arm a little more tightly to herself for just a moment. "And I am not certain it would be a better one. You have acted as a gentleman should. You have protected your right to decide your own future, without exposing her duplicity to the censure of the world."

He basked in her praise, and in the further lightening of the weight upon his mind for a moment, thinking how wonderful it would be to have her always by his side, there to laud, scold, or condole, as circumstances warranted. He gazed upon that beloved profile and ventured to ask, "Miss Elizabeth, have you happened to consider what we spoke of when I first learnt of her schemes?"

"I confess, I have thought of little else," she said, averting her eyes. "I was very surprised, sir, and even now I can hardly credit it. I am entirely willing to know you better, but please, you must explain to me why, how, you came to think—"

"To admire you? To think you the most worthy woman of my acquaintance?" Her cheeks took on a most becoming tinge of pink, and the desire to continue to provoke such a reaction loosened his tongue. "I was early intrigued by your wit, your laughter, and your beautiful eyes. And how could I not admire the way you refused to be moved from your sister's bedside, when many would be glad of any excuse to absent themselves from such toil and suffering? I found myself wishing for such devotion. And then, when Miss Bennet began to recover, and we were in company for more than a few moments at a time, I came to understand that there was no lady in the whole of my acquaintance whose society and conversation I preferred, or whose beauty so moved me."

"I was not aware that you could be so loquacious in your admiration," she said, her cheeks a lovely shade of rose.

"No other lady has prompted me to exercise my hidden talents." He studied her for a moment. "Is there anything else you wish to know of me?"

She laughed lightly, her cheeks flushing a deeper red. "Of your character I have no doubts, but I have known you only as a guest in another man's home. There is much I do not understand about your life and the society you move in, except that I suspect it would not easily admit someone of my background."

"Is it London society that truly concerns you?"

"I concede that it is so," she replied, abashed at having been seen through so easily.

"I shall not sport with your intelligence and claim that you would be welcomed with open arms," he said seriously. "But the Darcy name has *some* power, and your own attributes will earn the approbation of those with the wit to see you clearly. I myself am not well-liked," he admitted wryly, "only accepted for my name. You will not be surprised to hear that I should happily do nothing in London but conduct business and attend performances."

She laughed softly. "No, that is no shock at all. But your position will not allow such a withdrawal, I think."

"It will not. For my sister's sake and that of the children I hope one day to have, connexions must be maintained. I believe that my uncle and aunt, the earl and countess of Matlock, would soon come to accept you, and their assistance in society would be more valuable to you than mine. With their help, I would expect you to be very quickly established. But even without them, I cannot imagine that you would not make a place for yourself, enchanting as you are."

She looked away bashfully at this extravagant praise. "I think, sir, you are viewing me through the eyes of a suitor and not those of society."

Darcy brightened as an idea struck him. "Mrs Annesley is in the business of preparing young ladies for that very milieu. Should you like to speak with her on the subject? I can certainly arrange it."

"That is...an unusual idea," she replied thoughtfully. "I shall consider it."

"And I may call upon you?"

She agreed that he might, and soon learnt that Mr Darcy had a way of sweeping aside any obstacle put before him. Every question of hers, however minor, was answered with a sincerity and thoroughness few would expect from such a taciturn man. With her agreement, it was arranged that she should spend an afternoon with Mrs Annesley, from which she emerged thinking that there would be a great number of rules to learn, but that with such assistance available it might not be insurmountable. And with every intelligent sentence he spoke, every moment he indulged her sisters in their choice of conversation and activity, and every tender, beseeching look he cast upon her, she felt herself falling a little more into his power.

Then, one bright morning, she went with Jane by the shortcut between Longbourn and the church to place flowers on their mother's grave. They came round the hedge to find Mr Darcy standing before the shining new marble stone, his back to them.

"...that Bingley—and I, if I am so fortunate to win Miss Elizabeth—will always see to the care of your daughters," he was saying. "They shall want for nothing in our power to provide. Rest well, Mrs Bennet." He laid a single late daffodil at the base of the stone, and after a moment standing with bowed head over the grave, strode off in the direction of Meryton.

The sisters stood frozen by the hedge until he was lost to sight, then Jane turned to her and whispered, eyes glistening, "Oh, Lizzy..." Elizabeth, hand over her mouth and tears spilling from her eyes, at last acknowledged to herself that her heart was no longer her own.

"He really does love me," she whispered.

"Of course he does!" Jane's expression was a study in amazement. "Did you doubt it? Charles and I have been wondering when you would put him out of his misery and accept him, you know. It is apparent to us how perfectly suited you are."

"I did not doubt his affections," she replied hesitantly, "only whether they were enough to overcome the difference in our stations. I have feared his regard would die at the first obstacle, at my first mistake."

"Lizzy, do you really think him so mean as to withhold his forgiveness for any mistake of yours? I think you could spill a pot of tea on a royal duchess and he would simply offer his cravat and handkerchief to her to mop it up!"

Elizabeth laughed through tears at that ridiculous picture. "I should hope I would never fail *that* spectacularly. I was thinking more along the lines of failing to curtsey deeply enough to that duchess you mention."

"Honestly," Jane said with some impatience. "You are too clever for your own good, at times. Stop thinking so much and accept the man you love! What could be simpler?"

"What indeed?" Elizabeth wondered, her smile becoming luminous. "I have been silly, have I not?"

"*Very* silly!"

———

When Darcy entered the parlour at Longbourn later that day, Elizabeth greeted him with such a smile as he had not the power to describe. It stopped him in his tracks for a stunned moment, after which he could not possibly do aught but what he did: he moved directly to her and, holding out his hand, asked, "Miss Elizabeth, will you come walking with me?" He had not greeted his host, nor any of the others present. Miss Lydia, Miss Kitty, and Georgiana giggled behind their hands at this lapse in civility, as a certain sign of love. Captain Carter, who had arrived only a few minutes previously, exchanged a discreet, amused look with Miss Mary.

Smile never wavering, Elizabeth placed her hand into his and stood. "I should be delighted." He placed her hand on his arm and escorted her from the room with fond solicitude, sparing not a glance for anyone else and leaving behind him a room filled with whispers and laughter and one rather misty-eyed father.

"Miss Elizabeth," he ventured under the brilliant spring sunshine, "has something changed?"

"Something very substantial," she agreed cheerfully. "At last, I understand my own wishes."

"And...do those wishes include me?"

"I should rather say they are built upon you."

With a great indrawn breath, he released her from his arm, only to swing about and stand before her, claiming both of her hands within his own. "Then—dearest, loveliest Elizabeth—say you will marry me, and I will gladly be the foundation for all your wishes ever after."

"Oh! I want nothing more. I am only sorry that it has taken me so long to come to this point. Yes, I will marry you," she answered in a rush.

"Never apologise, my love," he insisted. "You deserved every proof of my affections, and every moment required to know your own." Having declared as much, he could wait no longer to seal their agreement.

He lowered his head towards hers, hesitating only a heartbeat to assure himself that she welcomed this liberty. He had schooled himself to bank his passions for her sake, and he was right to do so—the moment he set his lips upon hers his desire for her surged, eager to ignite into a conflagration to scorch them both. What he had not been at all prepared for was the even more overwhelming sensation that his questing soul had at last found its resting-place in her arms.

As her lips began to move sweetly, shyly beneath his own, he knew he must not linger there, however much he wished it. He pulled back and contented himself with avidly examining her beloved features and the expression of wonder stamped thereupon.

"Elizabeth," he breathed, "you can have no idea how I long to be married to you."

She dropped her gaze to one side, colour rising in her cheeks as a delicious, secretive smile played about her lips.

"I think, sir, I may understand a little better now."

Prudence be damned; he could do nothing in response to *that* but kiss her again. A cough from the direction of the house ended their embrace before it became too fervent, and they turned, blushing, to see Mr Bennet framed in the doorway. "I believe you have some business with me, Mr Darcy," he said mildly. With a look of regret, Darcy kissed his beloved's hand and led her to her father, whereupon they parted, he to the study and she to the parlour.

The interview between father and suitor was brief, for Mr Bennet had no doubts as to the young man's devotion to his daughter and certainly none regarding his ability to care for her. He required only an assurance that he might visit often and be admitted into the fabled Pemberley library when he did, and having received it, gave his consent. They shook hands upon it and returned to the parlour where the official announcement was made.

A chorus of shrieks and a great rustling of skirts followed. Darcy watched his beloved surrounded by her sisters and her future sister. Bingley, Mrs Hurst, and Captain Carter wisely kept their seats until the Bennet and Darcy ladies had done with their exclamations and embraces, whereupon they each in turn approached Elizabeth with their own felicitations.

"So, we are to be brothers," Bingley remarked with a broad grin as he pumped his friend's hand.

"I could not ask for a better one," Darcy replied.

Bingley lowered his voice. "Jane and I had considered this possibility, and were agreed that if you should settle your engagement in time, we would invite you to share our wedding day with us. Discuss it with Elizabeth, and if the idea appeals to you, let us know."

Darcy blinked with surprise. "It does appeal. I will ask her."

He saw Miss Bennet speaking quietly to Elizabeth, likely on the same topic, and it was not long before the newly-acknowledged couple were able to reunite in a corner of the room and agree they could neither of them imagine a more desirable plan. Mr Bennet was approached once more, and as he could have no objections to something that would save him a deal of expense as well as answering the wishes of his eldest daughters, all was easily decided. The couples would marry in a single ceremony on the third Tuesday of June.

———

Some few days later Mr and Mrs Jones were busy in their shop, he attending to customers and she carefully affixing labels to a row of bottles upon the preparation table, when an unfamiliar wagon pulled up on the street outside. The driver hopped down, retrieved a smallish, heavy crate from within and bore it inside the shop. Setting it upon the counter, he looked at the young apothecary.

"Mr Evan Jones?"

"I am he. How may I help you?"

"Delivery for you, sir, from London. I were bid to say there's a letter inside." With a tug of his forelock, the fellow departed.

"I do not recall you ordering anything from town, my dear," remarked Charlotte curiously, wiping the glue from her hands before she approached.

"That is because I have not." He made quick work with a knife, slicing the twine which held the lid on and placing it into a bucket behind the counter where they kept such oddments as might prove useful. With the lid removed, a sealed letter lay atop the straw packing, through which could be faintly seen the spine of several books and a handful of items wrapped in burlap.

Neither of them recognised the seal, and with mounting curiosity they opened the missive and read.

> *Mr Jones,*
>
> *Please accept, on behalf of the grateful residents of Meryton and its surrounds, these books and implements which will be required for your remaining term of study at the London Hospital Medical College to commence in August of this year. The fees have been paid, and lodging awaits you and your good wife for the duration of your residence in town with Mr and Mrs Gardiner of 29 Gracechurch Street.*
>
> *Your instructors at the College are anticipating your return, and Mr Edward Linley most particularly wishes that you will visit him immediately upon your arrival in London. God bless you, sir, and do not concern yourself with those you leave behind—Meryton is a growing town despite its recent setback, and we have no doubt that we may attract another apothecary in short order. Sir William Lucas and Mr Philips stand ready to assist in the transfer of your lease, when and if you wish it.*

There followed the signatures of every gentleman of property in the area, along with those of Mr Darcy, Mr Bingley, Mr Gardiner, and several of the more prosperous merchants and tenants. The young couple gaped at the letter in shock for some minutes before Charlotte, at least, regained a modicum of composure. "I suspected Papa was up to something, but I had no notion there was a conspiracy throughout the neighbourhood," she remarked in surprise.

"Do you think we ought to accept this, then?" Her husband's voice was rather faint with shock.

"The fees have been paid, my dear, and these items purchased." She squeezed his hand and smiled, the future beginning to open up before her like a gift unwrapped on Christmas morning. "To refuse would not only be a waste but an insult. They have recognised your qualities and your labours, and I rather think you have little choice but to allow it."

"Well, then, my dear, I suppose you had best run down to the stationers, for we have a great many letters of thanks to write."

CHAPTER THIRTY-ONE

IN THE FIRST WEEK OF MAY, JANE AND ELIZABETH ventured to town to shop for their trousseaux with the assistance of Mrs Gardiner. Mr Darcy and Mr Bingley went thither also, to meet with their attorneys and review the settlements which had been drafted. Mrs Hurst, Miss Darcy, and Mrs Annesley would stay at Longbourn during their absence, under the protection of Mr Bennet.

Mrs Hurst and Miss Darcy were already considered by the Bennets as part of the family, so their residence caused no anxiety on either side. One rainy day as they were all sat in the parlour, Mrs Hurst recommended to Kitty the novel she had just finished reading. Mr Bennet looked up from his own book to comment, "You go through those books at a prodigious pace, madam—might you like to borrow something more substantial from my library?"

Mrs Hurst drew herself up, looking somewhat offended. "I have read many books you would call *substantial*, sir, but I generally prefer a novel."

He tilted his head and regarded her curiously. "I

cannot understand why. You strike me as too intelligent to be always reading such silly things."

"And what right have you to call them silly, sir?" she retorted with uncharacteristic asperity. "Have you ever read one?"

"Certainly not!" he exclaimed.

"Really?" The corners of her mouth twitched upward. "You have not read the works of Fielding or Richardson, then? I understood them to be favourites among bookish gentlemen."

Mr Bennet closed his book and sat forward. "Those are not novels, they are literature!"

"Oh...then pray explain to me the difference between a novel and a work of literature." She smiled expectantly, and the young women hardly dared blink, lest they interrupt the exchange.

"A fictional story may be called literature if it deals with matters of substance, suitable for serious contemplation," he answered with assurance.

"I see." She nodded thoughtfully. "I am assuming you would not include matters of the heart in that category."

"Generally, no. Not as the primary topic, certainly."

"But a work of fiction which looked deeply into such issues as class, society, and economics, which also contained a romance between two of the many characters, that would be worthy of the higher designation?"

"Likely, yes," he agreed.

"I find it curious that by your standards, *The Taming of the Shrew* is not literature, while *Evelina* is."

Mr Bennet sputtered. "Shakespeare, not literature? Preposterous!"

Mrs Hurst smiled. "The play I mentioned centres

around two romances. There are other elements, of course, but those are at the core of it. And if you revise your definition to allow for matters of the heart to drive the plot, you will only be allowing for more of my *silly books* to be classed as literature."

"And what serious topics does that book you were just recommending to my daughter canvass?" he enquired acerbically, put out to find that he was suddenly losing an argument he thought he had well in hand.

"Class and morality," she answered without hesitation. "In particular, the poor manner in which the gentry may be treated by higher society, and the ruinous decadence of some in the highest spheres. I thought Kitty might like it because the heroine is just her age, and has lived entirely in the country before events unexpectedly take her to London."

"And there, I suppose, she meets and marries a lord?"

"You may read it, sir, and find out."

Mr Bennet laughed and held up his hands. "Very well, madam, you have bested me. I shall read this book of yours, if you will lend it."

———

Handing the book back to Mrs Hurst at breakfast the morning after he finished it, he said, "Madam, you were correct. I enjoyed the story and it certainly did give me much to think upon. I shall never deride novels in general again."

His daughters gaped, but Mrs Hurst smiled. "May I ask the substance of your reflections upon the story?"

"It put me in mind of Jane and Lizzy, and what they

may soon face," he replied with a furrowed brow. "Lizzy will not allow anyone to make her unhappy for long, but my Jane is not so indomitable, nor will she have the protection of the Darcy name, or the Darcy glower."

She nodded sympathetically. "I think she *will* have the protection of the Darcy glower, as she will be his sister, but I see what you mean. Unlike Darcy, however, my brother and Jane may easily retire to the country and give them all no further thought if they do not enjoy London. Or they may choose to move in less exalted circles."

"Does your brother not wish to raise the Bingley name?" Mr Bennet asked.

Mrs Hurst shrugged. "By purchasing an estate and marrying the daughter of a gentleman, he will do so. His children will be born into the gentry, which is no small thing."

"I simply do not wish to see Jane made unhappy, even long enough for them to decide they want no part of that circle."

"She will not have a life free of sorrow and trouble. That is not granted to any of us," she reminded him gently.

"No, indeed. But I would change that if I could." He was silent for a moment, and then regarded her with something of his usual droll humour. "Tell me, Mrs Hurst, do you read the papers, or only the ladies' magazines?"

She smiled to herself and answered demurely, "I have often heard it said that ladies who take the papers will end as bluestockings, scorned and ridiculed."

"You will not hear such a thing in this house, I assure you! My girls have always been encouraged to understand what is occurring around them, though some are more interested than others."

"Well, in that case, I shall admit to sneaking a peek on occasion," Mrs Hurst replied with a dimpled smirk.

Mr Bennet laughed. "Excellent, most excellent, indeed! Tell me, what think you of this business with the Welsh Calvinists?"

———

"Tell us all you can of this country girl Darcy has got himself entangled with," the earl of Matlock demanded gruffly.

His youngest son shrugged. "There is little to say against the lady herself, more's the pity. A beauty to be sure, witty, amiable, and well-read. Just the sort of lady to attract my dour, clever cousin. Seemed to genuinely like Darcy, too, though I cannot believe her heart was touched as his was. If she had anything at all in the way of fortune or connexions, I could be happy to support him in this, but she simply is not suitable. And with all these rumours going about, what was already far too imprudent is surely impossible."

"Good thing he's come to town, then, for I certainly cannot be spared from Parliament to gallivant off to Hert-fordshire to talk sense into him," Lord Matlock declared. "Will it be difficult to separate them, do you think?"

Richard shifted in his chair. "I hardly know. He had made no decisions when I was with him at Christmas, but when I saw him last month, he was quite close-mouthed about the whole business. Either he had realised her indif-ference and did not want to hear me say I had been right all along, or he had decided in her favour and wished not to argue the matter. I rather fear the latter, for I would expect him to have left Hertfordshire in the former case."

Lady Matlock listened quietly as her husband and younger son went on in this vein for a time, considering which arguments would work best upon her nephew. The young lady's supposed indifference was a favourite, but her ladyship was sceptical. If she understood rightly, Richard had met the girl only weeks after the death of her mother, and the serious illnesses of more than one of her sisters, not to mention any number of neighbours and friends. If she was not overflowing with admiration for Darcy in such a circumstance, it was hardly to be wondered at. That her handsome, intelligent, and wealthy nephew was capable of securing the affections of nearly any lady capable of feeling, she had little doubt. He often showed to poor advantage in company, it was undeniable, but if he were to lower his formidable mask and bend his considerable powers towards securing the heart of a lady, he would be difficult to resist. He had now had above four months to do so without Richard's discouraging commentary.

She returned her full attention to the conversation between the gentlemen, noting that her husband was becoming rather overwrought.

"He *shall* be made to see reason!" the earl declared, red-faced. "I am the head of this family, and if he is minded to be recalcitrant, he shall simply be made to obey!"

Lady Matlock cleared her throat delicately; her husband and son turned to regard her with a level of surprise which suggested they had entirely forgotten her presence. She fixed her stern gaze upon the earl. "I *will not* stand by and be sundered from my niece and nephew simply because you do not care to be diplomatic in this matter," she informed him crisply.

"Darcy would never break with family over a woman," he replied dismissively.

Although she felt her own temper rise at this cavalier disregard, the countess exerted herself to present a composed exterior.

"Have you met Fitzwilliam Darcy?" she asked, eyebrows raised. "Where he believes himself to be in the right, he is as immovable as the Peaks. If he has given his heart to this girl, I very much doubt he should be swayed from her by anyone other than the lady herself."

"Then we will pay her off."

"It may come to that," she said, nodding at the earl. "But recall, if you will, that Richard's information is several months old. Darcy may have won her affections in the interim, which would make her far less likely to accept any offer of ours. The lady you have described, Son, does not sound like a fool, and only a very great fool would turn down wealth, status, *and* felicity."

"What, then, would you suggest we do?" her husband enquired snappishly.

"We must speak to Darcy, and determine where matters truly stand, and we will judge better to do so without barking orders."

The earl nodded reluctant agreement to this plan, but Richard was not yet finished. "I agree more current intelligence is needed, if we are to stop him from making a mistake of this magnitude. He could have almost any lady in the land—he could aspire to the daughter of a duke! I can hardly credit his foolishness over Elizabeth Bennet. Charming as she is, she is far, far beneath him."

"I believe you said you have an engagement tomorrow morning, Richard?" Lady Matlock asked mildly. He confirmed this, and she nodded decisively. "I shall invite him to attend us then. We do not need you stoking his obstinacy into immovability."

As her youngest son sputtered, she regarded him with a frown. "I have noted that you praise the lady in one breath, and seek to separate her from Darcy in the next. I am very sorry, Son, that you are not able to disregard matters of fortune when selecting your bride, but this envy of your cousin's ability to do so is most unbecoming."

"Envy!" he cried. "Mother, you have got it all wrong! I am thinking of the credit of our family."

"I am sure that is some part of your motivation," she allowed. "But until today, you have been the least caring of such matters in all the family you claim to be thinking of. Whatever has caused this alteration, you will not be present when your father and I speak to Darcy about Miss Bennet. I hope very much that you have not been, and shall not be, involved in spreading these rumours," she concluded grimly. She then stood and moved to the escritoire to pen the invitation to her nephew, clearly indicating that the discussion had now ended.

———

"Darcy, we are glad you have come."

He noted with some concern that his uncle and aunt, Lord and Lady Matlock, seemed rather forbidding. "I am always happy to visit with you," he added, bowing to them both.

They enquired after his journey and its cause while tea

was served, but as soon as the servant had left the room his uncle spoke. "Darcy, you wrote to us of your intentions towards Miss Elizabeth Bennet, and knowing your character and discernment as we do, we had determined to accept your choice in spite of the vociferous protestations of my sister."

Darcy grimaced; Lord Matlock had long been at odds with Lady Catherine, and he regretted worsening their relations.

"However—" His uncle paused, consternation on his countenance. "A report of a most alarming nature has reached us. The two eldest Miss Bennets are being widely spoken of as adventuresses, who have lured your friend into engaging himself to a disfigured woman by claiming that his honour was engaged before her illness, and that her sister is in pursuit of your fortune, and playing upon this connexion to draw you in."

Darcy was furious and had no scruples about showing it. "This is utterly ridiculous! Bingley is quite desperately in love with Miss Bennet, and has been since before her illness. Her face is marked now, it is true, but he cares nothing for that. The poor girl was quite prepared for him to reject her when she rose from her sickbed, and surprised when he did not. I should know, for I was there! I have no doubts she would have gone away without a single protest had he wished to end their association, as she was not the sort to put herself forward even when she could claim more than her share of beauty, and is understandably even more retiring now."

Darcy took a breath, unable to quell his anger and uncaring of its effect on his relations.

"As for Miss Elizabeth, she has never pursued me. I

believe I explained some of the history of our acquaintance in my letters to you, and I stand by that description. I had to persuade her to consider me as a suitor. Fortunately for me, she did eventually agree. More fortunate still, she recently accepted my proposals, and is now in town to assemble her trousseau. I came here today specifically to acquaint you with this news, and to inform you that our wedding will take place in Meryton on the third Tuesday in June. I had hoped to introduce her to you during her stay."

"Impossible," declared the earl quickly. The countess laid a restraining hand upon his arm; he ignored it. "We cannot be seen to associate with her while such a cloud hangs about her. It is unfortunate that you have acted so precipitously, Nephew, for you will have to pay out quite a sum to be released from this betrothal, and likely your friend will, also."

Darcy shot to his feet. "I shall do no such thing. What care I for the wagging tongues of the *ton*? If Elizabeth is not welcome in town, we shall be very happy at Pemberley all the year round. I am confident that I may speak for Bingley when I say that neither engagement shall be broken."

"Think of Georgiana!" Lord Matlock thundered.

"I do! She already loves Elizabeth as a sister, and she knows the truth as well as I do. She will not wish me to give up my happiness so we may impress the preening wastrels of London!"

"Gentlemen, I will thank you to cease shouting in my parlour," said Lady Matlock, and both men turned to her with expressions of contrition.

"Your pardon, madam," said Darcy, as his uncle murmured, "Apologies, my dear."

"Sit down, both of you," she said, and they obeyed. "Nephew, I have no doubt of your honesty, or of the fact that you would never forsake your honour by ending this betrothal. For your sake, and your sister's, we must attempt to mend this situation. I will discover whence this gossip came, for if we can discredit the source, we can largely stop the talk. Secondly, I will meet this Miss Elizabeth Bennet and determine for myself if she is as genuine as you say."

"Absolutely not!" her husband objected. "I have already declared that we shall not associate with her!"

"Such rumours *can* be managed by those without your bluntness," she replied acerbically. "I have already lost my dear friend Lady Anne to an early grave, and I shall not lose her children to your intransigence!" Husband and wife glared at each other for a moment before Lord Matlock gave way by averting his eyes.

"Darcy," her ladyship resumed, "you will be led by me in this. I will help you, but you must concede that I am better placed to determine what actions must be taken than you are. Your young lady will call at Darcy House in two days. I will *happen* to call while she is there. We shall meet without any appearance that I have sought out the introduction." She raised her eyebrows at her husband, who nodded reluctantly.

"And if you approve of her, as I have no doubt you shall?" Darcy asked.

"Why, then I shall combat these rumours with every means in my power. I am not without influence."

When the gentlemen called at Gracechurch Street, Elizabeth immediately apprehended that Darcy was preoccupied. She promptly suggested they all walk out, and having won free of the house, with Jane and Mr Bingley distracted by each other, she turned to him and said, "Well, what is it?"

He looked briefly surprised, then laughed. "How well you know me already. I visited my aunt and uncle yesterday, and they had some news I was not pleased to hear. Apparently, there is already talk about you and your sister, and it is by no means flattering."

"How can that be?" she exclaimed. "Neither engagement has been in the papers yet."

"I do not know." He explained what had been told to him, and his aunt's plan.

"Naturally I shall be happy to meet Lady Matlock tomorrow," she said when he had related all. "And if it would be better to delay the wedding until the gossip dies down...?"

"Absolutely not. I will not be separated from you by lies."

"From the moment I knew of your interest, I feared that by accepting you I might harm you and your family," she admitted with a sigh.

"You have not done this," he insisted. "Someone, possibly someone who had decided I should marry *their* daughter, has elected to paint you and your sister in a poor light, and the tales have spread and been embellished, as always seems to happen."

"Do you mean to tell me," she replied with a look of

mingled amazement and humour, "that the great Lady Catherine de Bourgh is not the only one who has decided the course of your future without consulting you?"

Darcy's gaze flicked heavenward, and he sighed with exasperation. "A single man in possession of a good fortune is the rightful property of the ladies of his circle, and is not under any circumstances to be allowed to decide such weighty matters for himself."

"And now you are to be punished by that circle, for your defection?"

"So it would seem." He shrugged carelessly. "But we have my aunt's support, and that is no small thing. Lady Matlock is a bosom friend of several of the Patronesses of Almack's, and wields considerable social power in her own right. The earl is unhappy, but apparently willing to allow my aunt to work her magic upon the court of public opinion."

He frowned then, and Elizabeth waited as he seemed to struggle with something. At last he continued, "My aunt informs me that my cousin, Colonel Fitzwilliam, remains opposed. I do not know why. I was very surprised when he objected to the interest in you which I admitted while he was in Hertfordshire. He liked you very well, but decried your station. Richard has been as a brother to me all my life, and yet I cannot explain this attitude—he has never before seemed to care for such things. Indeed, he would often tease me for being too concerned with those considerations!"

Elizabeth felt a stab of guilt for being the cause of such dissension, but she could not think of herself now. She laid her hand upon his, and when he turned it to interlace their fingers, said, "Does your aunt understand this alteration in her son?"

"If she does, she did not explain it to me." He raised her hand to his lips, and smiled at her as he lowered it again. "It will be well, Elizabeth, so long as you do not cast me aside. I would bear a hundred confounding cousins and suspicious uncles for your sake, you know."

It did her a great deal of good to hear that, just then. She returned his smile. "I do not think I could let you go, unless you wished it yourself."

"That shall never happen."

CHAPTER THIRTY-TWO

LADY MATLOCK STOOD IN THE FORMAL DRAWING ROOM at Darcy House as her nephew gravely presented his betrothed, Miss Elizabeth Bennet of Longbourn, and her aunt, Mrs Gardiner. As the formalities were observed, she examined the girl. She had a description of Miss Bennet from her younger son, of course, but words could not adequately convey the animation of her expressions or the sparkle in her eyes. She had often hoped that her nephew would find for himself a cheerful lady to lighten his habitually sombre demeanour, and was pleased to see that in this, at least, he had met her wishes.

Of course, although Richard said she has little else to recommend her as Darcy's wife, he did admit she has a quick smile and is pleasant company, she recalled.

As they sat down to tea, Lady Matlock was reminded by the black trim on the young lady's lavender dress of some information Darcy had conveyed. "Please allow me, Miss Bennet, to offer my condolences on the loss of your mother."

"Thank you, my lady. She is much missed."

"I understand you have several sisters." The countess regarded the young lady with interest.

"There are five of us," Elizabeth said with a smile. "Jane is my elder, and is recently engaged to Mr Charles Bingley. After me come Mary, Catherine, and Lydia."

"I have been following the rumours which are circulating about you and your elder sister," Lady Matlock commented, pleased to note that whatever the young lady felt on that matter, her pleasant smile did not so much as flicker. "There has been mention of your younger sisters as well, painting them rather as hoydens."

"The younger two were a little rambunctious," Miss Bennet replied easily as her aunt nodded. "Which is not uncommon for girls aged seventeen and fifteen. Both of them have matured a great deal these last months, as have we all. Their carefree girlhood is quite over, I am afraid, but they have shouldered their burdens in such a way as to make us all proud."

"I can confirm that," said Darcy.

"My eldest and youngest sisters were afflicted with the disease," Miss Bennet continued quietly. "They are both very much marked by it, and Lydia, the youngest, has lost the sight in one eye. Their lives have been most materially altered. Even in the neighbourhood where they have been known from their births, they have not avoided a certain amount of disdain for their lost beauty, but they have not allowed it to make them bitter. They, and all our family, have overheard comments that it would have been better for them both—and particularly for Lydia—to have perished with my mother."

Darcy looked at her sharply. His aunt suspected he

had not been aware of these incidents. "And yet, they remain cheerful and loving despite these injuries," he said, his eyes fixed upon his betrothed's. "I have no patience for anyone who does not see their worth."

Lady Matlock nodded to him and returned her attention to Miss Bennet. "And what of your father? He must feel quite outnumbered, with five daughters."

"Oh, he certainly does!" she replied with a little laugh, her expression brightening. "Poor Papa is a quiet man who likes nothing better than a book. If he were more like Mr Bingley, we would vex him much less!"

The countess knew little of Miss Bingley's brother, but joined Mrs Gardiner in laughing at the observation.

Her nephew, however, remained grave. "Forgive me for interrupting, but I must know—have you made any progress in determining whence these tales came?"

She gave Darcy a look of disapproval for his impatience. "Indeed. I have traced them to Lady Symonds. Interestingly, Miss Bingley has stayed with her daughter for some weeks, and Miss Symonds is known to be enamoured of Mr Bingley."

"Miss Bingley," Darcy groaned. "I ought to have known. She has pursued me relentlessly for years, and was in Hertfordshire with her brother. She took an instant dislike to Elizabeth before she fled to London to escape the epidemic."

Lady Matlock watched as he gazed at his betrothed apologetically, and was surprised at the calm amusement she saw in the young lady's expression.

"I wonder why!" Miss Bennet said in a mocking tone. "Her feeling of possession over Mr Darcy was made clear early in our acquaintance."

The fondness in the smile she directed at Darcy heartened Lady Matlock, who said, "But it sounds as though she and her friend together have an interest in foiling both engagements, and a mother, desperate to marry off her unattractive and aging daughter, willing to be of assistance."

"What are we to do to combat these lies?" Darcy asked.

"If you will allow me to get to know Miss Bennet a little better, perhaps I can think of something," she told her nephew pointedly. His lips flattened at this rebuke, but he quickly turned to Mrs Gardiner and engaged her in talk of Derbyshire and Lambton. Lady Matlock bent her own attention to the young lady her nephew had chosen.

Within half an hour she was prepared to concede that either the girl was genuine, or the stage had lost a finer actress than it had ever known. "Miss Bennet, how long are you in town?"

"Another week, my lady."

"Very good. I will begin correcting the story today by calling upon some ladies of my acquaintance who will be delighted to spread the truth, if only because they dislike Lady Symonds. I confess that I am of their number," she added slyly.

Lady Matlock took some amusement in the astonished looks exchanged between Miss Bennet and her aunt. So many feared her power that to be the cause of such pleasant surprise was a novelty she found she enjoyed. She turned to her nephew, noting he had taken the young lady's hand in his, and was gazing at her warmly. She cleared her throat and went on to explain her scheme.

"Darcy, you will place a notice of your engagement in the *Times*, to run...three days hence, on Monday. That very day, Miss Bennet, you will visit Gunter's with me, and I shall introduce you to any of my acquaintance we happen to see. I expect there will be more than a few, and they will all have read the announcement. After this, you and Darcy shall take a walk in Hyde Park, so that society may see how easy you are with each other. Mr Bingley and your sister ought to join you for this, if your sister can bear the scrutiny and probable unkindness of strangers. The night before you leave, Lord Matlock and I shall have Darcy, Mr Bingley, you, and your sister to dinner."

She turned to the tradesman's wife. "I can see you are an elegant, ladylike person, madam. I hope you will forgive me for not including you. We are trying to raise your nieces in the estimation of society, you see, and it is best just at present not to remind anyone of their connexion to trade."

Mrs Gardiner inclined her head and replied with great composure, "I understand, my lady."

———

"What do you think of my aunt's scheme?" Darcy asked Elizabeth after Lady Matlock departed.

Elizabeth shook her head ruefully, smiling. "I am not sure that having an opinion is part of my role in this. But in all seriousness, I see nothing to criticise. Certainly she must know more of how society is to be managed than I. I had rather know *your* opinion."

"I am more versed in avoiding gossip than managing it," he replied with a bemused expression. "I am inclined to trust my aunt in this; as you say, she is the knowledgeable party here."

She reached for Darcy's hand, wishing to reassure him

as much as herself. "I do appreciate the effort she is willing to expend on our behalf—or rather, yours. She cannot yet trust me, much less *like* me, but she shows a faith in you that can only induce me to admire her."

"Then we shall follow her lead."

"And perhaps," suggested Mrs Gardiner, "we might hope someone else will stir up a greater scandal and divert attention."

This bit of levity lightened the mood for only a moment, for Elizabeth was quite concerned about a related matter, which she soon laid before the two people she most trusted to advise her. "If only it had been anyone but Caroline Bingley behind it all! Have Jane and Mr Bingley not suffered enough? This will hurt them both—in society, yes, but to discover that his sister has been so vicious? I hardly know how to tell Jane."

"You will leave that to me, Lizzy, and worry about your own future," Mrs Gardiner said firmly.

Darcy cast her a look full of gratitude and squeezed his betrothed's hand. "And I shall speak with Bingley tonight. He will be angry, more for your sister's sake than his own, I expect."

"It is amazing to me that she should so callously work to bring her brother down in society, even if she cares nothing for his personal happiness," said Elizabeth. "Would his descent not damage her own prospects?"

"If he could be enticed or dragged away from Miss Bennet, he would not be damaged in the eyes of society now that she is held in suspicion and disdain. That is, I believe, Miss Bingley's strategy. And if she can then attach him to the Symondses, the Bingleys would be thereby elevated and her own prospects improved. She is gambling that either Bingley will choose his standing over your sister or, if he does not, that her own loyalty to the Symondses and the very society which scorns *her brother* will protect *her*."

Mrs Gardiner shook her head and frowned in disapprobation. Elizabeth, realising that she was gaping at Darcy in horror, tried to school her expression. As much as the young ladies of Meryton had jockeyed for position on those rare occasions an eligible young man appeared, she did not believe any of the friends of her youth would maliciously blast the happiness and respectability of another—much less an excellent brother!—in pursuit of the married state. It seemed that in the higher circles, there was a great deal more to worry about than having punch deliberately spilled upon one's dress.

"Is her very own brother truly just a disposable piece in her game of social advancement?" Elizabeth wondered aloud, some of her dismay leaking into her voice. "I could not imagine feeling or behaving so."

Darcy squeezed her hand. "That is why she never had a chance with me, and you captured my heart without even trying."

———

Darcy had conferred with Bingley, and the notice of both engagements ran in the *Times* on Monday, one atop the other. This caused disturbances to breakfasts in many a fine house that day, as readers exclaimed over them. Miss Caroline Bingley and Miss Josephine Symonds were among those who could not allow the news to pass silently, and Sir Everard found it expedient to attend his club at a shockingly early hour as a result.

Elizabeth was conveyed by her uncle's carriage to Grosvenor Square, where she was to be introduced to Lord Matlock. He was polite but cool; to Elizabeth, it was clear the older man wondered what his nephew saw in a passably pretty girl of no apparent distinction. *I am tolerable, at least,* she laughed to herself.

In the plush Matlock carriage on the way to Gunter's, Elizabeth fixed her ladyship with an earnest look and said, "You must allow me to thank you for the generosity which induced you to take so much trouble for Mr Darcy's sake. I understand that you cannot know me well enough to be certain that I am no fortune hunter, and that your assistance is all for him, and for Georgiana. I hope to one day earn your trust and approbation on my own account, but for now I am grateful that you extend it on his."

Lady Matlock nodded graciously, clearly pleased that Elizabeth had the sense to comprehend her position and the courage to speak openly of it. "I share that hope, and my doubts about you are, I will admit, already rather slight. My nephew is perhaps not the best judge of character, but his misjudgements have tended towards convicting on slim evidence, rather than acquitting the guilty."

Elizabeth laughed and agreed.

"It will be best, I think, if we pretend to a closer relationship than we presently enjoy," she continued. "Might I call you Elizabeth?"

"Whatever your ladyship thinks best."

They sat at a table for two, so that no one could impose upon them for long. The refreshments were delicious, but

Elizabeth hardly had time to sample them, so constant was the stream of acquaintances who simply must speak with the countess and be introduced to her young companion. Although she was accustomed to gossip spreading quickly in a town the size of Meryton, Elizabeth found it astonishing, and somewhat amusing, how widely circulated in London were the conflicting rumours about the Bennet sisters—that they were adventuresses from a home devoid of all propriety who had ruthlessly trapped two eligible bachelors, or that Darcy and Bingley had fallen madly in love with sisters from a perfectly acceptable, if obscure, gentle family. Lady Matlock's open approval and Elizabeth's easy amiability lent credence to the latter. Her ladyship was quick to express her delight that her nephew was at last settling down, and that he had found a lady who, like himself, preferred the country. When anyone was so bold as to hint at the less salubrious rumours, Elizabeth was in open admiration of Lady Matlock's skill at turning them back on their source, swiftly and devastatingly, in a few words.

"Oh, you do know that tale was spread about by Miss Bingley, do you not? She has been chasing my nephew most blatantly these three years at least—as though he would marry a woman of her birth! I would feel sorry for her disappointment if she were not such a scheming mushroom, and had not spread such dreadful lies about our dear Elizabeth and her excellent sister."

Elizabeth could hardly keep from laughing at the comeuppance being given to Miss Bingley. She smiled to herself, thinking, *How Mama would have enjoyed such social gamesmanship!*

After a rather gruelling two hours at Gunter's, Lady Matlock gave Elizabeth over into Darcy's care at the most fashionable gate into Hyde Park. Jane and Bingley were there also, for Jane had determined that in braving the stares and whispers of society she would aid the two people she loved best, her future husband and her dearest sister. "Let them talk," she had told Elizabeth when they discussed the matter, "and let them stare. Only let them also see that we love our gentlemen and they, us."

After Elizabeth assured Darcy that all had gone well with his aunt, the quartet strolled Rotten Row at the fashionable hour, determined to enjoy each other's company. The stares and whispers commenced immediately, but it was some minutes before anyone dared approach them directly, though several acquaintances of the gentlemen did nod at them civilly in passing.

The first to breach the invisible perimeter about them was a gentleman of about six and twenty, who called heartily, "Darcy! Well met!" Elizabeth could see from her betrothed's relaxed expression that this was someone whose company he enjoyed, and when the man requested an introduction to the rest of Darcy's party, she learnt that he was Lord John FitzRoy, the second son of the Duke of Grafton, who had been at Cambridge with Darcy for two years. She and Jane sank into deep curtseys, and Bingley bowed with a look of near-terror.

"A pleasure, a real pleasure," Lord John said, studying the ladies with an ornate quizzing-glass on a velvet ribbon, an affectation made impish by the sly wink his magnified eye bestowed upon them. "And my congratulations upon your betrothals," he added, lowering the glass. "I would request an invitation to the wedding, but I am bound for Northamptonshire next week and shall be firmly fixed there until the new year. You will come for the Season, Darcy?"

"It is likely," the gentleman agreed.

"I will expect an invitation to dinner, then. Something intimate, so that I may come to know Mrs Darcy better." He gave a little bow in Elizabeth's direction. He clapped Darcy on the shoulder and murmured, so low that only Darcy and Elizabeth could hear, "Your friends are with you." He farewelled them all then and continued on his way, leaving Bingley and Jane to marvel at having met the scion of a duke, and Elizabeth to wonder pleasantly at the statement the young man had made by speaking so happily with them before all and sundry.

This was, unfortunately, to prove to have been the high point of the outing. The chatter and blatant observation of their party did not cease, or even perceptibly decrease, and now that one person had approached, others felt able to do so. Some were pleasant, it was true, and some merely curious, but neither was there a shortage of those willing to advance rude comments veiled as compliments or ask impertinent questions. These, Elizabeth felt she could not answer as she would have liked; Lady Matlock had impressed upon her that her task today was to display every characteristic that would sit ill upon the brazen fortune-hunter she had been painted as: modesty, restraint, gentility, and forbearance. So she gritted her teeth as she smiled and said only sweet, pleasant things, and cast her gaze bashfully downwards that none might see the annoyance simmering in her eyes.

As for those who ostentatiously turned their backs as the party approached, Elizabeth could laugh inwardly and be glad that she need not interact with them. A few others spoke of Elizabeth in carrying voices, without having the courage to voice their insults face to face. These, thought Elizabeth, seemed to irritate Darcy more than those willing to openly question his choice, and his face took on a thunderous aspect whenever one of those comments carried their way, until with a clear effort of will, he smoothed his expression and returned his attention to her.

"I am glad they are so focussed on me," she confided, when he quietly asked how she was holding up under the barrage of curiosity and scorn. "I am not at all concerned for myself, but for you and Georgiana, and Jane and Bingley. If my sister and your friend can escape the tumult, and I can demonstrate that I have not 'captured' you by underhanded means, perhaps the tide of gossip shall turn. Mayhap your cousin might even come to accept our union."

"What matters most to me is the happiness I find with you," he replied, his voice strong and sure. "Those who wish to see can recognise the truth. Every kind of partnership has its risks whether one weds for love, wealth, or family connexions, as my family is well aware."

She smiled up at him and opened her mouth to reply when a lady's exclamation cut through the air. "My word, I should never leave the house again were I so marked!" cried a very pretty young woman in a fine green gown and matching parasol. Her eyes were fixed upon Jane with an expression of affected horror. "What can she mean by it?"

Elizabeth turned immediately to her sister, and found her pale and struggling for composure. Bingley's hand rested over Jane's upon his arm, and he lost no time in leaning over to speak into her ear. Elizabeth wanted nothing more than to go to her and shield her from the eyes of the crowd, or to run up to that malicious miss and give her the sharp side of her tongue, but she could do neither. They were on a stage of sorts, and must cleave to their roles and their appointed lines. Deliberately, she turned to Darcy and put a pleasant smile upon her face.

"Who," she asked very quietly, "was that?"

"Miss Arbuthnot," Darcy replied, in much the same tone as he might have mentioned Wickham.

"I hope," Elizabeth answered, still smiling, "that she does not expect to be received at Darcy House when I am mistress there."

The look of pride and love he bestowed upon her caused several nearby conversations to stutter to a halt. Elizabeth's smile then became genuine, and glancing back, she was satisfied to see that the colour had returned to Jane's cheeks, and that she was smiling at something Bingley was saying. Elizabeth could not stop these people from speaking as they would, but neither would she be required to be more than civil to anyone who chose to belittle her or her dear sister. The man beside her, who would soon be her husband, would not expect or want it. Knowing this, she felt herself falling even more in love with him.

In the privacy of their shared chamber in Gracechurch Street that night, Jane would weep at the cruelty and thoughtlessness of those who were supposed to display the best of manners—all begun by the malicious lies of her beloved's very own sister!—and Elizabeth was at last able to be of use and comfort to her. But Elizabeth's confidence and Jane's optimism—bolstered by that early encounter with Lord John—that London was not devoid of their supporters was soon proved true. In the following days both Darcy and Bingley each received notes and calls from several of their acquaintance wishing them happy and requesting an introduction to their ladies when convenient.

———

Several days later, Bingley called upon his betrothed in a state of happy agitation, and requested to speak with her in private. Mrs Gardiner allowed them a quarter hour with the door ajar, and when she and Elizabeth had left the room, he turned to Jane with an odd expression of mixed delight and anxiety.

"My dear Jane," he said, nearly vibrating with excitement. "I have been attempting to arrange a very special wedding trip, but until this morning it did not seem as though it would come to fruition. If you like—and I will not be angry if you do not wish to be from home for so long—we may go...*to India!*"

She gasped, her hands coming to her mouth. "Oh my!" she cried, her head spinning. "Does it not take half a year to get there?"

"By the usual routes, yes, but with good winds we might make it in as little as twelve weeks if, rather than going around all of Africa, we instead sail through the Mediterranean, pass overland and by river through Mesopotamia, and thence sail to India by way of the Arabian Sea. I thought we might plan to be away for as much as a year."

"Can you leave Netherfield and all your other business for so long?"

He grinned. "The steward is a competent fellow, and I hope your father would agree to sit with him from time to time. I spoke to Darcy and your uncle when the idea first came to me, and between them they are willing to look after my business interests for a time. Louisa could visit our relations, engage a companion, or come with us."

"You have thought of everything." She smiled sweetly at him. "I should very much like to go to India with you, Charles."

"Ha!" he exclaimed joyously, picking her up by the waist and spinning them both about, before returning her to the ground only to plant a firm kiss on her lips. "Such sights we shall see, my love!"

———

"I feel rather dull and stodgy now," Darcy murmured to Elizabeth later that day, not long after Charles and Jane had shared their plans with the family. "For I have only planned to take you to the Lakes and thence, Pemberley."

"And that sounds entirely delightful to me," Elizabeth replied firmly, "as I long to see both of those places! Jane's grand adventure shall be India in the autumn, while mine will be London in the spring."

At the thought of attending the Season, he grimaced. "Travelling halfway across the globe suddenly sounds rather appealing."

Elizabeth laughed. "Come now, most of the reason you hated the Season was the relentless pursuit of your name and fortune without any regard to yourself. As a married man, you will be safe, and might actually enjoy the activities."

"I do look forward to attending the theatre and concerts with you," he allowed. "But I am concerned about your reception, given the gossip Miss Bingley's coterie has launched. And I dread the crowded balls and insipid dinner parties."

"You are going to be positively miserable the following year, when Georgiana makes her come-out and we must attend something almost every night, are you not?"

He groaned. "Do not remind me!"

CHAPTER THIRTY-THREE

ARDENCY AND JOY MARKED THE DAY ON WHICH MR Bennet relinquished his two eldest daughters. The sun shone brightly upon the Bennet brides with their bouquets of roses from their mother's garden as they made their way into the church upon their father's arms, and light streamed through the windows to rest upon the couples as they pronounced their vows with certainty and delight.

Elizabeth Darcy smiled happily as congratulations and toasts rang through the public rooms of Longbourn, driving out many a shadow of the past year, and held tightly to her new husband's arm as a great crowd of friends and relations saw the newly married couples off to London at the close of the festivities.

"At last," Darcy sighed a few hours later as he loosened his cravat and relaxed into an overstuffed settee in their private sitting room at Darcy House. Elizabeth smiled indulgently at her husband of half a day; the wedding, the boisterous breakfast, her own spate of tears upon leaving Longbourn, and the formal presentation of his new wife to his London servants—it had all been a great deal of activity for an unsociable man. They had been able to relax to a certain extent in the carriage, of course, but had been mindful that the instant they stepped from it they would be very much on display, so there could be no loosed cravats or removed hairpins. She set to work on those hairpins as she took her rightful place next to him, closing her eyes in relief as the heavy weight of her hair tumbled down. She tucked her newly unburdened head onto his shoulder and revelled in the freedom to touch him as she liked.

"It is longer than I imagined," he said softly, twining a thick curl around one finger.

"Do you like it, or shall I have it cut?" she asked with a smile.

"I like it very well indeed." He drew her close and she felt his lips brush the top of her head. "How do you fancy your new home, Mrs Darcy?"

"Oh, a great deal, and yet not nearly so much as I fancy my new husband," Elizabeth murmured. She felt his silent laugh beneath her cheek. "Mrs Darcy...how well that sounds."

"I am glad you think so," he said, "for I shall take great pleasure in saying it often. After all the effort required to convince you to take the name, I cannot soon grow weary of repeating it."

She raised her head and leant away a little, that she might see his face. He was smiling lazily, his eyes half closed, his fingers still languidly moving through her hair. Never had she seen him so at his ease, so unburdened and tranquil. She wanted nothing more than to ensure he reached that state often. She gasped as his fingers began gently stroking her neck, and she felt a frisson sweep over her.

"But what shall I call you," she whispered, "to enjoy the same novelty? For you have always been 'Mr Darcy' to me."

His eyes opened, his soft gaze replaced by smouldering desire. "Address me however it pleases you, and so long as you do not call me 'that man I wish I had not married', I dare say I shall like it."

"Very well...my love," she said, and set her lips to his.

———

"Oh, Jane, I shall miss you so!" cried Elizabeth the following morning after breakfast, as Mr and Mrs Bingley took their leave. "Though the mail is dreadfully slow from so far away, you will write to me nevertheless, will you not?"

"Of course I shall!" replied Jane, returning her sister's fierce embrace. "And you must write to me, no matter how stale your news will be when it reaches us. And when we meet again, we will have ever so much to tell each other!"

Darcy could see that although Elizabeth smiled, there was worry in her expression; clearly Jane saw it as well. "Do not fear, Lizzy," she said quietly. "Smallpox could not take me from you, and neither can the sea. I promise you, I shall return." She smiled, clasped her sister's hands, and continued, "Now, I know you shall be well-occupied before you depart for Pemberley, but I hope you will call upon Louisa while she is here in London, or have her and Cousin Portia around for tea. Perhaps you might all go to

Hatchard's together—that would no doubt delight all three of you!"

Elizabeth acquiesced easily. "Certainly I shall, dearest. *That* Miss Bingley has struck me as someone I should like to know better," she added pertly. "And when they return to Netherfield, our sisters will hardly allow Louisa to be forgotten. When you return, you will no doubt find the house and estate in perfect order, and your new sister as much a part of the community as Lady Lucas."

With such assurances, Jane appeared content. As the Bingleys' carriage pulled away, Darcy stood behind Elizabeth, holding her without care for the gaze of the servants, and spoke tenderly to her of all the adventures their own married life promised. His soft whispers led to kisses, and a somewhat hurried trip back to their chamber. Once there, it took all the persuasive power of a new husband to restore her good humour.

That evening the Darcys were roused from their rooms to go to Fitzwilliam House for a family dinner. Though the couple would both have preferred to wait a little longer before going out in company, Lady Matlock insisted that the family must signal its continued approval soon after the wedding. They would attend the theatre with the earl and countess the following week, and then retire to Pemberley until spring. Darcy was very much looking forward to a winter secluded at his home with the two ladies he loved best and very little other society.

Upon their arrival, his cousin, Viscount Hammond, had received the new Mrs Darcy with cool courtesy; Lady Hammond had been a little warmer. The colonel had greeted them with something of his usual amiability, but there was an undercurrent of reserve which Darcy could not ignore. Now that the deed was done, Lord Matlock had thawed a bit further, going so far as to compliment Mrs Darcy on her appearance. Lady Matlock, of course, had made a point of welcoming Elizabeth with open pleasure and a kiss to the cheek, and Georgiana, who was staying with her aunt and uncle for the nonce, was unabashedly delighted to greet Elizabeth as a sister.

Darcy smiled as he watched his wife speaking with the other ladies; his smile widened as the viscountess laughed delightedly at something Elizabeth had said while his aunt and sister looked on in approval. Out of the corner of his eye, he saw his cousin step up beside him, but made no move to acknowledge him.

"I want you to know that I never fed or even repeated the rumours about your lady," the colonel said quietly after a time.

Darcy nodded once. "Thank you for that."

"Are you happy with the bargain you have made? You shall need to work hard to dower your own daughters, since she brought you nothing."

"*She* brought me everything I wanted," Darcy replied quietly. "To save for my daughters will be a pleasure, not a burden. That is what you have not understood, I think— whatever is done in service of our life together cannot be a hardship. I have no cause to repine."

It was clear from his expression that the colonel did not understand, but he nodded and held out his hand. Darcy shook it, and allowed himself to hope that their close relationship would eventually be restored.

———

Louisa Hurst rose as the sitting room door opened and one of the hotel's maids showed her sister in. "Caroline. You look well."

Caroline Bingley swept into the room and took in its fine appointments with one comprehensive glance. "Louisa. It is good to see you. This suite is very elegant; I had not thought Hurst left you so well-settled."

"Charles took it for us, so that I might enjoy a fortnight in town and visit with those of my acquaintance who have remained for the summer," she answered, busying herself with the tea service.

"Us?" Caroline's brows rose.

"Cousin Portia is with me. I thought you would wish to speak privately, but I would be happy to ask her to join us."

Lips pursed with disdain, she replied only, "I thank you, but that will not be necessary."

Louisa handed her sister a cup and sat with her own. "I was surprised to receive your card. You have not written in months, and I had come to believe you no longer wished to know me. I am not sure how you discovered my where-abouts, to be honest."

Caroline shrugged. "One hears things. When I learnt that Charles and that creature he married had left England, I saw an opportunity to once again be in company with my dear sister." Her smile was everything smooth and insincere. Louisa wondered if Caroline had always regarded her so, and she had been too gullible to see it.

"Jane is our sister now."

Caroline sniffed. She had declined her brother's invita-tion to attend the wedding, and did not appear at all recon-ciled to the marriage. "It is the sister who sits before me now of whom I wish to think," she said in an ingratiating tone that instantly put Louisa on alert. "We are both independent now, and considering our closeness all these years, what would be more natural than setting up housekeeping together? Why should we burden ourselves with companions or indigent relations when we might more amiably keep propriety for each other? We might lease some comfortable rooms, and staying here in London will surely be more agreeable than living with our relations in Scarborough."

Louisa sipped her tea before replying. "I am not bound for Scarborough when this visit is over. Cousin Portia, who is, as you well know, far from indigent," she said with a stern glance that visibly surprised Caroline, "will be staying with me at Netherfield. Charles and Jane have invited me to make my home with them for a long as I wish, and I have accepted."

"Netherfield," Caroline pronounced with contempt. "No, you had much better stay here. You will be far better entertained, even with the constraints of your mourning."

"I disagree. I have found I enjoy living in the country, and I have good friends in Hertfordshire now, whose company I should be loath to forego."

"What friends could you possibly have in such a savage place?" her sister cried.

"The Bennet girls are delightful, as is their friend, Miss Maria Lucas," Louisa answered. "Mrs Jones, who you knew as Miss Lucas, is becoming a friend also, as is Mr Bennet." She recalled how, when she had confessed herself undecided as to whether to remain at Netherfield or join her relations in the north, the Bennet ladies had clamoured for her to remain, and Mr Bennet had added his own opinion that she would be greatly missed, without any of his usual sportive wit. She felt the rightness of her decision all over again, and faced her sister with renewed resolve.

"A pack of silly country chits, a dull stick of a woman, and a sad excuse for a gentleman?" Caroline's face was a picture of incredulity. "They are nothing to your friends here!"

"I have learnt," said Louisa sharply, "that some of my 'friends' in town have far less to say to me now that I am a widow with a small income. An income, I might add, that will go farther in the country, living in my brother's house."

"Your income would also go farther living with me." Her tone became cajoling, and she leant forward to place a hand on Louisa's arm and entreat, "It would be like old times, only better, with no gentlemen to dictate our movements."

"I am persuaded that your first reason is the true one," she replied with a mildness that belied the pounding of her heart. How she despised this fuss and bother! And how it hurt, to know she was but a means to a selfish end for someone to whom she had been so devoted. "If you wished for my company, you would not have forgotten me for all these months. But now that you have understood the cost of decent lodgings and a companion's wages, you look to me to alleviate your problems. I will not, Caroline. I return to Netherfield next week, and shall be glad to do so. If you have decided that you no longer wish to impose upon the Symondses' hospitality, you must set up your own establishment and resign yourself to a smaller wardrobe."

"It is such a bother, being always a guest! One must constantly give way to the preferences of others," Caroline retorted shrilly. "But it is far too expensive to live in London alone! You must help me, Louisa!"

"I cannot, nor do I wish to." She stood, signalling that the interview was at an end. "Stay here with friends, moderate your spending, or set yourself up elsewhere. You are not without options."

"You are no sister of mine!" Caroline retorted spitefully, and stalked from the room without another word.

Louisa sank back down onto her chair, clasping her trembling hands tightly together, and strove not to waste any tears on her unworthy sister. After a moment and several deep, restorative breaths, she began to feel just a little proud of herself.

CHAPTER THIRTY-FOUR

As Lydia returned from a visit to her aunt Philips several days after the weddings of her eldest sisters, she heard footsteps behind her and turned to find Captain Carter hurrying to catch her up.

"Miss Lydia!" he called cheerfully. "I was on my way to call at Longbourn when I spotted you on the path. May I walk with you?" He offered his arm as he drew abreast of her, and she accepted it with a smile.

"How fortunate that we should meet like this, Captain, for there is a matter I have been wishing to discuss with you, but not before all in my father's parlour."

"Oh?" He looked at her curiously. "Speak, then. I am happy to hear any concern of yours, Miss Lydia."

"What are your intentions towards my sister, Mary?" she asked bluntly. "And do not tell me you do not call upon her particularly—for I have noticed how you look at her, particularly when she is not looking at you!"

He laughed heartily. "I see I have no secrets from you. My intentions are entirely honourable—in fact, I have been attempting this last week to speak to your father, but have been thwarted at every turn. My time in Meryton grows short, and I have determined not to leave without pleading my suit. That is, of course, if you and your father will allow it."

Lydia looked surprised. "Why, what has my permission to do with anything?"

He grinned down at her. "I know very well that Miss Bennet would value your blessing at least as highly as your father's, and I fear I should have no chance with her at all if *you* spoke against me."

She made a pleased little sound in the back of her throat. "Well, you may be correct. But I should like it very well if you were my brother, sir, and I shall tell Mary so if she asks."

"I am flattered by your approval," he said lightly, and it was her turn to laugh.

"As well you should be! There are few gentlemen to whom I should be willing to trust her happiness, you know. I have worked very hard these last months to increase her confidence, and I should hate to see it reduced by an unworthy fellow," she concluded with a toss of her head.

———

Mary's curiosity was piqued when she heard a familiar voice inside her father's book-room. Her surprise was even greater a few minutes later, when Mr Bennet came to her and told her she had a visitor waiting for her there.

"Why, Captain Carter! Papa told me I had a caller, but..." She trailed off, her hands twisting together before her, then drew breath and continued. "Will you not come into the parlour? Lydia would be disappointed to miss your visit."

He stepped up to her, possessing himself of her restless hands. "I shall not speak if you had rather I do not, Miss Bennet, but I do have your father's permission for a brief, private meeting."

"Speak of what? ...Oh!" Her eyes widened.

He smiled. "Surely you are not *very* surprised? I have called upon you most faithfully these last weeks, and we have been known to one another for many months. The regiment are to Brighton in a fortnight, and I cannot bear the thought of leaving you behind forever. I have little to give you now, but you know my prospects—we have spoken of Morton Grange and my plans for its improvement, on some distant day. Will you cast your lot in with mine, my dear Mary, and be my wife?"

Mary ducked her head, concealing her shocked expression. When she felt tears misting her eyes, she took a shuddering breath and lifted her face and said, in a shaking voice, "If you will give me yourself, I need no more. Yes... my answer is yes."

He whooped with joy and swept her up into his arms, swinging her about in a delirious spin before setting her gently back onto her own feet again and even more gently setting his lips against hers. She melted into him for a moment, and then drew back, murmuring, "And that will keep until we are married, sir." She smiled and placed her hand on his cheek, hoping to convey some inkling of the warmth and joy he stirred in her.

"Then we had better join your family in the parlour, and give them our news."

She blushed then, and blushed even more moments

later, when he communicated the news to Kitty, Lydia, and their father, and they were surrounded by embraces and well-wishes.

"I told him not an hour ago that I should very much like to have him for a brother, but I did not expect him to act *quite* so speedily!" Lydia exclaimed, nearly squeezing the breath from Mary's lungs in her enthusiasm.

———

Two weeks after their betrothal, Captain Carter was off to Brighton with the regiment. Their betrothal gave them licence to write to each other, and the letters positively flew between Brighton and Meryton during those weeks.

Mr Bennet smiled wistfully at Mary's eagerness to claim the latest page from her betrothed one afternoon in the parlour. "Kitty, Lydia," he addressed his other daughters, "I hope you will not be quite as eager as your elder sisters to wed and leave your poor papa all alone."

"Do not worry," said Lydia, "It is likely I shan't marry at all, and no one has caught Kitty's eye yet."

"I shall wish for you to visit me on occasion, Lydia, and you, too, Kitty, if Longbourn can spare you," Mary remarked, peering over the top of her letter at her family. "But perhaps I might wait until Jane has returned, so our father will still have a daughter in the county."

She quirked an eyebrow at her father, who chuckled before noticing that Kitty was regarding him with rare intensity. That evening after dinner his second youngest daughter knocked upon the door of his study and slipped inside when he called out.

He set his book aside and looked at her curiously.

"Good evening, Kitty, this is a surprise. What brings you here?"

She sat in the chair across the desk from him and, visibly gathering her courage, spoke haltingly. "It is only...I have been thinking about what you said earlier, about being all alone when Lydia and I marry." She could not quite bring herself to meet his gaze.

"You will be mourning Mama for some months yet, but...*later*, I really think you ought to consider remarrying. You might live another forty years and I do not see why you should not have a pleasant companion if you wish it. You have your own estate and are quite handsome for your age—surely many ladies would wish to receive your attentions."

Mr Bennet was thrown into red-faced silence for a moment by this speech. "Would not you and your sisters resent me for replacing your mother?"

"Mama will always be our mother and we are all grown or nearly so—we need no other. So long as you pick a lady who will be pleasant to us, I do not see why any of us would be angry with you for seeking happiness."

"Well, I cannot at present imagine actively seeking a wife when my mourning ends, but I shall think upon what you have said, and perhaps fate will be kind enough to place an amiable widow in my path in a year or two."

Kitty rose and came around the desk to kiss his cheek. "Just do not insist that being alone is your only option, Papa, and I shall be content."

———

On a late December afternoon at Pemberley, Elizabeth was startled from her contemplation of the household ledgers by a discreet cough in the doorway.

"Pardon me, madam," said Mr Harding, the butler. "But I believe you have been in anticipation of this letter for some time." He held forth a silver salver upon which lay an envelope which had obviously travelled no little distance, addressed in a flowing feminine hand.

Elizabeth gasped. "Another letter from Jane! At last!" She hurried to secure the precious missive, beaming at the senior servant who had lowered himself to deliver it personally. "Thank you for seeing this into my hands at the first possible moment. Would you see that Mr Darcy is told? I believe he is in his study."

With a bow, Mr Harding acquiesced, a rare twinkle in his hazel eyes; Mrs Darcy had won over the entire household within a fortnight of her advent, and the master was only one of many who now went about his work with a lighter heart. Darcy soon joined his wife, and together they read their sister's news.

Dearest Lizzy and Fitzwilliam,

I write for both my husband and myself, as he declares that his correspondence is not legible enough to be worth sending across the globe. I cannot disagree.

Darcy muffled an inelegant snort and continued reading.

We have arrived safely in Bombay after our unplanned stop in Gibraltar, detailed in my last, which I hope you received.

When the ship was repaired, we made our way across the Mediterranean, which is very beautiful, to Mesopotamia. In Basrah, I made many more sketches, and Charles rode a camel! The journey across the Arabian Sea went smoothly and we completed our voyage to Bombay without incident.

Oh, Lizzy, I can hardly describe this place. There are great numbers of English here, so everywhere one turns there is some reminder of home, and yet it is so very different also. We have only been here a few days, so I shall certainly have more to tell in my next, but for now you must believe me entirely happy, except for the distance from you.

I remain your devoted sister,
Jane Bingley

———

When the old year gave way to the new, as it generally does, Parliament opened and the London Season launched. The Darcys dutifully made their way to town, though they would not remain for the whole of the Season, as Lady Matlock had wished. Elizabeth was in expectation of a happy event near the first anniversary of their wedding and would have to retire from the social whirl when her condition became too apparent. They would remain through Easter and no longer. After several months in company with her new sister, Georgiana was actually looking forward to attending a few small dinners and musical evenings in preparation for her come-out the following spring.

It was immediately clear that society was still of two

minds regarding Mrs Darcy. Though a goodly number could not believe that the upright, clever Mr Darcy could fall prey to entrapment or base desire, or that Lord and Lady Matlock would admit into their company such a lady as the slander described, others found it more gratifying to believe the worst. The young ladies who had wanted Mr Darcy for themselves, and the mothers who had wanted him for their daughters, comprised much of this latter company, along with a number of gentlemen who had long scorned Darcy for his inflexible morals and clear disapproval of their own profligate ways.

Unlike her husband, Elizabeth was more amused than angered by the insinuations some chose to make in her presence. She was more than capable of dealing out genteel set-downs, but once she became known for her wit and warmth—and society saw the genuine affection between the couple—she saw more smiles than frowns directed her way and new acquaintances became friends.

There were old friends to be met with, as well, for Mr and Mrs Jones were now residing with the Gardiners while Mr Jones completed his training. Visits to Gracechurch Street were now an even greater joy for Elizabeth, made all the sweeter as she watched the regard between her beloved husband, her dear relations, and her cherished friend deepen and grow.

Two acquaintances who were not to be seen, on this visit or any future ones, were Mr Wickham and Caroline Bingley. He had been taken up for debt while the Darcys wintered at Pemberley, and was unlikely to ever win free. She, and, by extension, the Symondses with whom she stayed, had found invitations were in short supply after Lady Matlock's disdain for her and her lies became widely known. Darcy returned home one afternoon from White's and regaled his wife and sister with the story of the chilly reception Sir Everard had received there on account of the wagging tongues of his wife, daughter, and houseguest. Furious, he had declared that Miss Bingley would be removed from his home forthwith. A letter from Louisa confirmed the tale, including her refusal to receive her sister at Netherfield. Miss Bingley had had no choice but to seek refuge with her relations in Scarborough.

CHAPTER THIRTY-FIVE

A FEW MONTHS LATER, ELIZABETH STROLLED THE paths of Pemberley's formal garden, a riot of colours on a pleasant late July day, smiling as the bundle in her arms squirmed. "Yes, darling," she murmured, "I'm happy to be out of doors, too."

Footsteps behind her heralded the arrival of her husband. She smirked. It had taken him all of ten minutes, this time, to seek her out. As he took his place beside her, she regarded him with one eyebrow cocked, almost daring him to object.

He shook his head with a little sigh. "I do wish you would have a maid carry Bennet, at least."

"I am perfectly well, Fitzwilliam. I am not going to faint and drop our son. Indeed, I am entirely convinced that staying abed for a month would have made me ill, and that easing back into my routines has helped me to recover more quickly from what was, I am assured, a very easy birth."

"You got up after five days. *Five*, Elizabeth," he

grumbled.

"Which is more than twice as long as I have ever known a tenant's wife to stay abed after an uncomplicated delivery," she retorted. "I am not delicate. And besides, Ben loves the sunshine. Do not you, my sweet?" she cooed at the heir to Pemberley. "You are a fortnight old today! How quickly it goes."

"Before we know it, he will be answering back," the proud father said with a fond smile at the two most important people in his life. "I hover because I care, you know."

"I do know, which is why I have not lost my temper with you over it, though it has been a near thing at times," she replied cheerfully. "He is the dearest little creature, is he not? Worth every moment of swollen ankles and being smothered by my well-meaning husband. Though I do wish his arrival had been a bit more conveniently timed. I am sorry to miss Papa's wedding today."

"Well, as to that, the post has come, and with it a letter from the lady who, by this hour, should now be Mrs Bennet." He drew the missive from his pocket with a smile. "Shall I take him while you read?"

Elizabeth handed the baby to him and accepted the letter in return, opening it eagerly. Her eyes flew over the lines, penned in Louisa's elegant copperplate hand. "Oh! Jane and Charles have returned!" she exclaimed. "That is a relief. I could not be entirely easy until they were in England once more."

She read further, then chuckled. "Let me read to you what Louisa says."

They were, as you might imagine, most surprised to learn that Mr Bennet and I are to wed next week. Dear Jane looked as though the world had turned inside-out, and my poor brother nearly swallowed his tongue. But once they had got used to the notion, I believe they were happy for us.

"It must be strange," Darcy commented, "to know that your friend is now your step-mother."

"Oh, I doubt I shall ever think of Louisa that way. She will have no motherly role to play with me. I only hope they shall be happy together."

"I do not see why they should not be. They both prefer country to town, and books to people. Perhaps it is no grand romance, but I expect they each will work to please the other and end contented, at the very least." He blanched suddenly. Slowly, he shifted the baby and held him out, and Elizabeth saw that both Bennet's swaddling and her husband's sleeve were thoroughly soaked.

She threw her head back and laughed.

———

October 1815

Elizabeth sank into a soft chair and gazed around Bramley Hall's warm, comfortable parlour. "You have done wonders with this house," she said to Jane.

All five Bennet sisters were gathered for the first time since she and Jane had wed. They were assembled now at the Derbyshire estate the Bingleys had taken eight months prior. The interior had been positively dreadful the last time Elizabeth had seen it, so dreadful that the Bingleys had lived five and twenty miles away at Pemberley for the first three months of their ownership, while the plaster was repaired and new furnishings bought.

"It was a great deal of work, but it is finally finished. And just in time," Jane replied, laying a hand over her belly. There was a great furore as the younger sisters rushed to congratulate the eldest.

Having offered her own wishes, Elizabeth withdrew slightly to watch her sisters so happily occupied with talk of the coming child. Mary was all genuine smiles, though Elizabeth knew her to be disappointed by her own childless state, while the more newly-married Kitty had an absent, dreamy look about her and Lydia made outrageous, laughing claims about all the mischief she intended to support her sisters' children in during the coming years.

Lydia had adapted well to her altered vision, though the process had been long and arduous. She had regained much of her former liveliness and Jane, much of her serene good cheer. Both were greatly improved in appearance, their scars faded to almost nothing, the distinctive pitting of smallpox softened by time. The milky white cast of Lydia's damaged eye could not be hidden, however, and she had early resigned herself to the role of spinster.

Mary soon mentioned that she had news of her own. "Uncle Carter has asked us to make our home at Morton Grange, and begin to oversee it while he is still there to help us along. Nathaniel has already begun the process of separating from the militia, and we expect to be in our new home by Christmas."

Elizabeth and Jane expressed their pleasure in having Mary and Mr Carter so amiably settled; the news did not seem to be a surprise to their younger sisters, who had travelled to Derbyshire with Mary. Kitty had wed Sir William

Lucas's heir, Matthew, the previous year, and relieved Lady Lucas's nerves by immediately taking over the running of Lucas Lodge. Lydia was still at Longbourn, though Elizabeth suspected she would be installed at Morton Grange not long after Mary.

"What news from Meryton?"

Lydia smiled mischievously. "I know nothing for a certainty, but Louisa has been rather unwell in the mornings of late. I believe Papa's issues with drainage are not as severe as he has painted them; they could have come here, if Louisa were able to travel."

"Well, I hope she may give us another brother!" Elizabeth cried. "If only to spite Mr Collins. He had the temerity to write to my husband after our brother Tommy was born and supplanted him as heir to Longbourn, asking him to restrain my father from 'continuing to subvert the will of God in the matter of the entail', and that both he and Lady Catherine would be 'most seriously displeased' should Mrs Bennet produce a 'spare'. He even had the utter gall to write that he still considered himself the heir presumptive, as so many children do not reach their majority."

While Mary and Lydia were quick to voice their outrage, Kitty only raised her eyebrows. "I wonder if he wrote to Darcy before or after he wrote much the same to Papa, and received a most scathing reply."

"He did not! Oh, of course he did. Insufferable man!" cried Elizabeth.

"Are Darcy and Lady Catherine still at odds?" Jane asked.

"Matters have settled into a detente of sorts. Once a year, in January, she writes to inform him that she is still offended by his breach of the supposed betrothal with her daughter, and that as a consequence, he will not be welcome at Rosings for the visit he was used to make each spring. And every year, in February, he replies that he had formed no intention of going in any case. And that is the sum of congress between Pemberley and Rosings," she concluded with a laugh.

———

July 1818

"What word from Hampshire? Is Mary well?" Darcy asked as his wife folded the letter from her sister and set it aside. She turned a shining face to him, and his heart still caught at the sight, six years and three children after she became Mrs Darcy. With the summer sun reaching through the window to bring out glimmers of copper and gold in her dark curls, he thought she looked not a day older than when she had first taken his name.

"Very well indeed. Despite the long wait, her expectancy is proceeding as easily as any of ours, for which she is thankful—as am I. But she had other news, the best possible news—Lydia is engaged!"

He smiled in return, his pleasure real. His brotherly relationship with the youngest Bennet daughter had been slow to form, no doubt because they were so different in essentials, but he truly liked her now. She had faced her altered life with a courage and cheer he could not but admire, and he flattered himself to think she had, in time, come to appreciate his own steadiness and his care for Elizabeth and all her family.

"Did Mr Harman finally convince her that he did not merely wish for a closer tie to his patron?"

"It seems so. Silly girl—it has been plain for two years at least that he was simply mad for her." Elizabeth shook her head with a fond expression. "As confident as she seems, I do not think she ever believed a man would be able to look past her appearance."

Darcy nodded. Even he, who was not at all attuned to the romantic inclinations of others, had seen that Mr Carter's parson was desperately smitten with the last Miss Bennet.

"How strange," Elizabeth added with a grin, "to think that Mary should have wed a soldier, while Lydia will be a clergyman's wife!"

He chuckled. "I am glad she allowed him to persuade her. Should I give Mr Harman the Branxton living, do you think? It is smaller than the one he has, but he might install a curate and enjoy some additional income."

She rose from her chair and demonstrated with a lingering kiss her approval of that notion.

———

Later that year, as winter dawned, Elizabeth and Georgiana were practising the waltz, which had only been allowed at Almack's for the last two seasons, and they feared forgetting the steps if they passed too many months without rehearsal. Elizabeth knew that her sister was particularly fond of dancing the waltz with her betrothed, with whom she was to be united towards the end of the next Season, in a splendid ceremony at St George's in

London. Both bride and groom would have preferred something quieter, but between the Matlocks and Mr Hardwick's father—a member of high standing in the Commons —a more elaborate scheme had been pressed upon them.

Darcy entered the parlour, and rather than enjoy their performance, called out her name. "Elizabeth, there are letters for you. Will you not sit and read them?" he asked, waving the presumably tempting missives.

Elizabeth stretched her face into a smile which she was fairly sure did not convey any real pleasure. Five months into her fourth expectancy, with nary a hint of real trouble in the previous three, and yet he *would* hover. "When we are finished, my dear," she said.

Georgiana, the traitor, immediately pulled away and, claiming an urgent need to write to Mr Hardwick, vanished. Husband and wife faced each other, the former looking rather smug.

"My letters, if you please," she said, holding out a hand. He deposited three missives onto her palm, and made as if to escort her to a chair. This gesture she affected not to notice, flipping through the letters. "Oh! Here is one from Papa! Do you know, I think I shall take it up to the gallery, and read it while I take a stroll, since my other exercise was interrupted," she said pointedly.

He sighed, shoulders slumping. "Will you at least accept my escort?"

She smiled at him then, really smiled. "I should love to walk with you." Throwing her thick woollen shawl about her shoulders, she took his arm and leant against him as they ascended to the second floor and its long gallery. As vexing as Darcy could be when she was with child, he was in all other ways a near-perfect husband, and she treasured their times alone together.

They strolled along the gallery under the painted eyes of Darcys past, the November wind rattling the windows in their casements, in companionable silence for some moments before Darcy gently reminded her of the letter in her hand. She laughed and shook her head; expectancy always seemed to make her terribly forgetful.

"Oh, my," she breathed, after reading through the short letter twice, unsure whether to be angry or burst out laughing. She glanced up at her husband. "Papa, Louisa, and the boys are well, but I am not sure I should tell you what Mr Collins has done this time."

Darcy's eyes rolled at the mere mention of that man. "You might as well."

"Now that my younger brother has survived infancy, Mr Collins has—" She had to stop and laugh, shaking her head. "He has brought a suit against my father for, 'wilfully and with malice sundering him from his expected inheritance'. Lady Catherine's solicitor is representing him, a fact apparently intended to set my father quaking in his boots."

Her husband regarded her with an expression of sheer disbelief. "Mad, the both of them," he muttered. He paced over to a window and stared out for a moment at the early-winter landscape. Then he turned, with a smirk on his lips and glint in his eye.

"Let us write to your father and tell him that my solicitors are at his disposal, and I shall pay the fees. There is no chance of such a suit succeeding, but neither my aunt nor Collins have an understanding of chess, war, or legal strategies."

Elizabeth grinned. "Nor a lick of common sense. And does my clever husband have anything in mind aside from quashing this preposterous suit like a bug?"

"Oh, I have any number of plans," he said, returning to her. Instead of offering his arm, however, he seized one of her hands, placed his other at her waist, and began to waltz her gently down the long gallery. "I plan to dance with my beautiful wife, and then I hope to convince her to take a little rest before dinner. Cunningly, I mean to read to her once I have lured her into bed, to keep her there. Then, of course, there will be dinner, and no doubt a great deal of talk about my sister's wedding, followed by tea in the parlour and more wedding talk. And after that, well...some things are best left to spontaneity, do you not agree?"

———

April 1823

"How is Mrs Jones? She was to visit you this morning, as I recall," Darcy asked as they climbed into bed after a night at the theatre.

"She did, and she is very well, as are the children. She is recently returned from attending Maria's latest confinement, and is delighted with her new nephew." Elizabeth snuggled up to her husband's side, smiling as his lips brushed the top of her head. "Seeing Charlotte regularly is my favourite part of spending the Season in town each year, you know."

"She is not your only friend here."

"No, but she is the dearest." She turned and peered at him through the gloom, and saw that he seemed concerned. "I do know many lovely people here, it is true, but it is likewise true that despite having navigated a decade of marriage, and nearly as many Seasons, without dragging your name into disrepute, there are still some who sneer at me. I suppose they always shall, and I would happily bear twenty times their number for the privilege of being Mrs Darcy." This reassurance she punctuated with a kiss. "But it is a little trying at times."

He nodded. "When all of our children are grown, perhaps we could retire to Pemberley and allow Bennet to uphold the family name. He is certainly more sociable than his father!"

Elizabeth chuckled with him, but said, "You will not separate me from Charlotte—or from Drury Lane and Hatchard's—so easily! When that day comes, however, I do think we may be a great deal more selective in our invitations, both proffered and accepted. But that is many years in the future."

"Only fifteen years or so until Mathilda makes her come-out," he replied hopefully.

"Ah, but I am only one and thirty, my love. I am not as certain as you are that our family is complete." She laughed at the expression of surprise upon his face. "In any case, we will wish to be there for Edward's first Season, also, and he will most likely enter Cambridge the year before Mattie makes her come-out. No, we will be in London in the spring for some time to come."

He sighed, and then asked, "And Mr Jones? Does his practice continue to prosper?"

"He remains the most fashionable physician in London, thanks to you."

"I recommended him for years before anyone took

notice. It was his good work in saving the life of the viscount that sent the peerage flocking to him," Darcy demurred.

"Your uncle would never have summoned him in place of that bloodletting quack they used to employ, if not for your insistence. He and Charlotte are quite sensible of your role in their elevation, as am I." She kissed his cheek, and they lay in silence for a while before she said, contemplatively, "She and I spoke a great deal today about the autumn you and I met."

"Oh? Were you remembering what a boor I was at that dratted assembly?" he asked lightly.

"It was mentioned," she admitted drily. "But only in the context of wondering what our lives might have been, had the smallpox not come upon us. Would you and I have found our way to each other, after such a beginning? Would she and Mr Jones have come together in some different circumstance? Would any of us be where we are now? It was so terrible at the time, and so many died, but it does seem to have worked out to the betterment of many of those who survived, does it not?"

"It does," he agreed quietly. "I did not suffer as you and your family did, but what I witnessed during that time..." He shook his head. "It showed me what I truly valued, and what was all show and nothingness. I hope I should have had the good sense to pursue you in any case, but we cannot be certain. We can only be grateful for what we have, and ensure that our life is a worthy testament to those who were lost."

She hugged him more closely to her. "I believe it has been, my darling, and that so long as we are motivated by love, it shall continue to be so."

GET A FREE EBOOK!

The Course of True Love, a contemporary Pride & Prejudice variation is free for subscribers of the Quills & Quartos newsletter. CLICK HERE to join us today!

Cover image shown is a vector based depiction of a man and a woman embracing with a sketch of London behind them.

ABOUT THE AUTHOR

Frances Reynolds fell madly in love with *Doctor Who* at the tender age of seven. This, in turn, led her to embrace other quintessentially British delights such as tea, scones, Dickens, and Austen. When she is not wrangling wild data for a large financial firm, she is generally to be found reading, writing, or watching her favorite series (*see above*) while knitting.

Frances lives slightly south of Canada with her spouse and a small herd of cats, in a house which is continually upset that it has been obliged to remain standing since 1916.

SCAN HERE
to be taken to
Frances Reynolds's
books on Amazon

ACKNOWLEDGMENTS

I wrote the first few scenes of *In Sickness & In Health* in the fall of 2018, then filed it away because it wasn't really speaking to me and moved on to other projects. I picked it up a year and a half later, in late spring/early summer 2020, just after my spouse came home from a stay in the hospital due to COVID-19. In some ways it was amazingly easy to write, because such unique and trying times need to be put into words. In other ways, it was extraordinarily difficult, because what words can adequately describe our individual and communal experiences during those long, strange months? Perhaps none truly can, but I hope you have found within these pages something that resonates with you.

To the team at Quills & Quartos, many thanks. This story wouldn't be half of what it is without your thoughtful suggestions.

To my family—Nan, Ryan, Charlie, Rebecca, Victoria —all my love, and eternal gratitude for your support.

And to my dearest friends: Rebecca, AJ, Jessica, Aaron. Thanks for everything, and the next round's on me. Sláinte.